The Afterlife of a Threadbare Jester

The Afterlife of a Threadbare Jester

a novel

Khanh Ha

Red Hen Press | *Pasadena, CA*

Portions of this novel have previously appeared in somewhat different form in the following publications: *Saranac Review; Pangyrus Literary Magazine; The Blackwater Press Short Story Collection* (as the prize story).

Book design by Mark E. Cull

Library of Congress Cataloging-in-Publication Data

Names: Ha, Khanh author
Title: The afterlife of a threadbare jester: a novel / Khanh Ha.
Description: First edition. | Pasadena, CA: Red Hen Press, 2026.
Identifiers: LCCN 2025034337 (print) | LCCN 2025034338 (ebook) | ISBN 9781636284675 paperback | ISBN 9781636284705 library binding | ISBN 9781636284699 ebook
Subjects: LCSH: Vietnam War, 1961–1975—Fiction | LCGFT: Historical fiction | War fiction | Novels | Fiction
Classification: LCC PS3558.A13 A65 2026 (print) | LCC PS3558.A13 (ebook)
LC record available at https://lccn.loc.gov/2025034337
LC ebook record available at https://lccn.loc.gov/2025034338

The National Endowment for the Arts, the Los Angeles County Arts Commission, the Ahmanson Foundation, the Dwight Stuart Youth Fund, the Max Factor Family Foundation, the Pasadena Tournament of Roses Foundation, the Pasadena Arts & Culture Commission and the City of Pasadena Cultural Affairs Division, the City of Los Angeles Department of Cultural Affairs, the Audrey & Sydney Irmas Charitable Foundation, the Meta & George Rosenberg Foundation, the Albert and Elaine Borchard Foundation, the Adams Family Foundation, Amazon Literary Partnership, the Sam Francis Foundation, and the Mara W. Breech Foundation partially support Red Hen Press.

First Edition
Published by Red Hen Press
www.redhen.org

In loving memory of
Mr. and Mrs. Nguyễn Xuân Nhị,
with gratitude

The Afterlife of a Threadbare Jester

CHAPTER 1

Cổng Trời, Heavenly Gate

Autumn 1978

Whoever goes to Cổng Trời shall never return;
Give flesh when you're in love with him;
Send him off to Cổng Trời when you hate him.
—Folktale

I was hung butterfly style on a barbed-wire pole.

My arms bent back, I felt the twine cut into my thumbs strapped together, both wrists clamped by the 8-shaped cuffs tied to a rope that was looped around the pole behind me. On this cold night, so cold at zero degrees Celsius, I could no longer remember time. I sweated as hoar frost clung to my eyebrows. The camp commies called this folded-butterfly-wing cuffing "trói cánh tiên," or "fairy-wing restraint." Some flowery name.

Several feet to my left, my escape consort, Captain Bé, was awake, his head lolling. To my right, my other escape companion, Father Ninh, was a goner.

They had not applied the fairy-wing restraint to Father Ninh. When they tried to bend his arms back, pushing so far his thumbs touched and his wrists met, his piercing screams made me forget my evil pain. Eventually they improvised a new kind of contortion, flinging his right arm over his shoulder then pulling his left arm up behind his back so his thumbs met. I could see him now, dimly lit by the bulb hung on the tree that shaded the lookout post. Silhouetted against the yellow light, his twisted body toppled forward, chest jutted out.

The two guards paced back and forth on the dirt courtyard in front of the three poles. The penal poles, solitary, skeletal, stood in the center of the bare courtyard. Each morning, leaving the camp on our labor trips, we would pass them; evenings, coming back to the camp we would pass them again. They were fixtures, almost non-existent, until we ran afoul of the cadres.

Sweat beads collected on my brow and dripped down to my lips. They tasted salty. The sweat stung the cut on the corner of my mouth and the torn skin on my cheeks. The guards had beaten the three of us where they had captured us.

They banged us with the butts of their rifles and while we rolled on the ground they kicked us, soccer-style. I could not hear the screams of my companions for the cries of my own. I covered my face with my hands and doubled up into the fetal position, but each blow sent flashes inside my head, behind my eyes. I tasted something salty in my mouth, felt something torn in my ears, something ruptured in my eyes. They dragged me and Captain Bé by the armpits but carried Father Ninh like a corpse. He had passed out.

Someone came out of the darkness. In his hand was an unlit storm lantern. The two guards saluted him. He was lanky in his sage-green uniform adorned with yellow-striped, red epaulettes. A senior lieutenant security cadre. He stopped in front of the guards. Without his pith helmet, his hair was slicked back with a sheen from the light.

"Now," he said, looking at us, "now, you can have a taste of the physical deprivation we used to suffer from." He spat. "Leeches!"

I eyed him. I disliked his heavy northern accent, though I was born in the North.

Father Ninh moaned. He had finally come around. He puffed, his voice strained. "I'm asking God . . . to give me the nobility not to despise you . . . Without freedom—"

The cadre cut in. "What is freedom in your opinion? Consider us equal."

"You're the victor . . . I'm the vanquished . . . So, what is freedom, sir cadre? When you lose it . . . you'll know."

Father Ninh, a thorn in their side, had formed the Association of Political Prisoners in the camp. For that, the camp security had him quarantined in solitary confinement. He had his supporters, mainly the Catholic devotees. In exchange for his release from solitary confinement, the camp administrator had asked him to tell his followers the three words that symbolized the Socialist Republic of Vietnam: Independence, Freedom, Happiness. With the cadres sitting in a gathering in the courtyard, Father Ninh had calmly addressed the assembly: "We are living in a new regime by the name of the Socialist Republic of Vietnam. Under this regime, what used to make a man a free human being has vanished. No independence. No freedom. No happiness." He had since earned the sobriquet: "Father Three No's."

To my left, Captain Bé raised his voice, "To this day . . . our people have disavowed your so-called Party and Revolution."

I had known about Captain Bé. The *Chính Luận Daily News—Political Discussion*—had run a five-column, front-page story on him after the Battle of An

Lộc in 1972. Now, its publisher was condemned in another camp for heralding such a hero. Captain Bé came from the Fifth Airborne Battalion of First Airborne Brigade. He was a hero of the Battle of An Lộc during the North Vietnamese Spring Offensive in 1972. The battle lasted over two months, pitching three NVA and Viet Cong divisions against one ARVN Fifth Division. In the end, with staggering losses on both sides, An Lộc stood victoriously as the decimated NVA withdrew from Saigon.

"We don't bear any animosity toward you," said the senior lieutenant as he took a sharp breath and held it. Slowly, he set the storm lantern on the ground. "Remember those words by our beloved Uncle Hồ:

Like a swath of red crepe covering an altar relic from dust,
Cast aside differences, countrymen, love one another.

"That's exactly the goal of our reform program: to make you a better person, so that we, as a whole, can love one another."

Those pontificated words, in fact, came from one of our proverbs!

The cadre cupped his hands, pointing his pressed fingers toward us. "I welcome your opinions. By exchanging our ideas, we will broaden our knowledge of the Revolution, the Party, and the State, and hence pave the way to your successful reform program."

His openness was ominous, especially with his smile. I could sense it. Whatever stated, worded, or declared by their Party was absolute—maxim unchallengeable. What we, the anti-communists, lacked was a collective knowledge of communism. All we were good at was to shout, "Down with communism."

"Sir cadre," Captain Bé finally said with an effort, "your Revolution was based on Marxism-Leninism, which has followers like Mao Zedong and Hồ Chí Minh. There's nothing wrong with your political theory which advocates to end capitalism and replace it with socialism, favoring the proletariat after you seize power." He strained his neck to speak louder. "But what is wrong with your theory is that, in reality, it was not affected by the workers, but by your Party and its leaders. One of them is Hồ Chí Minh. You proclaim him as the greatest leader of our country. Is he?" The captain panted, out of breath. The cadre waited, his breath pluming. Captain Bé puffed, half of his face swollen. "What is the quality of a great leader? Bringing peace and prosperity to the people . . . Those who live in peace and in prosperity will crown him as a great leader . . . But are we all living in peace and prosperity?" He strained to breathe. "Look around you, sir comrade

... Your leader Hồ Chí Minh bred animosity among his countrymen, extending genocide from one war to another. To kill a human is an unforgivable crime ... But it's justifiable for a righteous cause for your communists to kill many humans ... That's the illusion of the communist psychosis." He coughed, his mouth drooling. Finally, he regained his breath. "You're treating your southern countrymen like the enemy. Cast aside our differences and love one another?"

The cadre clasped his hands, musing, then nodded. "We rose up as proletariat because we live for our ideology. By defeating the American imperialists, we brought peace, disposed of the yokes, and united the nation as one." He glanced at the two guards, then turned his face back toward Captain Bé. "We can't have differences in ideologies. That breeds division, and we can't have division among ourselves."

Captain Bé finally opened his eyes, his neck thrust out, his voice gruff. "No division? Look at your Party in Hanoi. The moment you retook Hanoi from the French, each of your privileged Party members occupied a villa left behind by the French personnel, or the wealthy local residents who'd fled communism. Each of your bureaucrats had a chauffeur, a cook, a secretary. You even have divisions in what automobile each Party member is allowed to drive. Bureau chiefs share a Moskvitch car; ministers have a Pobeda for himself with rear-window curtains; Politburo members ride in Vogas with window curtains all around; Hồ Chí Minh had a Tsaika. Now look at yourself. Out here, teeth clenched in the cold. Your Hanoi cadres' daily leftover meals are a feast to us compared to our daily rations." He gasped for air. "Whoever robs you at night is just a thief; but if they rob you in daylight, they are your Party officials."

The cadre turned quickly to the two guards behind him. "Report to me everything you see and hear after I'm gone." He lit the storm lantern with a cigarette lighter and walked across the courtyard, past the lookout post to the camp officer housing quarter, lightless, misty gray.

By now the pains in my arms had passed excruciating agony and turned into throbbing dull aches. My shoulders twinged, and I toppled forward, sucking air. *Will you stop haranguing*, I moaned in my head at Captain Bé. In some camps, I heard, they had rigged up a bridle-like contraption and used it on any orally malfeasant inmates.

I was floating on air. I had stopped sweating and the cold seeped into every pore of my body. My arms were no longer part of my body. The pains burned at my shoulders. I floated in my head, in and out of my mind. It was catnaps, throbbing with twinges. I saw one of the guards pointing his rifle at my temple. I felt grateful. My head exploded.

I woke and saw the two guards still pacing back and forth. An owl hooted.

The catnaps were dreams broken by the reality of the sounds of night birds, at times the whooping of owls, and at times the sight of the sentries standing still like statues in the night. Then there was light. And the light bulb, hung on a tree that shaded the lookout post, went out. Soon the sun rose. Dimly, I heard my thoughts cry out for water. The gong sounded. The commotion at daybreak from roll call. My body, parched like a dried-up leaf, quivered. Once, I opened my eyes and saw line after line of inmates filing out of the gate. I felt chilled then hot, hot then chilled, with a fever.

I woke again. The sun was hot. It burned my skin. But I did not sweat. The lines of inmates coming back appeared in my blurred vision. Then the sunlight blinded my eyes, bursting with thousands of eddying stars now red, now white, now yellow, and the light intensified its glow until it emitted an enveloping heat of molten steel and I convulsed with a long twisting spasm that seemed only in my thought, and then everything felt cool, the light now dim, and the stillness seemed to float gently in an immense dimension that smelled of camphor like in the old clothes drawers back home.

The guards took us down when the inmates had gathered in the courtyard. Half-conscious, I sensed it was past noon. Everyone must have had their noon meals and were ready to head back out. With my face pressed against the dirt, I could see the shapes of my escape companions lying face down to my right. Standing over us was the camp administrator in his quilted jacket, the left sleeve dangling, hiding his amputated arm. Silhouetted against the sun, he held in his good hand a sheet of paper. Then his voice came over me. I heard my name, then Captain Bé's, and Father Ninh's, the date of our escape, the teams we belonged to, the shack where we dwelled.

"On behalf of Cổng Trời's overseeing committee, the security committee, the proctor committee, I hereby issue a decree that the three offenders be put in the dungeons for one month with their feet shackled twenty-four hours a day, and each be given meals up to nine kilograms a month. The sentence shall vary in accordance with each offender's progressive behavior in light of the Revolution's clemency. The camp's Order Maintaining Committee shall execute this decree as of today without further delay."

CHAPTER 2

Remembrance

Remember me, and a part of me will always be with you.
—Martha Carrier

When I was a fourteen-year-old northern boy, I used to worship General Võ Nguyên Giáp as our national hero.

On the day his army marched through Hanoi, October 10, 1954, five months after their victory over the French Union at Điện Biên Phủ, I stood on the street among boys my age, waving a gold-star red banner.

My father, a noted writer, had extolled Hồ Chí Minh as our messiah. But the following year, 1955, my father was arrested at home by the secret police for his advocacy of the arts and letters renaissance. A literary man, he allied himself with the artists from the Army's Arts & Entertainment Bureau to demand autonomy for freedom of literary expression, creativity, and human rights in the military and private media.

That year, my mother asked my paternal uncle to take me to the South, as my uncle was ready to leave the North. The Geneva Accords, signed in July 1954, allowed a 300-day grace period, ending on May 18, 1955, during which people could move freely between the two Vietnams before the border was sealed. On that day, my uncle told me, "We're leaving. Those communists believe in nothing—no family, no religion—only the Party. They have no souls. Remember my words."

I did. My father died in Hỏa Lò prison in 1958, the same year when all his literary friends from the two journals, *Nhân Văn* and *Giai Phẩm*—Humanism & Masterpieces—were imprisoned for their literary reform movement.

Years later, I became an intelligence officer of the Republic of Vietnam; but I never forgot my early illusions about communism, which had me confuse the Nationalists with the Communists. President Hồ Chí Minh was head of North Vietnam from 1945 until his death in 1969, the epitome of a stable, well-oiled regime in the eye of many of my acquaintances in the South. They downplayed the economic and political upheavals that had taken place in China: its Great Leap Forward campaign resulting in over a million deaths, its Cultural Revolution movement causing a half million casualties. Such disasters, in their minds, would never befall our northern communist government. They made light of the inhumaneness of the Soviet collective labor camp system that killed millions of detainees. Yet such transnational political repressions had never warned them about the northern communist in nature. Neither did the Land Reform in the North in the 1950s persuade them of its savagery, its immorality, which lead to children denouncing their parents, families turning against one another. Nor did the communist massacres of innocent citizens in the remote areas of the South during the war. These southerners had told themselves that it was merely another propaganda trick of their South's government.

Like the younger me, they believed communism was patriotism.

In those days before the collapse of the South, I would read the daily dispatches that passed through our Central Intelligence Office. March came. Things did not look good. Our President had ordered a military withdrawal from the highland of Ban Mê Thuột. In panic, a massive wave of citizens fled, following the troops, clogging up Road 7B. Twenty thousand civilians died from enemy shelling, and tens of thousands of soldiers perished. The reports offered a name for that inter-provincial road: Corridor of Bloodbath. Twenty-one years before, the exodus of one million northerners after the Geneva Accords had made southerners gasp; they scorned those refugees as wretched poor who had left their homeland to seek out the wealth of the South. Misery had come full circle.

Though our office kept daily contact with the Office of the President, we received no plans from it. We thought it must have had a strategy, or at least a proposal. Alas, no proposal nor strategy came, but daily news from foreign media assailed us. Did the BBC, Reuters, the AP, the UPI all lie to us?

On the day the communists entered Saigon, I comforted myself with a thought: Regardless of who the victor was, they would find ways to improve people's lives. After a century of being exploited by the colonizing French and then the civil war between the North and the South, I believed we were due for prosperity in peace time. Following the American Civil War, the North and the South became a single nation; the United States became a singular noun.

Three days after the communists had taken the South, I still kept that thought.

In hindsight, I should have recognized the premonition I'd received in the days when we watched the American troops withdraw from our homeland. It was January 1973, following the Paris Peace Accords. At our Central Intelligence Office, we met with William Sullivan, chief deputy to Henry A. Kissinger. Here was a proconsul who had his finger on the pulse of the war, so aware of the operations in the country that "there wasn't a bag of rice dropped in Laos that he didn't know about." Summarily, he said that the continued opening of the door to China would advance more easily, should positive steps toward removing Vietnam as an issue between the two countries be clearly evident.

One of our senior agents let out an exasperated sigh. "The Americans are shaking hands with the Chinese," he said. "Break China away from Russia. That is of paramount importance to them and takes precedence over winning the war. I hope we're not sitting under a guillotine."

Many of us at the CIO counseled one another that we should all report to the Reform Program, which had been announced to the public by the Transitional Revolutionary Government. Perhaps by subjecting ourselves to be reformed, we would receive the mercy of our Socialist government. Did the Soviet Union's political prisoners and ordinary criminals, who were sentenced to forced labor after the October Revolution, receive clemency? Most of them died in the Siberian labor camps. What happened to those Chinese nationalists, hundreds of thousands of them, after Mao Zedong's triumph? They were sent to Xinjiang reform camps and ceased to exist.

One senior member of our staff told us that "reform" by the communists meant "brainwashing." We, the people of the South, after two decades living under the maligned puppet regime and the overseeing imperial Yankees, must be cleansed inside out to become a new species under the Socialist government. As a new species, we would be valued as working capital to develop a new nation. And as an investment, we would cease to be human.

His words were an omen.

As part of the communist victory celebration, May 17, 1975, the Commissioner of the Central Committee of the Communist Party declared: "Of the former regime's puppets' private properties, and assets: they shall be ours; of their sons and daughters: they shall be our slaves; of their wives: they shall be used at our discretion; of their husbands: they shall be banished to remote zones where they will languish in labor work to pay back the blood debts to our people."

Once we reported to the Reform Program, we entered the abattoirs and the butchering began.

CHAPTER 3

Cống Trời, Heavenly Gate

Autumn 1978

If you love someone, say it.
If you hate somebody, say so.
—Phùng Quán

When I woke, I shivered and realized I was lying on a slab of concrete. The floor was a foot below. The air was so cold it stung when I breathed in, carrying a stink. Darkness only made the smell sharper: vomit and blood and sweat and feces and urine all having dried and refused to go away. I tried to shift my weight and stopped. The openings of the shackles were serrated. My ankles pounded. They must have bled.

I listened to the throbbing pains in my shoulders and arms. *They don't belong to you anymore.* My left arm hung limply, and a pain flared in the shoulder blade. I tried to turn onto my back and felt every part of my body stiff and raw with the cold. *Rest. You obstinate counter-revolutionary element.*

That was who I was. As a former CIO intelligence officer, I had monitored every political transpiration in the North and known well of their Resolution No. 49 that spelled out the reform of the obstinate counter-revolutionary elements. I could never imagine that one day I would be one of these elements. Forget the crimes against humanity. That does not exist in the communist law. Imprisonment without a formal charge or trial? That is their law. Now sleep. You are in no mind to think philosophically. But that is their law. They imprison you and deprive you of physical liberty, and all along they know they are violating the basic rules of international law so that they can brand you with counter-revolutionary crimes which, if convicted, will put you away for at least twenty years, or worse, a life sentence. Only then shall you feel grateful when they tell you, owing to the Party's clemency, that you will now be spared from a court judgment and sent to the reform camp instead.

The cellar was built from rocks. I shivered in my thin clothes. My stomach gnawed. Evening came. I knew it was evening when the trusty—a favorable inmate chosen by the camp—appeared with a tin can in one hand, a ceramic bowl in the other. He set down the storm lantern on the threshold of the door. In its glimmer, I spotted handwriting on the concrete slab. Just names. Those who had lain here had carved their names perhaps with something pointed. After the trusty left, darkness returned. I did not touch my meal, both the water and food, that sat on the floor within my reach.

I thought of carving my name. *Why? To be immortal after you die? For someone who would someday be lying here to say a prayer for you?* I killed the thought. From that day on, I never looked at those names again.

The concrete cell was narrow, damp with condensation that created a cold film of water on the floor. My fingers touched the moistness as I reached down for the bowl. It was rice. Thank Heaven. It smelled like moldy rice and tasted rough. *Eat. Don't think.* I ate the whole bowl and found out there was nothing else in the rice except a taste of salt. I drank half the can and saved the rest. The water tasted metallic. Was it boiled? *Drink it. Think not.*

The next evening, I asked the trusty who brought me water and food where they had taken Father Ninh and Captain Bé, and he said, "The dungeons."

Somewhere in this quarter were my two companions.

Sleep did not come easily. The wracking pains from my ankles troubled me throughout the night. They had swollen so badly; tears filled my eyes. Every slight movement of my body would cause bursting stars in my head. My elbows hurt from having had to support my raised weight so that, after a while, I gave up and laid down flat on my back. That brought out a groan from my scratchy throat. You must become stick thin and your ankles must shrink, I told myself. Then you could turn, and that shall be the greatest favor to your ankles.

I had found that my thoughts as a captive became limited in their range. At first, during the day I functioned and thought as a prisoner, but at night I could think freely; I could go anywhere; I could speak out loud my deep-seated liberal thinking. However, it did not last long. Once the physical freedom was taken away, a man could not think freely anymore. He would think as a prisoner.

Hunger returned.

Our great patriot Phan Bội Châu said, "When your stomach is empty, you can always dig up weeds and grass and stuff it; but when your head is empty, your nation is endangered."

Both my stomach and head were empty after days in the dark. Someone had said to me that one might not think of hunger on the first day of solitary confinement, simply because one was still beset with anxiety. It was not too far from the truth. The trusty would come in with my food and water and soon, by seeing him, I could tell a day had passed. I only had one meal a day. If not rice, then corn sprinkled with coarse salt. I would feel the corn kernels with my fingers. Out of curiosity, I counted each kernel as I chewed unhurriedly. Time had stopped. I need not hurry. I counted a hundred and five kernels. When I thought deeper, it came to me that I had one eighth of an ear of corn. I held a tiny pellet of salt in my mouth. *Do not suck on it. Let it melt.* Precious salt. Once I had a fist-sized ball made of wheat flour. It had been boiled and balled up with salt inside, each the size of a pea. I collected them. After the meal, I put each one of them back in my mouth, holding each pellet long enough to feel the taste seep through my tongue. Then I drank. I cherished my water, always saving it. *Do not dehydrate.*

Then the cold came back, sharp and clammy. I lay still. I was a hibernating rodent. I counted each throb in my ankles, felt the saw-like bite of each throb. I did not give up on my count until, like counting sheep, I slept.

I knew it was daytime from the sounds of the gong. I kept count of it the first day, imagining our daily routine, from morning to dusk. Then I forgot the time and lost track of it. Vaguely, I placed the passing of time at one week at the moment when I suddenly felt I could turn my ankles in the shackles. The ankles had thinned enough to lose the painful constriction, and now I could turn onto my side.

I trained my eyes to make out the shape of the cell, the cement bed, the chamber pot. I measured in my head the width, then the length, of the cell. One and a half meters by two and a half meters. Meals were brought in the evening. Most of the time, a bowl of cold rice mixed with salt. No spoon, no chopsticks. I ate in the dark, feeling the rice cold to my fingertips. I ate slowly. I chewed each morsel until it melted before I swallowed. I could taste a sweetness. Now I knew a secret. This could substitute for sugar. During the night, I was roused from sleep every three hours by a loud bang on the door. The metal sound dinged my ears and dazed my nerves. I found out that was the torment intended for the isolation confined inmates.

Through the bottom gap of the door, daylight would tell the passing of the day, except when it was weak, a dead gray, then it must be a cloudy day. Through the bottom gap, sometimes a rat would scurry in. I saw it darting around in the dimness, then it was gone. It might have gone down the drain hole in a corner into which one could urinate, if one was not permanently shackled.

I had not had a bowel movement for some time now. A toilet pot sat on the floor by the raised cement bed. When I drank, I sipped. I must make it last a whole day until the trusty came back with a fresh can of water. A few times I urinated into the pot, and it demanded a great effort on my part to try to place the pot between my legs and perform my function. I could feel the warm liquid coursing down the inside of my thighs, none of it going into the pot. I did not want to think further of defecating.

Once, I was asleep when the trusty came in. After waking, I knew it was evening by touching the can of water and the bowl of food on the floor. The rice had gone cold. In fact, I had never had warm rice served. Except this time, as I put a morsel of rice into my mouth, I touched something that moved. I could smell a stink. It must be a cockroach that had gotten into my rice while the bowl sat on the floor.

I imagined I was lying prone on the floor next to the door's bottom gap. The cold air filled my nostrils. Such pure air. It smelled of fresh dirt after the rain. I could smell mint from the foliaged mountain marigolds.

Then one evening I had my first bowel movement.

I pushed down my pants and, with my legs still crossed at the ankles, I tried to force it out. Nothing. I pushed myself up on my elbows and tried again. Nothing. Then I spread my buttocks and grunted. Nothing moved. I flopped back down. The cold of the concrete felt like a shock. After regaining myself, I raised up and tried again. The stool moved and stopped, and I could feel it when I touched it with my finger. The tip of the protruding stool was hard. Stuck there, it caused a great discomfort between the buttocks. I spat on my thumb and forefinger and tried to pull the stool out, all the while forcing down on it with my rectum. I felt that piece break off. It dropped with a tiny sound on the concrete bed. The inside of my buttocks felt wet. It took me a while to guess. It was blood.

The trusty appeared at the door. I did not hear the familiar clanging of his keys during my catnap. In his hands was a metal canteen of water and a wooden bowl of something. He placed them next to me. Daylight was mild coming through the opened door. For the first time, I could read some scribbled words on the wall.

Inside the bowl was dark broth and some sort of vegetable, perhaps water spinach, and floating in the broth were two dough-like cuts in white.

"It ain't much," he spoke with a southern accent.

"Brother, are you from the South?" I asked him.

He flicked his eyes at me and nodded.

"So, you've never been back?"

He said nothing, turned, and banged the door shut.

Sometime in the night, I woke. My big toe hurt. I wriggled my foot, cross-locked over the other, and there came the hissing sound of a rat. It was gnawing my toe. I thrashed my body. That brought out a loud cough from my otherwise dry throat. The rat sprung off in the dark.

I reached down for the chamber pot. The effort to bring it to my crotch caused sharp pains in my ankles. I kept still to wait out the discomfort. Darkness seemed to have condensed the air and sharpened its bad odor. *When was the last time this cell was cleaned?* I tried to hold my bladder and waited for the trusty to return. It would be some time before the evening meal.

On the cold cement bed, I opened then closed my eyes. The same blackness. Outside, quiet. Only at night were you saved from the clanging of the gong, which, hearing it the first time, made one think of medievalism. In the stillness, the words on the wall came back to me.

Once here, stay here
No return, not even after those baby trees
Have reached ten meters tall.

Some tenant had stayed in this cell, slept on this concrete bed, perhaps shat on this bed, perhaps coughed up blood. Perhaps he had used his own blood to write that poem on the wall.

Hunger gnawed at my stomach day and night. In this timeless blackness, hunger became malignant. I was consoled by the free movements of my shackled ankles. They had thinned enough for me to turn my body and ease the numbness on my back. Hunger had a blessing, though. It reduced the urge to defecate. An empty stomach equated breathable air. If you could last two days on a near-empty stomach, you soon became inured to hunger. My eyesight seemed to sharpen, something I noticed on one occasion when the door was opened to let in the trusty. I saw the tiny, ragged edges on the wooden shackles' openings, and spotted dark spots around my ankles—they were scabbing.

I constantly felt itchy, sometimes on my head, sometimes on my limbs. When I smacked myself at the itchy spots and smelled my hand, it smelled rancid. I did not know if I was plagued with bedbugs or biting midges. I fought them. I became the smacking sounds, the only sounds in the otherwise quiet cell.

One evening my meal came with a boiled manioc tuber and some cooked rice. The tuber felt slimy and tasted sour. I ate only the rice. I left the unfinished tuber in the bowl and set it on the floor. When I woke, not knowing the time, my stomach groaned from hunger. I felt around in the dark for the bowl and touched the tuber. In my hand it felt sticky. I ate it like eating a stick of glue, registering the sourness in every bite. It's just food, I thought.

I had lost track of time, but I knew it must have been many days since I entered the dungeon. The telltale of that was my craving for salt.

The rice would come every meal, with or without salt, depending on the cook's level of neglect that day. The body deprived of salt felt sluggish. I felt it in every fiber of my muscles. The lethargy left me lying like a decomposed log. A barn owl hooted outside. Then the wind whooshed. The cold slab of concrete did not bother me anymore because I kept drifting away. I commanded myself to wake, fully wake, to ward off the lifelessness in my limbs. I began massaging my body. I breathed in deeply and kept breathing in and out to keep my brain awake. I wiggled my feet, forcing the pain to flare up and bring me to life. This was going to be a long battle, I thought.

Before arriving at Cổng Trời I had nursed a hope of being freed after three years. Call it naiveté. Call it despair.

I thought back on what the camp educator, a lieutenant cadre, said to us on that first day, following the welcoming lecture by the Cổng Trời's camp administrator.

"You are here as a sole collective existence. For the one thousand of you, this is your real world. There is no outside world. There shall be absolutely no visitations, no correspondence. But you have one another, the one thousand of you. For those of you who nurse the intention to escape from this camp, my advice to you is this: Do not try. No monkey-browed, buffalo-headed lot like you have ever done that successfully out of this camp. There are two paths that you can choose. One going into this camp—you have already traveled that path to be here safe and sound. The other path is in the rear of this camp. That path leads to our camp graveyard on Bà Then Hill where, if opportunity allows, you will see the graves of your predecessors—those who have attempted escape and failed. Remember: Ascending to Heaven is easier than escaping from Heavenly Gate."

When I stopped reminiscing, I felt the cold deep in my bones. The mind was your worst enemy. It was autumn when I came to this camp, and it was autumn again now. We were on an elevation of three thousand feet in the Hà Giang province bordering China. The camp sat high up on a rocky mountain, so high that when you lifted your face you could breathe into the clouds. The mountain sides dropped steeply into a valley, and from high above you could see glittering reflections, like broken pieces of glass in the coursing streams. It was rare to see the sun in a cloudless sky, and every day was the same. A cloudy sky, foggy and damp. In its permanent grayness, rain fell, and the sky and the earth were a shivering pall of gray, and winds hurled across the mountain sides, hissing over the deep rocky furrows. Then the rain stopped. Twilight. Clouds sagged so low the valley disappeared, and in that whiteness, you could hear a cuckoo calling *bo-ko-ta-ko*, always four mournful notes. At night, sometimes it plunged to zero degrees Celsius, and the surrounding mountains stood frigid, rocky surfaces veiled in gray. The forest below lay black and, as the night grew, old fog descended thickly white until you could see nothing down below, and all was quiet except for the occasional growls of tigers and the hooting of owls, one calling after another, resounding like sounds in a bottle.

A spark of hope had kindled within me to break free of this camp after I ran into another group of inmates from another camp sector.

At the creek during a break from labor, I saw two men, not from our group, coming down to the water's edge, each hauling a bundle of fresh-cut bamboo on his back. They swung down the loads on their backs. The taller man, leaning on his machete, asked me, "Did you fellows just arrive in camp?"

"Yes," I said.

Both of them straightened their backs and saluted me like a soldier. "Our greetings to you. We're the forgotten commandos."

To my disbelief, the taller man named Văn told me he was part of the South Vietnam commandos who had parachuted into the North between 1963 and 1968. As captives, they had been granted the freedom of movement in permitted areas, working mainly for the camp cadres. They had been moved around, they said, before arriving in this camp, with many years in between. The last two notorious camps were in Cao Bằng, a nameless camp with a moniker "Rotted Bones," and another unnamed camp in Sơn La they called "Foggy Mountains." The longest detainees had seen twenty years pass by; the rest had at least seventeen years in captivity. In those years, they had seen many reform inmates finally released. But they, the former commandos, had been forgotten. Since their capture, over three hundred of them had died in different camps and now only forty had survived.

To see us, talk to us—the vanquished—they had finally believed the South had surrendered.

"All of us have been waiting for you for twenty years now. For the day you come north to liberate us. But it isn't so. What irony!"

I admired them. But I wondered why any of these commandos had not tried to escape. So, I asked Văn. He squinted at me. "Had you that thought?"

He touched his forehead and peered up at me. "Several of us have tried. Some died out there, some were killed by the guards, some were captured by the militias. I myself have stayed put. Only one of us made it out of here successfully."

"How?"

"How? Pick the right time. And be resilient. But we believe he did what nobody else could." Văn touched his lips with his forefinger as he measured me with his eyes. "Be warned that we are surrounded by mountains and forests that stretch beyond the horizon. Unhealthy miasma in the woods. Unclean creek waters from organic decay. Avoid them. Avoid speaking to the locals. If you must, change your accent. Your southern accent is your death sentence. Never trust the locals. They will turn you in to collect rewards from the camp. In case you don't know: If they capture you, they'll receive better rice ration, a merit certificate which will exempt them from labor work at their commune, and coupons to buy rare commodities most common folks aren't allowed to buy. So, to capture any escapee is their serious business. We, the political prisoners, are worth much more than those common criminals. The bounties on our heads are too valuable for these northerners to ignore. Once they hear three gunshots, they will drop everything and go hunt you down."

I said nothing; yet I felt the graveness he had conveyed to me. Then he smacked his lips, as if he had just forgotten something. "Let me make it clear to you about the consequences of escape. Any escape attempt will put the entire camp's administration in the Party's negative view. And any successful escape will discredit such a camp from top to bottom." Văn nodded at me. "But listen, do not lose heart. Man proposes; God disposes."

In my head, time did not exist. But, I must admit, our biological clock still ticked on its own. It left impressions of time beyond this blackness I was in. It must be a month passed.

To keep my rationality, I recollected the literary works I had read. I found that it was easier to relive them with my eyes closed. Albeit in darkness, the mind focused better with closed eyes. I let myself greet Edmond Dantès in *The Count of Monte Cristo* when the *Pharaon* came into the port of Marseilles. I kept track of time by the coming and going of the trusty, bringing the only meal in the late afternoon. I would then stop reliving the story and resume after my meal. It must have taken three days, three nights for me to journey through the life of the young sailor who was framed as a suspected Bonapartist and accused of treason for attempting to aid Napoleon to return to power. Reliving his suffering and retribution, I remembered some of the words he spoke. "It is necessary to have wished for death in order to know how good it is to live." I found comfort in them. When I arrived in the ending, the words which had stayed the longest in my mind to this day were: "Human wisdom is summed up in two words: Wait and hope." *Fac et spera*.

My daily food ration had changed. Now it was two meals—lunch and supper.

Each meal, sometimes stale rice, sometimes corn mixed with rice, or rice mixed with sliced manioc, came with pellet-like, unroasted salt. I would save half of what I had in a bowl and, later, dissolve them in my can of water to wash the wounds on my ankles and the bites from bedbugs. Cleaning those cuts, I could feel my bones in every part of my body. I had lost so much fat that it hurt to lie flat on my back, because my tailbone would rub against the concrete slab. I felt cold all the time as if I wore nothing; yet my mind had hardened against it, even accepting it, so that the clammy air and the ice-cold concrete slab were not something I fought against. I was the cold.

I woke. My body simmered with heat. The air was so cold it hurt when I breathed in. The heat did not leave my body. My chest felt painful. The feeling of being in a vacuum, in an eternal blackness, came back. What was wrong with my body? I touched my face; it felt damp. My throat was so dry it felt scratchy. In that blackness I felt absolutely alone. No use to call out, I thought, feeling my life ebbing.

I drifted in and out, enveloped in a suffocating darkness. I defecated and urinated on the cement bed, as my body acted on its own. The door opened. The clanging of keys. Barely was I conscious of the food brought into the cell. The door closed. The food sat untouched. My thoughts ceased. My body, drained of energy, was coal hot. Once I smelled the stench of my body waste and the urine. I was going away. In that blackness came a light. Some presence hovered over me. Then a voice, "Is he dead?"

When I woke again the door was open and, silhouetted in the doorway, were two figures. One of them said, "He's coming to." And they moved toward where I lay. My body was simmering hot and damp with perspiration. I barely made out the face looking down at me. "Are you awake?" he asked. The trusty and his familiar voice. He told me the doctor from the camp infirmary had injected me with a shot of Streptomycin. "Your lungs had fluid," said the trusty. "He'll give you more antibiotics in the next few days."

That evening, when the trusty came in with my meal, I saw a spider on the wall crawling towards a cockroach. From the overglow of his lantern, I made out some smeared words handwritten in blood and coal. I was in a minuscule prison cell, of a miniature prison, that existed among countless others in a colossal camp. Be grateful, I told myself, for you still have a roof and four walls to protect you from the squalls and the harsh sun when you could have been kept in a three-meter-deep pit large enough to hold three detainees, all standing and leaning onto each other, pissing and shitting in one place, and midday meals came rationed in half, the only meal each day. This way, they treated us a thousand times worse than just shooting us dead. One of our shack mates had died from eating goosegrass which he masticated like a cow; after three days he died, mouth open, still full of half-chewed yellowed grass and *bo bo*—the sorghum—which we had cultivated day after day for their Party, and for them to feed their pigs. One day before my failed escape, I had stopped at a pit that belonged to the human-waste team and watched a man crouching on all fours over two baskets ready to be dumped. He seemed oblivious to the surroundings and the biting cold. You could see the shape of his spine under his threadbare shirt. The excrement had a yellowish-brown color, and it looked like mud as he dug his hands in it.

"What're you looking for?" I asked him.

"Here they are," he said without turning his head.

"That's disgusting," I said, nauseated, as I saw the round ivory color of the bo bo. Strangely, I smelled nothing from those two baskets heaped with excrement. Then it dawned on me that what we had eaten contained no meat, no fish, and so our waste had no smell. He already had a handful of the bo bo grains, his hands covered with brownish gunk, as he moved to the other basket. Those grains had no signs of being digested in a human's stomach. Pearly, hardy grains for livestock. Something told me he was not going to eat them raw.

"You will cook them?" I asked.

"That's the intention," he said, busily churning the putty-looking heap of excrement with his free hand. I held my breath, turned away. Hunger had spared no one from grace. From political prisoners to common-criminal inmates—those with monkey foreheads, foul of smell. Hunger had brought us down to the animal level.

I kept track of the days every time the camp doctor came in with the trusty to give me a shot. It must have been on the seventh day when he stopped coming. My fever had gone down sometime on the third day, and I began noticing how cold it was in the cell and realized that I had beaten back death. In that moment, I breathed in the bad odor that came from my cement bed I had soiled with everything that had come out of my body.

I heard a gong. The first gong. It must be early morning. Then the door was opened with the clanging of keys. The same trusty came in. Behind him, standing in the doorway, was another man. The trusty unlocked the foot shackles; I felt the omnipresent weight gone. Yet my feet did not belong to me.

"Get up," said the trusty, backing away from the oppressive smells from the concrete bed and from my body.

Was I being freed from this dungeon? That was all I could muster up in my concrete brain. The moment I slid off the bed I collapsed to the floor. The men waited. Finally, the one in the doorway said, "Help him up." The trusty did not move; then I felt his grip under my armpits to pull me up. I leaned on him as he dragged me out, his head tilting away from me. The morning light was mild. Yet, it bothered my eyes. It was cold and I clenched my teeth. Was winter here? I wondered, as we made it to the pond behind the kitchen. I was out of breath the moment the trusty loosened his grip. On my hands and knees, I heard him say, "Wash yourself. You're now out of the isolation cell and back to the penal cell." He paused and gestured toward the man behind us. "You'll have a working-together session with Cadre Bảo later this morning."

On my haunches, I saw that my ankles had festered, caked, and scabbed. The skin looked purplish. The morning breeze fanned the bad odor from my crotch to my nose. I crawled to the edge of the pond and lowered my head and drank. I felt like a dry sponge being soaked. Lightheaded, I slid into the pond with my clothes on. The water was brown. It was not as cold as I had thought. The kitchen would boil the water they fetched here to cook rice. The green team would come here to fill their buckets to water the vegetable patches, and the human-waste team would rinse their buckets with the pond water at the end of the day. I felt grateful for being allowed to use the precious water for my cleanliness.

When I turned to get out of the water the cadre was gone. The trusty, with his arm under my armpit, walked me slowly to the disciplinary housing quarter. We entered the second cell. Next to one cement platform bed sat a wooden crate. I recognized it. An old ARVN ammunition crate.

"Your clothes are in there," said the trusty. "Get changed before you catch a cold."

I stood shivering in my wet clothes. Yet his soft tone made my heart flutter. I opened the crate. My old shirt and pants were folded on top of a bundle wrapped in banana leaves. I did not want to touch it. At my hesitancy the trusty said, "For you. You need to eat well to live."

I looked at him and saw his face clearly for the first time. He was about my age and height. His oval-shaped face looked gentle; the high forehead glimmered. Narrow-shouldered, he had a smaller appearance, as if he was born to be unnoticed. I unwrapped the bundle. Inside there were three thick cuts of manioc tubers, pale yellow, still warm. The fragrance had me close my eyes.

"Listen," he said, "you need to realize the situation you're in. They have the upper hand. If you cause no troubles, you'll be released in the near future. But you are on a blacklist of the incorrigibles. You're on that list based on your personal record from the previous camp in the South. If they can't have their way with you, they'll transfer you to another camp, and each time your chance of release gets smaller. My advice: Give them free labor and be invisible. Then you might live to see the outside world again." He breathed in deeply and squinted at me. "You'll be locked up only at night—not cross-locked with both feet this time. Only one. I'll be back in an hour to take you in for the working session with Cadre Bảo."

Something came to me as I was holding the banana wrapped bundle in my hands. "What's your name, brother?"

"Luân."

"What did you do before?"

"I was an aide-de-camp." He turned to look over his shoulder toward the door. "I must leave."

I did not want to press him to tell me which general's personal staff he'd served on. I said, "You shouldn't give me food. If they catch you . . ."

"You need to take care of yourself." He glanced back at me and left.

Alone, I sat down on the cement bed and brought a manioc tuber to my nose and inhaled its warm fragrance. It was the first time in a long time my mouth watered.

I noticed two bamboo tubes lying in the walkway between the beds. They were empty, and yet the cell smelled of rotten eggs. Those would be used for my urination and defecation. There were bloodstains on the foot of the bed around the shackles.

I ate my food, chewing slowly to savor the taste I had long missed. Each precious bite of it seeped into every fiber of my being. As I chewed, I sniffed the aroma of the tuber and felt grateful to my trusty. I ignored the evil smell that permeated the cell. By the time I ate the whole tuber, the hardness around my mistrust of humans had softened.

The cadre introduced himself as the security aide, a senior lieutenant by rank from the Military Justice Bureau. I sat down across from him, squeezing my hands between my thighs. I shivered. He offered me a cup of hot tea and, as I thanked him, my hands shook. Dressed in his sage-green uniform he appeared warm, while I had only a shirt on and could not stop shuddering against the cold. He leaned forward, tapped out a cigarette and nodded at me. In silence I received the cigarette as he struck a match. The first puff had me double up, coughing. After a few puffs, I helped myself to a first sip of tea. I began to calm down. I glanced up; he was brushing something off his yellow-striped, red epaulet. He said, "Since you were admitted into this camp, has anyone from the camp staff, from the cadres to the guards, broken the law while dealing with you?"

"I think not, sir cadre," I said.

"Then what was the reason for your escape?"

"As a prisoner, I was seeking freedom."

"Freedom? That will come after you repent for your crimes against the People."

I remembered him and his exchange of opinions with Father Ninh and Captain Bé that night. I did not know what to make of him. The cigarette was at my lips. I decided not to take a drag. "Sir cadre," I said, letting the cigarette smolder, "To be more exact, it's safe when you have the upper hand."

So much of this interaction was about the upper hand, as the trusty had warned me. So much of this was about playing safe and being invisible.

"Brother Khang," said the cadre, paused to light his cigarette. He let out a long exhalation and tilted his head looking at me. "It is not a mantra that we have repeated to you. It's a fact. We the proletariat believe in it. If we let you write home and receive letters from home, do you think that would help you see our new society in a better light? Perhaps you will realize that your hostility has been misplaced."

"What do you think, sir cadre? Once you get hold of my letters, you'll look for my sentiments. Despair. Hope." I took a quick puff and leaned back in my chair.

"If you do not change your way of thinking, we cannot and shall not release you."

"I understand, sir cadre."

The cadre looked at my cigarette burning to a stub between my fingers. I noticed it and stamped it out with my foot. He offered me another cigarette. I inhaled the bitter smoke, he refilled my cup. "Did you know that the American bombing ten years ago claimed the life of your mother here in the North?"

"I'm aware of it, sir cadre." I looked into my cup and spoke without engaging his eyes.

"You southerners had no ideology. That was why you were willing to become worms for the Americans to step on."

"Those are harsh words, sir cadre. We southerners were peace-loving people. Yes, we had no ideology, because we had freedom and democracy. And, sir cadre, freedom and democracy is not ideology." I looked across the table at him and, for the first time, I looked into his eyes and met an unflinching gaze. A trained interrogator, I thought.

The cadre lifted the teacup to his lips while the other hand slowly opened a folder. He leaned across the table and handed me a picture. "This came with a letter forwarded to this camp from our security bureau in Hanoi. I cannot let you read the letter from your wife, but you can look at this picture."

My hand shook. The cold came back, colder this time. In the black-and-white picture, my wife was holding our baby girl. She was six months old when the picture was taken, and I was the photographer of that picture. Our daughter must be six years old now. The last time I saw my father, before leaving the North in 1955, I was fifteen years old. At least we had had time to know each other before he died in Hỏa Lò prison in Hanoi. I had not had time to see my daughter grow up. Everything was drained from me.

The cadre refilled my cup, still almost full. "Nothing has changed back home," he said, fingering the envelope which had the picture and the letter from home. "Your wife is still teaching at a high school; your daughter can sing very well, so your wife said. I am sure she has an angelic voice."

I noticed the word "angelic" and wondered if the cadre was Catholic, a fact he must have guarded with his life. I said nothing. In fact, I had nothing to say. My shivering bothered me so much I felt as if I had a bout of malaria. Then I heard him say, "Brother Khang, do you remember Mr. Phong, your old director of Planning at the CIO?"

"I do, sir cadre."

"He has told us everything he knew as a former director. In fact, he did his best to help our government with whatever knowledge he had. By the way, he did mention you, Brother Khang. He held you in high esteem."

My old director had disappeared shortly after a brief stay at this camp. Nobody knew where they had taken him. The more you proclaimed to know, I thought, the more you entangled yourself with their interrogators.

At my silence the cadre said, "Brother Khang, you will rewrite your confession until I am satisfied that everything you put down in words is written with your utmost sincerity."

From then on, trusty Luân only shackled me at night. I thanked him for his kindness. He said to me, "You should thank the camp committee. Perhaps you played the invisible role very well." I said nothing.

I began to practice defecating using the two bamboo tubes. The smaller one served as receptacle for urinating, the bigger one for defecating. I felt grateful to have both of my feet unshackled during the day; and I had trained myself to do my bodily functions only during this time. At night, trusty Luân would come in to shackle my feet—not cross-locking, which was a merciful act. It was difficult for me to employ both bamboo tubes in the beginning, owing to the trembling of my already weak legs. At first, I had to make use of the concrete bed, raised two feet high, and lean my knees against it during my trials. In time my legs became stronger, and I could stand on my own, my stance spread and bent at the knees, concentrating on steadying the bamboo tubes, one in front, one behind, so the human waste would not spill onto the floor. A few times I had to sacrifice my own precious water to clean the spillage off the floor, water I had saved to wash myself after each defecation.

For an entire week, Cadre Bảo and I worked together on my new confession, covering lengthy subjects like socioeconomics, social and news media, cultural and social affairs, arts and letters, everything to do with our old South Vietnam and my association with it. On the last day of his stay, Cadre Bảo, looking more relaxed, remarked, "I will be transferred to another camp. This is my last day here, Brother Khang."

I refrained from asking him of his future whereabouts. I held no animosity toward him because he had neither verbally abused me nor physically maltreated me. Outside I could hear the loudspeakers blaring out the daily news. We had all grown so familiar with its strident tones of voice and vociferous hullabaloos that we called their broadcast LOV—Lies of Vietnam.

"Are there any small things that you might need?" Cadre Bảo asked me.

"I'd like to have a Bible."

"Aren't you Buddhist?"

"No, sir cadre. But this is for my priest companion. His only treasure was confiscated when he was admitted into camp."

"You know very well I can't do that."

"But I've heard from the camp lectures that you still have churches and pagodas in the North, and worshippers are still allowed to go there. That's the fact, isn't it, sir cadre?"

"We have religious freedom in the North, and plenty of worship sites in Hanoi."

I took it in, said, "With all due respect, sir cadre, I haven't lived in the North long enough to be its truthful observer. But I do believe my ears. Here, sir cadre, we're surrounded by villages. I've heard the people talking, I've seen them going about their chores every day. Most of our people are Buddhists. When there're Buddhists, there're pagodas. When there're pagodas, there're bells. If there're bells, why didn't I hear them? I haven't heard the sound of bells for months. Only the gongs. Why, sir cadre?"

Cadre Bảo smiled and said, "You're mistaken. Our pagodas in the North don't use bells. Only gongs." He nodded at me. "Do you still wish to write home?"

"No, sir cadre."

He blinked. "Well, then."

He rose and fetched from a chair a paper-wrapped item. He unwrapped it. I dropped my gaze to an enameled pan, its bright blue the only cheerful color in the drab shack of brown and gray. I wondered why an austere man like him would own such a nice-looking item.

"It was a gift," he said to me. "Given to me while I was at that 'Rotted Bone' camp in Cao Bằng. Brother Khang, consider this a parting gift from me."

I was speechless. It was like hearing a cadre shouting, "Foxy Hồ, you scoundrel!"

But from a camp security aide?

He turned the pan upside down to show me the Chinese characters printed in black on the pan's bottom. It said Guangzhou, where it was made. He took his time to contemplate the word only he could read—he was well-read in Chinese, he had told me.

"You will need this the next time you go bathing." He tapped the pan as he peered up at me. "Take this pan. It was made in Guangzhou, a valuable item."

"I can't, sir cadre."

"Do not worry. I have instructed the proctor committee not to confiscate it from you."

The next day, after he was gone, trusty Luân came in. He was not surprised when he saw the pan sitting on the floor, still unused. "A parting gift from the camp security aide, huh?" He smiled a rare smile. "You must've prayed a lot lately."

I wish I had. Perhaps to our Mother of Jesus, and when that proved not enough to keep me sane, I would start praying to our Guan Yin Buddha.

A few days later, the camp summoned all the inmates to the meeting hall. It was a Sunday morning, and the cold was in the air. All the inmates must attend. Those in the dungeons and the disciplinary cells were ordered to sit in the back, watched over by the guards, and were allowed no verbal communications with the assembled inmates. There were two other fellows from the disciplinary quarter. We sat far apart from one another. I looked for Father Ninh and Captain Bé and concluded that they were still in the dungeons for some reason; otherwise, they would have been with me, the unwanted.

The proctor committee sat behind a long table facing the congregation, then one of them rose and walked up to the podium. He took a megaphone that had been set on the only chair next to him and addressed the crowd.

"We are here this morning . . ." He stopped to adjust the volume, then put his finger back on the trigger. "We are here this morning to share some wonderful news with our camp attendees. It has to do with reconnecting with your families by way of correspondence." He stopped because of a hubbub in the hall. He gestured with his other hand for everyone to quiet down. "All of us proctors here have spent half of our lives on the B front, and during our time in the South fighting the Americans and the *ngụy* soldiers, none of us received family visits. That was unheard of then. The only news we received from home was via letters, and I myself received only five letters in my twelve years in the South. One of them was the news of my oldest son being bestowed with the honor of joining the B front. He was sixteen then. We never dreamed of receiving gifts from our families."

He seemed either agitated by the thought, or simply nostalgic for his own youth. The word "ngụy" still hung in my head; a pejorative the commies called our ARVN. Brainwashed by his Party, he must have believed that he had been fighting a resistance war against America, and we, aided by the Americans, were *ngụy quân, ngụy quyền*—puppet army, puppet government.

"Now listen well," the warden continued. "The Party and the Revolution are showing compassion for all of our camp attendees by allowing family gifts for the first time. Not visitation, but gifts. You are now allowed to write home, of course using the camp designated mailbox for location confidentiality. You are allowed such correspondence once a month. Consider this the highest privilege the Party and the Revolution have granted you. Your letters will be read by the camp security committee. There is no censorship here: Your letters must conform to the camp's protocols by always being positive, and by revealing nothing about the camp's location, name, and such. Any negative writing shall result in having your letters rescinded and you being disciplined." He paused as the congregation looked on. Many had a worrisome look. The warden fished out a much-folded piece of paper. "In one camp, we had an attendee describing in his letter the landscape where he currently resided. Very detailed. 'Panoramic, full of the cries of monkeys; at night you can sleep soundly to the roaring of tigers on the hunt.' One other wrote, 'I intend to save my only pair of sandals given to me by the camp. They're precious footwear, ingeniously made out of American automobile tires, which outclass any of the Italian dress shoes I had back home. To save this pair, I'm willing to walk barefoot into the forest every day. I don't mind having cuts and bruises on my feet. Thanks to the Revolution, I'm primed to become closer to my primate distant cousins: apes and monkeys.'" He eyed the assembly, nodding to himself as if to admit the gravity of such insinuation. He returned to the sheet in hand. "This letter I am going to read to you shall serve as a warning to those who may look to distort the noble policy instituted by the camp in the name of humanity and compassion. The attendee wrote, 'It's wonderful to see how the Revolution synchronizes human productivity with food rations. The former goes up in sync with the latter going down. It's done so to embody the grand scheme of the Party and the State. To substitute for rice, the Revolution gives us boiled manioc, which is, to our delight, a most delectable staple. At home you must try it. A rare find.'" The warden folded the sheet and put it back in his pants pocket. He cleared his throat. "The camp administrator in charge of the camp in question called that attendee into his office where he had laid out two bowls: one filled with white rice, the other boiled manioc tubers. 'Which bowl do you pick for your meal?' he asked the attendee. Without hesitation, the attendee pointed at the bowl of white rice. The administrator then produced the letter the attendee wrote home." He paused again as if to let everyone ponder the consequence of such aberration. "The Revolution grants you clemency so you can improve your health; and with body and mind in unison you can reform yourself in time to reunite with your family. To malign such clemency is anti-Revolution, and consequently self-destructive."

A silence fell upon the congregation. From afar, I watched and felt squeamish. The more you desire comfort to be provided for your meager existence, the more dependent you become on the camp's mercy. If I chose to write home, I would be held hostage by the camp.

The next day, toward evening, I had a new cell mate. He was an ex-commie, as I later found out. I never asked him what crime he had committed. He came in, bruised and bloodstained, and took up the other bed on the long iron rod that traversed the width of the cell. Mr. Vinh, the new cell mate, was in his early forties. He was bucktoothed and his thin hair was salt-and-pepper.

At noon the iron door was unbolted and a trusty came in with our meals. He left at my shackled feet a bowl and a cup of water. That cup was for both of us. He glanced at the newcomer and dropped his bowl beyond the rod. The man's eyes had more whites than pupil. He spat. Lanky and dark-skinned, his brief stare unsettled me. I could see saliva seeping at the corner of his mouth.

"Where's brother Luân?" I asked him about my kindhearted trusty.

"I'm your new trusty," he said, flatly.

After he left, Mr. Vinh sighed. In the dim light, I was not sure if he smirked or grinned.

"He worked me over yesterday," he said to me. "That watchdog."

"After they brought you in?" I asked.

"Yes."

"Who's he?"

"A former captain of your lost country. Now he's a trusty. His family are Catholics who fled North Vietnam in 1954. His father was a Catholic priest in Bùi Chu."

Bùi Chu was a Roman Catholic diocese of North Vietnam. After 1954, its Catholic devotees fled to the South and formed their Catholic stronghold near Saigon.

"So? Is he a good Catholic?"

Mr. Vinh's face was scrunched up. Finally, he said, "When he was put in charge of us out there, the first thing he said to us was, 'If any of you ever cause problems to my early release, I'll kill you.'" Mr. Vinh smacked his lips. "Completely reformed! That's what he wanted to be, so he could go home."

That trusty, Mr. Vinh said, had been here three years, and in that time had gained enough trust among the camp overseers that they allowed him to work offsite, sometimes unsupervised, and at times even engaging with the locals. Mr. Vinh had noticed that the trusty had received no visits from relatives. One day recently, Mr. Vinh gave him a few gifts and some petty cash to spend in the camp. Then he slipped him a piece of paper and asked if he could pass it on to one of those locals who had business dealings with the camp. The trusty read the note, said nothing, then nodded. A few days later, Mr. Vinh had been summoned to the camp's office and presented with his own handwritten note, having been laid on the chief warden's table, as if awaiting him. The note said to an intended recipient, who was a member of a gang in Hanoi, to bring weapons and manpower to attack the camp.

I looked at the bowl at my feet: a bowl half filled with bo bo. I picked it up while Mr. Vinh strained to reach for his bowl, the one the new trusty had put on the floor. A hand span closer would have been enough, I thought. I let out a silent curse, then handed my bowl to Mr. Vinh.

"Let's share this," I said. "Save your bowl for tonight." At night we could sleep, with one foot unshackled.

"We'll share my bowl tonight," said Mr. Vinh as he grabbed a handful of bo bo and fed a few grains into his mouth.

I wanted to eat it, one at a time, and count them as I had done before. That way you slowed down your thought and gave yourself ample time to break down a hardy grain. You would find out, to your surprise, that it tasted sweet when it was completely mashed.

In the evenings we would return to our shackles with one foot locked. Mr. Vinh would fall asleep with both arms crossed, hands covering his face. After a few days I began noticing his habit and asked him.

"Brother Khang," he said to me, "I've been locked up, both feet and hands, for so long that I'm afraid I might lose my hands for good should I leave them down there." He pointed at the through-wall rod. "Do you know that these shackles are power personified when they use them on us? From wardens to guards to trusties. The shackles empower them." Then pointing at the walls, still visible in the early evening weak light, he said, "Ever wonder why they painted the upper parts of these walls black?"

"Aren't they the same in every cell?"

"Only this cell. It used to hold inmates to be executed by decapitation in the old days."

"Would that such a privilege be reserved for us," I exclaimed. "Some of us living deserve death. And some of us already dead deserve life."

"Sometimes it's crueler to deprive a man of death."

I could not agree more.

The next day, the new and unfriendly trusty came in with our meals at noon. The tin cup that held drinking water for both of us was only half full. Mr. Vinh examined the cup and measured it with the length of his forefinger. He peered up at the trusty just as he was leaving.

"This much water for the two of us?" he said with a restrained voice. "Will you reconsider our water portion, please?"

"That's all you receive," said the trusty. "Be frugal."

We said nothing. We had learned not to pick a fight with our trusties. After he was gone, Mr. Vinh turned to me. "We'll have to save our own pee from here on."

"Maybe he'll change his mind the next time. We're not that desperate yet." Then on second thought I said, "Have you ever drunk your own pee?"

"Yes, Brother Khang. Have you?"

"No. And I don't want to try either."

"It's tolerable. First time it might be disagreeable. But if you keep drinking water, no matter how little, it'll help dilute your pee and make it less distasteful."

I kept such notion with me. The less judgmental you were, the more tolerable your life would be.

The next day it was hot. At midday, our thirst had reached its limit. Mr. Vinh banged his fist on the wall and screamed. "Water! We need water!"

His voice was loud; soon it turned into screams. The unfriendly trusty came to the door. I could hear him outside the door. "Water?" Then I saw his eyes through the air hole.

Moments later I heard water splashed against the door. Water droplets flew in through the air hole and I felt them on my face. It was then I reconsidered Mr. Vinh's suggestion. It would turn cold quickly after dark. The cold air would come in through the air hole on the door, and the cell would become bone-chill toward midnight. I found out that we could urinate more because of the cold, as it helped us retain our body fluid for longer.

Our food, on the other hand, was salty, be it rice or rice mixed with bo bo or corn. I silently thanked the kitchen for its mercy by making our food overly salty; otherwise, it would have been tasteless. But the salty food would drive us to quench our thirst quickly. Mr. Vinh came up with a solution. He took our pee in our shared cup and washed our food with it to dilute the content of salt. Now our food tasted as flat as a monk's meal, and we found out we could last the night. Nights when it rained, I would wake and listen to the gurgling sound of the water as it ran down the draining channels. I saw myself prostrating over a drain, lapping up water in my cupped hands.

One day our midday meal was made up of rice—nothing but rice. It was freshly cooked rice, still warm. I inhaled its fragrance, amazed that it did not smell stale for the first time. Mr. Vinh took no time in making a rice ball with his bare hands. He packed it tight, wasting no grains by wetting the palms of his hands with our precious water as he balled up the rice. I must admit when packed, the rice tasted better, so I made myself a fist-sized rice ball. The cooked rice came with a sprinkle of granulated salt, and it tasted so good I had to slow down to enjoy each bite. Then Mr. Vinh said, "I have an idea."

I looked over at him and saw that he had eaten his share. He pointed at the rice ball in my hand. "Can you break that in half and give me one half. And then tonight you can take half of my share. Does that sound reasonable to you?"

I thought of tontine. Perhaps it had begun this way, a poor man's common fund scheme.

I let him eat my other half and, that evening, I had a double meal that was so much for my already shrunken stomach that I gave him back a quarter of the share he owed me. Mr. Vinh was happy with his scheme because he always ended up with more to eat. Not that I was a naturally light eater but, in fact, I had trained myself to eat less, and my stomach had obeyed my command.

Whenever we received boiled manioc tubers, Mr. Vinh would break up his share into small chunks and let them soak in his bowl with salt. He would refrain from eating until an hour later—which was a torment for him—when the manioc cubes had expanded in the bowl to twice their original sizes. After each meal like that, he was full and fell asleep soundly.

"The difference is in the form," he quipped. "The expanded manioc lumps give a more satisfactory taste in the mouth than in the stomach."

By this time, I had become skilled in emptying my bladder and stomach using the bamboo tubes. Mr. Vinh was no novice to such practice either. We both had become contortionists by our own volition. We split our garments, with him giving up one sleeve of his only shirt, I one leg of my only pair of trousers, to wipe ourselves clean after such a routine. Then we waited until we were let outside to wash at the pond. We would bring with us those rags, and we would wash them at the same time we washed ourselves.

Once a week we were allowed outside for self-cleaning. We had adopted a new word from the commies: "improvement." From their repeated use when they interacted with us, we came to understand that "improvement" meant to better something—and we applied this to our daily meals. We would be allowed to forage food as supplements to our daily rations. Before long "improvement" meant a multiform food improvement. We foraged vegetables and animals—frogs, rats, snakes, even scorpions. On the way back from the pond to our cell, I would sometimes quickly pluck a handful of sorrel, sometimes purslane, sometimes wild water celery. Once I brought back a fistful of duckfoot herb and found out that this animal food was too tough to chew.

One morning, I woke up with a pinging toothache. It came from one of the molars in my upper jaw. I said nothing to Mr. Vinh. I fought back the throbbing by not thinking about it. I noticed the pain seemed to grow sharper whenever I closed my eyes. It pounded against my temple, and I felt as if my eyes were falling out of their sockets.

At noon, the trusty came in with our usual meals and shared water. I blinked to see him better. "Can you spare me some fresh salt?"

"There's salt in your meal."

"It's for my toothache."

"Never heard of such thing."

He left as quickly as he had come in. I could understand his refusal if I had been in a common shack. It was true that some inmates had used salt to break the metal bars in the shack windows. They would wrap the bars with rags and then wet those with saline water. Over time, with much patience, the metal gave. But while an inmate could crawl through a window to get outside at night, he would never make it in the end. I knew it now.

Mr. Vinh, hearing me moan, suddenly tapped his head. "Don't despair. Consider this heretic if you think it's a bitter remedy."

I raised my brows at his statement.

"This," he said, "might be your first time. But it'll work. Drink your own pee now."

I had eaten my food with our urine for weeks now, as we had used it to wash off the salt laced rice. I gave it a thought, not wanting to ask for a scientific explanation. I picked up our shared cup and filled it halfway full. I looked at the cup in my hand as my temples pulsed with each jab of pain. I drank. My own pee tasted salty-bitter. Warm with an ammoniac smell. I took only three sips and set the cup down unfinished.

The next day when the trusty came in with our meals, I had to drink up my unfinished cup so he could take it back. The first night the toothache had kept me awake, and I was tired when daylight grayed off the wall of the cell. During the day I did not talk to Mr. Vinh. The pains kept me mum. I heard him but could not retain what he was talking about. The following night I drank the remainder of my own pee and fell asleep despite the pains. Perhaps I was simply so exhausted that the pain mattered no more.

I woke in the night as if I had come to an abrupt stop in a dream. Coming to, I had expected the pain to return, but in the quiet I felt only tiny pulses in my temples. They were not from the pain. I slept, feeling grateful. Perhaps, like a ceasefire, the wicked bacteria needed time to regroup.

The next day, I drank this new home remedy with a renewed confidence. That night I could sleep, not soundly, but not in pain. When I asked Mr. Vinh, now my resident doctor, how this could be possible, he said there was a toxin in our urine that forced our body to develop antibodies to fight off infections. I did not buy his theory, but deep down, I owed it to him.

One morning the cell door opened. The unfriendly trusty came in with a guard. The cool air and the morning light filled the cell. The guard wrinkled his nose. "It smells in here. Didn't you make them clean the cell?"

"If you wish," said the trusty. "It hasn't been the rule, as far as I know."

Hearing him, I thought it must be the unspoken rule to let the detainees breathe the unhealthy air of their own muck.

"Do as you wish," said the guard as he stepped out of the cell for fresh air. "They're your responsibility."

The trusty unlocked only me, freeing my foot. "Come with me," he said. His breath smelled of onion. "Put on your clean clothes. I'll be waiting outside." He gave me a fresh set of blue-striped garments.

I changed as Mr. Vinh watched in silence. Then he said in a low voice, "Are you thinking what I'm thinking?"

"I'm thinking it may be another interrogation—not being released back to the shack."

"Don't lose faith."

"I have none."

I caught his smirk. Perhaps he agreed with me.

The moment I stepped into the camp administrator's office, I was surprised. He was not the same administrator I had seen before I was put in the dungeon and then the disciplinary cell. He looked in his fifties and was small in stature. In fact, he resembled a shrunken version of a mummy, except for his eyes. They were beady, glittering, like the eyes of a hawk. From the number of stars on his red epaulettes I could tell he was a captain.

After the trusty and the guard withdrew and closed the door, the administrator greeted me with a nod and a smile. The corners of his mouth pinched. His teeth were badly stained, perhaps from smoking or drinking tea, which he offered me by pouring it with the reverent gesture of a tea lover. Respectfully, I raised my cup with a slight nod at him and sipped. It was subduedly fragrant. I felt buoyed.

After some formality during which he introduced himself as the new camp commander, the administrator opened a book to an earmarked page. "Read this," he said, pushing the book toward me. "Then tell me what you think."

Unsettled, not knowing what his subterfuge was, I reluctantly lowered my eyes and read:

> Our nation is rich in fauna and flora. In Cát Bà National Park we have the near-extinct white-headed langurs, the world's rarest primates. There are rare species of trees, such as the weeping fig, some of which are over a thousand years old. Intruders have, in the past, sold their stems for gold. Our Soviet Union ally has asked us to exchange one strangler fig for one power plant capable of providing electricity for a whole city. But with our excellent engineers who are working to build many electrical facilities for our people, we are determined to preserve our precious fauna and flora at any cost.

"That's hard to believe," I said, carefully, "if I may volunteer my thought, sir administrator."

"This book is authored by our comrade Lê Duẩn, general secretary of the Party's Central Committee. Don't you believe it?"

"I'd rather not say, sir administrator. But personally, I read discerningly; otherwise, I worry I will fall for propaganda, which, sir administrator, is the word I'm afraid to use."

"Will you be honest with me, Brother Khang?" he asked, blinking. "Do you equate this camp to death, and the world outside to life?"

For one brief moment, I could not place him as a philosopher or a communist, because I had never heard of a communist turned philosopher. "Sir administrator," I said, "if I could ask the dead from this camp, I'm certain that our opinions would agree; and if you, sir administrator, could ask any southerners about life—life in our beloved South—I'm certain that you would know what life really is."

He seemed to muse, his hand slowly turning his teacup. He looked straight into my eyes. "If you never leave this camp, or any camp in the North, would you have any regrets?"

"If I added nothing to this world when I came into it, then I won't mind if I don't leave anything behind when I depart from it."

The administrator kept a neutral look as he fixed his gaze on me. Slowly, he opened a file folder. The top sheet had my name and, below, inked in black, were the words: "Incorrigible Element." That was the first time I saw my personal file. He closed the folder.

"At least you speak your mind," said the administrator, his tone mild. "Now, the reason I called for you is to inform you that you are now released from disciplinary confinement and back to your common lodging. Your daily ration is back to normal." He dropped his voice with his eyes lifted at me. "Brother Khang, you shall conduct yourself in accordance with our rules and regulations. It will help you work towards a favorable end. Don't you wish to see your family again?" Without me replying, he nodded. "I wish you well."

I left the administrator's dwelling and blinked against the bright morning light. The trusty and the guard, who had been waiting outside, escorted me back to the cell. They stood outside, leaving the door open for me to gather my only belongings—a camp shirt, camp trousers, and the enameled pan. Mr. Vinh, shocked, seized my hand. "You're going back to the shack, aren't you?"

I nodded, aware of the stares of the two men at the door.

Mr. Vinh pumped my hand. "I told you." His voice was shaken.

I felt his companionship, however brief it might be.

As we approached the inmate shacks, I saw a long line of men standing outside each one. At our shack, the trusty briefly exchanged words with our shack leader and handed me over to him. I realized that it was Sunday, and that on this day the inmates received the privilege of going to bathe in the creek. They all looked like beggars with pans and *Guigoz* can in hands—*goz* for short among us—and the rags they had used to wipe themselves that now helped them wash in the creek. It was chilly, but nobody seemed to mind. Sunday was the best day, not only to rest but to cleanse one's body of filth, to scavenge edible herbs and vegetables, and to stock up water for private cooking.

I met Bee's stare. Five years older than me, he was a satirical poet, a literary critic, and a political analyst in the South's glory days. He had one eye smaller than the other and, when he squinted, the small eye closed. I limped up to him in the line. Immediately he turned his face away. Hurt, I simply stood, head hung. Had I done something wrong in order to alienate myself from the group? He turned back to me, his hand on his nose. "You need a bath, Khang!"

A man behind Bee chimed in. "We all do, Brother Khang. But you smell worse than a rat."

Bee touched my shoulder. "You'll need to eat. I want to see you live."

I tried to smile. For one moment I had thought that he, my best shack mate, my best companion from the old days, had disassociated from me because of my offense against the camp. His real name was Lau. His moniker came from a Japanese Bureau Chief of the Saigon-based *The Daily Yomiuri,* the English-language newspaper that came out in the morning and evening editions. The bureau chief, who was versed in Vietnamese, took a liking to Lau, especially his satirical works, and called him "The Bee." I could not agree more when I thought of the barbs in his work, as nuanced as they were.

In the old days, whenever I could not find him in his newspaper office, I would walk down the street to an alley several blocks away and find him among opium smokers in a smoke-filmed den. Some of the patrons were journalists and writers and artists, and more than once they would offer me a draw, which I refused. One time he quit going there. It lasted several weeks during which he dedicated himself to writing investigative journalism on a topic arising from the Mekong Delta. A homegrown boy of the region, he was one of the most vociferous voices criticizing the Saigon regime for its stance against opening a university in the delta. Verifiable sources backed up his belief that the regime viewed the delta as a southern haven of Viet Cong. They believed that opening an educational institution there would only entice their infiltrators to infest the academy. To fuel the fire, he accused the Saigon regime of using this policy to stunt the delta's inhabitants' intellectual standard so it could reign over an untaught population. There were truths on both sides of the argument, and I never wanted to challenge him on that, knowing how plagued the delta was with Viet Cong moles. In fact, I would hate to be his satirical target. While his satire was a beloved feature, accounting for the large sales volume of his newspaper, it would often be held up on the censor's desk, causing delays to the release of the newspaper due to the affected pages having to be re-typeset.

He had had a repertoire of poems he wrote, which found their home in some of the vanguards of literary journals like *Sáng Tạo*—Creativity—which published groundbreaking new forms of poetry where form and rhythm found their free styles that broke away from the structures of traditional rhythmic verses. I never knew he was a poet until I read his poems in one of those magazines. Then his poetry took on more challenging subjects, when he began satirizing the second Republic of South Vietnam for its repression and corruption. His satirical attacks were not one-sided, for he also stung the megalomaniac Party leaders of the North, calling them ignoramus, and lumping them in with the junta of generals in the South. Though antipodal, in Bee's eye, the two regimes were twins, using extreme measures to impose censorship and suspend civil liberties. I was more attracted to his attacks directed against the North, because I was working for the CIO of the South. To exemplify the repression the North used to suppress or silence its dissidents, he published, in place of one of his own editorials, a poem by Phùng Quán, a writer and a member of the *Nhân Văn-Giai Phẩm* movement. That poem had originally come out in the wave of criticism, primarily from those two journals, against the Land Reform campaign. When the Party shut down the movement, the author, and many of his fellow writers and artists, were sent to hard labor. I remembered that poem:

I am now twenty-five years old
The orphan-turned writer
Yet I never forget my mother's words
Still fresh as a red-ink stain
Ever since I was five
How dangerous it is for a circus tightrope walker
But if truth be told it isn't as dangerous as being a writer
When he chooses to speak the truth
If you love someone, say it
If you hate somebody, say so.

Now we marched single file to the creek under the watchful eyes of the guards. The creek, a kilometer away, ran high all year round. Halfway there I realized how tired I was. My legs gave. Bee stood me up. Wrapping one of my arms around his neck and leaning into him, I dragged on. His gray hair fluttered and tickled my face. Even his stubble was all gray. We were of the same height; only, I was stauncher in my build. But now I felt more like a skeleton next to him. I closed my eyes as I kept up with him and heard him say, "I had my daily ration reduced for three days because of you."

"What did I do?" I asked without opening my eyes.

"It's what I did by volunteering to bring food and water to your cell ten days ago so I could slip you a few vitamin B pills." He chortled. "Damnation!"

"Go on."

He had attempted to slip me a few vitamin B pills, he went on, by bribing the trusty—the unfriendly one—only he had no idea that the trusty he had bribed was a snitch. The following day, Bee was taken to the camp security quarters. The first question coming out of the security cadre was the source of those health supplement pills.

"I told him," Bee said to me, "'I borrowed one here and one there from our shack mates.' He said, 'Nonsense! Who could've spared you even half of a pill of that precious drug.' I wondered, could a vitamin be a drug? Well, vitamins are safe, while many drugs are not. But I couldn't tell him that."

"You underestimated them."

"Nothing surprises me," Bee said, huffing. "You know, I was late in reporting to their reform program. They came into my house, and guess who handcuffed me? This kid who used to be our newspaper's hot-metal typesetter. He didn't even greet me out of respect. Just slapped the cuffs on me, said, 'Now it's the time of our life. Write a poem for that, you reactionary!'" He coughed up phlegm and spat. "They arrested me and several other newspaper fellows. You might not know this, but the commies gave us a name: The Pen Commando Faction. First they accused us of espionage, then changed it to anti-Revolutionary propaganda. Twelve years to death sentence for committing espionage. Two to twelve years for being anti the commie's half-truths."

"Compare your offense to those involved in the *Nhân Văn-Giai Phẩm* movement, you, at least, have a chance."

Bee grinned. It looked like pain on his face. "If they were as smart as they always self-proclaimed, wouldn't they make use of our knowledge and skills?"

"No. If they did, there's a chance they'd lose control over us. The commies want absolute control or else." I raised my voice as we neared the creek; the men began talking excitedly like children in a candy store. "Have you still been writing poems while I was gone?"

"Just one. This one is pure poetry." He went on to say he had composed it in his head while crossing a mountain pass to a distant work site a week before.

Serpentine passes, plumping a gorge
at times kissing the clouds with the tip of your hoe.

I thought of his counterparts living in the North as poets and their stunted creativity, long snuffed out by the Party. What they produced now were propaganda poems, folk verses. To live out your creativity, you need freedom. I did not have to tell him that. He already knew. I admired him though for his undying will, this force that drove him to keep his creative mind alive.

With the guards' permission, we walked into the creek to wash ourselves. In summertime, we could not wait to get here; but the evil cold of wintertime had discouraged many of us to take off our clothes and wade into the icy water. Everyone stood along the edge of the creek, shivering, some having removed their shirts, hunched in their skeletal postures, pale and gaunt.

I got out of my clothes and calmly walked into the creek with my blue-enameled pan. Bee hesitated. "Just get it over with," I said to him as I filled the pan with water and splashed it onto my body. After my ablutions, I refilled the pan and buried my face into it. The wind had many men moaning. I walked back up to the pebbled bank and put on my clothes quickly. I turned to Bee who was squatting on the water's edge, washing his limbs with a piece of cloth.

"I thought you must've got used to the cold by now," I said.

"Easier for you than me," Bee said, and rubbed his face with the cloth. "You're the one who needs a good bath."

For the next three days I was exempted from daily labor. On the third day, I saw Father Ninh escorted to the security shack. Later that day he came back to our shack with a trusty. He looked emaciated, which did not surprise me. We were merely skeletons once we left the dungeons. In fact, he had lost so much weight, his once plumpness was now gone. As we greeted each other in the narrow walkway of the shack, I noticed his legs trembling. I could not help but sympathize with him. My legs, though not shaking any more, still felt rubbery, the ankles scarred and pained. Yet his equanimity put me at ease.

"Brother Khang," he said, puffing, "did you know that Captain Bé died?"

That froze me. "Died? When—"

"Last night."

Before I could ask him how Captain Bé had died, Father Ninh made a hand gesture for me to wait as he made his way to his bed. Only two of us were in the shack in the mid-afternoon. Seated, he regained his breath then crossed himself, mumbling. "Have mercy on us, the repentants. Amen."

Their cells were next to each other, Father Ninh told me. Though the concrete walls between cells were thick, he could hear Captain Bé, and the sounds he had heard were not pleasant. As time went by, he found out from the trusty that the guards had applied the saddle torture every day to inflict as much pain as possible on Captain Bé. With his feet cross-locked at the ankles in the wooden shackles, the guards raised his body with a square pole under his buttocks. The pole went through the wall and, subsequently, through a vertical post outside. The rectangular opening the pole went through allowed the guards to raise it at will. Each time they raised the pole, Captain Bé's ankles were squeezed. Father Ninh could hear him, and the sounds had him wishing he had gone deaf. Each day, Captain Bé's meal ration was a small bowl of something edible and a small can of water worth a few sips. They carried his body out of his cell at midnight the night before.

That night, unable to sleep, I lay on my back, eyes open, and in the darkness, I felt as if I had no eyes. *Captain Bé is dead*. I did not know him well except for the time together before and during the escape. I had asked him what he remembered most during his military career. He said it had to be the night he delivered the Funeral Oration for the Dead Commemoration. The night was cool. In the stillness of the night, he orated while the dead soldiers, once his comrades, must have been listening to his bass voice from another plane. In the coolness of the night, filled with the yellow flickering of torchlights, there was only his voice calling to the dead, vowing to sacrifice for the nation. A gritty man he was. A fanatic who believed in self-righteousness and spoke his mind to whomever, whether they were ready for his honesty or not. He had once said to me, "Brother Khang, were I a captain under our President Diệm's regime, would I ever be promoted to the rank of major? Tell me."

"What made you say that?" I had asked him.

"I'd heard that President Diệm would call any candidate who was a captain, and only from the rank of captain up, into his palace. He would consult his physiognomist to determine if the candidate was worthy of the promotion."

"Based on his facial features?"

"Yes. They're the indicators of the person's characters."

I laughed, avoiding looking at his facial features.

The next day, Sunday, it rained in the morning. In late September it was chilly. Bee and I left our shack and headed to the latrine.

Bee said, "You're as pale as a fish's belly."

He helped me to the trough by a latrine at the end of a row of shacks. I leaned my forehead against the slatted bamboo wall of the latrine, my head swimming away. "I'll get you some B1 vitamins," he said. "You'll need it to get back on your feet."

I urinated, eyes closed, hearing the sound of it hit the trough.

"Strange though," he said, hand on my back, "something about a human viscerocranium doesn't change. You still have your high forehead."

I tried to grin, my eyes fluttering. Even smiling was an effort.

"You need to brush your teeth," said Bee. "They're yellow like a dog's."

Done with our morning hygiene, we walked back, crossing the courtyard, when I saw a small group of elderly inmates sitting under the thatched eaves of a shack, weaving basketry. The oldest looking one, dressed in a blue-striped prison shirt, was also the gauntest. In shirtsleeves, his arms were mummy thin. Despite his poorly groomed, stubbled hair, his head was well shaped. It was cold and blowy. He saw us looking and nodded with a gentle smile. Bee bowed slightly to the old man, then looked at me. "You know who that is?"

"No."

"Well, you're not a Buddhist." He shrugged. "That's *Thầy* Thanh Tâm, head of the Buddhist Chaplain Commission."

The Venerable, later Bee told me, had been in the camp several months before I came. His dharma name was Thanh Tâm. We would address him in private as *Thầy* Thanh Tâm—Venerable Thanh Tâm. He would ask me more than once, "Please call me 'anh,' to save you from troubles." *Anh* is "brother" in Vietnamese name addressing etiquette. I understood. The camp had commanded us to address one another as "anh," never using our former pronouns, such as "Ông" or "Thầy," which accorded with the addressees' former titles or ranks. But, in this hell where most of us for the unforeseeable future had already resigned ourselves to our fates, "born south, die north," we still respected our old country's decorum.

Under the overhang dripping with rain, we stood. Bee sat down beside the old monk. He was rubbing his stubbled head, cropped unevenly. He was shivering in the cold wind.

"Where're your warm clothes, *Thầy*?" Bee asked him. "How can you sit out here like this?"

The monk smiled, a serene smile that held my gaze. "I'm more concerned about you young people. You're not well fed, poorly clothed, and not accustomed to hard labor. I often wonder how you survive. Many of you were not made for this. As for me, I grew up poor. I'm used to hardships . . ."

"*Thầy*—" Bee cut in. "Last week you fainted out there on a vegetable plot. That's just barely outside the camp. Imagine if they'd sent you to our labor sites, an hour or two on foot, you'd have perished." He and I caught the gaze of other elderly inmates who had stopped weaving. Some nodded in agreement.

"Do not fear for me," the monk said. "Fear takes the joy of living out of you."

One of the elderly motioned with his head toward the courtyard. A cadre was walking toward us. Bee grabbed the old monk's hands and then rose to his feet. I could see the old monk's gnarled hands, now mostly just bones.

Later, Bee disclosed to me that the old monk never cared about his daily meal allocations. Each team would divide equally the allocation among members, often under everybody's scrutinizing gaze while the food was portioned out. The old monk would sit on his cot and meditate when the portion was brought to him. "They steal his portion every day," Bee said, snorting. "He even gave some of his already skimpy meal to someone who complained about still being hungry. Those louts!"

After the cadres walked past, the old monk looked at my swollen ankles.

"Do you want to sit down for a breather?" he asked me.

I nodded. His calm gaze put me at ease. In his presence, I somehow felt light as paper. Perhaps that was a blessing for me. I sat down with Bee under the shade of an olive tree that canopied the thatched roof. In the shade, I could see some of the leaves had turned red. Sometimes we stole its oval fruits when the guards were not around.

I heard the old monk from where he sat.

"There had been a death in that cell, Brother Khang."

He meant the dungeon cell I had been in. "I didn't know that, *Thầy*." I looked over to him. "How did you know?"

"I passed by there the day you went in. I sensed a spirit's presence. Brother Khang, I prayed for him as I pray for all of you, every day."

Bee narrowed his smaller eye at the old monk. "*Thầy*, your prayer might guide his soul to a better place. But for us, the fools, nothing can free us from the everyday cycle of misery."

"That too shall pass," the old monk said.

Perhaps, I thought, he had no fear of death because he had lived wisely.

"Where do the souls go after death?" I asked him.

The old monk rose and came over. He stood in front of us, his hands folded on his abdomen. "Brother Khang, you asked because you are curious for the sake of your spirituality, or merely a thought of flirtation?"

I thought then shrugged. "*Thầy*, I did not believe in an afterlife, but I have begun to ponder the meaning of our existence. Sometimes I ponder how vast the universe is, or if there is a God, a Creator. But I often ask myself, 'Why am I here?'"

The monk's eyes turned pensive. He did not speak. His face was shadowed by the sun behind him. Then, after a moment, he cleared his throat and said, "You exist because of your mind. When the mind becomes still, no thoughts active, then your physical existence is unbound. Every action has its counteraction, good or bad. We exist because of our binding karma. The mind is that which drives everything. There is no God acting as Creator."

I contemplated. I had never bought into that "God the Creator" concept.

I thought of something else. If the retribution of one's karma was individually unique, why were we all here, in this camp? Had we all committed identical offenses in times past?

"Dear *Thầy*," I muttered, "I often wonder why the communists hate religion."

Thầy Thanh Tâm kept his gaze on a puddle of yellow light on the veranda. "Absolute power is the cause of such hatred."

I could not get up from my cot at the sound of the morning gong. When Bee tried to lift me up, my limbs were like rice noodles. I was exempted from that day's hard labor. But the following morning I did not get any better; my limbs dead, my breathing ragged. Another man and Bee carried me to the infirmary. The young male nurse was a northerner who was new to the camp. He gave me one brown pill he called "the subduer," which he said could fix any kind of illness. The following day, I was so low on energy I could not speak. Those in the shack speculated about when I would die. Bee decided there might still be a cure, so he and another shack mate carried me back to the infirmary. A man walked in.

"What ails him?" he asked Bee.

He told him.

The cadre scowled. Then he asked us what shack we stayed in and promised us proper treatment when he returned. Half an hour later he came into our shack with a black pouch. He took out a syringe. "This is vitamin B12. It will boost his vitality."

He gave me a shot in the chest and said to Bee, "Tell the cook to give him a can of pig feed every day. Boil it and have him drink all of it."

After Bee told the cook, he came back and said to me, "That's the camp's doctor. There's only one doctor for several camps. You don't see him often though."

The next day I received another B12 shot from the young nurse—the doctor must have ordered him to do so. Bee continued to boil pig feed—rice bran and leftover cabbage, all minced together—and I drank that blend for three days, and each day with a shot of vitamin B12.

Toward the end of the week, I was able to rise from the cot. The morning I was able to get up from my cot, I saw, to my abhorrence, I had defecated during the night. Unable to clean up my mess, I asked the shack leader's permission to move to the infirmary. But still, I was too weak to move around on my own. So, with the camp doctor's permission and the aid of a pair of crutches, I limped into the infirmary. But that night, I woke and felt a dampness in my crotch. I had wet the bed. I began to condition myself from enuresis and bowel incontinence. I believed that thought controlled things or, as the old monk Thanh Tâm had said, thought was behind everything. I did not have another similar incident, except one night toward dawn I woke and found that I was on the verge of urinating.

My body had aged terribly as a result of the corporeal punishment I had received in the dungeons. My body had become desiccated. During the day, with mild sunlight, I could look at my pale limbs and the wrinkled skin. The skin peeled when I scratched. Soon I could shed skin like a snake.

The next evening, Mr. Liên, who lived in another shack, came to visit me. He brought with him his *goz* can half filled with bo bo gruel—the hardy sorghum. Mr. Liên had been imprisoned since 1959 because of his involvement in the pro-*Nhân Văn-Giai Phẩm* movement. He had been on the editorial staff with my father, though he was several years younger. Spindly looking with a tuft of white hair on his head, he reminded me of a crane. He sat down on my cot and fed me one spoon of bo bo after another. The cursed sorghum was most hated among us because it was so tough that most of us had to pound them to separate their husks before cooking. This harsh winter saw the food supply dwindle: Meals were mainly made up of rice, and the camp brought in bo bo that came from India, where it was used as cattle fodder. The sight of him feeding me must have been comical because it drew giggles from the other two patients in the shack. I was not dead yet, but he did not let me feed myself. Much later, I learned from him that he had a daughter living in Hanoi. Perhaps by spoon-feeding me, he relived his love for his own daughter. I had not seen my little daughter for three years; whereas he had not seen his own daughter for twenty. Most of those from my father's generation, who had gone to Cổng Trời in the 1960s, had died by the time I arrived. Mr. Liên was one of a few left.

The next evening Mr. Liên came into the infirmary before the curfew. He slipped a piece of paper into my hand. "Read it and chant it with all sincerity," he said. "This is the *Great Compassion Dhāraṇī*. Your health will come back to you."

He said he could only copy a portion of the text of the *Invocation of the Great Compassionate One*, but in time he would copy the entirety of its eighty-four verses as a transliteration of the Sanskrit.

He was a devout Buddhist. "How will it help me, Mr. Liên?" I asked.

"Like saying a prayer, it will ease your mind. Chant it so you can calm your thoughts. Another thing: Less is more—do not speak freely; eat less to condition your body in case you have nothing to eat for days. Last: Karma must be paid in full before you are liberated. Understanding that shall take your grief away."

After he left, I opened the small piece of paper. The paper was the kind smokers used for their hand-rolled cigarettes. His tiny handwriting was unreadable in the poorly lit shack. I folded it and put it away in my shirt pocket. I never intended to read it, though I never forgot the concern shown on his unkempt face when he looked at me.

Sometime in the night I had an uncontrollable bowel movement. I soiled my cot, my pants. In the wavering light of the oil lamp, I could see the yellow bo bo, most of them still intact. Strangely, I did not smell the familiar odor of human waste. Was I dying?

Morning came and I could hear a chopping sound coming from the kitchen. *Chop-chop-chop.* Firm, crisp. If it sounded dry, that would mean they must be chopping gourds. But this was different. It must be meat. Today was Hanoi's Liberation Day. Inmates would be allowed fresh meat. Apart from national holidays, there were no other days in the year that the camp could afford fresh meat for us: those burnt-caramel-colored cuts of meat, those beef bones floating in a pot of broth glistening with fatty dots like fish eyes. Those narrow cuts of fried meat still covered with fat. Yes, the kitchen left the fat on. It saved time for them to skip trimming fat, but to inmates this was a treat. Sink your teeth into that strip of fat, feel it pop and release that rich greasy taste that spread all the way up your palate.

The last meal with fresh meat seemed eons past. Based on the camp's unwritten policy, inmates received fresh meat once a month. But it had been two months now and no fresh-meat supply had arrived in the kitchen. It started with our elaborate escape from the camp. The camp committee convened, and what came out of that office was a loud verdict: no fresh meat for inmates again until someone came forward to volunteer information on how the escape had been hatched and who knew about it.

I heard footsteps and opened my eyes. The young nurse stood looking down at me and at the mess now caked on my cot. "You miserable piece of spoiled meat. You still breathing? Stop that purring. Just die."

Indeed, I was dying. From my cot rose a stink, not of waste, but of me. No matter what I had washed this decrepit body with, it smelled like meat gone bad. Worse, the foul odor of the sick permeated the infirmary.

"Water," I muttered.

"Urgh! Hear this: Too much water will get you sooner to the grave."

I bit my lips, dry, cracked.

"Just hang on. You might get some fresh meat tonight before you leave us for good. Hanoi's Liberation Day. Ring a bell? Die now and those undertakers will get your share when they bury you."

Toward evening, the kitchen brought meals for the sick and the chief nurse. I could hear him talk to one patient who had feigned an illness to avoid labor. "Join me in my quarters. I have the spirits." The chief nurse had just finished concocting some intoxicant by mixing some ethylene, that colorless, sweet smelling flammable gas, with several tablets of multivitamins and some molasses. He had saved the ethylene by not wasting it on patients; he treated their external wounds by washing them with warm water. The chief nurse, appointed by the camp administrator, used to be a district nurse before serving a five-year sentence on a rape charge. He did favors for the camp's inmates in return for personal contributions. With his signature, an inmate could get a day off, at times several days, from hard labor, and rest in the infirmary. The kitchen was his ally, always saving good portions of fresh food for him.

Sunday came.

A gray morning. The infirmary was quiet. I was the only one who was awake; the other two patients were still asleep in their cots. I imagined the shacks across the courtyard would come alive soon, the men boiling water to make tea, to draw on their water pipes, the festive mood rising in the thick odor of wild tobacco smoke. I thought of my family. I allowed myself to do so out of my weakness. I conjured the face of my wife and then my little girl. I could imagine my wife, but I drew a blank when I envisioned my daughter. I could remember pains. They marked you. But all that remained of memories of love was elusive. I had thought the absence of their love would make my heart grow stronger; now I knew it was an unavoidable absence. In these moments, I could listen to my heart. It told me the truth of things which could not be touched or seen. And my heart was barren.

The mist had lifted toward noon when Bee came in. He slipped me a round piece of peanut brittle the size of a tangerine in diameter, spotted with black sesame seeds. I smelled the fragrance that came from the thin, reddish-brown layer of molasses that held together the burnt-brown bits of roasted peanut. Also wrapped in the paper were several broken pieces of brown sugar.

"You need sugar, brother," he said softly. "But you look like you're going to live. Whatever they feed you here, eat it. Eat it all. Or die."

"Where did you get all these?" I asked.

"The peanut brittle from the wife. She's been sending it since we were allowed to write home many moons ago. The sugar chunks from those goodhearted fellows in our shack. Late last night we heard the sound of hammering from the carpentry shack. Some fellow said they were making a coffin for you. I couldn't wait for morning to come." He looked at me. His concern touched a tender nerve. He put in my hand a much-folded piece of brown paper. "Read it at your leisure. My latest brainchild is now tangible in a piece of paper we wipe our asses with."

"I'll memorize it on your behalf," I said, "and dispose of it before they search me."

Bee looked out toward the kitchen at the end of the row of shacks, from which came the sound of utensils. It was almost lunch. He snickered. "We still have 400 grams of food a day, and that's a hodgepodge of rice and corn and manioc paste. But I've heard today we'll have meat. Damnation! Pork! Well, at least a portion of the stuff the size of two fingers for each person and cabbage soup boiled with pig's bones. Picture that!"

He left. I ate his treat. It had been a long time since I had something sweet in my body. I did not know that sugar tasted like a miraculous nectar, and my body shivered. The sweet taste spread through me, and I felt like a rejuvenated man. I salivated so profusely I had to swallow the spit. Sunlight made glittering coins on the earth floor. Slowly they moved and disappeared as dark clouds gathered. I liked watching the bulbous spots of sunlight in transit to become aware of the passage of time, something completely lost on me during my solitary confinement. I believed, as humans, we belonged to time like slaves to masters; the past lived through us in our present, and the future was merely the present projected. I never knew why, as the living, we kept thinking about time; even when I was completely shut off from the outside world, alone in darkness, I heard time tick on. The biological clock. I remembered the words written by William Faulkner in *The Sound and the Fury* about time, in a story where a father gave his son an heirloom watch: "I give it to you not that you may remember time, but that you might forget it now and then for a moment, and not spend all your breath trying to conquer it."

Rain fell tick-tacking on the thatched roof. Then rain came down in a gray sheet, thumping the dirt ground, pattering against the bamboo laced walls of the infirmary shack. Remembering the crumbled piece of paper from Bee, I took it out of my shirt pocket. In fact, I pulled out two pieces: one from Mr. Liên, still unread, and one from Bee. He had written a poem in pencil:

I have met the most simple-minded among the imbeciles
And lived among them like an ascetic
Consider me one of those dolts
Living a double life.

For us sinners, Christians or Buddhists or atheists like myself, we led double lives, and I surmised that none of us were happy with both of them. But with Bee, he was a man of two truths. In this odyssey he had been my steadfast companion, beginning with our two-year stay at an internment camp in the South, then to Cổng Trời exactly a year to date since the previous autumn.

I must have drifted off to the sound of the rain. I could smell it, the rain-soaked earth and vegetation. The seaside air would smell like this in my first camp, perhaps more briny and moist, more acrid and thin, and the air would echo with the calls of shorebirds, and out on the sand-brown beach there would be sanderlings, and, far out on the sandbars, the high-pitched cries of willets. After a rain, the air was cool and fresh. The morning was gray, a steely gray of water and sand. In the early light one could not tell where the calm water's edge met the sand. The shallows brought skimmers from the sandbars where they had rested; the air rang with the birds' harsh sounds. *Ha-a-a-Ha-a-a*! I pictured them as migrants who had flown south through Vietnam to escape the cold in the North. I envied them; their freedom, coming and going with the seasons. Mornings when we would come through this coastal flat from our nameless camp in the South, I could see far out in the ocean beyond the clanging buoy and imagined a ship to take me there away from shore where the bitter tang of the sea was the smell of freedom.

On one of those mornings, I met a little girl selling dumplings. She would cross the beach in the early morning light on her way to the commune market, half an hour on foot away. She said to me she was ten years old, four years older than my little daughter, who was only three when I left. That morning, I gave her two *Lu Petit Beurre* biscuits I had brought with me during our excursion to the commune where we would trade the produce of our camp for meat and rice. I told her the next time I would give her a book to read, if I could lay my hands on one.

"What kind of book, *chú*?" she said, referring to me as uncle.

"Any book. Reading is good for a child your age."

"Books are useless," she said, pouting.

"They are not. Why would you say that?"

"The new regime said if things are not edible, they're useless."

"And you believe them?" I was not surprised. The propaganda of the North had begun its strangulation of the South in every aspect of life; schooling was no different. It was disturbing to see a girl her age who already had a sour outlook on life.

"Flowers are useless too, chú," she said, as if having read my thoughts on this topsy-turvy society. "I used to sell flowers after school. Now I'm selling dumplings."

"Your mommy made these?"

"Yes, chú. Would you buy some?"

"I don't have money."

"It's fine, chú. *Tù* like chú don't have anything."

I did not have to guess. She could read the initials "CT" for "Cải Tạo" on the back of our shirts that branded us as reform prisoners.

"Daddy is tù," she said, brushing her hair on her forehead. "Mommy said the regime sent him to the North. Very far away."

"What did he do before?"

"He was a soldier. He'd lost a leg during the war, but they still sent him away."

That morning, she could not sell us her dumplings; we were penniless. However, one time we pooled the rare amount of money we had between us and bought the whole tray. It was more a treat for her than to us. Most of the time when we met on the beach, she would follow us to the commune. Some days she could sell the whole tray, but most of the time she would carry back the tray half empty, and her dejection would make me sad. On the way back one afternoon, as we crossed the sand-brown beach, a russet color caught my eyes from under a deep pile of saturated moss.

"Something in there, chú," the little girl called out.

I pushed the moss with my toes.

"A crab," she exclaimed.

The big crab stirred, then became still in its sedentary position. We all loved eating crabs but, with our shabby fates, none could make a meal out of those sea creatures—it was not possible to carry them back to camp, or to eat them on the spot. On the sand flat rested the shorebirds, shifting as the wind changed direction. I thought of a meal—the plump sandpipers, the terns, the skimmers. Overhead I heard the gulls calling and quickly covered the crab with the mound of moss.

"Why, chú?" she asked, lifting her face at me.

"Those gulls will have him for a meal if they spot him."

One afternoon as she followed us back from the commune, we rounded a dune and walked upon the faint footprints of some shorebird.

"Chú, look!" She pointed out a fox a short distance ahead of us. A red fox. I held her hand, kept her still. It took but a moment before I knew what the fox was after.

"Clever fox," I said to her, and explained in a low voice that the fox was following the footmarks to a bird's resting place. I added that if the bird had been smart, it would have walked on the wet sand and never left a print of its feet. The fox, impervious to the cries of shore birds, kept on trotting after the track, its fur ruffled by the wind that carried the clear bell note of a plover.

In those days we had had guards escorting us to the commune and back. After one year we had gained enough trust from the camp, so that our team, all twelve of us, guarded only by two *bộ đội* youths, was tasked to leave camp early in the morning and carry our homegrown produce to a commune near the seaside. In the afternoon we would return, bringing back with us the provisions we often lacked such as sugar, salt, cooking oil, and, at times, rice. By mid-morning, after leaving the camp, we could smell the brine in the breeze and the ground was rough with fine bits of shells. Bent under a burlap bag stuffed with the camp's produce, each man labored in his climb to cross the dunes. I weaved my way between clumps of low-lying saw palmetto and crested the dune ridge among nodding sea oats. The long climb sucked the air out of my lungs. The salt laden breeze was warm on my face, and the sea boomed below. We took a short break, sitting on the sand, away from the waxy looking pear cactus. Some of us plucked the red fruits and ate them. I never tried it, though some the men said it was sweet.

The last time we were in each other's company we saw a one-legged sandpiper. The little girl stood transfixed by the bird's determination as it probed and jabbed at the water's edge, where the white foam was a sign of mollusks carried in by the waves. The wader retreated, hopping away from the swift surf only briefly before skipping again toward the water's edge. It did not have the nimble movement of the normal birds of its kind, their legs twinkling as they flitted about on the sand.

"Chú," she said, as she looked up at me, "can you make his leg normal again?"

I was surprised she did not ask, What happened to his legs? I shook my head. A pause, then, "I can't. Nobody can. I don't know what's injured him. A trap might've hurt him, or a fox might've gotten him. He might heal again, or he might not, ever."

Thinking of her, I could not help imagining the precarious lives of the sea creatures, and those of humans like hers and mine. There were times when, walking on the sandy shore with her, we would spot small lives living deep in the sand, away from fish that rode the tide ashore to feed on them, and out of sight from foraging birds stepping along the water's edge at low tide. She said there were times, before she met me, when she forgot to go home because she had followed some tracks winding across the sand and had not stopped until she found the creature that had left them behind.

"What'd surprised you most?" I asked her once.

"They all surprised me when I came upon them."

I thought then of my daughter, wishfully imagining holding her by the hand as we walked across the sand after a V-shaped track a burrower had made, and she would ask what animal's track, *Ba*? And I said, just wait, and she broke off running and then stopped a good distance up the beach and yelled, I found it. It was a sea creature covered in brown bristles. What's it called? she asked. A sea mouse, I said. I could tell how fascinated she was by the iridescent blue-green hair on its sides. She said, I don't see its eyes, *Ba*, as she bent over the wide worm, afraid to touch it. I said, it has no eyes, but it protects itself with its bright colored hair to warn off predators.

That afternoon we came back through the coastal flat. It dawned on me that I had not even known the little girl's name. Something told me it was the last time we would see each other, and I felt empty as if she were my own daughter about to say farewell to me for the last time. We were walking above the tide line, sometimes kicking up litter of sticks and seaweeds and shells, catching sight of crows pecking at dead crabs and sea refuse. The air was full of sounds of the stirring of wings, the sound of bird voices, of sweet pipings, and the occasional cries, like laughter, of newcome birds squeaking across the empty sky. These sounds marked the passage of time for me. Yet, for us, time was indeed measured by the sound of gongs, morning to dusk; for these shore creatures it was the rise and fall of tides.

Before we crossed the dune, where we parted ways, and she would get on home, going straight down the flat, I stopped and said to her, "I don't know your name."

"Hải Yến."

Her voice was innocent, and she did not look surprised when I asked for her name.

"Pretty name," I said, picturing the graceful swallow known for its tireless wings.

CHAPTER 4

Cống Trời, Heavenly Gate

Autumn 1977

The evil that men do lives after them;
The good is oft interred with their bones.
—William Shakespeare

I was one of the seventy-nine captives the victorious Revolution had identified from various camps in the South at the start of autumn 1977 to send to Cống Trời, the most notorious punitive camp in the North run by the Ministry of Public Security. Our group included fifty-eight political prisoners and twenty-one Catholic priests. Based on our anti-Revolution behaviors—constantly confronting the camp authorities during lecturing sessions, organizing hunger strikes, masterminding escapes—the communist regime had come to categorize us as the most dangerous reform camp attendees.

Before arriving at the camp, I had heard rumors about the place: once entering, never exiting. A slaughterhouse hidden in the remote mountains in the year-round cold, foggy northwest. A burial ground for hundreds of the Republic of Vietnam's intelligence agents, political warfare officers, and thousands of northern Catholic priests, Buddhist monks, and political activists.

When we arrived at Cống Trời camp, winter, which lasted from September to April, had begun. The weather was cold, and at night it would drop to near freezing point. The sky was gray, and inside the meeting hall, it was cold. All the wardens huddled on the podium; you could see their breath in the air. The megaphone blared out: "All seated!"

The camp administrator was a cross-eyed cadre. He welcomed us with his heavy northern accented voice.

"On behalf of our proctor committee, our security staff, and our administrative personnel, I welcome you to our camp, where you will have the special privilege to continue your reeducation program." He straightened his back and dropped his gaze towards us sitting on the floor, and his face became stern. "To be here is to begin the new phase of the reform program. Now hear this: We, the People's Public Security, run the camp and directly report to the Ministry of Public Security. We require that you shall obey the name addressing etiquette in this camp. Address the camp personnel as 'cadre' and yourself as 'I,' and we shall address you as 'brother' and ourselves as 'I'. Now, hear another fact: You are not camp attendees as you might have been called elsewhere; you are prisoners. The camp shall exercise its absolute authority to assess your reform progress and shall determine whether or not to release or continue to detain you. As manager of the camp, we shall perform our duty to the fullest to assure your safe return to your family; but, at the same time, we have the vested authority to keep you here indefinitely."

Very soon I knew about the camp's infrastructure. Each camp was a self-sustaining, self-producing unit in this vast gulag. We, the inmates, must labor in the fields and turn out the appropriate yields to feed the camp cadres, who, in turn, fed us with food rations below the prisoner's standard allowance. Beyond that, we were expected to build our own prison. We built bamboo shacks to house ourselves, and tall fences surrounded by moats to keep ourselves from escaping.

Every day we had to walk three kilometers from the camp to where we could find sand to cart it back for housing construction. Other teams had to break rocks or fell *luồng* bamboo to build houses for the camp cadres. The *luồng*—giant, thick-walled bamboo clumps—were tall, and many of us had met our end while felling them. Some were impaled by a *luồng* trunk; others, while breaking rocks, were crushed during a landslide. So many had died, the dead filled up the Bà Then graveyard on one side of a manioc hill behind the camp. By this time, death was no longer something we feared, but something many of us had wished for.

Our shacks had mud-enforced bamboo walls. Each shack had parallel bamboo platforms for bunk beds running the length of the shack, leaving an earth walkway between them where wild turmeric sprouted, yellow-flowered, their bracts tipped with pink. We ate their leaves on nights when hunger caused us to lay awake. At the end of the shack was the water closet housing a single wooden barrel for human waste. Our bamboo cots' stems were our hidey-holes; carved, drilled, to keep our precious personal items the camp labeled as "illegal," "forbidden," "dangerous."

All of us dwelled in the section for political prisoners. Separated from our section by a bamboo fence was the section for common criminals. Beyond the cluster of our dwellings were the quarters of the penal house, partitioned into cells, and beyond it, the dungeons.

During morning roll call, the shack trusties would walk from row to row checking the back of our shirts. They looked for any shirts missing the ink-and-oil black stamped "CT"—Cải Tạo—bold, a hand-span tall, that would tell outsiders we were reform prisoners. Escapees would have no way to blend in with the locals unless they stripped themselves bare. In time the stamped initials would fade from sweat and sun and rain, then they would be superimposed by a fresh stamp.

It was the last day of July, and the weather was mild because the camp was high up, almost touching the clouds. On our way back into camp after the afternoon labor, we were ordered to line up in the courtyard. We stood in columns, team after team, in the bronze afternoon sunlight.

Waving a piece of paper in his hand, the camp administrator roved his eyes from face to face, all grimy and tired looking. Finally, he spoke, his lips barely moving. "Someone among you had a creative mind which he has misused to deliberately malign the Party and the Revolution. Worse, he slimed our beloved Uncle with his petty words. His little mind came up with verse, not poetry, on this thirty-first day of July. Fittingly, he called his verse *Remember the Land Reform Campaign*."

We looked at one another. Today, I thought, was the day the Land Reform campaign ended twenty-one years ago. July 31, 1956.

The administrator held the piece of paper away from him as if it were a live snake. "I have decided against reading the content of this verse because of its unworthy nature. However, the Revolution is always fair-minded and Uncle Hồ, I can imagine, would have a benign smile for even the benighted lot. So, I am going to ask a team leader to read this to you. Afterward you will meet among your team members to discuss this aberrant behavior and how it helps toward your ultimate release. Keep that in mind."

Our team leader was called forth, since our team stood nearest to the administrator. A fixed gaze on the piece of paper brought an uneasy look on our team leader's face. Then, squaring his shoulders, he read out loud: "*Remember the Land Reform Campaign*?" He paused to signify such was the title, then read on, lowering his voice:

Uncle Hồ! Uncle Hồ!
See the upheaval by ebb and flow?
See those innocents against the poles, dead by execution?
See those accusing evils in People's Court, your new breed?
Gone are our beloved hamlets, gone our country
Gone is our morality, gone family tradition
Sunk so low is our motherland
Spiraling to Heaven are our people's cries

He stopped, not moving, and held the paper away from him in much the same way the administrator had. We quickly stole glances at each other. I looked over to Bee. That poem had his satirical sting in it. As his confidant, I knew he would spend nights composing a single poem, whether free verse or rhythm verse, picking the words, the cadence, the nuances, revising them mentally then memorizing them. During the day he would rework the poem in his free time, repeating it in his head, and at night he would recite it again and again until he locked it away in his memory.

The administrator turned to one of the wardens behind him and nodded. He was not our warden. He was short in stature, his complexion livid. Bucktoothed, his receding chin barely moved as he spoke. "We are about to have a general inspection of personal items. Everyone will stay in the same place until your shack is called, then you will go back with the guards to your shack and bring out all of your belongings."

The old monk, *Thầy* Thanh Tâm, had given Bee, a devout Buddhist, a Buddha statuette the monk had carved himself. "If you wish," he had said to Bee, "then give it to your son by any means you can. Instill some faith in the child because you're here and not home. Otherwise, the soulless, moral-less communist teaching will turn children into haters, atheists."

The monk had used only nails and a handmade knife someone had made for him to carve the statuette. That afternoon when camp security launched a surprise shack search, going through each inmate's belongings, I seized the statuette before the security cadre saw it in Bee's cloth sack. The guard found it in my knapsack.

"Who made this?" the sallow-faced security cadre asked me as a guard handed him the statuette.

"I always had it with me, sir cadre," I said, looking at his two front gold teeth.

"Liar!" He slapped me across the face. "When you were admitted into this camp, your personal items had been declared. Except for those registered with our security office, your belongings did not include *this*—" He waved the statuette in front of my face, still stinging from his smack.

At my silence, he snarled. "You received it from *thằng* Thanh Tâm, didn't you?"

His insolence towards the old monk riled me. "No, sir cadre." I kept my voice even.

"Are you covering up for him? That's conspiracy. Are you conspiring against the Revolution? Is he your cohort?"

"No, sir cadre."

He threw the statuette on the ground and stomped it. It did not break. But something in me broke.

The cadre took from the guard another item from my knapsack: the black prayer beads. I had accepted it from the old monk on the same day Bee received his Buddha statuette. The cadre dangled the beads in front of me.

"It was reported to the camp committee that you practiced rosary praying every morning." He shook the beads noisily. "Is it true?"

"It is true, sir warden. I believe in religion. Also, our country under the new regime does respect the freedom of religion."

"That's a fact. Except that you do not have the entitled right to religion, which belongs only to rightful citizens. You are only working towards claiming back such right as legitimate citizen. The only right given to you for the time being is the right to live, so you can reform yourself. Until then, your religious practice is revoked. When the time comes for you to practice religion again, you are entitled to it fully, only after you have registered it with the State and then pay taxes, just like any other profession. Of course, with the exception of two forbidden trades: prostitution and robbery."

That was the first time I had the taste of a penal cell. The camp had a twelve-cell concrete house in its penal detention quarter. I was not shackled by both hands and feet. Only one foot was locked to the iron rod that traversed the width of the cell from wall to wall. Serious violators would have their feet and hands shackled. The worst offenders had their feet cross-locked. At night the guards on their rounds would make roll call by stomping the traverse rod, one end of which protruded outside the wall into the walkway. One would have to shout to answer above his racking pain. Some sadistic guards would entertain themselves at night by stamping the rods of those whose feet were cross-locked. I could hear the guards laugh from their sickening pleasures. The victims' screams had, ever since, lodged in my head.

When I had time to reflect on the statuette happenstance, I would blame it on coincidence. Much later, after I had known the old monk, I learned that nothing in this world, in our lives, ever depended on chance. Everything, he said, was karma induced. Then I must presume that the incident with the Buddha statuette was no coincidence at all.

Several weeks after I had returned to our shack from disciplinary confinement, autumn leaves turned red and yellow. One Sunday, the camp conducted an initiation rite. It began with shaving our heads. All of us became hairless like Buddhist monks, except the monks themselves. They, however, were forced to let their hair grow back to be like us, the mortals, before we lost our hair. *Thầy* Thanh Tâm was silent as always in his calm, dignified self; but one of the monks, Vĩnh Đăng, who was my age, protested against such practice. The barber, a common criminal, said to him plainly, "Cổng Trời's policy speaks louder than any of your Buddhist canons."

Because of his protest, the monk was disciplined. He disappeared from us. After asking around, I found out that he was quarantined in the dungeons, a stone's throw away from the disciplinary house.

In late autumn, the temperature dropped to near zero degrees Celsius at night. I heard that there was snow on the peak of Fansipan mountain. I thought of the monk alone in that concrete dungeon, in complete darkness, and I remembered my three days in the penal cell. How would the monk survive in such an ice-cold cell at night? Could he meditate and become oblivious to the surroundings? I thought of the old monk Thanh Tâm, and how detached he was all the time from his milieu. Perhaps such a mind could calm the body's physical suffering, especially a balanced mind.

Lying next to me was Bee who, every night, said a prayer to Guanyin, the bodhisattva who embodies compassion, to save the monk from suffering. I had never believed in praying; I had no faith in religion. I was an atheist. But, unlike the communists, I could sense the compassion of one human to another in distress through the words, the sound of such prayer.

One evening, the gong sounded for the last roll call of the day. We were lined up before our shacks when two guards dragged a human toward us. They were coming from the dungeon quarter. They stopped in front of a shack and called out the shack supervisor to take the inmate back. It was monk Vĩnh Đăng.

At first, I did not recognize him and thought he was a commoner. I stared at him: He was my age, but his hair was white. The hair was not long; but after only one month, it had covered the monk's head and he looked like a white-haired old man.

The guards dropped him. Without their restraint he sank to his hands and knees in a heap of shrunken flesh, barely clothed in a bloodstained shirt and yellowish stained pants. Half his shirt was gone, baring his back where his ribcage sharply protruded. There were dark welts on his back; those familiar marks left there by lashes. From his slumped position, he looked up as his shack supervisor took hold of his hand to lift him. His sunken eyes were two empty sockets, soulless. On his feet he trembled, the spindly legs unable to support him. Bruises covered his legs. There were bloodstains on the front of his shirt. He did not resemble a human. Something beyond human cruelty overwhelmed me. I shivered.

What haunted me was the inhuman shape of monk Vĩnh Đăng that spoke of evil reigning the earth. Yet what troubled me even more was the thought of comparing the monk's action to *Thầy* Thanh Tâm's. Why did the younger monk have to protest? Why could he not keep his faith to himself and live it?

The old monk, after listening to my question, let out a sigh and lapsed into silence.

"One," he finally broke the silence, "should not attach any significance to words or the nature of rules and regulations. These mind-induced attachments speak volumes of an ego still asserting itself. All is empty. Emptiness is all." The old monk stopped. He looked serene despite his malnourished paleness. I wished I had his serenity. What came back to me were the words he had once chanted in his nightly prayer:

Swallows wheel across the sky
Shadows in the water
Which they don't mean to cast
And water means to hold none of them

But was it wrong to fight for what one believed in? The monk Vĩnh Đăng fought for human dignity. Was it illusion? Was it vanity? The Catholic priests kept their faith at any cost despite their banished lives. They feared nothing. Heads could roll; Death could wait at the door, yet their hearts never surrendered. I had no answers.

It was too hot in the shack after our midday meals. Such was the vagaries of the weather in Cổng Trời. Out on the veranda, I sat down under the overhanging roof, my face tingling with the heat. I dozed off, my head lolling. I sensed somebody's presence next to me and woke. Mr. Liên was smoking a pipe. He did not seem sleepy.

A pig squealed, then more pigs went oinking. The plot where they roamed was behind the camp committee's house. The man who tended them was an inmate whom Mr. Liên had known since the day they were with the *Nhân Văn* journal. I listened to the ruckus the pigs made. Something came to my mind.

"*Bác* Liên," I said to him, "do you think he's doing what the other fellow did to his pig?"

"Who?" Mr. Liên took the pipe off his lips. "Bình? The guy who tended that big fat pig for our warden?"

"Yes."

Both Mr. Liên and I snickered at the same time. One day recently, one of our team leaders heard the squealing from the chief warden's dwelling's pigpen and decided to investigate. The warden's pig was black with a pink abdomen, a rare kind. There he saw the swineherd in an inappropriate relation with the female pig. There was a struggle on the swineherd's part as he tried to disengage from the pig. He was stuck in the pig's vagina. The team leader with his quick wit fetched some water and poured on the offender's manhood until he was free. He would have spent a week in a cold cell for such an act had the other man reported the incident to the chief warden.

"What do you think they would call such an offense?" Mr. Liên asked.

"Fouling the Revolution's property?"

Chortling, Mr. Liên turned his face toward the camp committee's house. "They have six pigs. All females. You know why?"

"For breeding?"

"I said all females. No breeding here."

I shook my head; I had not a clue.

"Female pigs," Mr. Liên said, "might yield lesser meat quantity than males, but they're easier to raise, less hostile, and you won't have to worry about castrating them. But I don't think old Khâm is into bestiality like the other fellow."

"Not at his age—those pigs are strong, *Bác* Liên."

Mr. Liên coughed and spat. "When you get to be our age, Brother Khang, there're other things to worry about."

"I've never asked you about Mr. Khâm. Was he a writer like you with the *Nhân Văn* journal back in those days?"

"No. He was our archivist."

"Then why was he arrested because of the *Nhân Văn-Giai Phẩm* movement?"

"Because they found him in possession of the reading materials deemed anti-Revolution."

I felt jolted. But nothing these communists did would shock me anymore. Like Mr. Liên, Mr. Khâm was arrested, detained, moved around from one reform camp to another, sent to work farms, and for twenty years he was a prisoner without a trial, much less a sentence. "They can't release you," Mr. Liên said in a toneless voice, "if there's no sentence declared on you."

"Just like you, *Bác* Liên."

Someone came around the corner of the shack. I looked up. Our warden. I tensed up. *Did he hear everything we have just said*?

The warden wagged a finger at me. "What did you just call him?"

I spotted a gleam of anger in the warden's small eyes. "I addressed him as *bác* out of respect. He's as old as my father."

"Rubbish!" The warden's spit flew, his face tensed up. "Only one *bác* and that's *Bác* Hồ."

Yes, Uncle Hồ. I quickly nodded.

"It proves that you haven't digested the camp's regulations. What is our bylaw of addressing one another? Everyone is on equal footing. You are forbidden to call him *bác*, *ông*, or by his former rank. Absolutely no former rank addressing, be it general, colonel, or captain. Understood?" He fixed us with a supercilious stare. "How dare you compare him," he shifted his gaze to Mr. Liên, "to our uncle by calling him *bác*? Did you intend to mock our Revolution's culture?"

"No, sir warden," I said, shaking my head. "I will remember my mistake and it won't happen again."

What a hemorrhage of the nation's morality, I thought, as the warden pivoted on his heel and left as quickly as he had appeared. Whatever you said, I thought, these commies would twist it to make it sound hazardous and, conversely, whatever they spoke they would color it to elevate themselves to some higher species of mankind.

After making sure that the warden had gone, I turned to Mr. Liên. "They treat Lenin's words in the same way a Catholic reveres his Bible, don't they?"

Mr. Liên's mouth curled up at the corner as he puffed on his pipe. I could tell he was grinning.

Sometime back, the camp had proudly announced to us that the camp library—the camp called it the "Cultural House"—was open to anyone who was interested in improving his knowledge of socialism. They were welcome to borrow books from the library. It boasted a variety of books in Russian, Chinese, English, French, and among them, the Vietnamese translations from those original languages. "The intellectuals like me and you," Mr. Liên had said to me as I broached the subject of propaganda using the library as a tool, "are the number one enemies of the Communist Party. You can join them. They will accept you only so they can exploit you until you offer them no more value. Then they will find ways to liquidate you. Who said, 'Send the intellectuals to clean the latrines. If necessary, execute a few of them to set the example'?" I had told him I did not know the source. He said, "Read Lenin's *How to Organize Competition*. Why? If you want to fight communism, you will need to understand Marxism-Leninism better than any of their commissars." Then a week went by. I had read that book Mr. Liên recommended, which I borrowed from the intercamp library. "I found that remark," I said to Mr. Liên, "about how the intellectuals are worth less than garbage in Lenin's eye."

Since our acquaintance, I had revised my knowledge of our enemy—they were far worse than I had thought. Courtesy of Mr. Liên, the purged victim of our northern communists, I had learned some important advice to keep in mind: Lie low, hide your hatred of them, then you shall live to see your family again.

Now, Mr. Liên took the pipe out of his mouth. He scratched his head then combed his fingers through his salt-white, thin tuft of hair.

"Both your father and I shared the same fate: betrayed by friends. One of my close friends led the secret police to my house to arrest me. And that man had been a good friend of mine over the years. I was his source of information—his eyes and ears. Before he had me handcuffed, he asked me, 'When did Trần Hoàng'"—He paused with a nod at me—"your father—'get you involved in this movement?' Of course, your father and I were pro-Revisionism in the early 1950s. At that time your father was already in prison; I felt no need to make it worse. I denied everything, gave the man no satisfaction. Then he probed deeper. 'What did the Soviets instruct you to do within our media circle?' Again, I gave him no satisfaction with my denial. But I was deeply troubled by seeing friends turned into adversaries." He paused to inhale deeply then said, "It's a close-minded regime, self-governed, self-executing. At least the members of an organized crime group have a life outside its circle. The Party members do not. The Party owns them, hears them, reads their thoughts with ears and eyes everywhere."

"Then, *Bác* Liên, what freedom do non-Party citizens like yourself have?"

Lips puckered, Mr. Liên looked absorbed. "Freedom is a luxurious word in a communist state. Freedom of movement, freedom of thought, freedom of expression. When you're stripped of all freedom, what then?" He glanced at me and, before I could form a thought, answered, "You stop the people from progressing. That's the Party's obscurantist vision for the people, its own people."

"It was exactly what the French did to us during the colonial time—preventing people from getting smarter."

The camp announced that all of us must attend a three-day self-profile assessment session. It was a fancy phrase for writing self-confessions.

Since my first camp in the South, we had gone through self-confession so many times that some of us had memorized what we had written in those personal history declarations. Many of us had to redo our written confessions because of factual inconsistencies, which were cross-checked by the Defense Department's Security Bureau, which led to cross-examinations of those deemed as liars. Aside from our personal history, we were forced to detail our relatives' backgrounds, those immediately related to us and going back as far as three generations. We had to put down their home addresses and afterward begin to assess each person mentioned regarding his or her social class and political affiliation. On our personal history, we were to account for our past periods segmented into three timelines: from the distant past up to 1945; from 1945 to 1954; and from 1954 to 1975. For each period, we were to list our major activities related to our jobs and how they had affected the society of the South, as well as any hidden effects on the North. We had to declare who we knew, their names, their jobs, their activities, and where they were now. We had to identify our superiors in the administration or in the army and describe each of them based on his rank and political outlook. Once that was done, we moved on to declare our personal assets—our bank accounts domestically and overseas. We had to declare if these accounts were listed under our names or our spouses' names. More importantly, we had to cite the sources of these funds.

In the end, the Revolution had succeeded in gaining insights into our former intelligence network as well as our natural, fixed, and moveable assets. As they seized all our assets, they succeeded in tracking down those we declared our associates or superiors, those who had managed to avoid the reform camps, and were now blacklisted as fugitives.

To kick-start the session, a political educator came to our camp from the regiment's headquarters. He opened the session by orating on the clemency of the Party and the State, on how to confess your crimes sincerely to pave the way for your release. We had heard this symptomatic echolalia so many times that most of us sat with our heads bent obediently, our eyes half closed. I came wide awake when I heard him say, "Brother Ninh, please stand up."

That was Father Ninh. How did the political cadre know his name? I figured that these commies must have singled out certain individuals based on inside information to showcase their pontification. Smiling, the cadre rubbed his hands excitedly, as if he had just been lauded by an admirer. "Brother Ninh, you are a Christian priest, are you not?"

Father Ninh calmly nodded. "Yes, sir cadre, that is correct."

"Christianity has been in existence for nearly two thousand years and its followers number in the low hundreds of millions. Communism is only fifty years old and has one third of the world's population as followers. My question to you is: Between Christianity and Communism, which is superior?"

I began to notice his shifting eyes for the first time. *Sly devil.* I wished Father Ninh could avoid the confrontation. Calmly and politely, he said, "Sir cadre, I honestly don't know the answer. However, I remain humble to hear your thoughts, should you care to elucidate further. As humans, sir cadre, we only live a short span of time on earth. I wish I could live two thousand years longer to see if Communism still exists by then."

Some of us laughed, and their laughs did not go unnoticed. The cadre smiled suavely, his pea-sized eyes darting to check our reactions. Father Ninh sat down just as the cadre said, "The Party and the State esteem your honesty and your willingness to listen to their wisdom. Brother Ninh, the people's welfare is dealt with in the now; only dreamers and procrastinators project their thoughts into future to find answers. We do not need to wait two thousand years to find out about our purportedly extended existence; we do not promise so-called Heaven to the people; we do not pretend to be so-called God's designators to hear their confessions every Sunday. In fact, we exist in front of your eyes—not in Heaven. Your confessions to the Party and the State are well received—we listen. We shall correct what is correctable when confessed to us. As for your Christians, ask yourself why you keep confessing to your God every Sunday and the crimes you have committed, if not repeated crimes, have never been dealt with? Where is your God?"

I felt as if he had hammered a bolt into our heads. The audience was silent. Father Ninh crossed himself surreptitiously.

The cadre measured our reactions with his unblinking eyes. Obviously pleased, he smiled. "I am asking you to have absolute faith in the Party and the State while you conduct your self-confession. Our question is: Do you feel at peace while doing your utmost to become a better citizen?" He scanned the hall. I was thinking that he was trying to assess our receptivity just as I met his gaze. He made a grand gesture with his hands toward me, as if he knew me. "Brother Khang, please stand up."

I was not surprised anymore. Some of us had become marked objects. I rose to my feet. He smiled again charmingly. "If you do not mind, please opine on my question just asked. Do you feel at peace while you are here to reform yourself?"

I tensed up. I felt the nervous silence around me. I met the cadre's stare. I was his prey.

"Sir cadre," I said, paused to clear my throat, "you were asking us to be honest with the Revolution, the Party, the State." I took a quick look around me. There were eyes like fisheyes blankly looking back at me. The cadre had sat down on the only chair on the podium. He appeared on edge. A heavy silence hung. I looked back at the cadre. "Sir cadre, you asked a question, one that is very convenient for you but very difficult for us. Look at it as a two-edged sword. Whoever answers it won't come out intact."

I sat down. The cadre fidgeted in his seat. The audience also squirmed. Then someone clapped. It sounded lonely in the silence. Then someone else clapped. Then a loud applause followed. They were applauding me for being a martyr. The ovation drew the cadre to his feet. He gestured with his hands for quiet. He coughed a short cough then turned his face toward me.

"Brother Khang, I can see that your one-sided emotions had the better of you. We are cleaning the South of the filth left behind by the Americans. But we take your opinion seriously, Brother Khang. On behalf of the Party and the State, I wish you success in the reform program."

We left the hall and went back to our shacks, and our self-assessment began. During this "brain stimulation" session, as coined by the camp's Machiavellian architects, our meals increased.

I understood their tactics. Reform. Reeducation. These misnomers, concocted by the commies to disguise hard-labor concentration camps, were soon adopted by the media.

In this socialist regime, we were *Homo erectus*. We crawled and slunk away when we had stolen their food. Everything grown around the camp—manioc, corn, potato—belonged to the camp, and stealing it was to rob the socialist state of its properties.

At mealtime we stopped writing as kitchen helpers brought food into each shack. As usual, Father Ninh and two other priests ate together in the center of the shack. I joined them at Father's invitation. The guards remained outside, and the cadres who supervised the self-assessment session returned to their own shacks. One of them stopped and stared down at the priests.

"Stop all that nonsense!" He glared at the three priests, the only three Catholics in the shack, as they were crossing themselves. "Prayer! Making the sign of the cross! Hm. No Jesus humbug, no Maria slattern can give you food. The Party, the State are the only ones who can give you food. If you wish to pray, pray to the Party, the State before you eat."

None of the priests answered him. They dropped their hands and did not touch their food. I watched them and waited. "Please, Brother Khang," Father Ninh said to me. "Eat your food."

I ate. I was hungry. I ate without looking at the priests, at the angry cadre. He left. Something told me that his outburst must have been rooted in our confrontation with their political cadre earlier in the meeting hall.

The priests sat quietly, eyes downcast. But I could see their lips moving. A silent prayer perhaps. Their rosaries, their Bibles, their crosses had been confiscated. Only their faith remained. The commies knew that. They hated the intangibles, the untouchables. In their eyes, each Catholic priest was a potential detonator. So, they defused them. Put them away in camps such as this. I had learned that the youngest of the three priests came from the North. Two years earlier he had been handcuffed then taken away from his seminary after someone reported that he had lectured to his class from the forbidden textbook, *The Vietnamese Essential Literary History*. The commies had rewritten the history and literature textbooks. The oldest one of the three, the President of the now defunct Northern Catholic Congregation, had been brought to this camp because of a youth informer in his class ratting on him about his philosophical take on the subject of "Labor Is Glory" as duly interpreted by The Catholic Church of Vietnam.

The commies considered us "progressive" because we prayed to no one, never crossed ourselves, neither observed nor fasted on Resurrection Sunday, or celebrated Christmas. We were allowed more food. We survived. None of us came from the seminaries now being used as grain storehouses or cattle barns; and, of course, we did not come from the churches now being converted to cooperatives. They had arrested as many seminary students as they could before those students had a chance to be ordained. Without the seminaries, the commies believed that there would be no future generation of priests, and the North was willing to wait for the next forty years until most, if not all, of the Catholic priests died.

Only then Catholicism in the North would cease to exist.

One cold December morning, we were gathered in the courtyard before filing out on our daily labor trip; we waited longer than usual, and then the camp administrator appeared unexpectedly to make a brief announcement. I knew what he was going to say. We sat on our haunches, knots in our stomachs.

The day before, there was an escape by three inmates who had lived in one of the other shacks. One was a former commissioner of the Military Court Front of South Vietnam, another was a former lieutenant colonel of the Office of Special Commissioners, and the last one was a former service chief of the National Institute of Administration. They had a gun with them. Nobody knew how they had secured it. But one guard had been killed by a gunshot when the escapees fired back during the chase. The guards had carried his body back while the rest remained in the forest to hunt down the criminals. "We shall capture these offenders," the administrator said with breath pluming from his mouth in the cold. "We will exact the maximum penalty for the crime they committed."

The guards' casualty hung like a bad omen. It had a deathly odor. I wished the escapees the best of luck.

The next day, past noon, the guards returned from the hunt. They entered the camp with two escapees, chained by the feet to each other, trailing behind. I had eaten my meager meal and stepped outside for fresh air when I saw them. Everyone went outside their shacks and the security guards rushed in to order us inside. I wondered what happened to the third runaway.

It did not take long to discover the conclusion of the three men's crusade. The gong called us back earlier than usual. At four o'clock, the sun still bright before the descending fog, we arrived at the camp just in time to see the guards bring out the bodies of the captives. One look at them knotted my stomach. They were still tied by their hands and feet like pigs being carried to the market. Their heads were misshapen: the temples dented, the hair matted down with dark blood, the eyes not even seated in their own sockets. One man's jaw was askew. I found it hard to breathe and felt the same horror in everyone else around me. The dead had been violated by direct blows to their heads by some blunt instrument; blood still oozed from the head wounds. The guards had not even bothered to reseat the eyeballs. The dead man with the displaced jaw had his face turned toward where I sat on the ground. His face was a horror mask of welts and bruises with dangling eyeballs.

To make sure we had time to contemplate the scene with its graphic display, the administrator waited. Then he spoke.

"On behalf of our security committee and the proctor committee, I ask for a brief moment of silence to pay respects to our deceased guard, who put his life at risk when he went after the offenders." He dropped his head, closing his eyes while afternoon sunlight gilded his face. We followed his gesture. I put my mind on our dead comrades, not knowing what to say or pray. Words meant nothing. The administrator lifted his face and squinted at us. "We now close the book on this regrettable incident. The camp suffers one casualty. But our security forces never fail in their duties. They shot and killed one of the offenders in the forest, the one who had wielded a gun. Now know this: Once you kill our personnel, there is no going back. Look at this incident, remember it, memorize this scene today, then ask yourself: What can I do under the guidance of the Party and the State to shed my old self, and become a model citizen?" He pointed at the corpses. "On behalf of Cổng Trời camp and the intercamp authority, I hereby issue the edict of having these criminals buried without coffins. The camp will continue to monitor the deceased's families back home for any suspicious activities that might cause harm to the Revolution. This decree shall enforce the camp curfew from five in the afternoon to six in the morning. Any camp attendees seen within three meters of the camp fences shall be shot by the guards."

The guards asked for volunteers to bury the dead. Four men, one from our shack, stepped forward. We saved the meal portion for our shack mate until he returned after sunset. His face and hands smeared with red dirt; he said they could only dig two shallow graves because it was laterite soil. How deep, somebody asked. A foot, he replied. With some leaves he had plucked, he covered the unsightly faces of the deceased.

I met Văn, the radio man for the camp and an ex-commando, on the day he snuck us a handmade set he had built himself from parts that'd come into his possession.

Three criteria to judge a northern man for being a "successful progressive man" were: his ownership of a bicycle, his wristwatch, and his portable radio. Most cadres of the People's Public Security had achieved the standard of the three "Must-Haves." In this camp, the item they kept having a reliability issue with was the portable radio. Fickle, their sets kept shorting out, forcing them to call on the commandos' handyman to fix their contraptions.

"Brother Khang," Văn said to me. "As a senior officer of the Central Intelligence Office, you must know a lot about the nature of information. So, last night I listened to Hanoi radio station, and this American four-star general was talking about the American service personnel missing in the Vietnam war, then the Vietnamese political prisoners. Then . . ." He paused, coughing nervously. ". . . he mentioned the Vietnamese commandos—that's us—who had parachuted into the North in the 1960s. For years now, Brother Khang, no one has mentioned us. How many times have I listened to those radio broadcasts? I've never heard the words 'South commandos' in those newscasts. We are forgotten, abandoned, considered dead. No military units, no military ID numbers, no names, no ages. We're completely isolated from the outside world. So, when I heard that general mentioning us, I thought I was dreaming. Dream or not, I cried."

"What else did you hear?" I asked him.

"I heard Chinese broadcasts of those who've fled North Vietnam to seek political refuge in China. Brother Khang, there seems to be some ongoing conflict between China and Vietnam. I've heard more than once that the two sides have taken shots at each other. Worse, they mentioned the possibility of using us, the prisoners, to fight the Chinese if there's an invasion."

Soon, this information wasn't secret. In the summer of that year, 1979, the Viet-Sino border conflict intensified. There were nights when the camp's loudspeakers would blare out frontline news, and the broadcasts always ended with name-calling. The insults of their long-time ally China, would spice up their commentaries and rhetoric, becoming the theme in their music and drama. No longer did we hear the slogans "Greatest China," or "Mountains stand connected; rivers flow side by side."

The broadcast continued. "We, the Socialist Republic of Vietnam, a workers' state, a workers' republic, had been friends with our northern neighbor China. Now, when we occupied our southern neighbor, the People's Republic of Kampuchea, as part of our humanitarian aim to liberate its people from the genocide committed by Pol Pot's Khmer Rouge, a puppet supported by China, we were called 'the invader' by China. China has sent us a message: 'We will teach you a lesson.' They are mobilizing massive military forces along our northern border to achieve one single objective: to colonize us. To defend ourselves, with the honorable goal of safeguarding our mother's soil, our army and our people will fight. We shall win with less manpower. We shall win by pitching our smaller self against their giant one. Our Great Cause shall prevail over our enemy's brutality. Our humanity shall take the place of their cruelty, as it has been passed down to us from President Hồ, our beloved leader."

Captain Bé approached me on Sunday that week. "China and Vietnam aren't on speaking terms now," he said to me. "This is the right time to get out. I've talked with Father Ninh. Say yes, and three of us will hatch a plan."

We had known each other well enough for me to trust them. Captain Bé had confirmed the news I had heard from Văn.

Captain Bé had decided for us when to make our escape.

"On a rainy night," he said to me and Father Ninh, who was at that time working in a team that tended pigs. Whenever he could, Father Ninh would pilfer pieces of burned rice from the pigs' meals and stock them up. At night, with a *goz* can and a candle, I would heat up a few spoonfuls of salt that came with our meals until the salt coalesced. Captain Bé had collected a handful of antimalarial pills and hid them with our contributions.

It had rained intermittently during the month of August; but I noticed the rain had come only during the day. We waited and kept hoarding up our provisions. Then one night it rained. Rain came down by the time the last gong sounded for curfew, and darkness fell on the camp, save for the electric lights from the watchtowers. The door opened and closed a few times when someone exited the shack to head for the latrine. They would make their way in the dark to the latrine and back, like scent hounds. Each time the door opened, I would strain my eyes to look outside. I could see guards draped in their nylon raincoats pass by. As the night wore on, I could no longer hear their footsteps. They had retreated to their dry hideouts as the rain had not let up.

It must have been past midnight when Captain Bé came by my cot. His stealthy move woke no one up except Bee. I got off my cot as he reached out and squeezed my hand. He had failed to talk me out of my escape plan; my heart had hardened. I squeezed his hand and left as quietly as I could. We might not see each other again, and we both knew this night could be the end of our friendship. I stopped by Father Ninh's cot. He was sitting up, saying a silent prayer. Captain Bé had already left the shack. I pulled at Father Ninh's arm. He kept praying. I thought he must have had a change of heart. I pulled at him again. Reluctantly, he moved. The cot squeaked. Quickly, I made my way out of the shack, past the oil lamp hung by the door, and looked back. Father Ninh had sat back down on his cot, head bent. I got out.

Captain Bé had been waiting outside. He whispered, "Where's Father?"

"Give him a few minutes," I said under my breath. "Then we'll go."

Both of us understood. This was no daily labor trip.

The clock in my head ticked and I nodded at Captain Bé. "Go," I said.

We hurried down the veranda just as the shack's door opened a crack and Father Ninh squeezed himself through. I stopped, took his hand, and pulled him along into the rain.

The cuts on my hand from when we had helped each other go over two barbed-wire barriers and then a stand of bamboo had stopped bleeding. Once outside the camp's perimeters, we could hear only our footsteps, like suction cups. The rain-soaked earth felt soft, mushy in places. The air smelled of wet vegetation and the earth was musky and moist.

We went north as Captain Bé assured us this was the direction that would lead us into China, a few days on foot.

At dawn, we stopped. Rain lingered at first light as we huddled up under the dripping canopy of foliage. "Rest during the day," Captain Bé said, "we can travel during the day only where nobody can see us." The locals. We knew. But moving at night made it twice as difficult to locate the terrain, thus affecting our distance traveled. We ate our food as day was graying. I watched the sky, hoping in vain to sight a mountain range to tell us we were near the border. The sky was gray, empty of clouds.

Our clothes dried during the day while we catnapped. At night it was chilly, as summer heat would turn to cold quickly after sunset. We moved twice under the sun, keeping ourselves closer to the edge of the forest and woodland. We ate frugally, sharing the hardened salt, the brittle rice pieces. Whenever we heard gurgling water, we would stop and find a creek and drink from it.

On the third day, I could smell a sour odor from my body. My shirt had been ripped at the shoulders by the low thorny branches of shrubbery. My companions did not fare well either. Father Ninh limped after slipping on a mossy rock at a creek and hurting his ankles. We stopped more often than we wanted to, to give him time to catch up with us. Captain Bé was most resilient, silent as the grave. That night we boarded down near a plain, on the edge of a woodland. I asked Captain Bé, "How far do you think we're from the border?"

"Another day," he said, as he gave us the last pieces of burned rice. Our salt supply had run out. I ate as my stomach grumbled. I could hear it too from my companions. We each had one piece of brittle rice. The night would be long on an empty stomach.

Father Ninh massaged his ankles. He mumbled a prayer in the winking lights of fireflies. After he prayed, he said, "Aren't we supposed to see a river near the border?"

"Yes, Father," said Captain Bé. "We'll see Chảy River if we keep this course due north. From the river it's five kilometers to the border."

That night, I slept fitfully. All of us had catnaps. I got up in the night and drank from our tin can filled with the creek water we had saved.

At dawn we rose and headed out. Without a compass, we had used the rising sun as east and reoriented ourselves at sunset. I felt weak. We did not move as briskly as we had. The day was not hot. We were at high elevation in the Hà Giang province. Yet at times my eyes saw glares from exhaustion. It came from a drained body that needed food.

At noon, like a miracle, we saw the river. Beyond the river was a bluish mountain on China's side.

We stood at the riverbank and watched the farmers tilling their land. They wore wide-brimmed palm-leaf hats. Captain Bé said they were Chinese farmers who had settled on our soil, on the strip of land that was closer to their homeland. He said it was the manioc season and assured us that we could find a manioc field on this side of the river.

We did, after having walked for a long time in the mild sun.

As Father Ninh kept watch, Captain Bé and I went into the field and cleared the dirt off one bush. Its leaves had not turned yellow, though a few had fallen on the ground. It could be another month before harvest. Captain Bé pointed at a handful of big roots, over a foot long, and we hacked them at the tapering necks. We had an armful and quickly headed back into the woodland.

We began cutting up the manioc roots. The flesh was white and smelled fresh. Captain Bé said, "Let's move in deeper. The locals might see us. Worse, the fire might tip them off."

Father Ninh was smelling the white-fleshed tuber and wiping flecks of dirt off its brown skin. "I think nobody could see us here, much less smoke from a cooking fire."

I agreed. He must have been as hungry as I was, and though we were not too far from the river, and barely within sight of the edge of the wood, I felt safe. "I haven't seen anybody the whole day," I said out of the urge to eat more than the safety concern. "The next village could be a way off from here."

Captain Bé said nothing. Quietly he started building a fire. It was getting late in the afternoon and the river was rising. I could see it overflowing the bank. I went back down and filled our can with fresh water. I could see wood bark and twigs among the driftwood floating downriver. There must be a lot of downed trees in the mountains upstream, I thought as I headed back.

We ate all the tubers after we cooked them over the fire. It got dark quickly, and we kept the fire going to keep us warm. I could no longer see the river after dark, only hear the sound of the rushing water and the wind hurling headlong.

After the meal, Captain Bé decided we should move downriver. His plan was to find a narrow waisted part of the river where we could cross at the most favorable time. Father Ninh said, "What about our provision for the next few days? Shouldn't we go back and stock up on more tubers?"

"No," said Captain Bé, his voice firm. "That'll give us away."

I seconded that. I recalled the commando's advice—never returning to the same field of manioc. Perhaps we should have listened to Captain Bé's instruction to move deeper into the woodland when we built the cooking fire.

In the dark we waded into the river, keeping close to the bank. We moved with the current downriver, at times losing our footing when the bottom dipped. We held hands with Father Ninh in the middle because he could not swim. I could only think of the ordeal when we must cross the river. After a long time in the water, we began shivering. The crosswind was strong. Captain Bé stopped and listened. We had been using our hands to feel our ways, grabbing bushes and tree roots. I heard Captain Bé. "We'll rest here."

Here? Then I saw him hoisting himself up by grabbing a tree root that snaked down the sloping bank. He must see things in the dark better than any of us, because what he found was a hollow, underneath a giant tree, with a mesh of roots branching downward.

We sat on the water-saturated bed of the tree. The cave-like hollow was damp and cold. I hugged myself to keep warm, and there were lights blinking outside the cave and over the river, and the fireflies were the only lights that made me feel alive whenever I woke. Captain Bé said something about a narrow part of the river that I could not make out completely. Some information he had gathered from a commando back in the camp. Find it and it will make your crossing much more feasible. He said we would resume our exploration at dawn and, once we reached the other bank, we were safe.

When I woke again, I heard footfall nearby. I was floating in my head, thinking it must be near dawn and the locals were up for the new day. The cold was damp, though the wind had abated. The fireflies had gone. In the stillness came the calls of coucals. Next to me, Father Ninh was breathing through his mouth in his sleep, and Captain Bé was asleep with his mouth open. We were all exhausted. I could see the sky now, gray and wispy with patches of clouds. Farther north was the mountain, dark against a pale horizon.

Then came human voices. Then dogs barking. My stomach knotted. Why the dogs? I thought and shook my companions. They woke. Captain Bé sat up. He blinked. The dogs' barking drew nearer. Footsteps quickened. Twigs snapped. A dog barked within earshot, then the clanging of firearms. A dog suddenly thrust its head into the cave and barked. I shrank. We bunched up. Someone stooped, peering in, in his hand a pistol.

"Come out," he shouted. "Now!"

He wore a pith helmet with a satchel slung across his shoulder. He pulled back the dog as we crawled out on hands and knees. Behind him stood four civilians, each wielding a rifle. They must be the village militia. Beyond them was a crowd of locals. Strident voices rose, hands pointing, slashing at the air. I knew we were their target.

Then came shouts. "Kill them!" "Those human-liver eaters!" We were pushed through the crowd and a rock hit my face. I covered up just as something blunt struck the back of my head. I staggered and regained my footing and heard cries from Father Ninh. My hands were streaked with blood. My head buzzed with a sharp pain where it was hit. We moved ahead of the militia and the crowd followed at a safe distance now and the dogs had stopped barking. One trotted alongside me, and when I dropped my arm, it licked off the blood in the palm of my hand. I patted its head, looking into its round black eyes, at its lolling tongue, as if it were my pet.

We were herded upriver, following the bank as far as the manioc field to the spot where we had arrived the day before. It was getting brighter, though gray and cold. The river flowed fast, and clear of debris. There were tree roots crawling off the bank into the water, and where they touched the bottom there were eddying pools.

We spent the day in the next village, the one that owned the field of manioc. Rain fell, tick-tacking on the thatched roof of a hut near the village entrance, under the spreading crown of a banyan. The man with the satchel told us we were to remain in the hut until the Cổng Trời guards arrived the next day. Before he left, he stood over us and said, "None of you southerners have gotten out of here. Do you ever learn your lesson? We have captured so many of your commandos. We captured them just as they had parachuted down. Captured them after they had just breathed our fresh air in the countryside. We knew in advance when they would land on our soil. We knew everything beforehand."

He left two men from the militia to post outside the hut. They were quiet; yet they chatted sometimes as they smoked some bitter, foul-smelling cigarettes. I could hear them in piecemeal, how a local buffalo boy had come upon the uprooted bush of manioc and the boy had reported it back to the village elders. The village sent out men to scout for any suspicious signs of intruders, and they saw smoke from the woodland.

We slept that night on the earth floor, our heads resting on a brick. The blood on my face had dripped to my shirt collar and dried there. I could only sleep on my side because it hurt to lie faceup with a lump on the back of my head. One of the men went in, looked at us, and cursed. His heavy northern accent was harsh to the ear.

"You can have wings," he said, cackling. "But you can never be out of our invisible net. Our militia of the North never loses to your southern boys."

He irked Captain Bé so much the captain snapped at him. "You backward nitwits. No wonder the lot of you have been slaves for two decades now, just to lick off the hands of Hồ Chí Minh and Lê Duẩn."

The man took three steps and kicked Captain Bé on the ground. He kicked him until the captain fell quiet. He spat on him, threw his cigarette butt at him, and walked back out. I wished that Captain Bé had kept his composure. I could hear him laboring in his breathing, and Father offered him some verbal comfort and a prayer. They were mere words that now did not strike a merciful chord in my mind. I felt nothing, empty as a shell. I lay, open-eyed, hearing rain that started again and hearing the men outside scrambling for shelter. Ironically, I felt as if they were afraid of us, or worse, afraid to share the same air we breathed in the hut. I dozed, then woke. Rain tapped the thatched roof, slackening late in the night, its tick-tacks steady as it dripped from the eave of the roof.

On the fringe of sleep, I smelled the wet earth, the damp chill air. Much like the early morning air at my first camp by the seaside.

CHAPTER 5

A Place Near the Sea

Summer 1975

> Some days in late August at home are like this, the air thin and eager like this, with something in it sad and nostalgic and familiar.
> —William Faulkner

After four hours on the road, the Molotova convoy stopped. Many of us had dozed off. Fifty bodies were jammed into the confined space of the tarp-covered truck bed. We were let out for the first time to stretch and relieve ourselves, and for the drivers to get food for themselves. It was mid-afternoon. None of us knew where we were. There was a market by the highway, and watching us from afar were people wearing palm-leaf hats and floral blouses. I knew we were still in the South.

Soon vendors began flocking to the trucks. Old women, young women, even children in faded blouses, patched-up pantaloons, each carrying a rattan sieve on which were laid tubers of cooked manioc, boiled potatoes, yellow bananas, sweet dumplings wrapped in jackfruit leaves. A woman pointed to us, shouted, "Cải Tạo!" That was us, reform prisoners. "Don't take money from them. Give them something to eat!" Her shout caused a ruckus.

We tried to pay. They shook their heads.

"Take it, uncle!"

"My poor son, you break my heart!"

More of them came running toward our trucks, from alleys, from ramshackle lean-tos. They tossed what they had in their baskets on to our trucks as the convoy was pulling out. The children ran after the convoy. I looked back, unblinking. Next to me, Bee wiped his eyes.

A young-looking fellow in tiger-striped fatigues leaned out and yelled. "Thank you, all the mothers, all the sisters. Forgive us. We didn't do our duties to protect you. I'm sorry!" I caught the pained look on the men's faces, all of them soldiers, many in army rangers' tiger-striped fatigues. I reached over to shake his hand.

"We'll live to see another day," I said to him. His hand was rough, on the forearm a bright red tattoo that read "Sát Cộng"—Kill Commies.

"Yeah, elder brother." He grinned, lips chapped. "We live heroic, live strong, but never live long."

We chatted. Fortunately, there were no commie guards sitting with us. I found out from him that he and his comrades in the truck were the remnants of the prisoners of war that had been captured six months before the South fell. Tùng—his name—was a lieutenant. He and those ranking as officers were turned over to Unit 76, which had managed prisoners of war since the 1950s, beginning with those captured in Điện Biên Phủ when the French Union surrendered.

"Elder brother," Tùng said, puffing on his Bastos, "those commies hung a giant map of Vietnam in the center of our prison camp. This was in March this year. They marked each province in each corps of our South Vietnam with a red piece of paper. Every morning, we came out to look at it, we saw more and more red dots. Are we losing? None of us believed it. It must be the commies faking it. Then, on May 1st, the whole map was completely red. Then we listened to their broadcast. General Big Minh was declaring the South had laid down its weapons. We were dazed, elder brother. We sat down and watched them commies shooting their rifles into the sky. They hooted while some of us cried."

I had to look away to hide my emotion. I did not want to listen to him anymore. I wished he'd stop lamenting, when someone called out, "Hey, isn't this Sóc Trăng?" everyone looked out. The sunbaked aluminum roofs, the red-dirt roads, the palm-leaf conical hats shimmering in the afternoon light.

"Damn right," Tùng said. "It's Sóc Trăng."

We were in Sóc Trăng province, which was above Bạc Liêu, his hometown in the Mekong Delta. Tùng lit another Bastos. He did not drop his voice as he told me he grew up in an anti-communist village, and his hatred of the Viet Cong began with his witnessing the murder of his village chief. Between us and the truck cab was a metal partition, which a tarp covered as part of the cargo bed. The driver and guards out front might not hear us.

"I knew Mr. Diễm," Tùng said to me, "our village chief under the former Republic of Vietnam, when I was growing up. He had gained notoriety in capturing the local Viet Cong, who would come out at night to mine the interprovincial road, to dynamite bridges, and to drop propaganda leaflets. After South Vietnam fell, the Viet Cong Regional Judgment Council sentenced him to death." He tapped to break the ash, took a deep drag, and continued. "They mobilized a mob. Once the sentence was read, they let loose the mob. Haters mauled him with clubs, sticks, and rocks until he was all bloodied, then they tied him up, gagged him, and blindfolded him on his way to an already dug grave. The mob followed him, and some broke the line and crashed his head with rocks. He was half dead when they reached the grave. The executioner shot him in the chest three times, then pulled up the corpse by the head and shot it in the temple."

Tùng stopped, out of breath. I pretended to be asleep. It was late in the afternoon when the convoy stopped. We got down and huddled up where the guards were yelling. I looked at a camp somewhere on a shrubbery-dense tract of land. The tall grass was littered with combat helmets, knapsacks, entrenching tools, water canteens. Something there knotted my stomach. These were remnants of an abandoned post.

There were a few huts roofed with aluminum corrugated sheets. Only one shack, bigger than the rest, looked fresh, with a bamboo roof. We lined up in front of that shack with gun porting guards watching over us. A dozen men wearing pith helmets went in and out of the shack, and eventually one of them came out with a megaphone. I could not make out what he said initially because of the static of his megaphone. After he tuned it, he said, "Everyone must find a place within the camp's perimeters for overnight lodging. Tomorrow we will start the camp construction that will become your housing. Be urgent. Be disciplined. We must finish our housing project before the rainy season. Or you will sleep with nature."

I was not sure if it was humor he intended, but nobody laughed.

Before sunset, the camp had handed out to each of us the camp outfit. Each shirt of the ash-gray getup was stamped on the back with bold, otter-black initials: "CT." The sun was setting, the heat still shimmering on the ground, as we lined up again and one by one stopped at a table where a cadre sat with a ledger open in front of him. Like everyone else, I emptied my pockets and laid my personal items on the table. The cadre looked at my wallet, my watch, a packet of gum. Still, he snapped at me, "Are these all? Do not hide anything, or else!"

I did. My wedding ring. Overnight I decided I must find a place to hide it.

After recording the items in the ledger, he explained once again that all belongings were now registered with the State and the Revolution and shall be returned to their owners upon their release. It sowed a notion in my head. Release? I was about to leave the line when the cadre called my name again. I stopped.

"Were you a senior officer at the Central Intelligence Office?" he asked. His face, shadowed by the setting sun, featured a low forehead, a snubbed nose.

I nodded, shielding my eyes from the sun.

"Your old barber sent you his regards," said the cadre.

My barber. My long-time barber. Before I left home to report to the Reform Program, he had dropped by to console me and give me encouraging words. Over the years, he must have known me inside out. Despite the churning of my stomach, I asked, "Is he with the Revolution, sir cadre?"

"He's one of our local cell chiefs," said the cadre, nodding with a grin.

I went back to join the line of those already fulfilling their duty, to have lost everything, to become a new species whose unique identity was "CT."

I saw Tùng emptying his pockets at the table. Within earshot came the cadre's voice. "Your father was a major? A provincial police commanding officer?"

"Yes."

"He owes our people a blood debt."

Tùng's voice rose. "Watch your mouth! Who owes who a blood debt? Who're the people? You? Or our Southerners?"

Two guards rushed up from behind the cadre and restrained Tùng. One pointed at Tùng's arm. "Look here!" He raised the arm he gripped for the cadre to see. I had seen it during the ride. I had also seen below the words "Sát Cộng," in black, a clip-point Bowie blade dripping blood from its serrated curved edge.

The cadre stared. Curtly he said, "Remove that tattoo or you'll be shot by tomorrow."

We boarded down that night, sleeping on the ground on the wooden planks scavenged among the grass. All night long I drifted in and out of my sleep, hearing the whines of mosquitoes and slapping myself on the side of my face as they buzzed close to my ears. I thought of Tùng. How would he manage to delete what was already fused into his flesh?

Surrounding the camp was waste ground which used to be rice fields, and coursing through them were narrow creeks bubbling over shallow pebbly beds. Beyond the waste ground were woodlands, an hour away on foot, where we heard our former Republic had laid mines to deter the Viet Cong from attacking this outpost. In the center of the dirt courtyard, framed by two parallel rows of shacks, stood a flagpole that flew a yellow-star red flag we must salute every morning. At the end of the shacks was the kitchen, then the pigsty, and beyond it was a row of five Conex metal containers.

I had occasionally passed these Conex containers during the day. At times, all you could hear was someone's laborious breathing as if the air was being sucked out of his lungs; at times, there was a faint sound of something being dragged on the floor, like a reptile crawling. Tùng had spent three days and nights in one of them. He had, indeed, removed the *Sát Cộng* tattoo. All he asked for from the camp was a razor blade and, with a guard looking on, he sliced off, piece by piece, his own flesh and with it, the tattoo.

That night Father Ninh came to Tùng's cot and prayed for him. Father Ninh was broad-shouldered and small in stature. A southerner in his forties, his salt-and-pepper hair was still youthfully thick, and his complexion was a shade darker than mine. Three cots from Tùng's, I listened to the priest praying with him. In silence, they crossed themselves.

The camp broke down the thousand of us into squads, which they called "A," platoon "B," and company "C." They made us aware that we were constantly watched over by a platoon of armed guards, that we must respect and abide by the camp's protocols for law and order. I often wondered about their law. Should there be law, why had we never been tried and sentenced?

One month had passed since the day we reported to the reform program centers. They had called upon all of us, the personnel of the former regime, to report to their chosen centers, encouraging us to bring enough clothing, food, and money to last one month while we attended the reform sessions. Only a month had passed since we came face to face with the Revolution on the morning their tanks entered Saigon. Those days, you could hear a voice on the radio, heavily southern accented, calling out to the citizens of the occupied city:

> Beloved People of the South,
>
> The Revolution is now victorious! The nation is now united, and peace restored. We ask you to remain calm and maintain order. Gone now are the once overbearing American imperialists and its unctuous puppet government. Should you wish to never see them return, welcome the Revolution with open arms. In the days to come, our authorities will visit with each of your families to ask for your support, to bridge the ideological gap, and to embrace one another in our brotherhood of love. Military authority during the transition will be in the hands of the City Military Administration Committee, and civil affairs will be handled by the Transitional Revolutionary Government. All citizens and former soldiers of the Republic of South Vietnam will have twenty-four hours to surrender any firearms or ordnance in their possession. Violation of this order will result in death by shooting. Under the new martial law an 8:00 p.m. curfew is in effect for all citizens.
>
> Victory Salute!
>
> Transitional Revolutionary Government

We woke at dawn to the sound of the gong.

They made the gong out of the shell of a dud. You could hear it eight times a day, and then you would never forget it because of its metallic echo seemingly spiraling across the land. The sound pierced the air, grating your nerves, and then the camp dog, the only canine in the camp, would howl so painfully you felt your hackles rise.

Eight times a day you had to listen to its strident sound. At reveille. At roll call before heading out to the work site. At mid-morning break. At the end of the break. At early afternoon roll call to head back out to the work site. At mid-afternoon break. At the end of the break. At roll call to file into your shacks for the night.

Those early days back home were so distant, and thinking about them felt like traveling back to the beginning of geologic time. In that nameless camp, we did corvée labor, day after day: chopping firewood for the kitchen, pulling weeds.

Many of us, when rising up, could not lift our legs, now too puffy from lack of vitamin B1. The everyday wear-and-tear began to show through our clothing after one month. I could not help recalling a cadre's response to one of us, who asked, "It's now past the one month you promised to keep us here. Please tell us, when is our release date?"

The cadre, stone-faced, shook his head. "Who said the Revolution would release you after one month? We asked all of you to bring enough of your belongings to last one month—not that you would go home after one month—while you attend school."

"Why does this school have barbed wire?"

"You have freedom of movement. Look around. See those freely going about? You have freedom of speech as long as you condemn the evil of the Americans and extol Uncle Hồ's virtue and our Revolution's greatness. Now, never think of yourself as a prisoner. I must remind you that you are not here as prisoners but as camp attendees. We, your wardens, are your educators. Trust us while you learn to become model citizens. And an individual's release depends on their progress."

"What is defined as 'progress'?" asked the same fellow.

"By completing all the ten reform lessons and embodying them every day in camp."

We were, at that time, beginning Lesson No. 1.

A man, tall, slightly stooped, donned with a green pith helmet, entered the hall. A senior lieutenant colonel, he carried a leather satchel. On his hip was a Type-54 Chinese pistol, its black grip engraved with a five-pointed star. He sat down behind a table facing us. We sat on the floor, many of us sitting on our sandals, roving our eyes from one wall banner to another. One under Hồ Chí Minh's framed picture read: "The Great President Hồ Chí Minh Lives Forever in Our Souls."

The cadre removed his pith helmet. He wore his slick hair parted in the middle. He made an upswept motion with his hand. "Let's sing *Pulling Our Cannons over the Mountain Pass!*"

Only he was singing.

Heigh-ho, let's pull the cannon over this mountain
Heigh-ho, let's pull the cannon over this gorge
One-two!

The lyrics sounded alien to my ears. The cadre stopped and clapped his hands. "Let's try again!"

None of us responded. Only a few lonely voices sang off-key.

The whole camp was quiet. The lecturer, the overseers, the commissars, the administrator showed no reactions. As if they had been mummified. The lecturer gathered himself and raised his hands, palms open toward us. "You are still obstinate and anti-Revo*n*ution. However, time will tell. Even mountains become eroded by the constant washing of rain. And time is what the Revo*n*ution has."

These northern commies had a tongue problem pronouncing letter "l" and for every "el" it came out as "n." I could not help thinking of the German "W" versus "V." His gaunt face was ghastly pale and his eyes, one smaller than the others, darted to measure our reactions. "The Revo*n*ution on*n*y regrets that it did not capture *thằng Foh*. He must have fled Vietnam before we entered Saigon. Otherwise, he would be paying for his crime in one of our reform camps now."

He meant Gerald Ford. We simply glanced at one another and remained poker-faced. I looked at him, at his eyebrows so bare I thought of the Japanese women who practiced *Hikimayu*, except that he had no fake eyebrows painted on his forehead. He removed his glasses, rubbed his eyes, then croaked on.

"To *n*ove your country is to *n*ove socia*n*ism. What is patriotism? *N*et me expound on that. We have one nation, then we have one Party. Are they separate?

No. They are one. To *n*ove the Party is to *n*ove our nation. What's good for the Party is good for the nation. Our Party *n*eaders know exactly what's good for the Party, which is good for our nation. Our duty is to be*n*ieve in the Party. Such faith is patriotism." He stopped, turned to the table behind him and picked up a glass of water. He took a healthy sip. The megaphone was now level at his mouth. I began hating the old red on that bullhorn. I tried to tune out his words but succeeded only briefly. They entered my ears and stayed.

He tapped the holster on his hip, roving his eyes across our faces. "You will have group discussion in the evening to vo*n*unteer your thought on the essence of each *n*ecture. Our po*n*itical instructors will be there to preside over each group. When you express your thought, do not genera*n*ize it. Be specific. Drill into the imperia*n*ist greed of the Americans, and the servitude offered them by your puppet government. Be mindful of our great *n*eader whose name, Hồ Chí Minh, is associated with the inte*nn*ectual crown of humanity."

The senior lieutenant colonel narrowed his eyes as he looked straight down at us. "Up till now, none of you have done hard *n*abor, but *n*ive off the people. Now you have *n*earned the *n*esson '*N*abor Is Glory.' Now you understand *n*abor can reform you. Uncle Hồ once said, 'With human efforts even stones and rocks can be turned to rice.'"

Bee leaned against me. "Damnation!" he hissed. "They all have a battery in their ass, haven't they? Turn it on and they'll speak. Same speech. Every time!"

"To refrain from speaking the truth is unfeeling; to speak half-truths is unrighteous." I said. "You know that old saying?"

Bee shook his head.

"And to speak the untruth is commie." I glanced up and caught his grin.

On day two of lectures, it rained, and we filed back into the meeting hall tired and grumpy. The meeting hall was an open-air hall; but we called it "the Colosseum," where the lecturers were slayers and us, the combatants, the slayed. Those who filed in last sat along the outer edges, where rain fell slanting in on their backs. At times, the winds blew rain into the hall, and I could feel raindrops on my face, but this at least kept us awake.

We had already covered such topics as "Crimes Committed by the Puppet Government and Its Army of the South." Today's new lecturer was a political commissar, who came to camp from the overseeing regiment to give a lecture with an appropriately embellished topic: "How the Yankee Imperialists Had Ruined Our Heaven-on-Earth Country."

He said, loud, in his southern accent, "To know the root of the imperialist evil is to treasure the words by comrade Nikita Khrushchev, who said, 'I worked at a factory owned by Germans, at coal pits owned by Frenchmen, and at a chemical plant owned by Belgians. There, I discovered something about capitalists. They are all alike, whatever their nationality. All they wanted from me was the most work for the least money that kept me alive.'"

He stopped and brought his hands to a hand span. "What I am about to tell you is a fact, not anecdote. During his revolutionary days, Uncle came upon a dead king cobra. This species eats other snakes and his own kind. Uncle had the king cobra skinned and had a pair of sandals made out of this snake's skin. He wore them throughout his resistance days and donated them to our National Museum after he became our first president. The Russian scientists came and inquired about the nature of his sandals because of their extraordinary durability. Aside from the fact that they were made of a king cobra's skin, the scientists wondered what else went into the making of these shoes. They never found out. It is still our nation's top secret. This is only a small tale from Uncle Hồ's sagacity."

We gasped. The commissar turned solemn; his lips crimped. "The common mistake that reactionaries like yourselves make, is to try to gauge the socialist loftiness with your lack of understanding of socialism. Ask yourself if you truly wish to return home to your family."

A hand shot up. The commissar eyed him long enough that perhaps his young-looking face put the cadre at ease.

"Sir cadre," Tùng said after the commissar granted him the permission to speak, "the Revolution should've let us go home after ten days of attending the reform program. Ten days. Why are we still here?"

"Who said you could go home after ten days?" the commissar's voice shot up. His loud voice startled many of us in the forward rows. "The Revolution simply requested that you bring supplies needed for ten days for the reform program. It never said that the program would end in ten days. I can play back that broadcast if you wish to hear it again."

"The Revolution made one statement and every one of us, the people, misunderstood it." Tùng cocked his head defiantly. "Whose fault is that?"

"To simplify the matter, know this: If you have not committed a crime, you shall not end up in a reform camp—not even for ten days."

"What crime, sir cadre?" Tùng shook his head vehemently.

"You have all committed crimes," the commissar barked out. "Let me give you an example. Among you here are your former officer details. You were assigned a special task. That's what *biệt phái* means. As a military officer, you were detailed to teach high schools, so you could earn your pay from both ends and, at the same time, fail as many students as you could, forcing them to enlist in the army. Some of you here were warrant officers of communications, who might claim that you had never fought the Revolution or killed any of its soldiers. But, in fact, you called in the B-52 to bomb the Revolution's troops. How severe is your crime? And some of you were officers in a *ngụy* military band, who claim innocence against the Revolution. But it was you who incited your soldiers with hate against the Revolution with your music, urging them to kill the Revolution's soldiers. You are one of the worst offenders."

Tùng raised his hand again. "Sir cadre, we, the soldiers of the Republic of Vietnam, fought the main force of North Vietnamese Army, the Viet Cong, your guerilla army in South Vietnam. That was whom we fought, not the people in the North nor the South. In my job as an army officer, I simply carried out my task to earn my pay and to serve my country. Why is that a crime? If I've committed a crime, why didn't you try me? What's my sentence? If I have committed no crime, release me. This is a sentenceless, life-labor camp!"

The commissar's face tensed for the first time. He flicked his tongue to wet his lips. "There you go again. You must have forgotten our lecture topic today: 'How the Yankee Imperialists Had Ruined Our Heaven-on-Earth Country.' When you decide to take up arms to fight for the Yankees, you have committed a crime against the Revolution and the People. You only beguile yourself into believing that you fight for your country, but in reality, you fight for who pays you. You are all mercenaries for the Yankees. Your muddled thinking needs thought reform. And that is part of this reform program."

The next day, during a break, Tùng grabbed me in the vegetable plot and pointed toward the kitchen. "Good news, elder brother. I found out the kitchen has run out of firewood and no fresh supply of firewood is on order. We're about to go home."

Later in the day, a truckload of firewood arrived. I reckoned that soon he would anticipate each convoy of trucks as a telltale sign of prisoners being released. But Tùng did not become a gate watcher; he hunted birds to supplement his diet and caught a white-bellied, brown-streaked skylark. I could hear the bird's long, liquid chirrup in the cage he built for the captive ground-nester.

One morning, after we had completed all the lecture sessions and gone out doing corvée, I saw Tùng with the birdcage in hand. The feathers on the bird's crest had fallen off and, as I looked on, it flew into the cage's slats, frantically beating its wings, until Tùng suddenly opened the cage and the bird shot out.

"Can't take care of it anymore?" I asked.

He nodded. "Kept banging itself against the cage. Wouldn't eat what I put in there. Kept hurting itself to get out. This much I can tell you, elder brother: It had more will than many of us here. So, I respected its freedom I took away."

After lunch, our warden instructed us to dig for fresh water. We asked for shovels and spades. He gave us a once-over.

"Be innovative," he said, seriously. "We lack everything here. Let me tell you something else. During the war, we fought the Americans to rescue our country from their imperial yoke, and there was this one time I had to use just a pair of pliers to loosen the bolts of a *ngụy* tank. But eventually I took the tank apart."

Pontificating and hyperbolizing. Before I could shake my head, Tùng blurted out, "Fuck!"

The warden looked his way just as I pulled on Tùng's arm. I could sense a volcano eruption working up in him. That precious second, as he relented, might have saved him from retaliation. He had been in this agitated state since he told me what they had done to his wife back home after they had searched their place and found several letters, those he had brought home on his leave, she had written him during the war. They read the letters and declared that those were the living proof of bourgeois decadence, and blatantly anti-Revolution. "What's in them?" I had asked him. "Maudlin, girly stuff," said he. "Like, it's getting cold on a rainy night like this, and I can't sleep just thinking of you now that you're so far away in some garrison, perhaps standing sentinel wrapped in your poncho. Do you think of me? Do you? Be brave, be strong when you fight our enemy. Kill them if you must, with a clean conscience for our country."

It's a death sentence, I thought. I did not tell him that.

The warden pointed his finger in Tùng's direction. "I will deal with you if you do not behave."

We scavenged the grounds and the storage shed, with the guards' permission, for anything we could use to dig. We found a shovel, a hoe, and a nicked machete and headed toward the rear of the camp where the ground sunk into a depression. At last, a fellow in our team told us this was a favorable area for underground water. He was a former civil engineer. He seemed knowledgeable about where we could find fresh water. "No need for a Y-shaped rod," he said to us. He surveyed the area, particularly looking at some trees, then pointed at a spot. "Here." He marked the spot with a stick of wood. "This is where we'll find our future," he said to us, the other four men of our team. "In the bottom of a well."

"Hope we won't have to dig deep," said one bespectacled man. He had the serious look of an old schoolteacher.

"How deep is deep?" I asked him.

"Five, seven meters, if groundwater is near the surface. Ten, twelve meters if groundwater is deep below."

Another fellow, whose rugged face was stubbled and eyes two slanted slits, spoke up. "I never like a deep well. If you fall and die down there, your soul will remain deep below. You must call on a sorcerer to help free your soul from down there."

"Who told you this?" asked the bespectacled man.

"Just folklore," said the rough-looking man. "It goes also for those who die in a prison. His soul will be trapped in his cell."

"You think the camp might let in a sorcerer to help free the man's soul?" I asked him.

"No," he said, his weathered face impassive. "The camp will have to issue a release certificate to set him free."

I tried not to laugh. The rest snickered.

The communists put us, the puppet regime and puppet army, into three categories in self-confession: Class 1—members of The Central Intelligence Office; Class 2—National Police force; Class 3—members of political parties. This was the order in which they filed away our confession documents.

Bee and I had found two disposed wooden crates which had previously been used to store ammunition. Sturdy, their lids were held together by two metal straps. Some of us used them as stools; others stored personal items in them. Bee and I used them as our writing tables.

"Write down whatever comes to your mind," Bee said to me as he glanced at the two sheets I had scribbled on as my outline. He had already filled five sheets. "Then you won't have much trouble rewriting. Keep it simple and consistent."

I mulled over his advice. I reread what I had written thus far. I did elaborate a few facts to justify the nature of my actions. Then I saw that I was more defensive than factual. I tore up two sheets and started over. Just lay down the facts from memory, I told myself. Do not dig too deep. Do not guess. Things assumed will become inconsistent, which is no good when you have to remember them to write your confession the second time.

"This won't be our last confession," Bee said as if he had read my mind. He dropped his voice as he leaned his head against mine. "You must have a formula to write confessions. But don't tell that to anyone. Any of them here could critique you for such an anti-Revolutionary attitude."

Two years later, at Cổng Trời, I would learn from Mr. Liên that overwriting your confession was hazardous. He had been on the *Nhân Văn* editorial staff with my father, and the pro-*Nhân Văn-Giai Phẩm* movement had had him imprisoned since 1959. He said many inmates had the urge to hyperbolize their self-confessions, and the more they embellished, the more the camp wanted them amplified. "You will find yourself writing full-time for them," Mr. Liên would say to me. "And your memory won't hold up well enough to keep things consistent. It would be simpler if you were the *bần cố nông* class. Tenant farmers, destitute laborers have no blood debts to the people. Try to keep things simple."

I made an outline. From that I wrote four sheets, and by the time I'd finished, the supervising cadre walked in. Three hours had passed. He began collecting from each man what he had assigned, then announced, "What you wrote this morning is only the draft. You will write your true confession tomorrow without your draft. Be true when you write, so that what you put down in your draft will come back to you naturally."

I had kept my outline. I felt fortunate for being alert.

Sleep was paramount at night. But sleep did not come easily; not for me, not for others. I lay awake listening to the heavy sighs, the curses. I began breathing in deeply, then letting out long exhalations. I forgot the count before I fell asleep.

The next day we were to rewrite our confessions, and as we labored with our thoughts before putting them down on paper, the same cadre from the previous day, before leaving, said, "In all your confessions you still addressed your former superiors as 'Mr.' and your former regime as 'Republic of South Vietnam.' The Revolution forbids the use of such words. Use 'hắn' for your former superiors and 'puppet regime' for your former government."

I could see the shock on everyone's faces. I was astounded. The third-person form *hắn*—he or him—referred to someone disrespected.

Before I could clear my mind, the cadre approached me with a sheaf of papers. "Because of your former profession," he said sternly, "you are to create an organization chart based on the information we have gathered from your former colleagues. It is all detailed in these sheets. You must write what you know about them in detail."

I thumbed through the sheets: a comprehensive structure of our former Central Intelligence Office. And its contributors were no one else but my previous associates: my special commissioner, my supervisor at the logistics support bureau, the head of my research unit, my chief of domestic policy, my superior in the information aggregation division.

I began building the chart. Out of habit, I addressed my former colleagues and superiors as "Mr." then quickly crossed out the taboo words. The moment I wrote "hắn" to refer to a former superior, something broke in me. Our age-old etiquette now crumbled.

I had heard that one of us, a former three-star general, had asked for more paper and, at one point, he had roughly one hundred sheets of paper filled with his thoughtful confession.

The education cadre spent some time poring over what Tùng had written. I imagined this cadre had marked Tùng as a troublesome element.

"What did you do during the period between 1960 and 1962?" the cadre snarled at Tùng.

"I don't remember, cadre," said Tùng. He deliberately dropped the word "sir." Then he shrugged nonchalantly. "Can you remember what you did when you were only eight years old?"

"If you did something meaningful for your parents at that age, you can and you will."

"All I did was to obey my parents by going to school, studying hard, and making good grades. That's meaningful to them. If you agree, I will write it down to your satisfaction."

The cadre's face hardened. "You are testing my patience. Think it through, and I will be back in an hour." He paced back and forth and stopped at someone near the door. Head and knees bent, he read what the man was writing. "Stop," he said. "Read out loud what you have just written."

The man timidly stood up and, hardly making eye contact with us in the shack, read out his own words: "I flew a reconnaissance plane and, when I spotted the

Revolution's presence in the jungle, I'd drop flares so the Revolution soldiers knew in advance to clear out of the area before our bombers came."

I could hear some snickers around me. The cadre snatched the sheet of paper from the man's hand. "What do you take the Revolution for?" he said gratingly. "You—" he pointed at the man, "when you dropped flares on our position, you marked our position for your bombers. Liar! You hold the Revolution in contempt."

The cadre shoved the sheet of paper back into his hand. After he gingerly sat down, the cadre paced up and down and then stood over another fellow. "What crime did you commit against the Revolution?" he asked.

The man rose to his feet. "Your permission to speak, sir cadre?" he said deferentially with a slight bow. He identified himself as a former artillery crew chief and, with the permission granted, he spoke. "I was awarded the National Order of Vietnam and Military Merit Medal for our fire support efforts during the retaking of Quảng Trị in the Blazing Summer of 1972. For the record, we had fired three days straight over 45,000 rounds of our long-ranged 155-millimeter artillery, and we had caused 30,000 casualties against the Revolution soldiers. Counting the wrecking of our artillery along the Hồ Chí Minh Trail, which destroyed one of the Revolution's ammunition depots that housed over 5,000 firearms of all sorts and over 10,000 tons of ammunition and fuel, we had killed over 10,000 soldiers of the Revolution. I am truly sorry for my past action and admit my guilt before the Revolution."

The cadre clapped, nodding like a self-winding toy. "Great! Simply great! That is what the Revolution has expected to hear from you. Sincerity and honesty. It is truly proportional to the crimes committed." His pale-skinned face flushed from excitement. "Remember, the Revolution knows everything about your parents, your grandparents—how they died. Do not say 'I know nothing' when answering questions about how they died. Give details. Died from what? Overindulging themselves in rich American foods? Depleting themselves of life energy in service of debauchery?"

His last words went through me like electricity—and through everyone else.

After three days, the supervising cadre took our manuscripts and told us the camp would make three copies of each document—one to be sent to our birthplace for verification, one to our current address to cross-reference with our family register, and one to their central office to cross-check with the former military register of the Army's General Staff.

By now, the drill was so taxing it was a menace just to hear the word "confession." Bee had a maternal uncle and a paternal uncle, both of whom were Party members in the North. His maternal uncle was Soviet Union-educated in economics and management and came back to Hanoi to manage the State-run enterprises. His paternal uncle was a three-star general who had been a part of the Soviet Pacific Fleet, deployed along the coast of Vietnam to relay the Chinese battlefield communications to the North Vietnamese forces. Bee never revealed his blood relations in his confession. "Can you imagine," he said to me, "that they would dare risk their status in the name of the Revolution to save the hide of their nephew?"

Years later, I learned about how our written confessions in those camps were categorized and filed away in the archive of the Ministry of Home Affairs. Each confession, a stapled booklet, was fitted with a cover and appended with a table of contents to guide the examiners to inquired topics.

It was close to nine o'clock in the evening when the group critique ended in our shack. The presiding cadres of the ten groups convened outside our shack and, minutes later, with everyone sitting in attention, came back in and announced a winner. He was from another group in my shack. A former marine lieutenant. According to his self-confession, during the war he was a company commander who personally killed more than one hundred Revolution soldiers, demolished a dozen T-54 tanks with his M72 anti-armor weapon, and was decorated with ten medals of honor. The cadre who made the announcement congratulated him on behalf of the camp and, after a pause to clear his throat, added with a smile that the former lieutenant would receive his release papers tomorrow. As everyone gasped, the cadre nodded and raised a finger as if to make a point. "Such a confession is what the Revolution is looking for from all of you. Sincerity, self-correction, and remorse. Our hero tonight will report to our camp's regiment office tomorrow morning, and from there he will be issued formal release papers to return home. Let us applaud him for his bravery and honesty!"

A chill went down my spine. I glanced at Bee at the same time he turned his head to me. We understood. Without doubt, there shall be more sincere confessions of that type in days to come. It would surprise no one to hear some more bizarre stories, as if out of a fantasy. I did not know if I should feel happy or curse the winner for his short, blissful moment. Tomorrow, Hell awaited him.

After one week of writing self-confessions, we reported one morning to the meeting hall to hear the administrator assessing the nature of our confessions and, possibly, the whereabouts of our progress.

The administrator was a plump bespectacled man in his forties. I had rarely seen a cadre of status wearing glasses. They seemed to identify such eyewear with the intellectual class whom they despised. The administrator went through the stack of papers on the table and picked up a single sheet. He briefly glanced up at us, then returned to the sheet in hand.

"We have had several model confessors in the past week," said the administrator with a firm nod. "Next week, during the revision of your first draft, your presiding cadres will guide you on how to negate your false thinking and channel it to something at least as close to what's been written by our vanguardists to make your time writing them worthwhile. It is all for you. The Revolution is only here to help. But it starts with you. For example, let's hear this confession and decide for yourself whether you have this confessor's utmost honesty to write such an eye-opening confession." He cleared his throat, briefly looked over the top edge of the sheet at the audience. "I," the administrator stopped, "the confessor, that is." He cleared his throat again. "I was a C-130 pilot. That day in March 1975, the Communists were advancing to Xuân Lộc. We flew in a pair of C-130 over Xuân Lộc, each plane carrying a CBU-55 bomb. We could see a long Communist convoy that stretched for several kilometers outside Xuân Lộc—tanks, armored trucks, artillery towing trucks, Molotova trucks full of soldiers. Then, swiftly overtaking us, were two, then four, then six of our A-37 Dragonflies. They were our attack aircraft. They nosedived then lifted up, and smoke and fire rose from the ground toward the rear of the long convoy. Ahead of us was our scout helicopter. It radioed us to drop the bombs and then took a vertical lift, just as we descended and released the two black parachuted bombs. We rose in altitude at the same time the jarring explosions hit us from below. Two green flashes. Then smoke. Then an incredible air pressure hurt our chests, and ahead of us our scout helicopter seemed to quake and then drop like a leaf. A vacuum sucked it down and we watched in horror. Then, it regained its balance and managed to lift up. But on the ground! Mercy! Trucks, tanks, cannons, all tossed about in different directions, and the bodies of the Communist soldiers lay on the highway, under toppled trees and in the ditches. Then our Dragonfly planes came back, strafing along the highway. There were no sounds of guns firing back. They were firing at dead bodies. Those CBU-55 bombs could kill humans and animals within a four-acre area by depletion of oxygen. The Americans had left behind twenty CBU-55 bombs for us to use in the most critical situations. They said it was an extremely powerful, non-nuclear weapon in the US arsenal. And I dropped one of the two bombs and witnessed its destruction on that day before Xuân Lộc fell."

My mouth dropped. The air seemed sucked out of the hall.

The next morning, I was called into a political cadre's shack after turning in my revision the previous afternoon.

"Today," he said, "we'll be working together."

He spoke with a heavy northern accent. His wrinkled white shirt was buttoned at the sleeves, and his baggy brown pants were hitched up and tied with a belt whose tail's excess loop hung down. This type of cadre, who came to the South from the North, I thought, had strictly kept their traditional attire and usually paid no attention to their appearance.

He offered me a cup of tea. I sipped, worried. I looked down at my sandaled feet. We inmates saved our sandals and wore them only when we were called upon for a "working-together" session.

"We will go over the revision of your confession," he said, tapping out a cigarette from a much-wrinkled pack. "You will orally tell the Revolution what you have written in the past two weeks."

"That will take some time, sir cadre."

"We have time."

I had made an extra copy of the first draft of my written confession in its entirety. When revising it, I dropped a few details to simplify the chronology. The more you confess your crime, I thought, the more information they will try to get out of you. That was what Bee and I had agreed on. The more information you spill, the longer it will take for you to go home.

He leaned forward, the cigarette smoldering between his fingers. His eyes had red veins as he peered into mine. "Your revision draft does not match your original draft. Why?"

"My memory failed me," I said calmly. "But if sir cadre wishes to see the consistency between the two drafts, I'd be more than happy to add what's been missing."

"Let's hold off what I have asked you earlier: to recount your confession verbally. Let's focus on what we have gathered from our records about your past activities in the South, a number of which you have not included in your confession."

He handed me a stack of photocopied sheets. I recognized it immediately, an editorial dated February 7, 1969. Quickly, I flipped through the rest of the sheets. I read my long-ago editorial; the parts underlined in black ink:

> The Viet Cong escalated terrorism in 1965 to disrupt the South Vietnam's civilian economy and break the morale of the people. When this failed, the terrorism ran amuck. Two-thirds of the victims of the terrorism were women and children.
>
> Who died but innocent civilians?
>
> In murdering South Vietnam civilians, the people became pigs, chickens, and water buffalo. When the Viet Cong set off a bomb in an urban area, where population density was ten thousand people per square mile, the effects could be readily guessed. The Vietnamese surgeons had become experts in removing metal fléchette embedded in the internal body wounds caused by "anti-personnel" bombs.
>
> Only the Viet Cong miscalculates its strategy. The terror of bombing has brought out an anger and a hatred in the people. It has turned them into enemies instead of friends.
>
> How can we win the war without the people's support?

I stopped and looked at him. I kept a neutral look. Now, not only had I to defend the authorship of what I had written but also defend what I denied.

"What grabs you from such an editorial?" asked the cadre.

"Can you win a war without winning the hearts and minds of the people?" I asked. "That's why the psychological warfare was so important during the Vietnam war. Go and tell the US leaders who thought bombs could beat a people's hunger for independence. They failed as much as you failed in wreaking havoc on the innocent people."

The cadre took a quick puff. "Then why did you leave it out in your confession? You only left things out when they bothered your conscience. So, it is a crime, is it not?" He dragged on his cigarette and snubbed it out with his heel.

"It was part of my job," I said evenly, "to gather intelligence information."

"It is all generalization, Brother Khang," he said, folding his hands together. It was the first time I heard my name on a cadre's lips. "You were defending a monstrous crime, and you claim yourself innocent? You even wrote lies in one of the editorials you authored. Here, read it." He seized what I was holding in my hands, flipped to a sheet, and turned the papers back to me. I glanced at it. I needed fresh air, yet I felt calmer. The worst scenario would be—

"Brother Khang," the cadre said, taking the cigarette from his lips, "you would not want a lengthy, dragged-out investigation. That is not our interest or intention either. So be truthful, and count on the clemency of the Revolution."

The clemency of the Revolution. How many times would I hear such a phrase again? I decided to oblige his overture. I would cut my own throat by resisting him. I must maintain a degree of innocence and take a defensive position on the logic. I realized I had put a noose around my neck. Yet I felt relieved from all the bile I had inside me. The outcome? Forget the outcome.

The cadre unclasped his hands and tilted his head, as if to reassess me with his narrowed eyes, his face bereft of emotion. "You had been, for so long, enslaved by the imperialist, your mind is so corrupted by luxury and the immoral western culture you can't see your own wrongdoings. How can we fix that without sending you to the reform camp? Only through such reform programs shall you be remade into a clean human, thanks to our Party."

"Your dogma extols the Party—an abstract." I no longer cared about what I was about to say next. "This dogma worships one individual—Hồ Chí Minh. This same dogma expunges religion and family. Whenever we mention our family, we are tearful. Family is real. Family is our foundation upon which is built our society, and upon which is built our nation. In the embrace of our family, we are in heaven, which you communists claim does not exist apart from in socialism, which is, to us, a dreamer's wet dream."

I could see his face tense. Then he relaxed. He must be trained as a professional interrogator to never lose his composure. He had been calm, never raising his voice or using profanity. He offered me a cigarette. I took it. I felt as if it was a cigarette a death row prisoner was offered before the firing squad.

"Your friend, Lau, did not mention you in his confession. Nor did you mention him in yours. He was a criminal in the eye of the Revolution."

I tried not to flinch. Whatever you put down in your statements might not work in your favor. *Think about what will happen to your old friends.*

"Your friend was one of the vociferous men of letters in the South. In one of his poems, *The Jester,* he wrote: 'Look at me, I'm a jester / A goateed clown.'" The cadre sipped his tea, then smacked his lips. "Brother Khang, our Uncle is worshipped by the millions, here and abroad. And your friend, a nobody, called him a clown."

I said nothing. I had not read Bee's poem. But it was a mild-toned poem. At his best, those others could be his ticket to his grave, courtesy of these commies.

"And here," the cadre continued, producing another sheet of paper he pulled out of a folder. "In this byline article you authored, you said that there was a total disconnection between the Party and the people. That the Party is absolute. That the Party oversteps its boundary of authority to rule over the National Congress. That, in the North, the National Congress and the Central Committee exist in name only, while the real entity is the Party. The Party secures its God-like power via the National Congress by disallowing any form of pluralism and multi-party system, so that such power now rests in the hands of a select few Party members for years to come." He stopped, out of breath. A suppressed burp, then he went on. "How wrong were you when you lectured your readers that our socialism was outdated? You reasoned that colonialism and imperialism were things of the past because of emerging global equality; hence communism had no more objectives to struggle against and, soon, would become a hell-bound incubus."

Listening, I felt that he had deliberately left out the stinger in that byline. That the communists thrived only in a swamp where impoverished people reside, where mosquitoes and leeches abounded. The moment they set foot in the South, they floundered. Too rich, too little animosity among the easygoing southerners to stir them to revolt. Fighting illiteracy? Women's equality? Land reform? The South had solved all of them. What slogan could the communists now use to rouse the masses?

He glanced back at the sheets on the table and, half looking at me, shook his head. "You even accused we northerners of having no ancestors, because we worship only the Party—"

"But that's true," I said, cutting in. "Families in the North all share the same kind of worship display. On the altar, in every house, is the portrait of Hồ Chí Minh, and on the sides are portraits of Lenin and Mao Zedong. Then families with sons in the People's Army are allowed to display, on the lower tier, two paper cutouts framed in glass; one of them reads 'Proud Family,' and the other 'Motherland Remembers You.' Where are the photographs of your ancestors?"

"The love of our ancestors is always in our hearts. That can't be measured by pictures or words. Only those corrupted by capitalist wantonness need pictures to remind them of what's not in their heart. But common people need visuals to remember our leaders, our heroes." He looked quickly down at the stack of paper and cut me a sidelong glance.

"Then you directed your diatribe against our standard of living, which you called 'a falling standard,' pointing to long lines of people waiting to buy their daily items for household needs. A tragic socialist meltdown, you concluded. In case you forgot, we were fighting the imperialist. Not only were we to feed our frontline troops, we were also obligated to feed the starving South that had long been robbed and exploited by the American capitalists and your phony government."

I had held my breath listening to him. I slowly exhaled. "If a segment of your people suffer food shortage every day, it's passable. For a whole socialist state, which loudly proclaimed its greatness as heaven on earth, it's tragical." In another byline, I had written that the Northern youths had been goaded by the Party to go south to fight the Americans, and the bait was the increased ration of rice for their families and, at the same time, the decreased ration for families whose coming-of-age sons had either dodged the draft or bolted from home. But even without the proof of that article, the yoke was already around my neck.

It took three weeks to go through writing self-confessions. I had the honor to sit with my political cadre through three "working-together" sessions. By the end of the third week, we had shared many cigarettes and many cups of tea and, on the afternoon when we had wrapped up the final session, I had agreed to add all the findings about my past activities in the South, courtesy of my political cadre, to my confession. I had sat in that shack, hunching over one sheet of paper after another, writing down what would be my silent sentence, while he watched me from across the table. I had felt disinterested. In fact, I had distanced me from myself. "What you have done, Brother Khang," he said, as he placed my written confession in a folder, "will facilitate the Revolution's process of determining your reform progress. On behalf of the State and the Party, I commend you." I felt transparent as we shook hands. At least I no longer feared retribution, nor did I have any trepidation of not returning home. I was now a persona non grata.

On that first day back to labor, we lined up in the courtyard, ready for a new day at the distant work sites for the first time. All our previous labor work had been in close proximity of the camp. Hung across the wood-framed entrance was a banner with red painted letters: *Labor Is Glory.* On the other side of the entrance was a long wooden board with cursive letters in red, which you could read when you returned in the late afternoon from the work sites. The board read: *Nothing Is More Precious Than Independence and Freedom.*

Before we headed out to different distant work sites, the camp administrator made a personal appearance. He said, "Today is your first day of real labor. However, the new *Homo sapiens* under our Socialism must labor, and only through labor could he turn into an honest, law-abiding citizen. Labor is glory."

Watching the administrator making his way back to his house, I had a second thought. Did he believe in what he lectured us?

I believed thoughts were things. Followers of Marxism, however, believed matter determined thoughts. The world, according to their creed, was matter magnified in motion, fueled by a struggle that paved the way to revolution through class conflict, whose undercurrent was economics that changed according to natural law inherent in kinetic matter. There was no God, as asserted by Marx and Engels, but humans as part of mass in progress, who created God. To Father Ninh, this might be abhorrent, to think that his God was conceived by humans whose sole existence abnegated Heaven and Hell and thus, the spiritual world was nil. I understood now why Christianity and Communism could never co-exist.

On the first day back, our team planted manioc roots. Our warden, after watching us going through the motions, approached me and said, "Wake a heron up after you have finished raising your hoe." Before I understood what he had implied, he tapped my shoulder. "Wake me up after you have brought your hoe to the ground." He spat at his feet. "Your thought reflects itself in action!"

Thought manifests itself in action. It struck me as irony, the slogan the commies used as a yardstick to measure our progress-embodied thoughts. Such a slogan created a mask to masquerade in public. Can you read his real thoughts? His cheerfulness masks his grief. His submissiveness masks his rebelliousness. His displayed love of Uncle Hồ masks his bubbling hate.

On a wooden footstool sat a guard. He looked barely eighteen. None of these guards wanted to sit on the lumpy ground, even under a shaded tree. To please them, I had had our men carpenter these stools to give them comfort while monitoring us. I wondered if the youth had finished high school.

"Just a duck herder or buffalo boy back where they come from," Bee smirked.

"And he's here to watch over us," I said, then added, "the intellectuals."

"Lose that thought," Bee snapped. "Many of our heroes didn't die on the battlefields but in the buffalo's hoof holes."

I glanced at the youth then back at Bee. "I don't intend to die in those holes."

That night, for the first time, the camp entertained us by showing an old movie, made during the French colonial days. The political cadre, before showing the movie, addressed the crowd.

"Because labor is glory, the Revolution has asked each of you to work your way toward the goal reified in such a slogan. We must be clever and adaptable when laboring. Lacking tools? Make them. Broken tools? Fix them, to protect and prolong their longevity and usefulness in the State's thrifty spirit. With only one tractor in the camp for farming, be adaptable. Pull the plows with your own strength. The movie will show you how our peasants of the *bần cố nông* class pulled their plows without a buffalo. They did it! Why can't we?"

Taking a deep breath, I refrained from shaking my head.

Many of us were beasts of burden in the fields, and many more were reduced to *Homo erectus* when, each morning, they would fight one another for the excrement in those latrines, sitting in a row, each elevated above a large bucket on the ground. The commies called the human waste "phân bắc," literally "northern waste," an indigenous name for night soil. All the communes under the northern socialist regime must follow the "Northern Waste" program: Each family must donate ten kilos of feces each month or face their rice ration being reduced that month. We, the extant southern *Homo sapiens*, learned the name from the camp's cadres, and became enlightened to distinguish this fresh kind of human waste from the "phân chuồng," pen-animal's waste, and the "phân xanh," green-fertilizing feces. Despite the bacteria-ridden wastes of all kinds, discharged every morning from diarrhea-infected or diabetic inmates or those plagued with tapeworms or roundworms, it was all valuable. Once those *Homo erectus* each had secured enough waste for his daily quota and brought his buckets to his counterparts tending the vegetable plots, they would mix such human waste with fresh urine, saved each morning when each inmate went to the latrine—everything unwasted—and fertilize their vegetables until the air started reeking with a head-numbing odor. In a week, the vegetables grew profusely. After harvest, the kitchen would receive the discarded, blighted parts, while the healthy parts were sold to the outside world, the profits of which were pocketed by the camp administrator and his aides. When we ate our meals with those rotted vegetables cooked into our rice, we heard in our heads the words barked out at us, day in, day out: "Labor Is Glory."

But, instead, we saw our meals becoming scanter as the months went by. Rice was replaced by half with manioc, or with the hard bo bo. After the meals, we were to sit in groups and begin self-criticizing with our group members until none of us could trust the others anymore. By the time it ended two hours later, our heads hurt, our bodies ached, and our limbs, after a long day's labor, wept for surrender.

This so-called reform by the communist regime was corrosive, wasting our minds, wearing away the camaraderie once fostered among us, the former free people of the Republic of Vietnam.

One day, it was so hot the brownish alum-laden water smelled strongly, hinting a stench. The wardens asked us, while we were laboring in the fields, to get clean water for them. The only clean water available came from hamlet dwellers nearby. But when they found out that we sought water for the camp cadres, they declined.

A new member joined our team. He was in his fifties, frail, jaundiced. On his first day with us, he shook hands with everyone and introduced himself as a former rector of the University of Cần Thơ—one of our provinces in the Mekong Delta. Mr. Quyền had been detained in a Conex for a week after an incident with our shack trusty. He had discovered a gold leaf Mr. Quyền had hidden in one of the soles of his sandals. When asked why he still had such a forbidden personal asset instead of registering it with camp security, he confessed that he had intended to give it to his wife when she had a chance to visit him. The trusty reported his finding to our camp warden. I was told by one of our former medical doctors that Mr. Quyền had liver cancer. That explained his jaundice. Here we trusted our former doctors more than those called "camp doctor" by the commies.

On the work site that day, Mr. Quyền came to me during a break, his face palely yellow, his breath hurried. "Brother Khang," he said, and paused to catch his breath, "I don't think I'll last much longer."

"Then sit and rest." I took his soiled hand and pulled him down beside me.

"No, I mean I'm dying."

"Sir Rector, we'll get through this together. Please."

"You shouldn't address me as such. I'm no longer what I used to be."

"We still have our decorum, Sir Rector. At least we haven't lost that yet."

It was near noontime. A gong sounded earlier than usual. Soon, every team followed its warden to a clearing. Only a few yellow-flowering cassias stood shading the ground. Under one tree stood a white-shirted cadre in black trousers. It jolted me the moment I saw him. He was my former high school mathematics teacher. Light-skinned, he still had the green sheen along the jawline where he had shaved, and his hair was still slickly pomaded. Clean, orderly.

Was he already a commie when he was teaching high school? I wondered as we stood under the glaring sun, listening to his lecture on "Equity and Crime: How to Redeem Yourself to Become Once Again a Model Citizen." It irked me to hear this parroted rhetoric as I saw that Mr. Quyền was struggling to stay on his feet. I felt helpless. It was then the speaker changed the topic.

"You are here today for a special task," the speaker said, his voice bringing back my memory of many years past, having listened to his southern tone three times a week on the subjects of algebra, arithmetic, and geometry. "After today's lunch, you will be removing land mines. These mines were laid during the war by the *ngụy* regime and its cohorts, the Americans, to kill our Revolution soldiers. Now, they hinder our grand plan for agricultural reform, as we strive to claim back every tract of land wasted by the war, so we can plant again, harvest again, and produce again for the State and the People."

He took out a white kerchief to dab at his forehead; none of us bothered to wipe our sweaty faces but listened on. "We do not have mine prodders at hand, nor do we have mine detectors, but we can use sticks. We can conquer everything if we put our minds to it. We succeeded because we conquered obstacles that you *ngụy* called insurmountable. We succeeded because we believe in our Party; their counsel is priceless wisdom. So now, lacking proper tools for this task, we shall conquer." He took out his kerchief again, this time to wipe his face. "I am going to let our mine expert explain to you the correct way to disarm and remove the field mines. For your own safety, follow his instructions when carrying out your task. Stop and ask questions when unsure."

It took only ten minutes for the mine specialist to explain the nature of the mines and how to disarm them. I found out that the mines were anti-personnel mines that could be triggered by a three-pronged pressure fuse.

"Use your stick and poke the ground for any possible mine," the man said. "You will be divided into columns, walking five abreast, one arm's length apart. We shall cover one hundred meters this afternoon and stay here overnight. We shall resume our task tomorrow morning until we cover the whole field . . ." He paused and gestured toward the stubbled field, yellow under the sun, behind us, and beyond that, the woodlands. "When you come upon a mine, call out 'Mine,' then mark the spot with a red pennant that you will be given. Wait until our specialist comes to your spot, then you can walk back to safety."

There were over a thousand inmates in this nameless camp, but only a hundred were tasked with mine detection while other groups were laboring somewhere else. The guards walked behind us. I could sense their tension as they kept a safe distance. It had rained hard the night before and the ground felt soft in places. The sun was slightly behind us, and I could see our shadows slanting ahead of us as we stepped carefully forward, stick in hand, probing the ground. The insects whirred. The heat smelled dry.

"Mine!" a fellow, two arms' distance to my right, yelled.

Everyone in my column stopped.

"The rest of you keep moving," one of the guards snapped.

We glanced back, my heart thumping. The fellow was driving a red pennant into the ground. He stood, looking around. I wish I were him, then I could have an early break.

My eyes strained searching for suspicious looking objects, my hand holding the stick, listening as I moved it carefully ahead of me among weeds and withered clumps of grass. A cricket jumped. A skink shot through the grass. Startled, I stopped. The coppery-brown sleek body slunk away. Then, an explosion to my right several columns away. Shouts erupted.

"Stay calm!" one of the wardens yelled. "Everyone stay where you are. Do not move!"

I could see the inmates and guards surrounding the scene where three inmates lay prone on the ground. Minutes later, several inmates came back with three makeshift stretchers, slapped together with sticks and cloths, and the victims were carried back to camp.

We continued our task with trepidation. Late in the afternoon, we stopped when the kitchen detail brought us our meals. It must have taken them an hour to get there on foot, and even longer with all the utensils and provisions. We camped overnight beyond the barren field. That night, I woke to the sound of an explosion coming from the land-mined field. A fox or a hare must have tripped a mine.

The next day, it rained heavily in the afternoon and our mine detecting task was stopped. We had found three mines before it rained. One of the specialists had cautioned us before we resumed our tasks that some of the mines must have turned sideways because of the rain-soaked ground. Probing it hard at a wrong angle might set it off. I felt tremors deep in my stomach whenever my stick hit something hard. Most of the time it was a rock buried near the surface of the ground. But the tremors in fact came from the sight of those victims the day before.

That evening, while waiting to receive our meals, we received bad news. One of the victims had died. It was Mr. Quyền. What he had said to me the day before came back to me. *I'm dying.* Such a premonition. After I ate, I went to see him in the carpentry shed where they had just assembled a rickety coffin made out of wood, some pieces still not shaved completely of bark. They had dressed him in his spare clothes: The shirt was not stamped with the bold, tar-black initials "CT" for *Cải Tạo*—reform. I followed the burial team to the grave site a good distance behind the camp. It drizzled and fireflies winked here and there in the drenched darkness. Desolate, the gravesite was fenceless.

Wild hogs would tear through his grave and stray cattle would trample on it and soon there would be nothing left but bones. But I'd remember you, Sir Rector, I thought as I walked back.

It was raining. A gloomy morning. Without a word from our warden on work continuation or stoppage due to bad weather, I, the team leader, went into his shack.

I sensed that he was watching us lining up outside in the rain.

"You are here to report to your warden, and you already committed a violation." Those were the first words out of his mouth.

I coughed a short cough, not bothering to wipe rain off my face. "Sir warden, what did I do wrong?"

"Take off your hat!" he almost shouted. "Now!"

I removed my hat and clutched it against my chest. "Reporting to you, sir warden. Do you wish to have our team set out to the work site this morning, despite the rain?"

He pursed his lips into a pout. "Everyone in your team must take off their hats. All of you. Once you obey the camp regulation then you may report to me."

The next morning it did not rain. Rather, it was hot at seven o'clock. The air was humid, foreboding a steaming day ahead. We were forming a line outside the warden's shack when Bee leaned to me, his hand on my shoulder. "Don't wear your hat."

I understood. Something perked up inside me. I turned to my teammates. "Everyone take off your hats."

They all took off their hats. Some smirked. I went into our warden's shack. He was watching us, I could tell, before I walked in.

"Reporting to you, sir warden. Everyone is present, no one is sick."

"Do you think it is going to be very hot today, Brother Khang?"

"Yes, sir, it will be hot today."

"Can you see that it will be detrimental to you and your teammates without headgear?"

I felt jolted. *This maladroit double-dealer.* At my silence he arched his brows. "What do you have to say?"

"Sir warden, it will be hot later in the day, but it is tolerable now."

"The act of taking off your hats is premeditated. That thinking is anti-revolutionary." He rose from his chair and walked to the entrance door. Without looking back at me, he spoke to the team, "Select a new team leader." He half turned his head at me. "Brother Khang, you will spend the next seven days in solitary confinement."

This was the same man who had read Bee's letter to his wife when we were allowed to contact our families once a month during our early months here. That was also in the time we were under the supervision of the People's Public Security Bureau. Bee had come back, dejected, to our shack. I called him a fool when he admitted his carelessness with his wording in that first letter home. He had said to her, "It has been a trying time, *Em*. We are all prisoners here. We are day laborers; but I will try my hardest to get good marks so I can see my release sooner. Pray for my return." He had been summoned to appear before the camp committee. "We read your letter home," said the committee chair to him. "How dare you to call this camp a prison? This is not a detention center. This is where you study and reform yourself to become a better citizen, a reformed person that fits into our socialist society, a much improved, people-oriented society in which everyone is equal. How can you compare it to a prison? How can you rely on your God for your release? You will be disciplined: No family correspondence for three months." I had felt enlightened by the cadre's remark about God. Here we shunned the word "God" and "prison." Especially the former. We had had natural disasters—it was part of the natural environment. Yet the commies condemned these catastrophes as "heavenly bandits."

It was just a can.

For decades now, those who had families with newborn babies who could not breastfeed would treasure this Guigoz infant formula milk that came from France in a light aluminum can. Now such a Guigoz powder milk can was a cult object inseparable from us. It was Guigozcanism as opposed to communism and socialism. The latter's objectives were to teach us by rote the philosophy of classlessness, and to instill in us the belief in such equality. Marxist theories or not, we were to be purged of individualism, so every bit of possessions we owned ought to be shared. Nights when we were inside our shacks, the doors bolted, Guigozcanism prevailed any *ism* there was. Some of us had craftily transformed their *goz* cans into a portable miniature kiln, fitted with a wire strap and lidded with a perforated cover, for drinking, cooking. At night, their owners would bring out items scavenged in the wilderness and drop them into their *goz*: sometimes a wormy potato, some red-vine spinach, a pinch of sodium glutamate, sometimes, by luck, a cut of a snake killed in the woods and, at the last minute, a handful of ramen. Sometimes someone would pull out earthworms he had caught and saved in his *goz* can. Now, with a sharp bamboo sliver, he slit open each earthworm and pried out its gizzard and intestine. He cleaned them, cut them into small pieces, and cooked them with his rice and wild herbs into what he called *earth dragon* pottage.

In those moments none of us cared about the people in the outside world, or who we had been, as we were often lectured on. We were progressing from a destitute existence to a socialist good life, in step with the fatherland that was becoming a prosperous socialist nation. In those precious moments, we were reformed by Guigozcanism.

One Sunday morning, our day off, we were summoned into the dirt courtyard before the camp administrator. Behind him stood the wardens and, behind them, guards pointing rifles. The plump man clasped his hands on his round belly, his pig eyes behind his glasses darting back and forth, measuring the faces watching him from the assembly. Finally, he spoke.

"To express your newfound spirit of socialist labor in light of your reform progress, every two weeks on Sunday, you will go into the forest and each come back with a bundle of wood which must weigh at least 50 kilos."

Such Sundays became "the commie Saturday" in our lingo. The strain of overworking, worsened by being underfed, had reduced each of us to a walking skeleton as light as a feather, leaving not even footprints on the dirt. We had been foraging food or greens while we were out laboring. Did the commies not encourage us to better our nourishment with supplements? "Cải thiện"—improvement—were the words they used. But truth be told, they would allow us to improve our diet—the camp diet—only after work, in our free time.

That day however, one of our men got caught during work boiling a raw manioc tuber in his *goz* can. The guard stood over him by the creek, startling him with his shout. "What are you doing while everyone else is working?"

The man looked up from his position, crouched down on his haunches, just as the guard brought down the rifle butt on his back. He fell forward, knocking over the steaming can. "Stand up," the guard said. "Hold your *goz* can in one hand, your tuber in the other. Raise both hands over your head and walk back to camp. You were stealing the people's properties."

"Sir," the man said, slowly rising to his feet, "I didn't steal. I dug it up in the woods."

"Liar!" The guard kicked him in the rump. The man stumbled, regained his bearing, and, arms raised, walked ahead of the guard toward the camp.

It was cold that night when we were ordered to gather in the courtyard. Each of us sat hunched on our heels, wrapped tightly in our thin blankets. They had already placed in the center of the court a bamboo table, lit by two flaming torches. The administrator stood behind the table, holding up our man's *goz* can in one hand and a machete in the other. The torches painted a lurid glow on his face. Unnerved, we held our breath.

"From this day on," the administrator spoke, "you are not allowed to have this can in your possession. Violators shall be punished. I loathe this can, for it speaks volumes of the petty bourgeoisie mindset still living inside you. Open your eyes!" He slammed the *goz* can on the table and, with one quick stroke, cleaved the can vertically in half.

On his order, we went back into our shacks and came out again each holding a *goz* can. Soon all the *goz* cans were confiscated, dumped clanking into the burlap bags the guards held opened in front of us.

Without our beloved *goz* cans, we had to resort to cutting bamboo trunks whose cavities allowed for storing water. Each of us had to improvise to make a plug or a cover for our bamboo receptacle. What riled us was the sight of our *goz* cans reappearing in the hands of the guards, the cadres.

So much for the loathing they had for our little vessels.

We had in our shack, like any other shack in the camp, an assortment of inmates, some of whom with sympathetic backgrounds, and others with eye-opening backgrounds.

One Sunday morning, with no work that day, we were relaxing on our cots when the warden ushered in a man, our newest shack member.

After putting his bundle of belongings in a corner, he took off his shirt and flung it over his shoulder. It was humidly hot in the shack, but his sinewy body did not sweat. He stood looking around. Suddenly he raised his voice, loud enough that it startled nearly everyone. "Let me introduce myself. My name is Quới. I was a former district cadre. My crime to the Party and the Revolution is corruption. I was a Viet Cong assassin in the sixties. Any of you here remember the hit on this guy at *Chính Luận Daily News*? It was me and my comrade who terminated him."

Stunned, we sat staring at him. He said again, dead toned, "The Party is right, I am wrong. While I am in this room, I won't tolerate any bashing of the Party or the Revolution. If you malign the Party or the Revolution, I shall report you."

More stunned than anyone else in the shack, I sat with my jaw dropped. I was a regular contributor to that *Political Opinions* newspaper, and who would edit my byline but the man who was assassinated on the next to last day of December 1965. The newspaper had received death threats from the local Viet Cong; yet it maintained its staunch anti-communist editorials. Shortly after it published my byline on the disconnection between the Party and its people in the North, the newspaper editor was gunned down outside his home. Our intelligence at the CIO later identified the assassination stemmed from the Viet Cong's Military Region Special Action Group, code-named F100.

I could not take my eyes off the man. He must have been in his early twenties when he killed my friend, the editor-in-chief. The man turned and walked back to the corner of the shack where he sat down, legs drawn up, resting his head on his folded arms. I heard expletives from behind me. Then I heard Tùng, his voice loud enough for everyone to hear, "Motherfucker! You're in a tiger cage now!"

Soon after his admission of his past crimes, the former VC assassin was removed from our shack. Perhaps a snitch had leaked information to the camp committee that the man would be in harm's way if he had stayed.

Another shack mate I had befriended was a former schoolteacher. He joined us late, after I had been in the camp for nearly eight months. But the thoughts he shared with me on the cancerous socialist regime back home had me thinking for days, and those thoughts he had had were the reason why he was in the camp with us.

Bespectacled, stooped, he looked much older than his age: mid-thirties, my age. I would have put him in his early forties from his receding hairline. When he talked, his protruding Adam's apple jerked up and down on his thin neck.

"Lies," he said to me, his voice surprisingly soft, "and fact falsifications were being taught in our schools back home." He quickly looked around, then spoke in a whisper. "Brother Khang, they replaced our principal with a man from the North. They also replaced all our textbooks with what they taught in the North. When I read our northern version of the geography textbook, I became aghast. It said, 'Russia came to aid the Nguyễn Dynasty in 1805 in building our national treasure, the Huế Citadel and its walled enclosures of Imperial City and Forbidden Purple City.' I brought this error to the principal's attention, who became agitated and went to consult with his local cell secretary of the jurisdictional schooling. He returned and said to me, 'All the textbooks were reviewed by our board of education and are free of errors. Therefore, you must abide by the rules.' I said, 'I cannot teach my students what is not correct. No Russians ever set foot on the soil of Vietnam in 1800s. They were, at that time, embroiled with the French in the Napoleonic Wars. The Huế Citadel, built by our people, was based on Vauban-styled architecture, the French military architect of the early eighteenth century.' He shouted at me, 'Don't you dare challenge the Revolution! I ask you to write a self-corrective report and submit it to me.' 'Then I shall resign,' I said. He shook his head vehemently. 'You cannot. You must stay and teach our younger generation the infallible knowledge the Revolution imparts to them.' So, I stayed."

"What if you stuck with your decision of resignation?" I asked.

"Then it would mean I was against the Revolution and its teachings. The consequences would be grave." He paused then spoke, but his eyes had a faraway look. "I went back to my class and gave the students an essay subject to write about. 'How Well Has Your Family Managed in Our New Society.' All the class responded with positive thoughts on the regime, praising Uncle Hồ for his guidance, the Party for its light, the Youth League for its inspiration. Only one girl stood out with a composition that described the loss of her father to the reform camps, the denial of employment to her mother, the untruths in school textbooks on geography and history. In conclusion, she wrote: 'My family and our school education share a lost identity. As citizens, we cannot be who we are anymore without getting discriminated against. As educators, we cannot teach what is true without getting indicted. This travesty of justice has become the norm of our new society.'" He paused while I felt the words sinking into me. "I read her composition to the class. The next day I was called into the principal's office—a student in the class had reported me. I faced the collective wrath of their tribe who called themselves educators." Then he rose, knees creaking. "And now I'm here. Brother Khang, the only regret I have is that I might have jeopardized my brave student's education when they reviewed her essay."

I never thought of escape until I met one of the shack mates. Born and raised in the Mekong Delta, he was a priest a few years younger than me.

The first thing I noticed about this priest, when he joined our shack, was his flair for storytelling. How he remembered those stories he had stockpiled in his brain, memorizing whole novels, was a wonder to me. On the practical side, he made many friends because of his amazing storytelling—not to discount his business acumen of getting gifts in return from his fans.

Some nights, we would gather around him to listen to him recounting saga after saga of the Chinese wuxia or swashbuckler, all coming from Jin Yong's novels. I was one of millions of Asian readers who were ardent fans of Jin Yong. Vy—the priest's name—would sip tea, sometimes sweetened lemonade, having been prepared by his servile fans much like churchgoers to their priests, and pause in between tales to feed into his mouth a ginger candy drop, or nibble a coconut candy stick, while his fans, including me, raptly looked on.

Once, we found out a guard was eavesdropping outside, not because he would report our activities, but because he was taken in by those tales, which I must assume he had never heard or ever had permission to read. For several nights he must have listened from outside to the colorful lives of heroes and heroines traveling through the *jianghu*—literally rivers and lakes which metaphorically implied the underworld—and he must have been wowed by the fanciful *I Ching*-inspired Kung Fu fighting forms; he must have been stirred to fantasize by the wistful romances between a hero and his female instructor, which, I was certain of, would never be allowed in his communist state; and what did he think, in his blindfolded view, when Vy described the heroine in *The Return of the Condor Heroes* as someone whose skin was white as snow, her beauty beyond convention, and who became a friend of a Taoist practitioner named Zhen Zhibing who eventually raped her?

How we found out he was listening was happenstance.

One night, Vy was halfway through telling tales from *The Heaven Sword and Dragon Saber*, which was part of a trilogy that includes two other novels, *The Legend of the Condor Heroes* and *The Return of the Condor Heroes*, when he stopped. But the part at which he paused was intentionally a cliffhanger in which the Good Sect was battling the Evil Sect on the Guangmingding Peak on Kunlun Mountains. The shack went up in an uproar. "Go on!" "Why have you stopped?" "Make another pot of tea for him!" Vy refused to go on, until suddenly the door was flung open and a guard poked his head in.

"You had no reason to stop there," he said in his backwater northern accent. "You must go with the majority. What happened to those men fighting on the mountain peak?"

Vy smiled. He looked at all the faces and at the young guard. "They all fell off the peak and died in the gorge."

Growing up in the Mekong Delta, he had told me, he first came to know about Viet Minh when boys his age began spotting human corpses floating downriver. Most of them floated facedown. The locals had a name for them: "thằng chổng"—*ass-up corpse.* Those fly-studded, hyacinth-entangled cadavers were sometimes naked, sometimes had on just a shirt, most of them with hands bound behind their backs. His father told him, "Those floating corpses were victims of the Viet Minh's executions."

He went to a Catholic school. In the classroom, the students would chat about "thằng chổng," and some of them bragged about pelting them with rocks. The teacher, who was a nun who had migrated to the South after the Geneva Accords, chided them and told them to pray for the dead. In those years there were more and more northerners coming to settle in his town. He looked at me, smiling. "It shocked me as a boy the first time I heard people from the north speak. They had accent like you, Brother Khang. I thought they came from a foreign country." He asked them why they left the North for the South, and one old woman, her teeth lacquered black, said to him, "Our priests told us that Jesus has gone south.'"

Then one morning toward noon, I did not see Vy on a work site when we gathered for roll call during our break. I heard that he had accidently chopped off one of his fingers and was brought back to the camp sick bay where he had been recuperating.

The next day, it rained before dawn and would not let up. The sky was pale, and so low you could see thick clouds in black and gray. Rain fell in white sheets, gurgling in narrow trenches around the camp. Gone were the sounds of peepers and birds. Past noon, the water rose and spilled into the shacks, and I grew alarmed when I spotted lumps of human waste floating in the water. The whole camp turned into a zoo when its animals broke loose. We hopped onto our cots and, in horror, watched the water continuously rising. Soon there were worms and bugs and maggots riding the water that kept flowing in.

There were cries coming from the row of Conexes. I yelled to our shack leader. "Our men in the Conexes! They'll drown!"

The leader hesitated, sitting on his haunches on his cot. Finally, he asked our watchdog—an inmate assigned by the camp to keep order among us—to go to rescue the detainees in those containers. The watchdog refused. I hopped down into the water just as Tùng left his cot in a corner. "Fuck," he said, glaring at the watchdog. "They're one of us. You yellow-bellied loafer!"

I waded toward the Conexes while Tùng moved toward the shack of the on-duty cadres. Outside the Conexes, I stood, waist deep in murky water, trying to calm down the detainees. Drenched, I watched the water rising above my hips when Tùng returned with the keys. We waded into each Conex and unlocked the leg irons for each detainee. By the time we got the five of them out, the water had reached our chests.

By sundown, the water had receded, and we had spent a whole evening cleaning up. The air was cool and smelled odorous. I slept fitfully, waking at times to hear someone in the shack cursing when he discovered a maggot crawling into his ear, or to see centipedes creeping up the wall above my head.

The next morning, the reveille gong sounded followed by gunshots. I could hear the footfall of the guards in the courtyard and then in the shacks, then the loudspeakers ordering us to stay put. No one was allowed outside. When three angry-looking guards burst into our shack, they kicked at everything in their way. One of us asked what happened and received a curt reply: "Shut your trap!"

In the afternoon, when things had quieted down, we learned that Vy had escaped from the infirmary during the flood.

The reveille gong sounded. Three quick, harsh sounds at five o'clock every morning.

Outside, it was dark. The only light that lit the shack during the night, a green sawed-off bottle that hung on a wooden peg on the partition separating the sleeping quarters from the water closet, had long gone out. After eight months, the lamp's oil had dried up, its wick a burned-down stub. In the lightless shack, men fumbled around. Those who were wise had risen before the gong to have the privilege of using the lavatory. The shack was full of the creaking noises the pallets made as men began to greet a new day ahead. The bamboo-slatted pallets were flat on the dirt floor, each a sanctuary of lice. Soon the human noises became a hubbub, the air tinged with a strong odor of fresh urine and body waste.

The morning was cool, with dew still wet on the ground. We lined up in teams, packing the dirt courtyard, a thousand strong of former personnel and civil servants of the Second Republic. We sat on our haunches, answering to our team leader during the roll call, their voices ringing from team to team, at times scattered in the wind that came from the sea. Each team would march out of the gate when the guard in the watchtower called its number through his bullhorn. The sea wind was damp and blowing. Line after line of drab-looking, thinly clothed men followed one another, some barefooted, some in sewn-up footgear, some bareheaded, passing through the gate. These were men who had once had families, a country, a future, and walking among them now were men of the victorious communists, of the opposite dogma—who had fallen from grace because of their corruption during the reign of their Transitional Revolutionary Government in Saigon. There were, in the assemblage, collaborators of the post-1975 Resistance, who would trek into the jungle with medical and food supplies to aid the resistance fighters, who had used their own cafés in various towns to recruit the old die-hard ultranationalists. Then, too, there was a coterie of double agents who, before 1975, were Viet Cong who were caught by our side and became turncoats. After 1975, they were heralded as local exemplars as they rode in the American jeeps through their towns to take over their districts. It took but a few days before somebody looked into their files in the archive of the Second Republic, where they found signed and sworn classified information on these sham heroes.

Column after column of men filed out of the camp. None of the men were allowed to walk with the aid of a stick—the sick and the injured had been denied exemption from work—after the camp deputy administrator had made himself clear. "Because a human act reflects a man's thought, it is evident that a man who walks with a stick has every intention to show the people how maltreated he is by the Revolution. From this day forward, everyone must learn to carry himself with dignity, to live up to the image of the Revolution. Every one of you must strive to become one of the new breed of socialist citizens. So, bring vigor to the work site. Physical weakness is a crime!"

Leading us out of the camp was our team leader, a former cabinet director of the Second Republic, whose optimism was always as lively as a hummingbird, and who had once told us, "Always be prepared for that day of our graduation. Have a tie and a clean white shirt ready for when we leave this place." As if this labor camp, disguised as reeducation center, was our Military National Defense College, and we, the inmates, were its students. Having been beguiled to turn ourselves in voluntarily, many of us were still buoyed with optimism about our imaginary release.

On our way to the seaside commune we would cross the dunes before reaching the coastal flat. That morning, the sea was rough, the waves crashing with loud booms. On the darkly wet rocks were round, spiny sea urchins lying together, as plum-colored as the part of the rocks washed by the waves. The little girl who sold dumplings once asked me when she saw those urchins, "*Chú*, why didn't they fall off?"

"They have tube feet," I said, and explained to her how the tube feet helped the sea urchins anchor themselves to the rock surfaces.

In the crevices of seaward rocks were pools of seawater. In those tide pools, the water was sometimes green from the bottom-living seaweeds, a clear green holding a sky in it. Once we came upon a tide pool whose water was crimson red. The red startled the little girl.

"Why the water is red, *chú*?" she asked me.

"I don't know." I left it as a conundrum to her. And to me. When I thought back, I imagined such a red in that tide pool must have come from some sort of minute plant that formed a colony in that pocket of water, and the water had taken on the color of the plant.

We sometimes found pieces of mollusk shells in those tide pools, pieces of crabs or mussels, a broken claw, broken shell, lying still in the clear water. They must have been the debris left there by the gulls who had dropped their prey on the rocks to break them up, so they could eat the soft parts inside.

The little girl was not on the beach this morning. Her small figure in the early hour was always a silhouette. A cane basket in her arms, wrapped with a white cloth, covered the meat dumplings inside. I would walk with her, trailing the men, as we both headed to the distant commune.

The beach was empty. The morning was gray. Along the shore lay mats of sodden rockweeds. Caught on them were opalescent jellyfish, cellophane-thin and gleaming. Out in the open, a vast sky above, an immense sea below, I felt the poignance of being free. But we had no sanctuaries, no place to hide or run to. In every tangle of drenched seaweed, every brine-filled crevice of rocks, and every forgotten pocket of water left on the sand by the sea, lived all sorts of sea-dwellers who sought out these sanctuaries from the harsh sea. We, on the other hand, were creatures of no special zone of life. The hunger that hounded us had deprived many of us of the vitality we needed to sustain life. Lacking food, we were like the swifts falling from the sky that died in multitudes when cold rains, day after day, had washed the skies clear of insects. So many of us had died from hunger, from sickness, from exhaustion. Or one might die in a solitary confinement cell when his life energy had drained out of him. Erased from the living, he was like the footprints left in a sand dune, momentarily, before the constantly shifting sands obliterated them and nobody would ever know who it was that had left those footmarks.

A few times, coming back together from the commune, the little girl and I would walk upon sand mudflats, brown and damp, between the high mark and low mark of tides. We went to the little holes, hundreds of them, in the sandy mud and caught ghost shrimps hiding in them. They looked clear as glass. We would wash them at the water's edge and yank the heads off so the meat came out of the shells.

Above the low-tide line, weeds hung in curtains over the rock walls. In the breeze, the glistening droplets of water were telltale signs of whelks living under the crinkly, moist weeds. "They're snails," I had said to her, picking up a coiled-shell whelk, and handing it to her. I explained to her the resiliency of the seaweeds, the red and the green seaweeds hanging from rocks in slippery fronds. "They hardly die," I told her. "They might dry during ebbing tides, becoming brittle, but their papery texture returned with the high tide, the push and pull of the sea."

She asked how I knew this, and I told her it came from my biology classes in high school and the four years at the Saigon University of Sciences. I did not tell her about my love for the sea, nor did I share with her my countless trips to the coast in my line of work to take the pulse of the tainted politics, where your friends during the day might turn out to be your enemy at night. She said, "Will you teach me biology?"

I smiled lovingly at her, nodded, and said, "In time."

She had barely finished elementary school when the northern communists overtook our South and now, with all the schools closing, she must stay home and help her mother who made meat dumplings for her to bring to the town market run by the commune.

At low tide, the red seaweeds looked dry and tattered, matted against the rocks. I had watched her running her hand under the papery red fronds and, as she lifted them, I could see, hidden under them, the pebble-like mollusks in black and sand colors.

"You can eat them," I said, "they're edible."

"The snails?" she asked, trying to dislodge one from the crusty rock surface.

"No, the algae," I said. "You can dry it and eat it." I had never known that what I just said would come true for me years later when, at times, we the inmates would eat even moss to calm our hunger.

We had both sat watching a crab digging through the mud. Finally, a clam appeared. The crab, gripping the clam with its walking legs, worked the shell of the clam with its pincers. When I turned to her, she was staring raptly at a crow several feet away. The crow was poking at the weeds and suddenly stopped. It found something. She dropped her voice as she spoke to me. The crow stepped up and I could see its dark toes holding a mollusk as it worked its beak feverishly on the mollusk's shell. She gasped the moment the crow jerked its head up and dangling in its beak was a snail.

I could hear the guards calling us to move on. "Go on home," I had said to her. We rose, me with the bulging burlap bag on my back, she with an empty cane basket in her arms. We went back now in different directions. At low tide, all the sand dwellers had retreated into their deep wet burrows or buried themselves under rocks, all waiting for the next high tide. Her footprints trailed her on the sand among those of swift waders, their legs seemingly lifted off the sand. Her figure became smaller.

Shortly after four on a Sunday afternoon, the gong sounded.

We were summoned to the courtyard. We stood in line facing the proctor committee, and behind them were guards carrying rifles. The chief warden raised the megaphone to his lips. He stopped, took a deep puff on his cigarette and blew the smoke out the corner of his mouth.

"Be attentive, everyone!" he said. "We have received the order to move some of you to another camp in order to take advantage of the liberal policy by the Party and the State, one that will allow you to progress well in our reform program. Before moving out we will conduct a thorough inspection of your belongings. When your name is called, step out of the line and answer 'Present.'"

None of us knew where we would be headed to. The commies were very good at guarding secrets. Even small matters. Not even the wardens knew the destination of the camp transfer.

Around me I saw faces I recognized. Faces of those who "owed a blood debt to the People"—Military Security, Political Warfare, Propaganda, and Open Arms; Police Special Branch, Special Commissioner Bureau—all stepping forward when their name was called.

All of us received a baguette. We were to move from our camp to somewhere presumably far away, judging from the day's meal.

The security chief issued the last warning. "We will stop once or twice for you to relieve yourselves. We will have security guarding the perimeters so you're protected against unruly civilians who want to stone you. But you all must stay put, no moving around. You must absolutely obey the order or security will shoot you. No chit-chatting. Understood?"

I could recite in my head the rhetoric used by the commies to deceive the People by extolling them as the holy relic all through the Revolution. *All for the People.* But after the Indochina War, and then the Vietnam War, who did they leave by the wayside? The People. To avoid incurring the People's wrath during transportation of camp attendees, they moved prisoners around at night. If they had to stop for them to relieve their bladders, they would pick a desolate location where no dwellers could glimpse the prisoners, like cats that hide their waste to avoid unwanted attention.

Despite the sense of threat, once we were in the Moltova I was able to doze off. Somewhere in my sleep, I saw the plough-shaped Big Dipper, then Venus, so bright in the dawning sky. When I woke, we were still in transit. It was so dark outside. There was not a speck of light.

We arrived at Saigon Newport at half past one in the morning.

We were the first to be shipped to the North, ranking from captain to general. In this same classification were people from the administrative side—ranking bureau chiefs, department secretaries, senators, congressmen, religious heads, political party chairmen. Now we knew why they had subjected us to a three-month long indoctrination on the ten lessons, lectured by members of the National Liberation Front, known as the Viet Cong, and then by their political cadres from the North. Now we could comprehend what the Revolution stood for and set our hearts and minds on our future settlement in the North.

A ship, lit with cabin lights, had been waiting for us.

Someone among us called out, "That must be our ship."

Someone else responded. "Our former Republic's ship all right."

A small group of cadres, clad in khaki outfits, broke off when one of them approached us. We had stood on the quay, waiting. I looked down at my feet. I was standing in a puddle of water. It was chilly.

The khaki-clad man spoke to us. "The reform camp you will be attending has all the facilities and amenities to help you get on with the program quickly and efficiently, so that you complete the program in due time, and can return to your families and become a respectable citizen who can contribute to the all-new socialist society. Only by fulfilling your duty and responsibility as a good citizen can you redeem yourselves from your past wrongdoings long associated with the American imperialists and the *ngụy* regime."

I kept my gaze downward. In the puddle of rainwater there were star-lights in tiny dots. A long time after the sermon, we were herded down into the ship's cargo hold. The air down below was dank. It smelled of cattle's waste. We sat bunched up on our heels; the floor was wet. I could see the sky, black and starry. Then the faces of the guards. All of them were northern youths. One of them shouted down at us. "You fuckers. Pretty wives, nice kids, cars, houses. This time we'll see you in the North and you'll die there."

I felt immune to their insults.

The seasickness began almost immediately. I slept, then woke, then slept again, remaining on my heels while many others had toppled over and slept on the wet floor. Meals came in buckets dropped down on a rope through the open hatch. Packets of instant ramen. We broke them up in chunks and ate them raw. Once the guards did us a favor by hauling up three metal containers full of human waste and urine. The containers sloshed and spilled halfway up, and people screamed. On the third day, the cargo hold smelled of ammonia and the human filth that had overflown from the containers and ran off across the floor.

On the fourth day, we arrived. Where, I did not know. We only knew we had reached our presumed destination when a cadre spoke to us through the open hatch. "This is the Hải Phòng port. You are now on the soil of the Democratic Republic of Vietnam."

As we climbed up out of the suffocating stench of the cargo hold, I blinked against the sun. The guards and the cadres had donned masks. They were like herdsmen, prodding us and corralling us until we were orderly placed facing a line of yellow-uniformed People's Public Security, all with pistols holstered at the hip. Beyond their line was a truck convoy. I could tell it was late in the afternoon by the setting sun.

A middle-aged man emerged from a black car that had only just arrived. He stood in front of the assembly, looking at us as if trying to acquaint himself with us in his mind. We were surely aliens to him, from the way we dressed to the images the North had created of us over the years for him and his kind. I looked at his short-sleeved white shirt and his gray cuffed pants, something that had gone out of fashion in the South in the late 1960s. Then he finally addressed us.

"On behalf of the Democratic Republic of Vietnam and our Ministry of Internal Affairs, I welcome you with open arms. You are here to benefit from the infrastructure our camps have set up, which is much better than those in the South, solely to aid your reform progress. You are only required to apply your diligence in assimilating with the reform program for three to five years. However, the number of years just cited is nominal. The result is based on individual fulfillment of the program's requirements. The Ministry of Internal Affairs shall exercise its best efforts to embody our Party and State's policy in helping you reform yourselves. That is the ultimate goal envisioned by the Party and the State for the benefit of your reform efforts. In such clemency, I wish you well with your endeavors."

The convoy took us through towns in the dusk, slowing down at times on bad roads, and, in the twilight, we could see the locals watching us go by; we could hear them.

Before midnight, we were transferred to a train. Boarding the train, I saw that all the iron ties were missing and in their places were wooden ties. I could not help imagining the locals or the transportation personnel had swapped them and sold them off for a profit. Packed fifty bodies in each lightless freight car, we slept in the unhealthy air, unventilated and smelly. In the night, I woke to cries for water and air when some people could not breathe. The train did not stop. In the constant clattering, the cries died out.

When the train finally stopped to let us out, it was noon. From our boxcar we carried out a body as the guards watched. The dead man was a former Head of Planning Bureau of Office of the Political Warfare. He had died of suffocation.

We lined up on a riverbank. A cadre told us it was Red River. Within a stone's throw was a crowd of locals in shabby clothing. They watched us as if we were exhibits in a museum. Looking at them, I thought they resembled prehistoric humans. One of them shouted, "Bloodthirsty!" Then another one, "Stone them!"

We only had time to cover our heads and faces as they pelted us with everything in their hands. We backed away. I felt rocks hitting me on the arms. Each hit smarted. There were cries and curses among us while the guards looked on. After they had seen enough—a staged event that drew blood—a guard shot into the air and the crowd relented. Bloodied and bruised, we slowly regained our bearings after the horror show. For the first time, I felt the vileness long harbored in our northern citizens; their animosity long cultivated in them by those at the top.

The barges were coming for us.

One by one we embarked on the freight boats. Sitting next to the boatman, an old man in a faded shirt the color of betel-juice brown, I watched him pole the barge in silence. "Where are we, sir?" I asked him.

He took a moment, then answered without looking at me. "Yên Bái province."

I tried to think of the remote northern provinces. I felt grim. I said to him, "Sir, you must've ferried so many more of us than you'd care to remember."

Again, he took a moment to answer me. "Yes. I've worked the river for twenty years. In recent years I've brought many of you across the river. I even remember some faces. None I've seen again."

The convoy of Molotova left the river and bounced on bad roads for several hours, stopping once for everyone to relieve themselves and then resuming the journey into the night. Several hours later, it was getting bone-chillingly cold when the trucks began climbing. Inside, I could feel the sharp air, and when I breathed it hurt my nose. When the convoy stopped, there were flashlights raking the dark, then shouts for us to dismount the trucks.

The moment my feet touched the ground, my knees gave. It was so cold my breaths plumed. My teeth chattered. The cold misted my eyes. Awaiting us was a large group of People's Public Security wearing Russian Ushanka hats and quilted jackets.

We were greeted by a security cadre, clad in yellow khakis, his trousers tucked into his knee-high black boots. He waved a rod in our faces, yelling out some incomprehensible order, and his underlings, two blue-uniformed inmates, ran up to herd the newcomers into line for roll call.

"On behalf of all the overseers," the security cadre addressed us through a megaphone, "I welcome you to our camp. You have now arrived at Quyết Tiến camp in Hà Giang Province. We are only ten kilometers from our brotherly neighbor China."

It did not take long for me to know that Quyết Tiến—*Forward Resolutely*—had another name much more popular among inmates: Cổng Trời camp. *Heavenly Gate*, a sinister epithet. The moniker Heavenly Gate spoke to its sky-reaching elevation; yet it meant, in fact, Heaven awaited you with no return. But if you really wanted to know its original name in the communist nomenclature, it was Hanoi Work Camp 75A. To ask of its whereabouts, you must go to the Bureau of Labor and Reform at the Ministry of Public Security in Hanoi.

In reality, no commoner knew where it was.

CHAPTER 6

Cổng Trời, Heavenly Gate

Autumn 1978

> At the going down of the sun and in the morning,
> We will remember them.
> —Lawrence Binyon

It was a harsh winter in the North that year. Our shacks' windows were never closed so the guards could check on us, and through the open windows the cold, and sometimes the rain, had us shivering like wet cats. Weak from malnutrition, many of us fell sick, and medication was rare as gold. Those who died were carried to the Farewell Hill, a moniker for Bà Then graveyard.

There was a man among us, Mr. Bìm, who had been to enough camps in the past fifteen years to earn a sobriquet, "Sir Inmate." He said it had become a routine for him to say a wordless prayer to the dead as he closed their eyes, before seeing them put in the ground. He did not remember how many inmates, many of whom were his friends, he had buried in other camps and, here, on the Farewell Hill.

Most of us fell victim to tuberculosis and pneumonia, and those who had been injured from severe beatings or deprived of the barest comfort like I had been in the dungeons, died sooner. Scores of cases of hepatitis and stomach ulcer went untreated for lack of medicine. I had been in the infirmary and had seen barely a dozen vials of Streptomycin, that dozen to be used only for those who had coughed up blood. The rest of the sick would be handed a few pills of King Bitters. The camp called its panacea *Xuyên Tâm Liên*, literally meaning radiating lotus. A pea-sized yellow pill, bitter tasting and acrid smelling. Most of the sick succumbed in the end.

At Cổng Trời, Mr. Bìm had been tasked with making coffins. He was good at it, but with the rate of accelerating deaths, he needed help. And so, I became his apprentice. However, it didn't matter how quickly we worked; soon there was no more land left to bury the dead, and the camp ordered us to move to the next hill to start a new graveyard.

One afternoon, two inmates escorted by a guard brought a corpse into our coffin-making workshop. His legs were still in shackles. One look at him and I concluded that he must have come from the dungeons. I could not help thinking of Captain Bé. A warden came in with an inmate turned blacksmith. "Take off his irons," the warden told the blacksmith, "so we can reuse them."

His words and his tone left me cold. No human feeling. The blacksmith lifted the feet of the dead onto a wooden block and turned the shackles a few times until he saw the rivet bolt. He positioned a nail on the head of the rivet nut and hammered it. The bolt did not move.

He hammered again. The metal clanged dryly. He peered up at the warden. "Sir warden," he said, "this nut is so rusted I can't . . ."

"You know what to do," the warden said. "Report back to me when done."

They both left. Moments later, only the blacksmith returned, this time with an axe. Mr. Bìm seemed to have a notion because he stepped back. The blacksmith positioned himself sideways and, with one clean blow, severed one foot at the ankle above the metal clasp. He chopped off the other foot as cleanly as hacking off a chicken's leg, then knelt and removed the irons from the lopped-off feet. He picked up his tools and the bloodstained shackles, saving the feet for us, and walked out of the shack.

Stunned, I asked Mr. Bìm, "Has this happened before?"

Mr. Bìm nodded, lit a cigarette, and drew deeply as if nothing had happened. I looked at his leathery, wrinkled face, his cloudy eyes, and wondered if there was any sensitivity still left in him. Then I knew I should not judge him. It was just one of my regrettable predispositions.

That day we received fresh planks of wood to make new coffins. Our tree-cutting team must have gone deeper into the forest to bring back additional timber for the carpentry team to make planks like these. We took the boards, already cut to the coffin dimensions, and nailed them into a rectangular box. The planks were thin because the camp wanted to conserve wood for other useful projects. Some of the boards had cracks, leaving gaps in the box. Mr. Bìm said not to worry, but I thought of coffin flies and corpse-eating beetles.

Late afternoon, when we had just finished a new coffin, the inmates carried in a fresh corpse. Shocked upon seeing it, I recognized the deceased. He was a former judge of the criminal court in Saigon. Though he used to live in another shack, I occasionally saw him with a green team, an amusing moniker for vegetable teams, whose members were the elderly. He must have been in his sixties, with a distinguished face. To see him struggle to carry a basket of fresh human waste to the vegetable plot, I thought of how we, the southerners, once had a country which we had abused and failed to save.

He once told me his wife had sold off all the window glass in their home. Then, she bought a whole live chicken and cooked for their family a hearty meal with meat for the first time since we lost our country. "Our northerners are also opportunists who're fast becoming red capitalists, Brother Khang," he had said to me after puffing on his still smoldering cigarette stub. "My wife wanted to sell our house to move to another city, but it wasn't easy. Selling or transferring your property must be reviewed and approved by the city block committee, then the district bureau. She said our city block had roughly thirty households, and ten of them were migrating northerners who came and took over those houses vacated by our people who had either left the country or were exiled to new economic zones."

"Why did your wife want to move out of Saigon?"

"She's a pretty woman." The judge took one quick puff. He looked intently at no objects through the smoke. "Many women back home had slept with those local cadres to curry favor with them. That or go hungry."

I did not know how the judge had died. It was certainly not from carrying baskets of northern waste. Later, I found out he died from hepatitis.

The warden requested our help to bury the dead, due to the lack of manpower. We carefully deposited the judge's body into the coffin and laid his belongings—a shirt without the stamped "CT" on the back, a pair of serge pants—on top of him. His serge pants were still new. Stories had circulated among us that some of those who buried the dead, unsupervised, would strip the deceased of his clothing for their good quality.

A grave had been procedurally dug by the common criminals beforehand. With the help of two other inmates, Mr. Bìm and I shouldered the coffin by a pole and carried it to the new graveyard. One man in the front had a shovel; the other carried a small basket that held a bowl of cooked rice and a boiled egg. Walking ahead of us was the warden holding a torch and behind us the two guards carrying rifles. It made me think of a funeral for a communist personage during the war, when he died deep in a southern jungle.

The new graveyard sat three kilometers from the camp. In the biting cold, we went past the old graveyard. Dusk fell and the humps of graves were nearly shapeless as we passed by. We crossed a scrubland overgrown with nut sedge and touch-me-not. There was only the sound of crickets and our heavy breathing. As we reached the new graveyard, our footsteps spooked a night bird to fly up from the grass.

As we lowered the coffin, Mr. Bìm said to the warden, "Sir warden, with your permission, can we let the deceased lie with his head pointing in the mountain's direction?"

"Why?" said the warden.

"So he could rest in peace, according to Feng Shui."

"That's superstition. Which side is the head in the coffin?"

Mr. Bìm tapped our side. We were standing with our backs toward the mountain. The warden lowered the torch, and I could see in the pit the white stubs of tree roots still unshorn.

"Drop it down where you are standing," said the warden. "It's a matter of convenience—not for his sake."

"Yes, sir warden," said Mr. Bìm.

The warden held the torch while we proceeded with the burial rite. The moment one of the two inmates put down the bowl of rice and the boiled egg on the coffin, I felt a tug in my heart. The dead could never enjoy this last meal, while the living, particularly the two haggard inmates, hungered for food. I could see a gleam of hope in their eyes as one of them looked over at the warden. Would he change his mind and let the inmates eat the rice and the egg?

When we were back in our coffin-making shack, I asked Mr. Bìm about Feng Shui. He said the direction of the coffin, considering the position of the deceased's head, favored the future of his offspring more than the deceased himself. I guessed he hid that fact to avoid the backlash from the warden. Still, I thought better of Mr. Bìm for his genuine concern for his countryman.

But it turned out that the former judge was the last deceased we would make a coffin for together.

Within a week, the camp received a live pig from the Rear Services. Everyone was happy. I had not had meat for months now and had forgotten what it would taste like.

On the way to our coffin-making shack, I visited Mr. Bìm in the infirmary to share the good news. He had been resting after he began coughing and, within a day, his lips had turned blue. He wheezed when he breathed. I thought the severe cold this winter must have gotten him. When I called in it was past noon. We could hear the chopping, *thwack-thwack-thwack*, coming from the kitchen. It brought back memories of the time I was convalescing in the sick bay, hearing those same sounds and craving the taste of fatty meat. Mr. Bìm's eyes fluttered open.

"Make sure they divide the meal portions equally," he said to me. He coughed. A bit of mucus, pink and frothy, dripped from his nose.

Late in the afternoon, done with a new coffin I had made myself, I stopped by the infirmary. I could smell the fried meat coming from the kitchen. Mr. Bìm was asleep. His lips were bluish. I looked at his fingernails. They were bluish, too. Alarmed, I called the young nurse. Casually, he walked over and said, "He coughed up blood earlier today. Probably from smoking too much."

He did nothing, even though I could hear Mr. Bìm's laborious breathing.

Shortly after our meals had arrived from the kitchen, the young nurse came into my shack and told me the old man had died on his cot.

I felt irate. I hurried to finish my precious meal of two finger-length cuts of fried pork and rare white rice and went back to the workshop.

The four men in the burial team and I managed to drop Mr. Bìm's skeletal body into the tight-fitting coffin I had made earlier. It was put together from thin planks because of the camp's low stock of natural wood.

One man carefully placed the deceased's last meal, still intact, next to his corpse. It was a blue-enameled tin bowl, filled with white cooked rice and two slices of fresh meat, fried and browned with crisp skin and fat. On this night, there was no warden and guards to supervise the burial; they were still feasting on the fried pork. The undertakers were inmates picked by the camp's overseers. They were trusted not to try to escape on those unsupervised trips.

With two ropes, the men hoisted the coffin and, walking in pair with two in front and two in back, made their way to the cemetery. I followed them to pay my last respects to the deceased. It was fortunate that no one in the sick bay had dared take the dead's last meal. The chief nurse said that if you die on the rooster hour you will keep looking for food like a chicken, so nobody wanted the dead to haunt them for stealing his last meal.

It was beginning to mist and a chill set in. During the day it was sultry, but the dampness in the valley turned cold quickly in the night.

Before lowering the coffin, with its lid still unfastened, one man bent and felt the corpse's quilted jacket. Irritated, he straightened his back. "Nothing. He travels light." They lowered the coffin into the pit and, just as it almost hit the bottom, dropped it with a thud. The same man said, "Hold it." He knelt and reached down to pick up the tin cup of rice. It had tipped over, spilling some rice and cuts of meat. The man gathered them back into the cup and rose to his knees, still holding the cup. "Good cup," he said. Another fellow grinned. "Don't waste the rice. And the meat."

They didn't bother to nail shut the lid and started shoveling dirt into the grave.

Rest, old man, I said under my breath. *You're now free.* I did not know if the dead could hear the living. I hoped he slept well. At least the undertakers had placed the coffin with the deceased's head toward the mountain. *No more coffins to be made, Mr. Bìm.* I headed back.

During the weeks of writing confessions, the supervising cadre had paid special attention to one particular man because of his name: Hồ Chí Mân. We had known each other since that first camp in the South, and he had been normal at that time, quiet and well behaved.

All that suddenly changed after we were moved to Cổng Trời. The first time all of us were put through another self-confession writing session, he claimed he had falsified his military record. He was, in fact, a warrant officer, not a political officer as major of his battalion. Therefore, he should not have been sent to the North like the rest of us.

"Speak no false words!" the cadre said with a hint of irritation. "It matters none where you're being reformed—in the South or in the North, you must be truthful. That's the objective of labor: Glorified labor corrects false thinking. What are the three most important lessons you've learned from the Revolution?"

"I don't remember, sir cadre," Hồ Chí Mân replied.

"The crimes of the American imperialists; the doctrine of the socialism; the clemency policy of the Party."

"I swear on my ancestors' graves," Hồ Chí Mân said to the supervising cadre, "I've falsified my declaration. If I am lying now then lightning will strike my wife, my sons, my parents."

"What solemn affirmation of truth!" said the cadre, raising his eyebrows. "Everyone else dies, except you. Write another confession. This time speak the truth."

"That's the truth, sir cadre. I can't die, because I'm a bastard child."

"What does it have to do with you speaking the truth?"

"My mother was killed by the order of Hồ Chí Minh. The one who should write his confession is Hồ Chí Minh. You talk about blood debt? That's the blood debt he owes to me and my mother. Where's that lecher Hồ Chí Minh? I have to find him. That louse forced himself upon my mother."

Mân spent three days in a penal cell after that incident. On the day he was let out, I saw him staggering in the bright sun. His eyes were sunken, his lips cracked, his shirt smeared with blotchy stains. He was muttering, "Fuck the commies . . . depraved motherfuckers . . ."

The guard quickly looked at the warden then back at Mân. "What did you just say?"

Mân nodded to himself. "Just cursing those who lied in their confessions . . ."

The warden, too, nodded. "Ah, so now you have seen to it that you lied to us, didn't you?"

"Lie? How? Where? Point it out for me, sir cadre."

"We have gone to your home district, and we had your statements in your confession verified."

Hồ Chí Mân laughed. "Viva the Communist Party!"

"Don't pretend you're not sound in the head. I can read you."

"Don't listen to what the communists said. Just watch what they do. Who said that?"

"You!"

Within earshot I heard the guard ask the warden. "Do you want to put him back in the penal cell, comrade warden?"

The warden calmly shook his head. He made a soft hand gesture as if to pacify the troubled man. "Come to your senses, Brother Mân."

"I'm not talking to you. All of you! Murderers!"

The warden raised his voice. "I'm your warden. Come to your senses now."

"You're a murderer!"

The warden snapped. "Shut your mouth! That's an order. You can't speak with malicious intent whether you're sick or not. Or you will go back to the penal cell."

Mân cut in. "Everywhere is home. For all the time I had last week I came up with a plan. Once I've got my airplane built, I'll fly to Hanoi to see what his mausoleum looks like. That old goat! Can you imagine if his goatee is a clump of pubic hair?"

"You asked for it," said the guard as he unslung his rifle.

The warden motioned for him to stop. He studied Mân. *A mad man*? From where I stood, I was sure we shared the same thought. Then Mân went into a rant.

"I've heard that they had a hard time before cutting him open to remove his guts for embalmment. The doctor who was supposed to slit him open cried so much they replaced him with another one, who too cried like a mourner, and comrade Lê Duẩn had to urge everybody present that it was a solemn task entrusted them by the Party and the People, but all the doctors couldn't stop crying and all said that they'd rather write self-critique than cut open the most revered figure of the world. I've heard that none of the one hundred doctors had the heart to disembowel him until the last doctor, the hundredth and first, finally willed his knife into the old goat's gut. Then our doctor fainted."

At the warden's order, the guard took Mân to the infirmary. They kept him there with his legs chained to his cot. One afternoon, Dr. Đàm was called in to treat Mân. As a bona fide medical doctor in the Republic of Vietnam army, Dr. Đàm now served these northern nurses, appointed as medical doctors by the Party, and watched them treat the sick, the near-death patients. He must have felt as if he was living in the nineteenth century. When Dr. Đàm returned to our shack, he told me and Bee that Mân had dreaded loud noises so much that, in the morning, he plugged his ears with chewing gums to block the noise from the blaring loudspeakers. Dr. Đàm had to dislodge the gum pieces that were pushed too far into his ear canals.

"Just the sight of a pith helmet," Dr. Đàm added, "also set something off in him."

After discharge he was by himself most of the time. He was relegated to tending a garden patch outside the gate. Edging one side of the plot was a row of kapok, which flowered white in summer, and you could spot him walking absent-mindedly up and down between the beds of bok choy. On all fours, he started pulling up a handful of cabbage, leaves and stalks, and stuffed them into his mouth. Some inmates rushed toward him. "Take it out of his mouth," one shouted. "He's eating cabbage and muck!"

It was the Sunday following Mr. Bìm's burial, and I wanted to rest but woke to some rustling noises. Someone was folding up his blanket and rush mat next to me. That used to be Bee's cot before the shack leader, under the warden's influence, moved him to another cot to separate us. I closed my eyes. Soon a wild tobacco odor stung my nose. I turned onto my side and raised myself up on my elbow. A white-haired old man was sitting cross-legged on his cot, drawing on a water pipe. Through the open window, the cold air felt sharp when I sat up. The old man turned his face to me.

"Are you up now, young man?" he said. He had a broad forehead. The eyebrows, though gray, curved gracefully. I considered he must have been handsome in his prime.

"Yes, sir. I gather that you're my new cot neighbor."

"I am an intruder. Look at what I have done to you. Young people need sleep as much as old people need wild tobacco." He offered me his water pipe. "This shall bond us."

I politely shook my head.

"Someday you will need its companionship," he said, then turned to fetch a *goz* can padded with rags. Smoke rose as he lifted the lid. Gently, lovingly, he poured the contents into an inox mug. The tea was amber-colored. The air smelled of its fragrance. I thought he must have done his morning ritual while everyone else was still deep in sleep. He handed me the mug. "Please have a sip of tribute tea. Are you a tea lover?"

Again, I shook my head. Then, afraid I had appeared unfriendly, I took hold of the mug with both hands and raised it to my lips. "You're very kind, sir." I sipped. My whole being woke with an alacrity. The tea's bitterness spread quickly on my tongue, its scent blossoming up through my nose. I handed the mug back to him. "You've just made a convert out of me. Where did you get such a good tea, sir?"

"It's a gift from home. On a cold morning like this, it's your best friend."

I could not agree more. Among the living, I thought, sometimes it was easier to lose friends than to find the true ones. I wondered if he had any best friends. He was a medium height, with a head of tousled white hair, much like Mr. Liên's. They must be of the same age. I noticed that he was sitting on a wooden plank veined with smoke stains. Something eccentric about him intrigued me.

"Where did you get that piece of wood, sir?" I asked.

"From the kitchen." He tapped the plank. "To help my back and to ward off bed bugs."

We passed back and forth the mug of tea. We spoke in low voices in the morning quiet. He came from the last shack on the housing row. Mr. Thạch had been to various prisons; on such a list was the notorious Hỏa Lò prison in Hanoi, and Cổng Trời. I told him about myself—just facts—not elaborating too much.

Mr. Thạch took interest in my new trade: making coffins. He knew about Mr. Bìm. I assumed that Mr. Thạch, for all his years spent in prisons, was something like a walking encyclopedia.

"From what you described," he said to me, "pulmonary edema was what ailed him and claimed his life." Then with a gleam in his eyes, he said, "From your accent, I presume that you were born in the North. I'd beg for your forgiveness if I am wrong."

I told him my name, my upbringing. I was born a northerner, but I considered myself a southerner for all the years I had spent in the South. The only thing tying me to the North was my father's past, his wrongful imprisonment that led to his death in prison.

"I knew your father," Mr. Thạch deadpanned. "We met once. Then I went to prison."

I asked him why he was moved into my shack.

"This cot was empty, was it not?" He pointed to his own cot, "They moved me by the same principle they moved your shack mate to another spot. They want no one to take roots in one place, even one spot. They want you to be in a state of anxiety, like a ship that cannot anchor itself on the high sea."

I took note of his remark. I thought of my transfer from that camp in the South to Cổng Trời, of my friends who were now in various camps in both the North and the South. I could see the fear factor the communists thrived on. At my nod, Mr. Thạch went on.

"The Party plays on people's fear," he said. "In fact, they parasitize it. Mutual fear. Collective fear. Here's a story: They were about to execute a female landlord, something so extraordinarily against our morality that the presiding committee had to ask the Party if it could find a guilty male landlord in the woman's place. The answer came back from the Party: 'Male or female tigers have no dithering about eating humans. Request denied.'"

I pulled the blanket tighter around me. After sipping his tea a few times, I felt wide awake.

Mr. Thạch stroked his chin. "I was, at that time, a commissar of the Land Reform Delegation. I saw the error of the campaign. Its focus was a result of our blind acceptance of China's Great Leap Forward—no private farming, and landowners deemed as counter-revolutionary. But in reality, my dear friend, those landowners, little or big, should have been complimented for their ability to rise above poverty and slavery. They should have been used as the prototype to reform our shabby economy. Would you, Brother Khang, build a nation by counting on those illiterates to grasp the meaning of Revolution? Who financed the Viet Minh before and after the August Revolution? But they counted on the uneducated, citing that only the proletarian can awake to the call of Revolution." He held me in his gaze and patted my hand. "Your father was a victim of the *Nhân Văn-Giai Phẩm* purge. They humiliated him and his colleagues and put them away. I used to hope for the day the Party would denounce me, then I would be free. You see, to live in the North you must always remember to say 'Yes' even though, deep down, you were ready to blurt out a 'No.' The 'Yes' will afford you a low-profile life. I had more than twenty years as a Party member, and it was all attributed to that magical word 'Yes.'"

I watched him slowly refilling the inox mug. The air was moist with the scent of tea. The tea, as he had said, came from his family.

"Are you still in touch with your wife?" I asked.

"The last time I heard from her, thirty-two years ago, was after she came to see Tố Hữu, our Party's celebrated poet and a good friend of mine. She pled with him that my arrest was made under a false pretext. He said to her, 'Let him have a taste of Hỏa Lò, then he'll be enlightened.'" Mr. Thạch smiled a crooked smile. The gentleness on his face was gone. "How unfathomable is a human heart. Once you begin to receive kingly treatment, you lose all your human virtue."

"What's the false pretext about?" I asked.

"Are you familiar with the Franco-Vietnamese Agreement that Hồ Chí Minh signed with the French on March 6th, 1946?"

I nodded. "The Hồ–Sainteny Agreement?"

"Yes, when Jean Sainteny came as a delegate from the High Commissioner of France and arrived in Vietnam to accept the surrender of the Imperial Japanese Army."

"Mr. Thạch, if I understand the agreement correctly, it recognizes the Republic of Vietnam as a free state. Yet it still belongs to the French Union."

"Correct. There's another clause in it that Hồ Chí Minh used as pretext for welcoming the French back into Indochina. That the government of Vietnam declares itself ready to accept the French army when it relieves the Chinese forces in Northern Vietnam. In other words, to use the French to drive out the Chinese."

"What does that pretext have to do with your arrest?"

"It's a pretext to fool the opposition, the public. It's a complex matter, but let me explain step by step." Mr. Thạch's eyes seemed like marbles as he stared blankly into the space between us. Slowly he exhaled. "We had been independent since August 1945, but no world powers had recognized our independence. The agreement with France opened the way to international recognition. Hồ Chí Minh made it public that French troops would only stay for five years. It was a show of political intelligence to negotiate rather than fight. Why should we sacrifice fifty or one hundred thousand men, when we can attain independence through negotiation? That was his reasoning."

"And you disagreed with that?"

"I will get to that. Here are the real reasons behind the Hồ-Sainteny Agreement. At that time the Kuomintang, or Chinese Nationalist Party, wanted to oust Hồ Chí Minh. Who would then benefit from the Kuomintang? The Vietnamese Nationalist Party. It was modeled after the Kuomintang, who assisted it with funds and military training to fight the French colonists and the Vietnamese Communist Party. Therefore, to welcome the French Union back into Vietnam, Hồ Chí Minh would have an ally to crush his major opposition: the Vietnamese Nationalist Party. However, he also wanted international recognition for his Viet Minh as a major political entity. At the same time, the French desired nothing more than to re-acquire Indochina." Mr. Thạch coughed and then continued. "I opposed his move to let the French back into Vietnam. That was treacherous. For that, I was arrested under the pretext of being an aider and abettor of the Viet Minh's opposition—the Vietnamese Nationalist Party." A long cough shook his body. He composed himself, eyes watery. "I was charged with anti-Revolution, opposition, nation betrayal, People betrayal, Party betrayal. The Five Betrayals."

When he stopped, I leaned back as if a blast of hot air just hit me. He had been detained as an ex-communist since 1946. If I had lived his life, I would have donned a mask, changed my identity and, as an impostor, lived the life of a persona non grata. Had a majority of our southerners lived one measly year under the communist regime, they would have woken from their naiveté about communism. How could I reconcile this mild-mannered man with his alter ego whose crimes—though they never existed, they were crimes nevertheless—had kept him detained for thirty-two years to date. Thirty-two years without a trial.

"But, Mr. Thạch, what sort of danger have you posed to them? Thirty-two years for opposing Hồ Chí Minh's collaboration with the French?"

"If truth be spoken," said Mr. Thạch, flicking the corner of his mouth, "I was an insider. An inner-circle man is the most potent threat if he turns against you. In fact, they imprison anyone who they believe could do them harm, even based on a conjectural notion. A friend of mine, also a Party member, had flyers printed and distributed to voice his remonstration of Hồ-Sainteny Agreement. They arrested him on the same pretext: sympathizer of the Vietnamese Nationalist Party. He committed suicide and left a note behind: 'I am innocent.'"

I let his words sink into my head. I knew everything he had just verbalized.

"Did you know those men well, Mr. Thạch? The Hồ Chí Minh, the Lê Duẩn, the Trường Chinh?"

"Yes, until they had gained enough power to become inaccessible. They embody the proletarian unintelligence. They are the most unforgiving. Their Party's persona isn't Marxism and Leninism. Far from it. What they personify is an ideal that had existed in the Viet Minh even in its nascent state: a philosophical vision of social equality, a haven free of class exploitation and blessed with sovereignty. They never reached that ideal."

I placed my hand over my heart. "That was the communism I used to believe in when I grew up in the North. I know many people were proud of being called a Viet Minh. Frankly, that's also the communism that many of us, young and old, have confused with nationalism."

"Honestly," said Mr. Thạch, "none of those Party members understand Marxism and Leninism."

Every morning we would repeat this cyclic dread, rising from sleep as the door of our shack was unbolted and the camp trusty barked out the order: "Shack number four, gather outside quickly for roll call!" We rushed out, many of us standing in the early morning chill twisting our bodies, flinging our arms to get warm from the all-night cramps caused by the fetal position we slept in.

The whistles blew three times, and, like robots, the inmates squatted on their haunches, every group of twelve in a line, answering to the team leader's call of his number. Confirmed, checked off. Then, dispersed, we rushed headlong to the kitchen to receive our meal portions for the day's labor trip. I put my meal in my sack, made from a sandbag with a shoulder strap. I checked my canteen to make sure it was full of water, enough for a day's labor, and inspected my nylon pouch for its condition. Sometimes after many uses from storing frogs, rats, or herbs, it could tear.

Many of us hurried into the latrines to relieve ourselves. Yet, in there, one could spot people exchanging personal items with inmates from another shack, or with the common criminals who shared the public latrines. Surreptitious, they were wary of the snitches, those who had slithered their way to curry favor from the camp higher-ups. One slip of the tongue and they would find themselves in a penal cell.

The gong sounded again, three times, and everyone ran back out onto the dirt courtyard, and squatted on their haunches. The camp watchdog called their team's numbers. Again, confirmed, checked off. Then the on-duty security, sitting in the shack by the entrance, looked up from his register and called out,

"Shack Number Four!" We rose and, in single file, passed our team leader, who counted our heads as we went through the gate. The on-duty gear guards brought up the rear, each with an armful of tools for the field job—machetes, axes, and shovels. All the axes and machetes were tied together and not given to us until we reached the labor site. The fatal mistake the camp had made in the early days was that they gave inmates these "weapons" while still inside the camp. That day, a riot resulted in the death of a camp security guard. But it was subdued, and the inmates' leader was court-martialed and sentenced to death. The rest of that group received fifteen years to life in prison.

Our team leader, once outside the camp, told us that we were to cut bamboo as our assignment. Each team was to meet the day's quota: twenty bamboo trunks, seven meters long for each trunk. It was a stiff quota but not impossible. Yet to find a bamboo grove still healthy, still abundant, in the nearby site posed a challenge. Most of the groves were already gone, having been repeatedly visited by inmates like us.

We walked ten kilometers and found a bamboo grove, dense and verdant. Our machetes were blunt, tearing the outer walls to mush. We had to bring our tools to a nearby creek and whet them. We lost considerable time before we could resume our work.

The grove was full of clumping bamboo, each clump bunching so tight that the inner columns had withered. We concentrated on hacking down the outer culms, working our way around the clumps to get the healthiest part of the plant.

Past noon, having cut down a culm that met the required specifications, I took a break. I went to the creek to wash, then sat down on the bank and ate my lunch. Our meals were cakes made from manioc paste, hard baked into squares. I ate the one cake, my share for the day. Some other men took time to build a fire by spreading a thin layer of twigs on the ground to keep the fire low and, with a flat stick cut from a lady palm to skewer the cake, toasted their cakes until brown. I could smell their warm, toasty scent, like when you broke open a freshly baked biscuit. I watched them savor each bite and understood the small pleasures they had waited for all morning long. It was a moment to live for.

Some other men went scavenging edibles to bring back to camp—the river-leaf creeper, the false oxtongue, the Chinese knotweed. They could enjoy their forage if they got past the guards. In time, it enriched my knowledge of herbs and plants, especially the edible varieties. They ate spiny amaranth which they picked along the road, sometimes blue-eyed grass or dwarf copperleaf or monkey grass or purslane. One man ate wild yam that looked like a potato and got sick. One of our former medical doctors in the shack inspected the yam and concluded that, like manioc tuber, it must be soaked in water for a few days to rid it of toxins.

I felt blessed for having a companion like Mr. Thạch. He worked in a vegetable team and knew much about the greens. Occasionally he brought back spinach or ragleaf, at times a bundle of sour-soup creeper. He would take pleasure in splitting the twigs that I fetched for him to build a fire between our cots, and he would drop the greens into his *goz* can and boil them. Our meals would taste more tolerable with vegetables. Once we had water spinach from the kitchen with our evening meal. I was about to shove a clump of spinach into my mouth when he grabbed my hand and said, "Pay attention, Brother Khang, when you eat this kind of vegetable cooked by the kitchen. Do you know how they went about cooking them? They never bother to pluck the dead leaves, never wash them, not even cutting off the strings that tie them into bundles. They simply dump them into the pot and boil them, then take them out and lay them on the floor and place another heap of greens on top of the one still smoking. One heap already boiled; one heap still uncooked. Just like that, Brother Khang, until they are through with all the greens for that evening. The uncooked greens will cook by the heat of the boiled ones. Save them time."

I went back to cut one more culm. By mid-afternoon, our twelve-member team had met the required daily quota of twenty bamboo trunks. We began hauling them to a staging area two kilometers away where a transportation team awaited. By then I felt the gnawing in my stomach again. I could hear my stomach growl, and the perpetual moaning from the men because of the pangs of hunger. We stood, hunched, shivering in the wind. Our monthly food ration had dropped to nine kilos, equal to the allowed ration of an inmate locked up in solitary confinement. I had seen a man eat paper. The wrapping paper that came from visitation gifts. I saw him ask each person who had received family gifts to spare the wrapping paper for him. Then, back in our shack, I came upon him sniffing at each piece of food wrapper before he started feeding.

If hunger could drive a wolf out of the wood, I believed a hunger-ravaged man could turn into an omnivore. Our daily meals were moldy rice with saltwater and some herbs floating in there. One day, a guard asked me what our meal standard in the South was like.

"What standard?" I asked him back. "We ate what we wanted. It was a free society."

His face turned red from anger, and he yelled at me. "Liar! How could you eat what you wanted? What were the food norms in your southern enslaved state?"

I was mad as well and said, "I could eat meat or seafood or even shit if I chose. Our food norms? Eat what you want, all you can."

Two days before, we had lost a man from our team and received no replacement. The fellow we lost, a former quartermaster captain, had been transferred somewhere else. Three days earlier, on a work site in the forest, I saw him carrying back a huge turtle the size of a watermelon. I was certain he would eat it—all of us inmates were predators. Our team leader said to him, "Be smart now. Don't eat it."

The fellow looked quizzical, said, "Why?"

"Just don't eat it," said our team leader, "bad luck will befall you."

The man walked on, grinning, the turtle cradled in his arms. He killed the turtle behind our shack and made a stew but kept the mottled black-and-brown shell. On its carapace he etched his name, the camp's name, the current year. He drilled a hole through the shell and, the next day, hung it on a tree in the forest where he had caught the turtle. It did not last long. A guard, with the warden, escorted him to the security committee's house just as we were lining up for morning roll call. That evening, after meal, I asked our team leader about that fellow.

"He's gone," said our team leader. "They suspected him of communicating with someone outside."

"So, it's bad luck after all to eat turtle meat."

"According to Chinese Feng Shui, the turtle is one of the four sacred animals. Black turtle, white tiger, red phoenix, azure dragon. Four celestial animals, each guarding a quadrant of Heaven."

Enlightened by our team leader's insight, I said, chuckling, "If you eat the slow turtle, it will slow your release."

He did not laugh.

It reminded me of the death of a man whose cot was next to Bee's. The fellow had stomach ulcers. He ate with a discriminating taste, though not by choice. He ate slowly, always the last one left with a *goz* can in his hands. He would take his time, eating long into the evening hours if the meal was corn or bo bo. He even took time to peel each bo bo kernel before putting them, one at a time, into his mouth. His leisurely chewing made an unnerving sound that kept Bee awake. Then, an illness struck him. He looked emaciated and said he was so sick he did not want to live any longer. He sold his personal pipe, intricately carved, to Bee, and with the money bought three cooked eggs—a luxury—some cured meat, a bowl of cooked white rice, and two *bánh gai*, a northern pastry with glossy otter-black skin. He ate most of his feast and fell asleep. When Bee got up in the early morning, he saw the fellow sitting, crouched, on his own cot. When Bee shook him, his body fell back. He had died.

Left on his cot was a lonely ball of *bánh gai* which he had not had time to finish. I did not know who got that last pastry, but I had thought about it afterward. I had always loved this kind of pastry when I was growing up in the North as a young child. Our *u già*—the old maid—would fill the center of a thick-layer of a dough made from glutinous rice with mung bean, split peanuts, mixed with heated molasses, and pack it into a ball of glossy black skin. The black skin came from finely ground ramie leaves, moss green when fresh, then ground to a shiny black hue.

I had heard Father Ninh furtively preach to a small group of his Catholic followers. He said, "When we are forsaken, forgotten, unloved, and uncared for, it is the greatest hunger of mankind, greater than poverty which robs a person of everything, food included." He said the words came from Mother Teresa. I hadn't given it much thought when I first listened in on his sermon until I had time to weigh his words again during the bleakest moments of our stark winter. I then construed that a man, any man, could turn into a thief when hunger possessed him. He could no longer tell right or wrong.

Gradually, I understood what it meant to be dehumanized. It meant you forfeited your human pride to satisfy your primitive urges. Take this man from our shack. Every morning, before roll call, we would stand outside our shack and go through a brief exercise. But this man, a former Bureau Chief of the Army Motion Picture Department, never put himself through that exercise. "Why?" I had asked him.

"Why waste your calories? Must preserve them for labor. If I was well fed, I wouldn't mind wriggling my ass like the rest of you."

One Sunday morning, I woke to hear a squeaking noise from the rafters. I saw him getting up to the sloped members by standing on somebody's shoulders. He dug his hand into the roof thatch and came out with three tiny pinkies. I rolled onto my other side to fall back asleep when I heard expletives from some men in the shack. I turned and, revulsed, saw him tearing one pinkie with his teeth. The blood dripped from his lips to his fingers.

Watching him, it dawned on me that dehumanization did not merely mean losing one's individuality. This man had descended into the realm of sub-human; from there he would not hesitate to do worse. In that moment I grasped the notion of how a human would behave while having a half-empty stomach every day. He would not die from starvation; but the gnawing hunger would drive him to thinking of food—not freedom, not democracy, not independence. His thoughts, when well fed, would copulate with the tantalizing challenge of fighting for liberty and self-government. Now, like me, he walked like a somnambulist, a cartoon character whose thought bubble read: God is dead.

I realized, the commies had us where they wanted. Cold and hungry. That harshest winter, to keep us alive from the cold that sometimes dropped to minus zero Celsius, the camp dished out quilted vests, blankets, and mosquito nets. Many of us received vests that were frayed or torn, some too tight, some too loose for the recipients. I took possession of a second-hand vest and, to my revulsion, found unwashable bloodstains on its collar. The vest must have come from a dead bộ đội. Bee, however, whispered into my ear when no one was within earshot, "Say a prayer to the dead before you wear it. Some spirits can be malevolent, and you don't want them to hang around you." I wore it, nevertheless.

Even with the aid of hand-me-down vests, many of us had scavenged rice bags discarded from the kitchen and sewed them to make burlap shirts to wear underneath our vests. It repulsed me one day to see these men giving up their crude clothing because some snitches had ratted on them, and the camp had been declared a disgrace to the Party and the State to see camp attendees in shabby clothing.

It was so cold that winter that most of us would keep our clothes on after work and sleep in them. Still, the bone-chilling nights were insufferable when the shacks' windows were open by regulations. The sleepers' breaths were wisps in the murky light. In the valley, I knew of the local people who would build a fire to keep their cattle warm all night long. We discussed our fate out loud. The camp, in the end, conceded and allowed each shack to build a hearth in the center of it. Each shack was responsible for fetching firewood to keep the hearth going throughout the night. Though my sleep was fitful, I had been conditioned to the cold after spending a month in the dungeon and another month in a penal cell. Those in our shack who bedded down around the hearth would sleep sitting up, forfeiting the comfort of their rickety cots. They were wrapped in blankets from head down, peering out from that hooded cavity that lit up occasionally with a drag on their cigarettes. The scene was picturesque, like a surreal painting.

One cold morning when the fog began to lift, we gathered in the courtyard for roll call. We heard a rumble and, through the fog, came two trucks. Word spread quickly. The food trucks had arrived.

Most men were excited, though we had to go out to our day labor jobs. We watched the kitchen detail take delivery of foods, and we told one another it was a good day after all.

Upon returning in the afternoon, I got hold of a fellow who worked in the kitchen that day and asked about the food relief. "What have you got from those trucks?"

"Fish," he said curtly.

"Any meat?" I asked.

"Just stinking fish. They smelled all the way from the trucks to the kitchen."

"Fish smell, don't they?"

"Not this kind of smell, brother. We've got spoiled fish." He quickly looked around and softened his voice. "They must have paid a hell of a cheap price for those two truckloads. The fish had rotted so bad even the cooks had to cover their noses with hankies when they prepared them for tonight's meals."

I had the first taste of it when our meal allocations arrived in our shack. The whole shack smelled of fish stink. I told myself, *Eat, don't think*, and held my breath, looking at the dark hue of chunks of fish in my bowl. The kitchen must have tried to mask the stench with black pepper, but a bad odor wafted up when I broke open a hunk of fish.

Noticing my hesitancy, another fellow said to me, "Don't throw it away. It's full of protein." I glared at him and recognized the man as a former army doctor, ranked colonel, of the Saigon General Hospital. I conceded that he might be right and held on to my meal. I drank a whole *goz* can of water after the meal, not because it was salty, but to deceive myself into thinking I was full. Most of us had done that so we could fall asleep not on an empty stomach. All had lost between twenty to thirty kilograms in weight. Even our pants would have dropped had we not drilled extra holes in our belts to cinch them tight.

I had watched myself and the rest of the men degenerate into skeletons, moving listlessly about in their somnambulism. Damn a morsel of food. But our curses did not reach Heaven.

Instead, what came back to us was a further cut in our daily ration. That year, the communist regime had emptied out all their granaries and shipped the threshed grain to China and Russia as a form of war payment. In October we had had three bowls of rice a day; then it became two bowls by the end of the month; then into November, one of two bowls of rice was replaced with bo bo, at times with manioc paste that had been cooked from long dried manioc tubers, diced up into slices still carrying in them grain weevils which would float up in the boiling pots.

However, lack of food came with lack of hygiene. The frigid cold had discouraged everyone from washing themselves, and worse, to refuse to shed their clothes to wash. Some of us had not bathed for six months. "You don't die from that," one of them declared. "Those opium addicts never bathe themselves."

The lack of hygiene, like an epidemic among us, was compounded by thriving head lice and bed bugs. You heated up your bamboo cot with a red glowing log, still smoking, and the lice started coming out like an army in disarray.

One morning the camp ordered us to sit naked to the waist in the courtyard under the mild sun, our shirts spread out in front of us, then, at the barking order, we picked up our shirts and shook them until the order to stop. On the dirt, to our horror, were crawling tiny brown specks of bed bugs, like a sieve just burst. Some shook their clothes over a puddle of stagnant water and the calm surface became alive with lice floating and moving.

The warden in charge looked at the scene in disgust. "Boil a couple of pots and soak your clothes."

One fellow, shivering in the cold in his bare torso, peered up at him. "Sir warden, we can roll a bottle over our clothes. That'll crush them blood suckers."

"You might," the warden said, "but again you might not. These crab lice can hide in the seams of your clothes and survive."

Then scabies broke out. Though spared from it, I felt assaulted by the reek of scabies and the constant scratching of the victims. At night, bed bugs the size of tangerine seeds and brown cockroaches came out of hiding and feasted on the pus-filled bodies.

Something had to give in the end. One morning a camp security guard came upon a poem someone had scrawled with black coal on the meeting hall's wooden platform:

You Revolution monkeys belong to the jungle
One day you catch smells of the cities beyond
One by one you come down the plains
You try to walk on hind legs but you can't hide your tails.

A week later it came time to harvest the manioc. The field used to be a vast bamboo grove, but that was slashed and burned, and the ashes became fertilizer for growing manioc. The camp erected watchtowers on the perimeters of the field to guard the crop from thieves—us. The camp would condemn such thievery as sabotage of the State's properties. I had sewn a pouch into the inside of my shirt beneath the armpit. In the hem of my pants, I hid a piece of metal that had been sharpened. We labored near the manioc field, lush with two-meter-tall plants. During noon break, I slunk into the field and began my work. I picked one plant in the middle of the field and, crouched under the dense foliage, dug. The manioc roots branched near the surface, and soon I hit the firmness of tubers. I brushed the dirt away and looked at the roots, bulging and long. Without a knife, I chose a slender tuber. I sawed it with the piece of metal. I could smell the acrid earth; the dry good smell of the tuber being severed. I could hear the wind in the field, and I was happy. I pushed dirt back into the hole I had dug and hid the tuber under my shirt as I came out of the field. At the creek, I washed the dirt off the tuber and began slicing it. I filled my *goz* with slices of manioc and put it back into my sack. On a good day, the guards at the gate would not check our *goz* cans, or else an unpleasant confrontation would ensue. That afternoon, I got back into my shack and found Mr. Thạch, my cot neighbor, preparing a water pipe on his cot.

"You look so perked up, Brother Khang," he said. "What's new?"

I told him. "I'll make *chè*, but I have no sugar."

"Worry no more," he said and reached down under his cot and brought up a wicker bin. He took a few things out and lay on his cot. One of them was a wooden tablet with words carved into it. Then he handed me a brown packet. Inside was a slab of dark molasses sugar the size of three fingers. "I'll make the fire. I still have some firewood I used for making tea this morning."

When I came back from the kitchen with water the fire was going, warming the space between our cots. I poured water into the *goz* can, dropped the slab of sugar into it, and began cooking the manioc. The last time we had a good smell of tuber was when we cooked the arrowroot with sugar, courtesy of Mr. Thạch lifting a root from the garden under his team's care.

Mr. Thạch leaned down from his cot and continued fanning the fire until a warm, rich smell began seeping through the air. I was lying on my cot with my eyes closed and my thoughts hovered over the *goz* can, bubbling with tiny sounds. A voice had me open my eyes with a start.

"What are you cooking in that can?"

Our warden was standing between our cots. Mr. Thạch looked up at the warden and said calmly, "We are cooking manioc, sir warden."

"That is not on our meal plan today, nor yesterday, nor tomorrow. Where did you get it?"

I sat up on my cot. I did not want to implicate Mr. Thạch in my stealing the

State's properties. "Please forgive me, sir warden. I got it from the field. And I'm not going to justify my act. Mr. Thạch has nothing to do with it."

"We are hungry, sir warden," said Mr. Thạch as he continued fanning the fire unhurriedly. "I gave Brother Khang my share of sugar."

"You must have done this repeatedly," the warden said. "This is not a first-time violation, I am sure." He looked around as if prying with his eyes into what we hid out of sight. Then he rested his eyes on the wooden tablet lying face up on Mr. Thạch's cot. It read, "Hoàng Thạch, born 1911, passed away xxxx, at the age of xx." He frowned with a puzzled look, then fixed the white-haired old man with a stare. "Is this to be your grave marker?"

"Yes, sir cadre," Mr. Thạch said, then added, "I'm not certain of my death date yet. I did ask my friend"—he nodded toward me—"to fill that in when the date is here."

Without saying a word, the warden turned and walked out of the shack. At the door he half-turned his head and said to us, "Just don't repeat this violation."

It was a very cold morning in early November when I woke with a fever. My body simmered, and my breath was hot. At the first gong, the door flung open and the trusty shouted at everyone to go outside. The brittle air pervaded the shack, yet I did not feel cold. I was sweating and wondered why my shrinking body still had fluid in it. Unable to shake me out of my torpor, Mr. Thạch came back with Bee. They lifted me up. I felt like a strand of noodle as my legs gave.

"He's burning up," Bee said to Mr. Thạch.

"Let me talk to them to have him stay home today," Mr. Thạch said. "Time for roll call now."

"Tell them, sir. Better yet, get him to the sick bay."

Alone with me, Bee said, "Did you have a fever in the night?"

I shook my head. In fact, I woke a few times shivering from a chill that came from inside me. I told him so.

"Sounds like you have malaria. You're a sick dog. Damnation!"

The shack leader and the trusty came in. They debated whether to give me a sick day or, if I was still able-bodied enough to work, send me out to the field. Mr. Thạch chimed in, "If you insist on having him work like a healthy man, then prepare a coffin today for him."

I believe Mr. Thạch's words carried weight. They all knew where he came from.

"Sir Thirty" was the sobriquet they gave him. When asked why he had such a nickname, he smiled charmingly as he explained to me that it implied his tenure as a prisoner. Then, good-humoredly he said, "They compare me to a tiger, Brother Khang. In medieval times, we, the Annamese, worshipped Lord Tiger. To be able to enjoy the New Year, on the New Year's Eve, the thirtieth each year, the villagers would sacrifice a living human to Lord Tiger. Hence, Lord Tiger is Sir Thirty." He smiled. "I am a tiger without teeth."

I was granted a cot in the sick bay. My temperature was forty degrees Celsius. The young nurse made me take Nivaquine. There were only a few vials of that antimalarial medication in the sick bay's cabinet. I knew that most of the sick whose fever hit just under thirty-nine degrees Celsius would receive a concoction made of Malaysian ginseng so bitter the patients would vomit.

My afternoon did not go by undisturbed. One of the three sick mates kept haranguing from his cot. "Have mercy, sir cadre . . ." His phlegmy voice drawled. "Give me my bowl of rice and the egg now . . . They'll be wasted when you put them on my coffin . . ." He became quiet, then his voice purred, "What kind of mercy is that?" I was relieved when the doctor finally ordered him to be removed from the infirmary and taken back to his shack. The doctor used to be a public health assistant from one of the North's hospitals. Here the camp appointed him medical doctor.

On the cot next to mine was a man they brought in the night before. Kidney stone. A curse to have in a camp like this. The night after the other sick mate was gone, the man suddenly screamed. The nurse-turned doctor held him down. The victim tore through the nurse's arm locks. Then the young nurse rushed in to help. He forced open the patient's mouth, and the doctor jammed in a spoon. I could hear the victim's teeth grating against the spoon. After he calmed down, the spoon bent. On his back, out of convulsions, he gasped, huffing. "Why? Why kidney stones? I . . . don't get it . . ."

The doctor looked at the spoon, its bowl's tip bowed. "You must have too much uric acid or calcium in your urine . . . that's why you have bladder grits."

"Grits my ass . . . hardly enough to eat . . . just rice, manioc . . . wild vegetables . . ."

"Whatever. Some wild herbs can contain higher calcium and magnesium. Like amaranth. I know some of you cooked and ate it. You should've looked for purslane. It helps urinary discharge."

"How?"

"I don't know. But if you keep eating amaranth and water spinach and don't drink much water, your kidneys won't be able to filter all of them, and what's not passed through remain as stones. Some are sharp, especially the little ones."

The doctor left; the patient lay like a corpse. I hoped he could fall into a deep sleep. A voice came, three cots from mine. "Don't listen to his crap," said the infirm, whose gangrened leg was odorous. Whenever he crawled out of his mosquito net, he would drag his leg, wrapped in his spare pants, to keep away flies during the day.

None of the men spoke again. I dozed and woke. All quiet. A night bird sang. Then only the nocturnal sounds of insects. During the night, someone was talking. It was the infirm with the gangrened leg.

"The saying went, 'Better be a slave of a wise man than be a teacher of an imbecile.' But being a servant of an imbecile is tragic."

No one said a word. I felt safe. No on-duty cadre, no guards, no snitches. Nighttime belonged to us. The man went on, reciting a poem:

A horde of skeletons
wading across a creek
priests and monks and laypersons
all naked alike
all stripped bare of proprietorship
all looking lost like newborn.

So true, I thought. I did not want to ask whether he was the author of the poem or merely an admirer of it. I felt so tired that nothing else mattered. Poetry was worthless compared to a bowl of hot gruel now.

In the morning, I took another Nivaquine tablet and lay listless. Meals came at midday. A cake of cooked manioc paste. I tried to chew it. Eat or die, I told myself. The cake was tasteless, my sense of taste gone. Past noon, the young nurse came back in and checked on the other two cots. He alerted the doctor. I saw the arm of the gangrenous patient hanging down the side of his cot. Death had come like a faint breath for him.

After three days I was removed from the infirmary. Outside, the midday sun was mild, the cold icy. I staggered as I headed back to my shack. A camp dog was sniffing at a clump of white rice some guards had tossed out. The dog wagged its tail and trotted off. I looked at the rice, gleaming white in the sun, untouched, and realized I had not eaten rice for a month now. The shack was empty; the air hung with a malevolent odor of unwashed bodies mixed with tobacco smell and things having been cooked on the fire. I fell onto my cot and slept.

When I woke, I saw Mr. Thạch making tea. I watched him until he turned his head and saw me. "Brother Khang," he said cordially, "tea is about ready."

"Thank you, sir." I was dying for a sip of fragrant tea to snap me out of my lethargy. With a great effort I helped myself up on my elbow just as Bee came to my cot. He stood looking at me as if appraising some merchandise.

"You look like you need a good meal," he said finally.

After our standard mealtime, that night saw the usual bo bo combined with yellow corn, Bee told me to wait until dark. In the shack, some older men with snaggleteeth had separated bo bo from corn in their bowls and mashed the bo bo to paste. They cooked the paste in their *goz* cans.

At nine o'clock, the final gong sounded. After roll call everyone stayed put in their shacks, the entrance door shut, the oil lamps turned up, and evening life began for us. Bee went to the kitchen and retrieved his *goz* can. It was steaming when he opened the lid. I smelled onion and my mouth watered. Mr. Thạch placed three bowls on his cot, one for each of us. I watched intensely as Bee poured white rice porridge into each bowl. He handed me my bowl.

"Eat," he said. "Don't ask." Then quickly he reached into the fold of his shirt sleeve and pulled out a handful of hot pepper. He gave me a most fiery red pepper.

Obligingly, I slurped the rice porridge and bit off half the pepper. The porridge washed down my throat with a rich taste of salt, onion, pepper. My mouth groaned from the stinging heat of the pepper, and I felt blood pumping fast through my veins. I felt invigorated.

Bee and I cleaned our bowls of the last grains of rice. I wiped the inside of my bowl with my fingers and licked them. Mr. Thạch was slowly spooning porridge into his mouth when Bee leaned into me and said, "Do you care to hear how I got the precious white rice?"

I nodded. My tongue still smarted from the pepper seeds stuck to my fingers.

"I was detailed this week to the kitchen," said Bee. "Have you seen the chicken coop behind the kitchen? Yes? Them guards fed those chickens with white rice, every day. They wanted to fatten them for their holidays. I saw so much rice wasted—even those fowls ignored the rice. So I gathered them into my *goz* can, found water in the kitchen to wash them of the chicken's feces and then boiled the rice with some spices I got my hands on." He patted me on the shoulder. "I talked with the young nurse in the sick bay and he told me they would kick you out after three days. So, this feast is for you."

By now, Mr. Thạch had finished his meal. He held his empty bowl in cupped hands as if to enjoy the last lingering heat. He took out his *goz* can from his wicker bin and set it down next to his only drinking cup. Slowly he poured the *goz*'s content into his cup and gave it to me.

"This is good for after-meal digestion and helps cool your body."

The liquid was pale green. I sipped. A light minty taste, faintly sweet, spread on my tongue and then coursed through my body. Whatever he had concocted it with, I found it so refreshing I took another sip before realizing I was such an oaf who had forgotten his manners. I gave the cup back to Mr. Thạch.

"What is this drink, sir?" I asked.

"From a vine called silvertop." He sipped and then gave Bee the cup. "Use only its leaves. I would crush them and soak them in water overnight, then strain the water, and boil it with some molasses sugar. Let it cool and it will do wonders for your health."

I felt deeply grateful to both of them. For a long time, I had not had a taste of salt or sugar. I had never known how much they meant to a human body until my body cried for them.

The last theft I committed was stealing two potatoes from the potato patch adjacent to the manioc field. These were property of the camp, hence, owned by the State. The crops, to be sold to the local commune, would help feed the camp attendees all year round and the rest would go into the camp personnel's pockets. Not that I craved potato; rather, I had remembered November 6th was Bee's mother's death anniversary. From those years together in the camp near the seaside in the South to Cổng Trời camp in the North, he had never missed paying respects on his parents' death anniversaries. He did it only once a year for both of them. "Simplify it," he had said to me. "Offerings overly done only get you in trouble."

That night, after the shack's entrance door was shut, I came to his cot where he had rigged a makeshift altar—three rocks and two incense sticks. Before the altar were the two potatoes I had thieved for him. Knowing him, I speculated that he must have bribed a guard for those aromatic joss sticks. Wedged between two rocks was a piece of paper, scribbled with his handwriting. He bowed and I bowed. He was saying a silent prayer to his parents. I never knew what the words were when people paid respects to the dead.

The incense smoke swirled when wind rushed in through the open barred windows. It was raining. It was safer for us when it rained because the guards, wrapped in their raincoats, would retreat to somewhere dry. Otherwise, they would peek into each shack on their rounds.

Bee handed me one potato. Both had been boiled. I noticed black scabs on the potato skin. I scraped off the scabs and ate the potato. These were the State's property. None of us had had potatoes for months. Among us in the shack were certainly some snitches; but I no longer cared. Neither did Bee. This cold norther blowing outside. This ash rain falling, falling. In my hand a blemished potato, more precious than gold. I had lost count of those fallen sick. Most would not last this stark winter. Me, a walking skeleton. Have mercy, Sir Winter. I fantasized about rice. I would bow to the ground, this gray-haired head dropped, and sing, *Hail to the holy rice.* I would chew slowly like a toothless senior masticating. But why did this stomach still feel empty? Look left, right, mouse-eyed. Chew quick! Before they seized your jaws.

After we ate our potatoes, Bee cleared the altar and snuffed out the joss sticks. I picked up the piece of paper. I read what was on it quickly. Slightly alarmed, I leaned into him. "Don't leave it out in the open," I whispered into his ear.

"For you to read," he said, then tapped the side of his head. "I have it locked in here."

I hoped his parents would read this poem and know that he was a man, not a maggot:

They learned from chairman Mao: / Intellect is worse than a clump of feces
They reform us the inmates / and we transformed feces into rice
We killed our self-respect slowly / through endless hard labor
until one day we lost / all our humanity
In the end they have succeeded / in transforming us
into what they are / the maggots.

I came to know Dr. Đàm after he received a diatribe from a lecturer one morning.

Holding up a book, the political lecturer said, "All the historical truths about the Democratic Republic of Vietnam and its allies are written in this textbook."

He showed us the cover. *History of the August Revolution*. "All the truths fabricated by the imperialists and your puppet government are corrected in this primer. For example, the Imperial Army of Japan surrendered to our ally, the Soviet Union, in Manchuria, which ended Japan's expansionist dreams." He ended his lecture with a rote motto, "The harder you work, the quicker you are reformed."

Dr. Đàm raised his hand. Allowed to speak, he said, "Sir cadre, Japan surrendered to the Allies after the United States dropped two atomic bombs on them, one on Hiroshima and the other Nagasaki. It is not a fabricated fact but a world fact, because every country in the world has this fact in its history textbook."

The cadre's hand holding the book slashed the air up and down. "There you go again. Of course, those nations are in cahoots with the imperialists. But you are a discontented element, one who spoke ill of our Revolution with your anti-propaganda and reactionary misinformation. All of you here are offenders, regardless of the nature of your profession. You—" He pointed at Dr. Đàm. "What was your former profession with the puppet government?"

"Sir cadre," Dr. Đàm said softly, "I was conscripted into the army during the First Republic and served through the Second Republic as a military physician. I was a major."

"A major," said the lecturer, snorting. "For over a decade you treated the sick and the wounded soldiers of the rebel government. You committed the unforgivable crime of strengthening the puppet regime. But you are not going to be brought to trial. That's the saving grace. Otherwise, you would be tried under our original laws enacted by the Democratic Republic of Vietnam, under which you would be imprisoned from three to twelve years for propagandizing the enslavement policy and depraved culture of imperialism."

I found out later from Mr. Thạch that Dr. Đàm was a member of his green team. They must have been of the same age; yet Dr. Đàm was frail and plagued with eye trouble. One morning I had diarrhea and, as I went to the infirmary, I passed through the alley between the two dwellings of the camp personnel. I saw him raking the ground. I stopped and asked him, "What are you doing here, sir?"

"I'm preparing the ground to grow sweet potato vine for our cadres," he said. "Are you in the same shack with Mr. Thạch?"

"Yes, sir." I rubbed my abdomen. "By the way, do you think our infirmary have antibiotics?" I had seen him work there occasionally whenever the nurses desperately needed a professional opinion on certain treatments.

"Your guess is as good as mine. Are you ailing?"

I told him.

He said nothing, quietly returning to his chores by continuing to rake the ground softly.

I arrived at the infirmary. There was already a line of five men outside. The familiar young male nurse was on call, sitting behind a wooden table which kept wobbling every time he leaned on it. He looked hostile, as if those standing in line were about to rob him. My turn came.

"May I have medication for diarrhea?" I asked.

"I have none. Next."

I went back to my shack, passing through the alley, and ran into Dr. Đàm again. He leaned on his rake, squinting at me. "Any luck?"

I shook my head. He appraised me with his rheumy eyes. "I'll ask around. Somebody might have antibiotics. By the way, what exactly did you ask him?"

"I said, 'May I have medication for diarrhea?'"

"That's why you got none. You played the doctor's role. You should let him be the doctor, and you the patient. Ask, 'Sir Doctor, I don't know why my stomach keeps twisting in pain and I let it out several times a day. Just watery discharge each time.' He'd say, 'That's diarrhea.' Understand? Play dumb. Let them be smart."

In time, I grew fond of him. A medical doctor with compassion. When the camp had allowed inmates to write home, most of us asked our families to buy the things we needed most to treat our illnesses. I was in the security shack with Bee, where letters and parcels were opened and inspected. Dr. Đàm received a gift from home. One of the security cadres, holding up the small glass vial, asked him, "What is this liquid?" It was amber brown.

"For my gastric ulcer, sir cadre," he said.

"What is gastric ulcer?" the cadre asked.

"Have you ever had constant stomach pains?"

The cadre looked quizzical at Dr. Đàm and shook his head.

"Such pains are often caused by gastric ulcers," Dr. Đàm said. "They come about when stomach acid causes open sores on the lining of the stomach."

Still looking quizzical, the cadre opened the vial, sniffed, then flicked his eyes at Dr. Đàm. "What is it made of?"

Dr. Đàm pointed at the vial in the cadre's hand but avoided his stare. "It's made mainly of honey and herbal extracts. Southern folk medicine, sir cadre."

"You people from the South have all kinds of unorthodox things, as far as I know." The cadre reluctantly gave the vial back to Dr. Đàm.

If Dr. Đàm had told him, as he had later told us once we were outside the security shack, that it was bear bile, which he needed to treat inmates for internal injuries caused by beatings, then he would have been sent to a penal cell and had his family gift confiscated.

The few times I stayed in the sick bay, I saw him work with the camp's antiquated medical equipment during surgery. Nobody from the camp personnel knew how to operate those devices: the autoclave that was used to sterilize equipment, the Ombrédanne Inhaler for administering anesthesia. They dated to World War I. With these devices, he once performed an appendicostomy on a patient, attaching his colon to his belly button to give him the enema for severe constipation. When so many inmates suffered edema, and the camp's infirmary had no cure for it, Dr. Đàm simply asked the cadre in charge of the kitchen to spare him every day a share of pig's mash. He made our edema victims eat it to give their body a dose of much-needed vitamin B1.

Because of his poor eyesight, Dr. Đàm would diagnose a patient by taking his pulse and asking him to describe his symptoms. Three typical cases among the inmates established his reputation and caught the camp's attention. One patient was a noted South Vietnam novelist, whose ailment was stomach cancer; another was a former senior officer of South Vietnam Ministry of Chiêu Hồi—*Open Arms*—who had hepatitis; and another was a former director of the South Vietnam Central Intelligence Office, who had diabetes. The first two eventually died from cancer and hepatitis; the third still lived, perhaps never forgetting Dr. Đàm's humorous remark: "The worst offender to diabetes is glucose. It comes from sugar. White rice causes spikes in blood sugar, which is bad for diabetes. But rest assured, you won't have to be on any diet for your ailment. How often do we get white rice here? How frequently do we receive sugar as a treat?"

The camp officials knew he was an authentic MD, for he was a former military doctor with a major rank. But they never called him "doctor." Smiling, he once said to me, "They regard me as a nurse. Just out of an inferiority complex." Then he added, "These medical doctors they brought in from the North are abysmally ignorant. Let's start with their education system. It's ten years from elementary to high school, not twelve like in our academic system. Those who studied medicine spent two, three years in medical school and then were rushed to the battlefield. Their reference sources came from Russian books, none from Western sources, much less American or British or French. Even with the aid of French medical books, many of them couldn't read French." He looked around then back at me, softening his voice. "You know why we don't have more medical doctors in any of these camps who came from our former administration? They were released and brought to Saigon to help those idiotic commies run the hospitals. The commies didn't trust their own doctors."

In the camp's infirmary, where he was called in occasionally to help, there was one cot reserved for him to display his medical instruments, all of them manufactured by us, the inmates, from scrap metal we scavenged from the GMC trucks the North had transported home after the war. Those scavenging days were miserable. Imagine carrying back all kinds of scrap metal in your sacks, so heavy your knees nearly buckled, as you trod in the spine-tingling heat at high noon. Out of those scraps, our smithy produced some heavy-duty pliers. Dr. Đàm used them, one day, to pull out one of my molars—one that hurt during my time in the penal cell with Mr. Vinh. Fortunately for me, one of my fellow inmates had donated a tube of local anesthetic, but even with the numbing effect, the reduction of pain was minimal, and I passed out.

One day I saw Dr. Đàm working among us in the manioc field because the camp had pulled many inmates from other teams to speed up the harvest. I stopped pulling up the tubers and went to him. "Why are you here, sir?" I asked him.

"Lost my status," he said, then continued. "Remember the visit last week from the Central Committee? Those inspectors they sent to our camp? I was flanked by our camp security when those men came to inquire about the camp living conditions. I'd been briefed to lie like a commie. Before I knew it, I said to those inspectors, 'All we have here to combat malaria is a limited quantity of quinine, and it came from the inmates who got them from our former administration. What we have in camp from the Revolution is herbal medicine, and the one we use mostly is that *Xuyên Tâm Liên*, the King of Bitters, as our panacea. That cure-all medicine does nothing to stop illnesses. As far as hygiene goes, our infirmary sits by our camp fertilizer shack where we store human waste from the latrines to feed our vegetables. The permanent odor in the infirmary is unhealthy to our patients. Moreover, the human waste as fertilizer leaves bacteria on our vegetables and causes sickness if not washed thoroughly.'" He shook his head as I understood the consequence of his outburst.

Moments after I went back to pulling manioc tubers from the ground, I heard his voice coming over. He was singing:

Arise, the damned of the world!
Arise, all the hungry people!

I stood up and saw the overseer walking toward him. "Why did you sing that song?" he asked our doctor.

"Sir cadre," said Dr. Đàm, "I was singing *The International*, the first Soviet Union national anthem. It's an official socialist and communist song."

"But why did you sing just the first two lines? Who rise up? Who? While you're laboring as such?"

"I memorized only those two lines. Whenever I'm tired, I sing those two lines. It's effective, sir cadre. It restores my enthusiasm for the Revolution."

"Liar! That song is holy to our Socialist State, to the world proletariat. You can't sing it with just two lines. It proves that you're lacking the spirit of reforming yourself."

The next morning, I did not see him during our roll call in the dirt courtyard. By evening, I learned that he was being detained in a penal cell with both feet shackled.

What saved Dr. Đàm from the calamity of the penal cell, considering his age, was a word from the camp's security chief who sent for him. I did not see Dr. Đàm for three days. I was worried. I asked Mr. Thạch, and his equanimity put me at ease. "Brother Khang, what would become of this world without medical doctors?"

The next day, to my surprise, Dr. Đàm joined our manioc harvesting team. Both he and Mr. Thạch were out on the field shoveling dirt, pulling up roots, and cutting off tubers. I looked over at the two old men and suppressed my outburst of enmity toward the wardens. That day, we had packed our meals when we left camp at daybreak. We were to stay at the work site without returning to camp for lunch. The four of us—me, Bee, Mr. Thạch, and Dr. Đàm—sat under the shade of a hornbeam. Before I brought out my *goz* can which contained my lunch—half bo bo and half yellow corn—Dr. Đàm said, "Save them. Let's enjoy our socialist premium porridge."

He set two *goz* cans on the grass. He opened one can and I the other. Inside was white porridge, thick and creamy. Dr. Đàm retrieved four tin cups from his sack as I watched him, wide-eyed. "Where're all these from, sir?" I asked.

"The cups?" He flicked a smile. "From the kitchen, courtesy of our camp's security chief." He poured the content of one *goz* can into the cups. "This porridge is no ordinary porridge. Taste it."

We spooned porridge into our mouths. I paused. It tasted sweet. A fine sweetness, not as coarse as with granular sugar. Dr. Đàm nodded. "That's cane sugar. The finest. Only for the camp's higher-ups."

Bee snickered. "Like the security chief?"

"Yes," Dr. Đàm grinned, blinking.

"What's the story here, sir?" I asked.

"The chief sent for me," Dr. Đàm said. He paused to taste the porridge and smacked his lips. "This is just right, not too sweet. Agreeable to everyone?"

We nodded. Dr. Đàm continued. "I assumed the worst when their doctor—the head nurse from the infirmary—came to fetch me. We went to the chief's dwelling. By the door there was a wire cage framed by sturdy looking bamboo trunks. Inside, there was a black python coiled up on its white-striped, yellow belly. The head nurse said it was the chief's pet. He said guards would catch rats to feed this reptile."

Dr. Đàm poured more porridge into Bee's cup which was near empty. Mine was still half full. "Have you ever seen the chief?" Dr. Đàm asked. "No? Neither have I. I heard he rarely showed his face during the day. Most of his work, including inspecting the security of the camp, was carried out at night. A fearsome figure even to his own people."

Dr. Đàm put down his cup and rubbed his eyes. Overhead, a finch tweeted. It must have come to feed on the hornbeam's nutlets. Dr. Đàm continued. "I've heard from guards that he was the one that bashed the heads of our escapees and ordered their corpses to be displayed on the courtyard for us to behold. I wasn't too eager to meet him. After the head nurse announced my arrival at the door, I heard a voice: 'Enter.' A heavy northern accent. I'm a born southerner, and if there's an accent that puts me on guard, it's a northern accent—not just any northern accent like yours, Brother Khang, and my friend Thạch's—but one that's heavy like from a backwater. We entered.

"It was the first time I saw his face. I was shocked. The interior was dim, but the face I saw was disfigured, its left side all shiny scars. His left ear was missing. He gestured for me to sit and dismissed the head nurse. That damaged left side affected him when he spoke, like someone was pinching the corner of his mouth. That's when I noticed his left hand. It had four fingers missing, and his left arm was all scarred. I wouldn't guess what had happened to him until later. But let me get to the point."

By then I had finished my cup at the same time as Mr. Thạch did. We received more porridge. Dr. Đàm still had his cup part full. He continued.

"The chief said to me, 'My daughter has come to visit me from Hanoi. She has complained about stomach pains on and off, even though in Hanoi she received treatments from one of our medical doctors. But the pains came back. I want you to diagnose her symptoms and come up with a remedy.' The chief called me into an interior room and his daughter came out. She must have been eighteen or nineteen. Sweet, innocent looking girl. A little pale though.

"The chief made a fist and brought it down onto the table, like when you rubber-stamp a document. He said, 'If you cause harm to her, I will see to it that you pay for your ineptitude.' I said to him, 'Sir cadre, I'm a physician. I cure people, not harm them.' The chief stood up, giving up his chair for his daughter. I said to her, 'When you have a bowel movement, what is the color of your stool?' She looked perplexed. Embarrassed, maybe. I repeated my question. She said, 'It was dark.' 'Recently, or was it like that in Hanoi?' I asked. 'Very recently,' she said.

"I asked for a pen and a piece of paper and said to the chief, 'She has stomach ulcers. Her dark stool is due to bleeding. If left untreated it'll cause holes through the wall of the stomach.' I glanced at her. She looked alarmed. The chief said, 'If you can treat her, you will deserve my praise. It is not a small matter, though it was malpractice on that doctor's part.' 'Yes, sir cadre. I'm going to write you a prescription. The two drugs: One will reduce acid to help heal the ulcer; the other is liquid medication to help cover the ulcer with a protective layer to prevent further damage from the acids.'

"The chief appeared relaxed and said, 'What about her daily nutrition? Anything that will help in her daily meals?' 'Yes, sir cadre. Put her on a brown-rice porridge diet and drink brown-rice extract after it's roasted—do not overly roast it. There are vitamins, fiber, minerals, and protein in brown-rice bran to help cope with stomach ulcers.'"

Overhead, the finch tweeted again then flew off. Dr. Đàm ate two spoonfuls and continued.

"He asked me to stay at the infirmary until he summoned me. After three days, he sent for me again—that was yesterday. He said, 'My daughter is free of pain now. She can eat without feeling discomfort, but she remains on brown-rice diet. The medicine worked wonders for her.' I said to him, 'Have her on that diet and continue taking medication for the next seven days. These ten days are critical. Do not miss medication and do not eat anything else but brown rice, and drink brown-rice extract.' He gave me a small carton. Inside there was granulated cane sugar. I could tell it was of good quality. He said, 'Tell the kitchen to spare you one kilo of white rice. Ask them to cook it for you, or you can cook at your leisure without being questioned by your shack leader or trusty or warden. You are a good doctor.'"

Such largess, I thought.

A finch came to perch on a branch above my head. I could not tell if it was the one from before or a different finch. I listened to its tweeting and asked Dr. Đàm, "Do you still have the vial of bear bile? Can you treat the girl with that?"

Dr. Đàm patted me on my shoulder. "Brother Khang, I lied to the security to save my hide. Bear bile is good for treating bruises, not for internal wounds."

Bee lit a cigarette. "That chief is something to be reckoned with, isn't he?" He squinted behind the coils of smoke. "What happened to his face anyway, sir?"

Dr. Đàm set his cup down on the grass. "From what his daughter told me—under her breath when he was out of sight—it came from the war. Artillery fragments during a battle in Pleiku." He licked the spoon clean, shaking his head. "That's my hometown. Fortunately, he must've not read my self-confession. The daughter said her father was handsome in his youth. Well, I couldn't be the judge of that. I never wanted to look at him squarely. He seemed to prefer darkness, and there's certainly something ominous about him. She asked me if I could think of any medication to help restore some of his facial qualities. I said I wasn't God. I wasn't sure if she was brought up as an atheist, fearing no God, respecting no one except those goons from the Party. I told her if her mother accepted him for who he was, that was that."

Mr. Thạch nodded but said nothing. I chimed in. "Did you see his wife?"

Dr. Đàm slowly capped one of the empty *goz* cans and peered up at me. "She was killed during the American bombing in 1972. They bombed Hanoi, Hải Phòng, Lạng Sơn, Bắc Giang, and Thái Nguyên. His family is from Thái Nguyên. I didn't say anything when she told me that; but I thought if their family had lived within ten miles from the border of China, her mother would've lived."

That was the buffer zone, I thought, as Dr. Đàm went on. "She was twelve years old then when her mother died, and she lived with her maternal grandparents while he was fighting in the South. I could tell he hated us, the people he'd fought against."

I thought of our two escape comrades who had died from gruesome head wounds, whose bodies were buried without coffins. I felt fortunate that it was senior lieutenant Bảo who interrogated and later worked with me on my self-confession. Had it been this man, the security chief, I could have received a different treatment.

"Brother Khang, you'll have to go with me now to the chief's quarter. You're needed there."

Alarmed, I looked quizzically at him. "Why me?"

Dr. Đàm smiled. "Easy now. It's the daughter. She liked this Russian song and wanted to read its lyrics in English. She said she loved the English language, and I thought of you."

"You told the chief I could transcribe the words?"

"Literally, yes." Dr. Đàm chuckled. "Not transliterating, of course."

"I don't know Russian from Chinese. How could I translate for her?"

"Don't worry. She's translated the lyrics from Russian to Vietnamese. Now all you'll have to do is go from Vietnamese to English."

Bee snickered. "If you can't, he'll feed you to his python."

Dr. Đàm and I entered the chief's house. I could smell a bad odor from the python as I crossed the threshold. The interior was dim. The chief sat in a chair farther into the unlit corner as he listened to his daughter playing her violin. The music was melodious, a tune I could not recognize.

Dr. Đàm introduced me to the chief, who remained in the shadow, and to his daughter, who rose politely and bowed to us, a gesture I had never seen among the northerners who had discriminated against us after the war. It helped soften my feeling toward her, and I bowed back. I could not make out the chief's face, nor did I want to look at him. The girl took me to a small round table near the door where sunlight fell on its brown wood on which lay scattered sheets of music and white sheets of paper. She picked up a sheet of paper with writing scribbled on it.

"This song," she said in her melodious northern accent, "was written by a Russian songwriter. I know the Russian language, but I would love to see the lyrics in English. I plan to study English when I return to Hanoi."

I read her handwriting of the song's translation in Vietnamese. "Two Shores" was the title. I read it from beginning to end and looked at her. She did not have the paleness Dr. Đàm had mentioned. Perhaps the prescribed medication had helped restore some of her vitality. She looked fresh.

"May I ask," I said to her, "if you can play this song again just to give me some sense, some feeling for it?"

"Much obliged," she said as she returned to her chair and picked up her violin.

I stood by Dr. Đàm, listening to the undulating notes of the tune. All the time, I avoided looking toward the shadowed corner. Yet I could feel his gaze on us. He must have compared me to those escapees whose lives he took. My gut trembled.

Perhaps I was still alive because I did not kill any guards. I still did not know his name, but it was better that way, and I'd rather remain a persona non grata after I had paid the price. But the music. It sounded like our "Yellow Music" of the South, which the Communists had banned throughout the country after winning. They, the North, reveled in "Red Music" which exalted its political-military power. I heard that to the northern victors, "Yellow Music," the slow-tempo music in bolero, ballade, and rumba sung in the South, represented decadence, melancholy. This tune I was listening to was mellow. Something sentimental in it stirred a yearning in me. Perhaps something irretrievable from my long gone past. I read the lyrics again and, half bent with a pen in hand, began turning them into English, guided by the mood I was in. She asked me to read it aloud. I read it out loud and, in one moment, felt as if I was speaking about my fate. Me and my family, the two shores.

Rain, rain, all night
Dawn is coming.
I am waiting
Though, no, says my heart.
You and I are two shores
Between us a river.

She seemed taken by the words spoken to her, saying she loved the sound of the English language. Momentarily, I forgot the shadowed man in the corner. When I finished, he rose and his daughter bowed to me and Dr. Đàm again. I bowed back, saying from the bottom of my heart that I loved the song rendered by her performance. In that moment, I felt no division, no barrier between us, of the North and the South, of the captor and the captive.

When we left, she stood in the doorway waving goodbye. The smell of the python followed me. Her father remained inside, in that somber interior. If I were him, living forever defaced, how would I bear it?

In the late autumn of that year, a border war erupted between Vietnam and China. Prisoners interned in camps near the northern border were forced to begin their exodus. I learned that our communist government had divided the North into three zones: one combining all the frontier provinces, one containing the midland, and one encompassing the Red River delta. We were to be relocated to zone two: the midland. I recalled having dug trenches in the early autumn, that had encircled the camp and ran the length of each dwelling, interconnecting them so we could move around in anticipation of the Chinese attack.

Every day the camp's loudspeakers would blare out anti-Chinese rhetoric and, in the evening, we were made to sit through a session on current events, listening to our shack leader read aloud the *People's Army Newspaper*, loaded with propaganda.

Our last outing came in early December when we were sent to a distant storehouse to bring back rice and salt in anticipation of a camp relocation. Rumor had it we were to move farther south of the border. Many of us rooted for a Chinese invasion to create chaos and therefore a remote feasibility of escape. I shared such sentiment, though I never wished to see a Chinese incursion thanks to a thousand-year deep-seated aversion to our northern neighbor.

It was raining heavily by the time we reached the repository with two teams of men and carts. The storehouse was built from wood, moss stained and weatherworn, with a corrugated sheet metal roof. It looked like a Native American longhouse.

We went inside and began loading up our carts. The rain had not let up by the time we were ready to depart. Many of us rested inside, lying on the packed dirt floor. I took shelter against the rain, standing under the rain-dripping eaves. A girl stood toward the far end of the storehouse, watching the rain. Seeing me, she turned and approached me. She looked in her twenties, dressed in a blue work shirt that factory girls usually wore. Her hair was plaited and flung over her shoulder. She wore rubber sandals like most of us, her toenails unpainted. Obviously, she was not from the city. When she was near enough, she stopped and tossed her plait back with a flick of her hand.

"Elder brother, are you from the camp?" she asked softly. There was a paleness about her, of someone malnourished.

I nodded.

"You don't smoke," she said, smiling faintly. "Most of your friends smoke like a smokestack."

I smiled, saying nothing, though I noticed her politeness, a rarity among these northerners who viewed us as rapists, hoodlums, human-liver-eaters. Finally, I said, "Aren't you cold, miss?" I had on an undershirt, a work shirt, and an army jacket, and I still felt the clammy cold. She was looking at me, then dropped her gaze as if to size me up. I could tell she seemed taken by the jacket I wore. It was an olive-green button-up army jacket that sported two large front flap pockets and airman insignia patches on both sleeves. More than once, some guards at the camp had asked to buy or trade for it, and I had politely declined.

"I'm used to the cold, elder brother," she finally said and came closer. She touched the insignia on my left arm.

I looked down at her. Her fingernails had flecks of black dirt; her hands had bluish veins of those frequently doing menial work. Her hair was wet; she must have come in from the rain when I went outside. I guessed she must have been one of the workers at the storehouse.

"How much is this jacket?" she asked without lifting her eyes up at me. "If I wanted to buy it."

"It's not for sale, miss," I said, keeping my voice even without sounding harsh.

"Can I trade for it with food?" She half lifted her gaze, her tone earnest.

"No, miss." I almost blurted out to her that she could never afford such a jacket, but something held me back. Perhaps pity.

She nodded. I saw her smile, her lips chapped. Then she stepped back, still gazing at my garment. Wind driven rain fell on my face and hers; she did not bother wiping it. I took off my jacket, folded it lengthwise, and handed it to her.

"Since you like it so much," I said, "please accept it as my gift to you."

Her eyes opened wide. In them I saw red veins. Her pale face brightened as she took hold of the jacket.

"Elder brother!" she exclaimed and stood looking at me.

I nodded at her. She stood in one place, wordless. I smiled and turned and headed back inside out of the rain.

News of China's impending offensive roused the inmates. Many perked up. "The enemy of our enemy is our ally." Yet others were sullen. "Them Chinese have been our enemy for centuries. Why all these celebrations?" I was aligned with the second camp. For nearly a quarter of a century, Vietnam and China had been on good terms with each other. To protect their reciprocal relationship at all costs was to avoid "pried lips, cold teeth," the famous motto repeatedly used by the Vietnamese commies. Every night the camp's loudspeakers blared out news of the border conflict. Listening, I felt neutral, though the broadcast's wording and its tone were acidic:

> Our socialist nation is on the mend after a decade-long war against imperialist America. It is when we need time and resources to rebuild our nation from north to south that we are faced with the new expansionist who had been our ally until now. Smelling a new opportunity to strike gold with the Yankees, China now exposes her true thousand-year-old identity as feudalist, a traitor to socialism. To invade our nation again, as she has done repeatedly in our four-thousand-year-old history, she now befouls our nation and its people with a war crime as thick as forest leaves and as immeasurable as the South Sea.

When the broadcast ended, someone in the shack cackled. He had a strange laugh, this former lecturer of the Thủ Đức Military Academy. Before I turned away, he recited a poem:

From the misery of hellhole I step out for fresh air
Stretch my limbs then walk back in!

"Damnation," Bee blurted.

Quickly I scanned the faces. No known snitches around. Give the man a silent applause, I thought. Nothing new. China invasion or not. Nothing ever changed.

Within a day I saw many inmates who were ethnic Chinese and Chinese mainlanders being rounded up and quarantined in a separate shack.

After days of following the news, we held our breath as we heard that China had launched six militarized divisions, fully supported by air and artillery power, along the 600 kilometers of the Viet-Sino border. Tense, harrowing, the cadres busied themselves with the task of relocating all of us inmates to an interior location, away from the border. At the same time, news came about our socialist state, having just ordered their Second Corps to pull out of Kampuchea and return to the north. A fresh army corps, Fifth Corps, was quickly formed by combining four infantry divisions: the 3rd, the 327th, 337th, and 338th. To maximize its defense, the Standing Committee of the National Assembly decreed a general mobilization of men above eighteen years of age.

It was midnight. A cold, moonless night. A gong sounded. Its shrill sound was strangely eerie at midnight. I heard the footfall of the guards and the cadres moving from shack to shack, rousing everyone awake.

"Line up outside your shack for roll call!"

Many of us stood at attention in the frosty cold, dozing off on our feet. Then we moved onto the courtyard while the guards poked through every corner of the shacks with flashlights. After they declared all was good, the administrator addressed us through a megaphone.

"Due to the recent political change in relations between China and Vietnam, the camp will move its attendees to various locations elsewhere. When your name is called, step out and return to your shack to gather your belongings. Come back out and line up on the far left of the courtyard until further notice. You shall depart in groups between now and daybreak. All must proceed quietly and in an orderly fashion." He turned sharply to his camp staff behind him. "Comrades! Carry out the order urgently!"

I belonged to the first group to leave. All of us in that group were former intelligence service officers, political warfare personnel, psy-op officials. Each of us received a packed meal for the journey. I understood that the kitchen had been notified in advance about the relocation. We said goodbye to one another and, in the dark, we parted ways.

On our way to the Molotova trucks, I asked Mr. Liên, "How far do you think the Chinese will go with their invasion?"

Looking quickly around, Mr. Liên kept his voice low. "If the Chinese decide to go all out without restraint, they could wipe out Vietnam in a matter of weeks. I doubt they intend to use all their strength to achieve such objective. Who's behind them on the other side of Heilongjiang river? A massive deployment of Russian troops along the Sino-Soviet border and Mongolian-Chinese border. The Russians might not intervene, but their troops massing at these borders would tie up the Chinese troops. Now, the caviar. If the Chinese aim to teach Vietnam a lesson, then it'd be a limited war. To fight a limited war, the advantage goes to Vietnam. Just imagine the scale of logistic supplies the Chinese must have to support and sustain the massive size of their forces, perhaps a quarter of a million men. Engaging their enemy, advancing then withdrawing, it'll be costly."

Once in the trucks, we sat in pairs, handcuffed together. I sat with Mr. Liên. The convoy began moving out into darkness. All that could be seen in the headlights was a mass of white fog.

Closing my eyes, I thought of all the camps near the Viet-Sino border being evacuated. Just getting out of Cổng Trời, the Heavenly Gate, was like a death sentence being lifted. Many inmates had not survived their stay there. The dead were buried in an eternal place, 2000 meters above the sea, where mountain peaks touched the clouds, thick and lifeless gray, which blocked out the sun year round, and the fog hung throughout the day making it damp and cold.

They said you could sense Death coming for you after only a short time spent there. I could not disagree. Yet that dreadful feeling did not leave me during the long ride, as I turned to look back. Gone from my sight were the peaks of those mountains at the Heavenly Gate. What came back was the scenes of those dying on the Bà Then Hill.

CHAPTER 7

Sơn La

Fall 1978–80

You were destined for me. Perhaps as a punishment.
—Fyodor Dostoevsky

I woke to the gong. My first day at the new camp.

We had marched for two days in drenching rains, each bent under his own sack, but I could guarantee that none of us cared where we were headed to. After two days on foot, we arrived at Sơn La Camp, sitting deep in the bowels of a forest.

Abruptly the gong died down and, in the stillness of dawn, I could hear the hooting of monkeys and the crowing of jungle fowl. The crowing cut off, then came the bird calls coming down from the woodlands.

Outside it was rock-frozen cold, and we shivered like rustling trees. One by one we came up to a long table where five security females in their mid-twenties sat. One of them, with her long hair tugged neatly inside a black army cap, peered up at me.

"Declare the contents of your previously registered belongings," she said.

"One Movado wristwatch, one wallet with money." I had kept my wedding ring with me by sewing it into the hem of my pants.

"How much is the value of your old money?"

"Between thirty or thirty-five đồng."

She handed me a cloth pouch. "You registered thirty-three đồng with Cổng Trời camp. Count it."

Everything was intact, except there was a greenish moldy film on the dial of my watch. The old self-winding Movado wristwatch my wife had bought for me shortly after we were married. Its crystal was marred by tiny scratches from years of use. My personal items now belonged to the Sơn La camp until I was officially released. The receipts given to me were a Note of Registered Personal Items and a Note of Registered Personal Money.

That night I slept soundly but suddenly woke in the night not knowing where I was. Then it came to me that I was no longer at Cổng Trời. The shack smelled different, absent of the nose-twitching odors and lighter perhaps from having been vacant until we lodged. My head rested on my rolled-up, sweat-ringed, salt-whitened shirt, my *goz* can hung on a peg on the wall next to my cot. I thought of the years past. I cut off the thought. There were new faces in the shack; the only thing common among us was that we were wrinkled and aged. I met an old face from Cổng Trời's camp personnel. He was a sergeant major there, whose daily duty was supervising the guards. Now, as second lieutenant, he was one of our wardens.

We had yellow corn for breakfast every morning. The kitchen helper told us the corn was in season. True, it tasted sweetly fresh and, chewing, I felt grateful. To whom I did not know; but every meal that came fresh would make us bow our heads and pray that the next meal would be as fresh.

The first morning on the work site, I saw a guard wearing a neck chain with a cross. At first, I did not notice until he took it out from under his shirt, wiped it, and quickly tucked it back in. A fellow in our team, who was Catholic, approached the guard and smiled.

"Comrade," he said, the charming smile lighting up his face. "I am happy to see with my eyes the all-harmony of religions, and I must thank Uncle Hồ for that."

The guard stared at him. "Why?"

"Uncle Hồ said, and I quote, 'Everyone is equal. Such equality encompasses freedom for human rights, freedom of religious faith. It goes without saying that such equality excludes virtually no other rights.'"

"Fuck that goat," the guard said under his breath as he looked around. "If he were still alive, I'd be damn dead for wearing my cross."

One late morning, during our break near a creek, I saw a fellow carry back a sizable striped bass. He asked me if I wanted to buy it.

"No money," I told him. "But I can find someone to buy it for you."

"What's your commission?"

Smart fellow. "One đồng," I said.

I brought the bass back to camp, wrapped in straw, by hiding it under the fresh ears of corn in my basket. Before the evening meals, I went to the quarters where our former high-ranking officers were segregated. After peddling the bass around, one former colonel agreed to buy it on one condition. I had to cook it for him. I used my handmade bamboo knife to scale the fish and used their little corner hearth to braise the fish in caramel sauce. All the ingredients came from the colonel. He paid me three đồng.

The following morning when I went out of the shack, I saw a film of ice on the ground. The December cold came with a norther, blowing all night and all day until the water in the receptacles we had stored now turned to ice. Fortunately, we were allowed to fetch firewood for ourselves in the woodlands during the day, not far from our normal work sites. On high elevation that morning, I could see mountain after mountain nesting and rolling away to a bluish horizon. I could spot the ochre-yellow serpentine trail dipping and rising in the folds of mountainsides, the one we used to go up in the morning. Sometimes we came upon the locals, walking barefoot, or walking a packhorse. They were Hmong. Sometimes we ran into the lowlanders, who were Vietnamese that had been banished from their homes after 1954 because they were associated with the French, or they were once the bourgeoisie. These people had turned over their assets to the North regime in return for the freedom to live in the mountains instead of prisons.

That ochre-yellow trail went past several hillside camps and ours was among them. The inter-camp layout occupied many kilometers, separating one camp from another by hillocks, one for our former generals, one for our former colonels and majors, and one for those like me, former intelligence officers. To get to these camps one could follow the trail on foot, or one could take a road used by vehicles.

Our shacks in this camp had cement floors. At night, if you ventured outside to relieve yourself, you would not want to walk barefoot. We each received a red blanket made in China—pre-border conflict aids—and still many of us had scoured the surroundings for remnants of cloth; some had found burlap bags and, at night, after crawling inside the bags, they still shook like leaves.

But there was a small wood fire in the center of the shack. The fire danced and the firewood crackled, throwing shadows on the wall and drenching the shack in the lurid red of the Chinese blankets.

Barely a week after we arrived, the camp executed two detainees. They must have been kept in solitary confinement cells for so long that they were now two skeletons. When they shot them dead, I swore the impact did not even jolt them. We looked away. Perhaps they did not have enough blood left to even bleed.

In the afternoon that day, the loudspeakers blared out an anti-Chinese broadcast. Listening, I believed it was the same rhetoric I had heard in Cổng Trời, except this time the tone was more acerbic, owing to the fact that Chinese troops had looted every border village in their first assault. They cleaned out every dwelling. In the midst of the broadcast came a couplet:

Your national flag will be made of our women's undies
Your national symbol will fashion after our chicken coop

The following year, in the midst of winter, the camp shocked us with an earth-shattering statement so un-communist we all gasped when we heard it: "We, the State and the camps, have faced a variety of economic difficulties, thus putting the State, the Party, and the camps in a bind to feed and nourish our camp attendees. Therefore, on behalf of the State and the camps, we are determined to amend our camp policies by allowing family gifts and visits."

We were granted once again the privilege of having correspondence with our families. Like everyone else, I was prepared to hear our security cadre orating on the clemency of the State and the Party in granting us such honorable opportunity, and then lambasting any one of us who dared go against the three "always" rules laid down by the camp for this privilege: always positive in writing home; always urging family members to believe the righteousness of the State and the Party; always expressing your satisfaction with the living and working condition in the camp. His speech sounded exactly like his counterparts at Cổng Trời. With home correspondence came family visitation. It was like fresh air in an unventilated latrine.

We were later told by visiting wives that, back home, the commies had let loose a plan called "Night-Blossoming Flowers." Those young wives, whose husbands were rotting in camps, were their prey—wives who could not support themselves or get help from relatives. Those of us who left them behind, the low-ranking personnel in the army who had received early release, came home to see a pith helmet on the table. After asking around, they knew they could not go home again.

Those of us who remained in camps found solace from the allowed visits—"alimentary visits," as we called them among ourselves—because we had not yet lost our wives. We had learned not to utter those two words in the presence of a camp committee member. The Revolution was adamant against such words. "No one needs to be nourished. The Party and the State never let any of our camp attendees go hungry. These are visiting trips, to be policy-correct."

But misfortune followed many of our families. One fellow's wife broke down crying while sitting across from him in a visitation hut and was immediately scolded by the overseeing guard. Do not shed tears to malign the Revolution as if it was the evil who caused your sorrow. She choked down her words, telling him their oldest son was laboring in the city to feed the family, and his younger brother was expelled from high school because of their father's anti-Revolutionary record as a former puppet regime employee. The youngest one, only nine, now sat beside her in the visitation hut. Malnourished, he looked no taller than a six-year-old, and was all skin and bones like his father, a walking-skeleton inmate.

In those early days, the visitors brought us basic food and condiments, some having been concocted as substitutes for the originals, like sesame oil cooked with hot peppers as a replacement for chili sauce. Each meal, we would gingerly skim it and mix it with our rice and, despite our miserly use of it, it lasted for only a few weeks.

Everyone back home was poor. Many famished. But they saved fresh fruits, salt, sugar, sesame seeds, even dried foods like beef jerky and stockfish, and brought us these edibles. They were our life saviors, the nutriment.

But nutriment from those visits brought us together. We shared. We came together in those moments. We bonded.

But those bonds only lasted so long. Most of our former superiors were inclined to keep their edible gifts to themselves. Words were spread among us that they used to enjoy privileges during the war and now, in hard times, showed their true colors. It was because of them that our country fell to the commies. Animosity then turned man against man. Snitches were born among us like an inevitable chemical reaction. Only those who maintained a high moral standard could resist such a downfall, Mr. Liên had told me.

Many of us received family gifts, among them money. Once declared, we were to register our money with the camp who would keep it and meter the allowed money to us on special occasions to buy items from the periodically conducted bulk purchases.

I had no gift money.

I had been frugal with the only sum I still had, but that now sat with the camp security. At night, occasionally a cart would creak by, peddling snacks. Its squeaky wheels would draw inmates to the barred windows. Out in the night the flickering lanterns hung on the cart's pull bars were like will-o'-the-wisps. I would watch them going through quick transactions. The snacks were usually manioc cakes, baked with brown sugar-sweetened potato paste in the center. I would watch them wolf down those snacks in a few bites and knew how much I would love to have a bite. Don't give in, I told myself. Then I fell asleep, before hunger began gnawing.

Two cots from me, a man would munch on his snack and mumble to himself. He would press against his face a gift from home. The first time I saw what he did it churned my gut. Perhaps I felt funny because of its perversion. It was a pair of women's sky-blue, white-lace panties. Our man was a former captain of the Armored Cavalry Corps, but during those moments, fondling his wife's underpants, he was a softy.

That was his wife's first trip to the North. Earlier in the evening, after the gong, I saw him rummaging through a bag. He saw me watching, paused and described the ordeal of his wife's journey from the South to the North.

Her journey had begun with her receiving the visitation paper issued by our camp administration. She brought it with her family register to her sub-district to have it verified and stamped, confirming that she was his wife and lived at such address. The sub-district sent her paperwork to the district which, after many days, would issue a travel pass. Like most inmates' wives, she had a small budget, which could not afford her a non-stop journey by train such as the *Reunification Express*. So, she joined many of the other women on a roundabout route, by boat, train—its passenger cars called "black coach" because they had no lights, and everybody slept on the grimy floor—then, when they arrived at the station many kilometers from the camp, they pooled money and then hired a buffalo cart.

The cart stopped a good distance from the camp's gate to unload the luggage, and a local boy no older than ten came running up and asked, "Hire me, will you?" Before she had caught her breath, a baby-faced guard walked up, poking the boy with his rifle. "You *n*azy good-for-nothing *n*ayabout. You don't produce, just want to be s*n*aves!" Eventually he turned to the visitors. "Wait here, all of you. Transportation will arrive shortly from the Cooperative. Anyone who disobeys the order will have their visit revoked." Soon, another buffalo cart arrived, and everyone followed it to the booth outside the gate. Seated behind a bamboo-slat table was a security youth. Her travel companion, a woman perhaps three times his age, approached him. "Sir," she said timidly.

"Cut out that feudal crap," he snapped at her.

"Dear brother . . ."

"Who's your brother?"

"What am I supposed to call you?"

"Cadre. Reporting to cadre. *N*et me hear it."

At this camp, among strange faces, were a few old ones. Bee was one of those in the opposite row. He invited me over to his cot after his family visit. We all suffered from hunger, so hungry even salt tasted like sugar on rare occasions. Yet whenever he had found something edible other than our regular meals, he would share with me.

"Eat!" Bee said, grinning, "so we won't look like a beggar on the day we return home."

"Beggar, huh?" I said. "We already are."

"My wife told me this man came to her neighbor's door. The son called out to his mother, 'There's a beggar at the door.' That poor fellow was his father, just released from a camp in the South. At least he wasn't interned in the North like us. That'd be worse than looking like a beggar, wouldn't it?"

Bee's cot neighbor joined us. He was a fortunate one, who had received permission to stay overnight with his wife the night before. After looking around, he lowered his head and spoke in a whisper.

"My wife's father, a former high school teacher, now pedaled a cycle to earn a living. In fact, he rented it from someone else when he took a break to rest. All the gasoline automobiles were seized by the State, and the gasoline ration cards were given only to their cadres. So, our people had no choice but sell their scooters to them at a cheap price."

Bee looked at the man and grinned. "How was the joy room with the wife? None of us here are progressive enough to receive such honor."

The man appeared evasive as he kept his eyes downward. I did not think he was a snitch; he could be obsequious, or a stickler for the rules. "The camp did try to protect my wife's respectability," he said meekly. "They issued a certificate stating that she has stayed overnight with me, the husband. So, in case she becomes pregnant, she'll have proof that her pregnancy isn't the result of adultery."

Bee and I looked at each other. In fact, I did not know what to think.

The man lit a cigarette and spoke evenly with smoke veiling his face. "My wife can't teach anymore. But she makes ends meet by selling knickknacks at the flea market. She said she knew others not as fortunate, who sold their bodies, and some of the husbands became pimps for their own wives." He nodded as I felt squeamish. "You know what's really abhorrent? More and more women become prostitutes while the younger ones, much younger, like your teenage daughter, earn their money by letting men fondle them."

I thought the commies had accused the South of being a giant brothel. Could they blame the Americans now for having corrupted their conquered South?

The border war was costly. Rumors had it that the North had suffered heavy casualties during the first wave of the Chinese massive assault. Most border towns were demolished, and civilian death tolls were staggering. Shortly after, we noticed our food paucity; even the camp guards griped about it. For us, we were helpless, but the guards had found a way to improve their rationed food: They looted several inmates' visiting families on their way to the camp. The victims later complained to their husbands that they were stopped on the only trail to the camp. However, the looting news angered many inmates, especially those who were on the visitation list.

I ran into Mr. Thạch that afternoon. He was coming back from his gardening duty to his shack next to mine. I had wished, when we were transferred from Cổng Trời, that we would once again be shack mates. Now I asked him if he had heard about the looting. "No, Brother Khang," he said. "My turn will come next time. Please drop by tonight. We have much to chat about."

That evening, I shared the water pipe with Mr. Thạch. We had an hour to reminisce before the curfew. In the scented smoke, Mr. Thạch told me that his only nephew was killed when the Chinese army swarmed the border.

"He was only nineteen," said Mr. Thạch. "The only boy in the family."

I said I was sorry. Mr. Thạch seemed lost in thought. "Was he in the army?" I asked.

"He was part of the outfit guarding Hà Giang border when the Chinese tanks crashed through. They overran the frontline outposts and moved farther south, annihilating everything in their way, including Cổng Trời camp."

"So, what's the situation now? Aren't we affected in some way?"

"At least we're not getting killed." Mr. Thạch handed me the pipe while he sipped at the tea. "Those found to be pro-Chinese were murdered. Many of them were dumped into the river. The number wasn't small."

I understood. With their two-decade old relationship, solid throughout the years, the pro-Chinese elements living on Vietnamese soil were a large number. I remembered the talk with Mr. Liên while we were still at Cổng Trời. He believed that it would be a limited war because Russia was still a staunch ally of Vietnam. I asked Mr. Thạch that.

"Even with the backing of Russia," Mr. Thạch said, "it's costly for Vietnam to go head-to-head against China. As you know, Brother Khang, China had had troops stationed in North Vietnam as far back as the Vietnam War against the Americans. The Chinese knew our strategic geography inside out. Our Defense Department even had military maps printed in China. Worse, there were pro-Chinese personnel in our military. What worked against Vietnam was the current armed conflict with Cambodia, who are an ally of China. Vietnam has committed several combat divisions in Cambodia. So, they were bogged down and became vulnerable in the North against China. Despite overwhelming losses on both sides, they both claimed victory. You know them, Brother Khang. They're lie inventors with bad intention."

I could not help visualizing the abandoned towns, many of them ruined; how many ghost towns awaited the returning inhabitants to rebuild their lives?

Then Tết, our Lunar New Year, came.

In mid-February the cold was bitter. At night, we would take turns to feed firewood into the metal drum in the center of our shack. More than ever now, I hated the sound of the gong at first light.

On the 29th, the chief warden gathered all the shack leaders in his office. Soon our shack leader came back and told us the camp would grant us the opportunity to use our own money to purchase pastries, candies, and wild tobacco so we could enjoy a memorable Tết. However, we took some time to discuss among ourselves and eventually agreed to use our money to buy fresh manioc tubers. We calculated the current market price of manioc and concluded that each of us would receive five kilograms. Starch would last in our stomachs much longer than pastry sugar. Then, each shack leader reported the decision back to the chief warden.

Our shack leader returned gloomily. He had gotten a tongue-lashing from the chief. The chief had said to him, "You all claim to be the intellectuals. Let's start with that. You must have known that Tết is our celebrated tradition for centuries. Each family, regardless of how poor it might be, will save up to have a meaningful Tết for its children. Now, you are the children of the Revolution. The Revolution is obligated to care for you on behalf of the Party's clemency and the People's forgiveness. The Tết celebration is for you, and the camp is here to help you celebrate it in the most meaningful way. When you think of Tết, you think of savory bánh chưng with pickled onions, leeks, and cabbage. You think of red *gấc* sticky rice and roasted melon seeds and candied tamarind. That is why the camp allowed you to buy these traditional edibles, so you can have a festive time while enjoying your delicious food. Instead, you malign the Revolution by asking it to buy manioc tubers with your money. Manioc to celebrate Tết! Indirectly you condemn the Revolution for having starved you. It is the damnedest insult to the Revolution. All other shacks honor and are grateful to the Revolution for its benevolence. Only your shack is anti-Revolution. Therefore, your privilege is rescinded."

On New Year's Eve, Mr. Thạch and I shared our Tết bánh chưng and drank tea that Mr. Thạch brewed in one of our *goz* cans.

Someone in Mr. Thạch's shack was playing a guitar. It was one of my favorite songs: "Mama, I'm Not Coming Home This New Year." We sipped at our tea. I kept my chin pressed against my chest. I was not sure if Mr. Thạch appreciated the song, especially its lyrics. For us, the southerners, it was achingly nostalgic.

I was leaning against the wall below the barred window. A voice came through the window, "Brother, hey."

A guard whose boyish face was pressed against the bars. I rose to my feet. "Yes, sir cadre?"

"What's the name of that song?"

"'Mama, I'm Not Coming Home This New Year.'"

"You know the *n*yrics? I'm sure you do. Can you copy them down for me?"

"So, you like our 'Yellow Music'?"

"They make me cry. I *n*ike these songs very much. I can't stomach those revo*n*utionary songs. They're *n*ike cat's *meow* to my ears."

"You still have your mama back home, sir cadre?"

"Yes. I miss her very much. How *n*ong have you been here?"

"Five years."

"Me too. We're prisoners on the outside. They told us we could take home *n*eave every two years, then they cancelled it. You still have visitation and gifts every three months. I have none of those."

I thought of all the guards like him, wasting their youth in their duties to guard us in these miasmal backwoods. "You must hate us very much, sir cadre?"

"I don't hate anyone. You know what I wish for? No more reform camps, so I can go home again."

I left the shack. Outside, the air was cool. The youth guard was sitting with his back against the bamboo wall of the shack. He peered up.

"Were you listening in to our nonsense songs, sir cadre?" I asked him.

"I *n*ove them. We have none of these in the North."

"What's your name, sir cadre?"

"Khôi."

He had been sitting under the window. I thought of a boy being disciplined by his parents, sitting outside and listening in to his parents telling bedtime stories to his siblings. I lit a cigarette, my last, took a puff, and gave it to him.

"Why don't you sit down?" he said, the smoke curling up and smelling bitter in the cool air.

"It's near curfew, sir cadre."

"It's Saturday night. If you're here with me, they won't bother you."

I could imagine him sitting by himself, listening to the crowd inside chattering and reveling.

"A cup of coffee would be nice," I said, letting him have my cigarette for himself.

"We're not a*nn*owed while on duty." He peered up into the sky. It was a cloudless night, and all the stars came out. He turned to me. "Did you drink coffee in the South?"

"Yes, cadre. Men and women both. Especially the *café sữa đá*."

"Iced coffee?"

"Yes, with condensed milk or sugar."

"Where did you get enough sugar for them? Every day?"

"Comrade! We had sugar available for customers in every restaurant, every café. You can use it as much as you want."

"I don't be*n*ieve it."

I decided not to convince him. How could I? When you were born in the North, and under that Socialist regime where everything was rationed, you received two hundred grams of sugar every three months per person.

Someone in the shack was playing a guitar and sang "Vietnam Our Proud Nation."

He turned to me. "I *n*ove this song. So exhi*n*arating."

"It's from a Cuban song," I said, lying.

"I think it's Vietnamese. I know it is."

"Yes," I said in a subdued tone. "You know how it is."

He simply nodded.

After a while I asked him, pointing out the Milky Way, "You know what that is?" He shook his head. "That's the Milky Way, our home constellation."

"I know about it through the Zhinü and Niu*n*ang folktale."

His mind on science was limited to the tale of *The Cowherd and the Weaver Fairy*. I explained to him that the Milky Way galaxy encompassed our solar system. Though I was not convinced that he understood a single word I said, I went on to tell him our earth was part of the solar system that held nine planets together by its gravity: Mercury, Venus, Earth, Mars, Jupiter, Saturn, Uranus, Neptune, and Pluto, and that our planet system sat on an outer spiral arm of the Milky Way galaxy. He was quiet, seemingly absorbed in my explanation, while I directed his gaze to the Ursa Major, Ursa Minor, and the North Star. I asked him if he knew about the speed of light. He simply shook his head.

"The first light you see at dawn," I said, "reaches you from the sun, and it takes eight minutes to travel 150 million kilometers at the speed of 300 thousand kilometers per second."

"The *n*ight speed?" His eyes opened wide. "In one blink of an eye?"

"Yes." I craved a puff of cigarette; but he was keeping the cigarette close to his mouth, as he dreamily gazed at the night sky. "It'd take two-hundred-thousand years for light to go across our Milky Way."

"Two . . . two-hundred-thousand . . ." Stuttering, he shook his head.

"Many of those stars in the sky," I said, pointing toward the sky studded with glittering sand-like dots, "are no longer there as we're seeing them now. They were long gone hundreds of thousands of years ago. And it took that long for their lights to reach us."

"So, the sources of those *n*ights no *n*onger exist," he said with a nod. "The stars themselves."

"True. And if there've been new stars, their lights won't reach us for the next hundreds of thousands of years."

"We don't *n*ive that *n*ong," he said, giggling.

"That's a good thing. We've created more problems even with our short life spans on earth."

On New Year's Day, the camp personnel went from shack to shack to greet us and wish us the most productive new year, to prosper in the benign spirit of the Party and the State. Inmates would also be expected to tidy themselves up—their dwellings and their personal appearance. Every one of us received a haircut. The camp would kill two live pigs, and everyone would feast with meat. Meat signified holidays. The grander the holiday the larger the meat portion.

Mid-morning we donned our clean clothes and, with our fresh haircuts, filed into the meeting hall. The camp administrator, a major by rank, stepped onto the stage. Wearing a pith helmet and a black leather belt, he puffed his chest as he stood facing us. On his chest was pinned a ribbon of medals, all gleaming. He pulled out from his front shirt pocket a folded sheet of paper.

"My greetings to all of our cadres . . ."

I stood in one of the columns behind the five rows of the camp personnel, listening to his long greetings full of titles and empty saluting words, and I began closing my eyes and dropping my head to hide my disrespect.

When we left the meeting hall, it was an hour to noon. There was a volleyball match to take place before mealtime. A match that pitted our undernourished players against their camp guards.

I was crossing the courtyard when I heard an explosion. It came from the barbed-wire fence outside the gate. In the melee, I hurried towards the explosion location. The guards were surrounding the spot. Some of them ordered us to back off. Soon, I saw them carrying two bodies toward the infirmary. Left on the scene were two black pigs, all bloodied.

When the guards went past us, I felt a twinge in my gut. One of the victims was Khôi, the youth guard I knew. The night before we were sitting outside Mr. Thạch's shack, talking about stars and the galaxy. The other victim was one of our men, a former chief of Recruitment and Enlistment Center. Late that afternoon, we learned that Khôi had died; our man was badly injured but lived. Both of them had been tasked to take possession of the two live pigs brought to camp by the Rear Services. They were pulling the pigs along when they accidently stepped on a spot booby-trapped with a hand grenade, one of many spots laid with grenades and mines.

I had written down for him the lyrics of his favorite song "Mama, I'm Not Coming Home This New Year." I never forgot the words he said: that we inmates were prisoners on the inside, while he and his fellow youth guards were prisoners on the outside. He had never visited Saigon, our beloved South. His youth atrophied in the North. His soldier's pay, after the camp deduction of meals, clothing, even soaps and cigarettes, left him with a meager sum each year. It would have taken him a few years to save up to buy a train ticket home on home leave. It was true, now, that he would not be coming home the next new year.

The weather warmed in the month of May, and it was time to plant seed potatoes. Our team, and two others, trenched the field for days and then began planting those green-sprouted potatoes and then hilled them. Every day, going to the field, we followed a trail that skirted a creek, sometimes losing sight of it then finding it again coming out of the woodland. I often saw a little girl sitting in a dinghy watching us go by. The first time I saw her, she was resting against a large bundle of firewood in her tiny boat. Other times her boat was empty. I stopped and asked her, "What're you doing out here by yourself?"

"I collect firewood," she said in a small voice. I noticed she had pretty brown eyes with thick lashes as she shaded her eyes against the morning sun.

"To sell?"

"Yes, chú."

I could not help thinking of the little girl by the seaside. Hải Yến. They were of the same age. "How old are you?"

"I'm fifteen."

That took me by surprise. She was small for her age. Most of the youngsters I had seen in the North were undersized. I thought of the shortage of food, of rationed food, of the dearth of all necessities.

"How far do you have to go to find firewood?"

"Sometimes very deep into the woodland."

I looked at the tied bundle in her little boat, the short-handled, chipped-edge knife. "You cut those with that knife?"

"Yes, chú, but not today. It's windy today, so I don't have to cut, I just pick these branches off the ground."

Then August came with the sun's heat. We returned to the field to harvest potatoes and, with meals packed every day, stayed out until late in the afternoon. We spent several weeks harvesting potatoes. The field was green, topped with white flowers toward the end of the season. There was no place to hide from the heat. I wore a bucket hat and would rest periodically in a trench under the cool bushes.

One morning, on the way to the field, I saw the girl again. Her boat was empty.

"Are you on the way to get firewood?" I asked.

"Yes, chú." She looked away toward the potato field before the creek curved out of sight. "Will you be coming back this way at noon?"

"No. I'll stay in the field. Just rest during our meal break."

"Chú . . ."

She looked at me, seemingly lost for words.

I nodded at her. "What?"

"Can you give me, like, a dozen potatoes? I'll wait here at noon."

I thought quickly. That would require some way to hide them from the guard's watchful eyes. I nodded again. "I'll find a way." Already I thought of what to say to the guards if they caught me leaving the field.

"Chú . . ." The girl hesitated. "You can do whatever you want with me . . . in this boat."

My breath caught. Pained, I felt a shock hit me then pass. "Don't say that." I patted her on the head. "But I'll get you the potatoes." I turned to leave to catch up with my team. Then I turned back to look at her. "Have you let any of the men do that to you?"

She nodded. "Once, chú . . . last year, before I met you."

I hurried up the trail. I could hear the creek and felt how heavy my heart was.

That night I lay awake for a long time. My heart ached the moment I conjured up the image of the young girl with her little boat. Then I thought of Hải Yến, the seaside girl. How would my own daughter grow up to be a decent human being in this mucked-up society of debauchery? I could have asked the old monk Thanh Tâm, had he been in the same camp. But as we were transferred from Cổng Trời, I heard later that he and Father Ninh were moved to Cốc camp. It sat deep in the northwestern forest of Yên Bái, nested against the foot of the Hoàng Liên Sơn mountain range, a tail of the Himalayas. Someone who had been there before said flowering on that mountain range was the goldthread evergreen, and the mountain was known by the eponymous flower. I prayed for both of them after I learned about that camp. All year round it was cold and rainy, and in that austere habitat, as the locals put it, dogs ate rocks, chickens pecked dirt, and monkeys were languid like zombies.

There were things I would have enlightened myself about had I lived with *thầy* Thanh Tâm or Father Ninh.

It had rained every day, falling gently like ash, and the ground gave way to a slick surface so slimy that, when you walked, you had to grip it with all your toes, and still you slipped. In this kind of weather, we were sent out to clear the woods surrounding our camp for cultivation. During a break, one of my shack mates told me a ghost story. He was the one who had asked me if I wanted to join him to escape. I declined—after my failed escape and the punishments that came with it, I no longer had the heart for it. Under a lone dragon plum tree in the woods, my shack mate had buried his cache—dried rice, dried manioc tubers, salt—for his escape. On a moonless night before he made his escape, he dreamed of a girl who told him, "Abort your escape." Then, before she disappeared, he saw his cache unearthed, perhaps by wild animals, under the dragon plum tree. The next morning, on the way to his task, he stopped to inspect his cache. It was indeed lying scattered on the ground. Bad omen, he thought. And he decided to end his plan. We had gone on to clear the woods. The dragon plum was cut down that morning. We saw a coffin.

I had never seen ghosts of my fellow inmates at Cổng Trời camp; I wondered why none of them had warned me before my escape.

Every three months, the camp subjected us to a political study session. They called it a "nourishment lecture." The only saving grace for us was that we were exempted from labor that day.

On this morning, the lecturer, after expounding on the subject of How the Party and the State Successfully Achieved the Post-War Reform Program, asked a volunteer from the assembly to express his thoughts on how such a successful reform program was applied to the surrendered puppet lot.

Mr. Tân, the judge, stood up.

"I understand the Revolution," he said to the lecturer, "and how it was conceived, born, and evolved to eventually effect an all-encompassing change in the People's consciousness. That is all good, because we the People, feeble-minded, with a herdlike mentality, have been shepherded for centuries, first by the scholars, then by the military officers, and at last by the anti-intellectuals. That is all for the greater good. This class of agnostic anti-intellectuals fit perfectly in Friedrich Nietzsche's concept of 'Superhuman' as he opines about the *Übermensch* as a goal for humanity in his book *Thus Spoke Zarathustra*. I can't agree with him more. Where do we go from here? Allow me to quote Nietzsche's most famous aphorism: 'When you stare into the abyss, the abyss stares back.'"

The cadres stared raptly at the judge. I could imagine what the convoluted deduction had done to their minds. The lecturer said nothing, but the administrator raised his voice, "Come into my office after lunch. You will then write down every word you have just said and clarify the sources they came from."

As we filed out, Mr. Tân said out loud:

On the Tương River
There's a mountain demon
White clouds stand still, a recluse you become.

A warden walked up from behind and stopped him. "What was that you just mumbled about?"

Mr. Tân lowered his voice. "I was reciting Li Bai's poem, sir cadre."

"Who is he? Is he here? Writing reactionary poetry?"

"No, sir cadre. He was a Chinese poet who died 1,220 years ago."

"Do you rea*n*ize that you just vio*n*ated one of the camp rules: No foreign *n*anguage a*nn*owed for reading, writing, speaking?"

"I was speaking Vietnamese, sir cadre."

"Then why did I not understand even one word of what you were speaking?"

"Because it's our *Nho*, the ancient Vietnamese language adapted phonetically from the Chinese language."

"You are talking in riddles. Are you mocking me, your educator?"

"I apologize for offending you, my educator, one of the superhumans of our Revolution."

"Si*n*ence! Go back and write a self-criticism. Turn it in in the morning and we will work together to sort this out."

CHAPTER 8

Sơn La

Fall 1981–82

Come back. Even as a shadow, even as a dream.
—Euripides

Winter drew to an end and summer came. It made traveling to the camp easier for the wives, the mothers, and the daughters.

Far from home, I had bred a sense of severance and felt emotionally safe being an observer, a spectator of those who, most if not all of them women, the wives, the sisters, the mothers, had traveled the arduous roads only to see their loved ones and exchange a few words in the short span of time allowed.

As much as I felt fortunate for not subjecting myself to those heart-breaking visits, I still felt the angst on the day of visitation. To see them, the visitor and the visited, restrain themselves from crying, from hugging each other under the watchful eyes of the security cadres, I realized my own callosity, an emotion-guarding shield. At least I still felt for them. I still had a heart.

I had not received family gifts or visitation or letters for so long now, I felt as if I was persona non grata. But if I wrote letters home, what would I say in them?

After writing home several times, Bee had said to me, "Each time you write, it's like rewriting those letters you wrote before. Every letter from home reads exactly the same. She would say, 'We're all doing well, as well as the whole nation is progressing grandly to fulfill Uncle Hồ's wishes. A proud people is Vietnam; one unique nation is Vietnam. Everyone is eager and enthusiastic, and you should not be worried about us back home. Do you understand what I mean?' In my letter home, two pages long, one and a half of those is to praise the Way of the Party and the Revolution, so that after all the hyperbole your family knows that you're still alive. It's the only way your letter will be sent and received, and its sender won't end up in a penal cell. When my wife came to visit me the first time here in Sơn La, she said to me, 'My mother who came from the North and fled for the South in 1954 was grief-stricken when I told her that you're now in Sơn La. "My dear," said Mother to me, "that's a miasma of forests and mountains where you die of mysterious diseases. He's there now, consider yourself a widow."'"

The morning of the first visitations, I tagged along with Bee to the gate and already there was a casualty. A warden was wagging his finger at a middle-aged inmate who cringed like a shrimp. "You are smearing the State and the Party! How could you think such a lowly thought of our local authorities? They were starving your wife and your family back home? Go back to your shack and write a self-critique and turn it in after visitation hours. You have lost your visitation privilege this time."

Soon we found out that the man had brought with him a pouch of dried rice, the cooked rice that made up part of our ration, which he had saved up each week, air-dried, then stored inside a nylon bag. He told the guard who searched him that he intended to give the rice to his wife, to relieve their burden back home.

After visitation was over, I helped Bee carry his gifts back into the camp, stopping at the customs shack where the guards would go through every item ruthlessly.

Bee fidgeted. "I have one hundred đồng..."

I knew he meant the new currency. It was against the regulations that allowed detainees to receive only up to twenty đồng. Quickly, I said to him, "Give it to me."

He slipped me the rolled-up bills. Hiding behind the man waiting his turn I took off one of my wooden clogs and jammed the bills inside a slit I had made on the sole. Whoever passed through the gate would be searched. So, I waited my turn. I could hear the warden in charge from inside the customs shack. "Put all of the money you received in front of you on the table. All the letters you received will be read. All the money and non-foodstuffs will be secured under care of the camp. Hiding any of these mentioned items will result in disciplinary measures."

I avoided talking to Bee. He must be thinking of his wife and daughter leaving the camp to return to the South. Deep down I felt revolted against the visitation. No, I did not hate it. I hated the loss of human dignity when I saw Bee take off his hat before a cadre, standing erect when answering his questions, *yes, sir cadre, yes, I understand, sir cadre*, while his wife and his daughter looked on. I felt relieved that I was not one of them; nevertheless, I felt less than human.

I watched the guards open parcels, then inside them the carton containers, cloth pouches, jars, vials, and tin cans. They used a knife to poke, to slit, to cut them open to examine the contents. Once the warden nodded at an item, it passed. Otherwise, misery ensued for the recipients.

Bee gave some of his fresh money to one of our shack mates we trusted, a former ordnance officer, who was in a blacksmithing team who could work outside the camp, so he could buy from the market some soja beans and rock sugar. The fellow who slept next to Bee received among his family gifts a set of pajamas. After reading his wife's letter, he began fumbling along the pajamas' elastic waistband. He caught my attention. I watched him turn his back toward the door, hunch forward, the trousers in his lap, and pull something out of the trousers waist. Four new currency's bills. He shushed me as he caught me looking. That was forty đồng, each new đồng worth five hundred đồng of our old currency.

It was the first time my wife visited me.

She came alone, traveling with other women from the South. During that visit, I detected something different in my wife. No longer a fragile woman, she looked self-assertive and confident. She appeared calm when I told her that I still loved her, but it would be better for her not to wait for me. I made it clear that I was a prisoner without a sentence, and my unforeseen release was what she must consider for our marriage. I put such a decision on her. It was also a decision I made perhaps out of unselfishness, or perhaps out of hopelessness.

We had half an hour with each other in the visitation shack. She was dressed in a peach-yellow blouse and black cotton pants. She looked fresh. This was not the fresh innocence I used to see six years before; but in her eyes I saw distraction. I reached for her hand. Startled, she withdrew it. My hand, gnarled and scarred, must have shocked her. She looked away. She was aloof; I sensed distance between us. We still had time when she rose from the table.

"I must head back," she said. "I don't want to be late for the train."

"Of course," I said and rose to my feet.

"There's something I must ask you." She drew a deep breath. "Will you agree to sign the paper to approve for our daughter to go to America with me?"

That gave me pause. I cleared my throat. "By yourself?"

"Yes, *anh*."

Our daughter was six years old now. I had not seen her growing up. In that brief visit, I had had barely the time to visualize her from bits of description my wife gave me. I nodded, despite the hollowness in me.

"Just send me the paper after you get back home," I said.

I bade her farewell outside the visitation shack and headed back to my own, carrying with me a sack of visitation gifts. She had brought me some money to spend, which I registered with a cadre in the visitation shack, who tallied it up to add to the sum I had registered with them upon my arrival here. I received a banknote as my receipt when my money went to the camp's bursary.

Outside the shack, after my wife was gone, I saw Bee. It was his third family visit. This time his wife brought along their young daughter. Bee said she was seven years old. I thought of my daughter and tried to picture her. Nothing came to my mind. Bee's little girl had been shy at first, from not knowing him after all these years. She hid behind his wife, peeking out at him. Was that man her father? I had such a thought, imagining if my daughter were here. We were no longer young, though we might have thought we were. Such a travesty of youth.

I waited for Bee until his family left. We walked back together, each with a gift bundle in his arms. At my quiet, Bee broke the silence.

"Do you have a male cousin?"

I turned to look at him. "A few. But none was in the army or in the same line of work as me. Why?"

He shrugged. I felt curious. Then he said, glancing at me. "I saw your wife coming in with a man. I thought he was one of your relatives. Someone to escort her to the North for her safety?"

The hollowness suddenly came back in me. I held my breath, said nothing.

"I thought you knew," Bee said.

"She didn't tell me." Now I thought back on her distraction, the distant look in her eyes. She had spent only half the time we were allowed to spend between us. "Was he waiting outside?"

"Of course."

I did not press him further. There was no need. Yet deep inside I wanted to know about his age and, perhaps, what he looked like. Was I deceiving myself after all? Why did I tell her to start a new life because of my unforeseen future, then feel sorry for myself when she did just that? There was truth to any paradox, I thought. And mine told me I was still very much attached to her.

In our shack, there were a few people who had just returned from the visitation. They were bubbling with small talk as they went through their gifts. I removed items from my sack and lay them on the cot. Three foil-wrapped, cooked rice balls. A large jar filled with salted pork, capped and sealed. A jar of salted ground sesame. A bundle of bananas beginning to ripen. A dozen packets of ramen. A vial of vitamin B and a vial of antibiotics. Three bars of soap. I sat and looked at them without registering them in my head. The hollowness did not go away. Was the man Bee saw an overseas Vietnamese? That might explain her request to have my daughter emigrate with her to America.

There were more people coming into the shack. Most of them had had no visitation for a long time. I watched them make their way to their cots, then I called them over. I decided to keep only the vials of vitamin B, the antibiotics and the bars of soap. I gave my shack mates the rest. I caught Bee looking at me. The second time I glanced his way he was shaking his head.

That night, Bee asked me if I wanted to hear a poem he had just composed in his head. "Not yet complete," he said. I knew his composition routine by now. He would keep adding and recalling the new verses until satisfied.

"Read to me," I said.

He turned on his side toward me, his voice dropped:

I am whitewashed of my past
and crippled for my future.

I grinned at him. "Aren't we all, brother?"

He, too, grinned and lay on his back gazing at the ceiling.

Our warden, Hưng, was a decent man. He was a lieutenant. The first time he led a surprise search of our shack, he found the Mala beads Bee wore around his neck. He said to Bee, "Hide it. Don't let them see it." I assumed that warden Hưng must be Buddhist, and one of the northern males conscripted into the army. He was not a trained communist. Later, Bee found a way to ask him how long we the inmates would have to endure the reform program before being released. Warden Hưng said, "It is not reform program you're in. It's prison. Stay well. So you don't die."

I asked him, "Why'd you sympathize with us? Because you also have a hard life here?"

"Maybe a little better than you . . . We all have uneven lives."

"I've heard all the communists are equal—no class discrimination."

"No, you're wrong," said he. His timbre seemed to have lost its familiar baritone. "They're worse than our former feudalists. You mentioned class discrimination. Their Ministry of Education in the South just issued a communiqué. It said, 'All high school students of the South, whose parents were former employees of the Second Republic, or combating soldiers of the *ngụy* army, are denied university matriculation . . .'"

I cut in. "I can't believe it."

He dropped his gaze, said nothing. This retardation of academic learning, I thought, brought back memories of the French colonial days. In fact, to the communists, the goodness in humans is a phenomenon; but the evil in humans is nature.

Mornings when we had a boiled manioc tuber for breakfast before heading out to the labor site, Warden Hưng would tell our team leader, with his permission, to bring us extra manioc tubers from the kitchen. "Have a stomach full," he said to us, "so you can last the whole morning." We agreed among ourselves that any northerners who had an opportunity to live in the South would likely have their thinking changed about their own regime in the North. Warden Hưng had spent a year in the South at one of the reform camps before being recalled. Once he knew some of us well—I was one of them—Warden Hưng would share some of his anecdotes. One of them was a revealing account of an army doctor ranking major who was head of Hải Phòng Hospital, where he had worked his way up as a nurse. After 1975, he traveled to the South and supervised all the infirmaries of an inter-camp network.

Hearing his story, I could imagine the time I had spent at the nameless camp in the South. I could have told him how pitiful the infirmary was concerning medical supplies, knowledge, and practice. Then warden Hưng said, "I was a warden at one of those camps and I knew him well. He had appendicitis and was taken to our Thống Nhất Hospital in Saigon. That's the new hospital with high standards reserved only for the Party's dignitaries and high-ranking cadres. But he requested to be treated at Grall Hospital. That's your South's old hospital. His request was denied. The Party would not lose face to have its own senior cadres treated by the former *ngụy* doctors. I caught news of his deteriorating condition, so I went to Saigon to visit him. He had a post-surgery infection. In his own words, he said to me, 'How complicated can it be to perform an appendectomy?'"

Then warden Hưng was gone for three months. I ran into him on the day he returned. He looked at me. I could see something had struck him. "Is that you, Brother Khang?" he asked.

"Yes, sir cadre," I said. "It's me."

"Your face . . . it's changed. Did you gain some weight?"

"No." I shrugged. "Sir cadre, we've been on the manioc diet for several months since you left. Every one of us looks this way, thanks to the Revolution."

He should have seen us shaping the manioc paste into round balls or conical-shaped lumps, wrapping them in banana leaves and boiling them. But a monkey was a monkey regardless of how you tried to alter its appearance. Our taste buds eventually became dead after having eaten manioc tubers for months until our faces all had that mumps-swelling look.

I mentioned to him the auspicious news that we the inmates were now allowed to read the *People Daily*. Its front page frequently ran big-headlined articles heralding the successful spring and summer crops. It lauded the co-ops that had exceeded the State's expectations in the recent harvests. Warden Hưng had a subdued look as he listened.

"Sir cadre," I said, "At this rate of plentiful crops, the State might be hard pressed to come up with enough granaries to store them, unless it finds a way to export the excess of crops."

I believed he could read my feigned concern and the slight mocking tone. He dropped his gaze, then quickly glanced up at me. "Brother Khang," he said, one of his eyes twitching, "On behalf of the State and the Party, I thank you for your concern. But rest assured that everything said in the newspaper is correct. Well, at least about the address of the newspaper's office."

The last time I saw Warden Hưng was on the day he asked me if I wanted to trade my ramen packets—six of them—for his three bundles of fresh-water spinach. I thought he craved dried noodles and asked him that.

"No," he said, "it's for my trip. It's more convenient to bring dry food."

"Are you on home leave, sir cadre?"

"No, it's a task." He went on to tell me that the inter-camp network had pooled the personnel resource from various sub-camps to go to nearby towns, where they would spy on arrivals at the bus station, train station, following a prisoner escape from a neighboring camp. "We receive fresh-water spinach which we have to dry to make it last longer. Then salt and rice for the road. I only eat my meals when nobody's around. At the market, I feel ill at ease when I see people eat in the food stalls."

"Don't you receive dry provisions, sir cadre?"

"Dry dung?" He grinned.

After that day I did not see Warden Hưng return. He must have been transferred.

Warden Hưng's replacement was a war veteran from B Front—our South. His name was Thái. He joined the Viet Minh at the age of sixteen as a true proletariat—the *bần cố nông* class of tenant farmers, destitute laborers. All his life he must have asked himself, "Why am I so poor? Why am I illiterate?" Eventually the answer came to him from the Party. "The poverty and misery that you, the People, have suffered at the hands of the American imperialists can only be lifted if you rise up as proletarian to end all imperialism." In the jungles in the South—the B Front—living in a waystation, he had been tasked to dig graves and bury the dead. His youth, then his adulthood, was married to the jungles, ostracized from civilization. Then came the North's victory over the South, a magnificent event that restored him from subhuman to human.

My firsthand experience of his unmerciful handling of his subordinates came on a day of scorching heat. We were building trellises for bottle gourds. One of the guards had retreated into the tree shade when Warden Thái appeared out of nowhere.

"Get out of that shade!" he yelled at the guard. "A Revolution's soldier like you shied away from sunlight?"

The next day was just as hot. We went into the patch of climbing vine where the smooth-skin green gourds dangled on the trellises. On the ground, amaranth grew wild, maroon-stemmed and crimson-bright leaves. While I plucked a handful of the leafy vegetable, Bee ducked under a trellis. I could hear him urinating.

"What were you doing in there?" came the shrill voice of Warden Thái.

Startled, I looked up. He was peering into the harbored shade of the trellises.

"I was relieving myself, sir," said Bee as he came out.

The warden bent to enter the trellis. On a piece of soiled brown paper, he spotted some scribbles. He dropped his head to look closer. He sprung around. "What the devil! Oh devil! How dare you write those blasphemous words!"

Bee turned to look. So did I. *Foxy Hồ the red devil!* The Vietnamese associate "hồ," among various meanings, with "hồ ly tinh"—huli jing—a fox spirit, which originates from animal deities, having nine tails, and can shapeshift into, or possess, young women.

"Not me, sir," Bee said, shaking his head vehemently. "I only went in to pee."

"Urinate, not pee," Warden Thái barked out. "And you were a journalist in your former life?"

"Yes—"

"You lowlife reactionary! I'm going to have a session with your team leader, and we'll see to it that you shall be properly disciplined."

Bee only had to write a self-critique to correct his wrong thoughts. But it had only taken one such incident to unleash Warden Thái's wrath on him.

Not far from our work site was a hillock rising in the middle of a stubbled field. The corn stalks of the past season had yellowed, and grass now grew wildly. There were no shade trees and the field lay bright, shimmering. Every time I looked toward it, the cowherd and the tawny cow, old and gaunt, were always together, the man following the cow slowly, sometimes leaning on it for support. He wore a prosthetic leg from the knee down.

Âu was about my age. He was tall and had a fine nose, a rarity among us. When he talked to me, his eyes never shifted, and when he listened, he had complete focus.

"Why did they send you to the North?" I once asked him. "You were only a lieutenant."

"I was with Political Warfare, Brother Khang." He smiled as if he were still on our southern soil and telling someone who he was.

"But you're an amputee."

"Political Warfare accepts no foe who has lost his limbs. It sees you as a potential convert. It uses you to heighten the sense of humiliation. Brother Khang, it's ferociously pragmatic."

I had seen him pushing a cart with the guards to a local commune, where they exchanged the whole cart of fresh manioc tubers for a cow. He was tending the gaunt looking cow. It had come from a herd of seven cows, and that put the family who owned them in the category of small bourgeoisie. Six of those cows were sold to the State at a giveaway price.

Hearing it only confirmed what I had known. There were less fortunate people around you, I thought. But these were not whom the communists always cited they served. I could relate to the real people; however, the communists' people-worshipping collective was Death itself. On its behalf, the Revolution and the Party sentenced you, executed you, robbed you with unchallenged power.

One day I saw Âu limping on a stick along the cow. I found a way to approach him during the noon break. I could hear in the quiet the cow pulling the stalks with its teeth; I could see its jaw slowly cycling, its eyes dull and empty. I looked at him standing with his weight bearing down on the bamboo stick.

"Why the stick?" I did not notice anything unusual about him, except his face was tired, sweaty.

"It helps me walk," he said. "I gave up my artificial leg."

I frowned. "What's wrong with it?"

"Nothing. Warden Thái told me that I owed the people a blood debt, and to pay for it, I must return my prosthetic leg to the camp. But the Revolution was benevolent and granted me an opportunity to make a crutch for myself."

Anger rose in me. The gong sounded and I hurried back to join my team. We continued to work until the gong sounded again for quitting time. It was late in the afternoon and, as shadows spread across the field, it felt cool to sit for a breather under the trellises. I saw two guards conversing with Warden Thái. One of them pointed toward us, sitting on the grass, waiting for roll call. Warden Thái approached us.

"Empty your sacks onto the grass," Warden Thái said, looking down at us.

We obeyed his order. One of the men did not lift his face the moment he poured out the contents of his sack. Besides his *goz* can, there were slices of a bottle gourd, white-fleshed and green-skinned.

"Empty your can," Warden Thái said again.

We did. Mine had a wad of amaranth; the same man emptied his *goz* can and out came chunks of bottle gourd.

Warden Thái took time to count the slices. He ordered us to rise. "Put a slice between your teeth—not in your mouth. Do not drop it. Move out!"

We walked single file back to the camp. I clenched my teeth to keep my slice from falling. Soon spit dripped freely from my mouth. We kept walking, none of us raising his head. I felt gazes as we entered the camp.

I learned from Âu that he came from a town in Sóc Trăng. I told him I'd spent almost two years in a nearby camp before being transferred to the North. That day I visited him in our sick bay. He had been admitted there because of some abnormal swelling of the abdomen. He lay on a cot that had a mosquito netting. I could tell that he was suffering. His abdomen looked unusually distended; his eyes jaundiced. I asked the nurse if his urine was yellow, and the nurse nodded. Over the years, I had seen many sick people and shared with them a slew of horror stories. I had a notion. It was not good for him.

Dr. Đàm came in later that day, because no one in the infirmary knew how to treat Âu. When I returned from the afternoon labor, I stopped by and Dr. Đàm was still there. I looked at Âu. He held down his suffering well, though his face was contorted in pain. The bamboo stick lay on the floor; earlier when I had stopped by it had been leaning against the head of the cot.

"What ails him?" I asked Dr. Đàm.

"Hepatitis," he said as he had just finished his round of checking on the other four patients. He glanced at Âu. "Swelling goes to his legs now."

"Will he live, sir?"

Dr. Đàm looked away. Then he shook his head.

Two days later Âu died. The coffin that came from the carpentry shack reminded me of those I used to make with Mr. Bìm at Cổng Trời. The wood planks were thin, having been salvaged from dilapidated shacks. Our shack leader, out of his kindness, consulted a monk among our inmates for a good day to bury the dead. There were no good days for the remainder of the week; so, we picked the next day, the least star-crossed. Also reclaimed was a sandbag which we used to wrap his body in after dressing him in a fresh camp outfit, without the black-inked "CT" stamped on the back of the shirt. I avoided looking at his stump. I helped by cushioning his head with his old shirt to make him more at rest. Our shack leader removed Âu's wedding ring and put it in an envelope to register with the camp. That night, I followed the "progressive cart" to the graveyard behind the camp. The diggers had a hard time digging a deep hole in the rock-filled ground. It was a shallow grave.

Later, our shack leader asked me to write to his family, using the return address on the gift parcel still unclaimed in the security office.

Dr. Đàm was no stranger to the penal cell. He himself had a first taste of it two years before at Cổng Trời. His trouble with the camp stemmed from the cash he had hoarded, gifted by his wife on a few alimentary visits. As they harassed him, Warden Thái pulled out a book from my haversack. He knitted his brows. *Under the Party's Glorious Flag* by Lê Duẩn, secretary-general of the Central Committee of the Communist Party.

"Where did you get this book from?" he asked.

"I borrowed it from our library," I said.

"What is your intention?"

"I wanted to know more about the Party and the Revolution."

"So you can find ways to be more anti-revolutionary?"

"Absolutely not, sir cadre."

"When you finish it, discuss it with me."

"Absolutely, sir cadre." I was certain that whatever topics I would be discoursing with him were beyond his grasp.

That Sunday, the camp showed a movie. Everyone was expected to attend. We watched *Điện Biên Phủ Victory*. It was not purely for entertainment, because afterward each of us was to write a paper expressing his thoughts about the Revolution's magnificent triumph. The following Sunday we reconvened to hear critique from the proctor committee.

Each team warden took their turn to read out loud the expositions which favored their views. I listened. They all sounded the same, unilateral and submissive. Then Warden Thái took the stage. He held a sheet of paper in one hand and brought the megaphone to his mouth with the other.

"Brother Lau, please stand up," he said, scanning the audience.

Bee rose. I sat next to him. My gut told me the spiteful warden must have something for Bee after the incident in the trellises. Warden Thái gave the audience enough time to take in the candidate he picked to praise, then motioned for Bee to sit down.

"In light of our Điện Biên Phủ victory over the French colonists, Brother Lau contributed to such a colossal achievement with his analysis of the *ngụy* regime of the South, that enlightens us on why it collapsed. Let's start with the South's military officers when the Americans entered the South. Who were they?" He paused and moved his gaze across the audience. "They were native guards and colonial infantry soldiers. Many were reserved non-commissioned officers for the French. All of them failed high school or fell for the better pay by the French. The French needed a native army, as a reserve force to maintain law and order, and did not hesitate to promote ranks as bait to lure our people. These people rose to the ranks of general by seniority. None earned their ranks by combat merit. Their military junta, after having killed their master Ngô Đình Diệm, fought one another for power. These same generals, after the death of their boss, divided his slush fund of seventeen million đồng among themselves."

Warden Thái nodded toward Bee. "On behalf of the Party and the State, I salute you, Brother Lau, for your honest assessment of your former *ngụy* military leaders. It only confirms what the Party has said all along: 'Their generals are replicates of their American master. Just paper tigers.'"

Astonished, I looked at Bee. I could feel the wrath in the crowd, especially from our former generals. I could not believe he wrote such a demeaning critique. I thought I knew him, but this troubled me. Then Bee raised his hand.

"Sir warden," Bee said, "may I have your permission to speak to our friends here about the significance of winning back our independence? It's not so much about the movie, despite its historical value, it's the implication of how the French had our nation under its thumb for so long."

A puzzled look passed over the warden's face but quickly he said, "Permission granted."

Bee slightly bowed his head. "Thank you, sir warden." He turned and let his eyes drift across the faces in the assembly. "Tonight, we're supposed to hear praise for the *Điện Biên Phủ Victory* movie. But alas, before we call such an event a historical masterpiece, does any one of us here tonight have any knowledge of what had failed our nation for so long?"

At the blank looks from the crowd, the warden gestured with his hand toward Bee. "Speak."

"Let me tell you an anecdote," Bee said. "In the South where I was born and raised, we had crops of all kinds. My father raised corn. One year we had a new enemy. Marauding monkeys had raided our corn field. My father trapped them and captured several monkeys. He proceeded to shave each monkey's head, then painted their heads and faces red, black, and yellow. Then he set them free. Those monkeys ran back into the jungle. They sought out their troops. But none were welcomed back. Eventually, if they kept after their old tribes, the leaders of the troupes would kill them." He stopped. I tried to process his story just as he continued. "So, you see, the French were able to rule our country by the same tactics. They divided and conquered. They pitted Christianity against Buddhism, French-trained natives against deep-rooted natives. Such shenanigan is used everywhere by rulers over their captives. They tell half the story to one side and the other half to the other side, then sit back and watch you ruin one another. To heal such division, you shall need another *Điện Biên Phủ* to dispose of the ruler. Otherwise, my dear friends, we shall be those painted monkeys in human form."

Blank faces stared at him, then at the warden. Then heads nodded. I began to get the gist of Bee's story. There might be more from Bee's paper than Warden Thái had wanted us to hear. Some quick-witted cadres might not be satisfied with Bee's metaphor, but Warden Thái appeared to take it at face value.

We went back to our shack. I kept quiet as I walked alongside him. He looked unperturbed. "Let's have some tea," he said, as we arrived at our shack.

I sat down on the edge of his cot while he heated water in his *goz* can. Then my cot neighbor came over. Cung was a former major of the airborne division, a colonial French-trained paratrooper who jumped into Điện Biên Phủ in 1954. He watched Bee blowing the twigs into flames then said, "Is it true what the warden read to us?"

Bee nodded without looking up. The fire caught. The flames rose licking the bottom of the *goz* can. He signaled for me to get his tea pouch. We sat and watched him. After he dropped a pinch of tea leaves into the *goz*, he said, "That's half of what I wrote. The other half he would never want us to hear."

The major nodded. "I had such an inkling after listening to what you had to say to the audience."

"Tell us the other half," I said.

Bee sat cross-legged on the floor. The cement floor was cool during the day, but ice cold at night. "Our best crop was the middle-ranking officers. Like you." He nodded at the former major. "Those were well trained, well-schooled officers. They were the true patriots. They weren't leftovers from the French colonial days. If we needed another Điện Biên Phủ, we'd need those elements. We also need to wrest control of the Party from China's dominance, and we need a free economy to build an independent nation. Then we won't need another Điện Biên Phủ."

The major listened attentively. Then he said, "President Diệm was our strongman. His Strategic Hamlet Program was a thorn in the side of the communists. Those we captured during the war told us that the coup d'etat in 1963, that had President Diệm killed, was a heaven-sent gift to the communists. But you were right. Several of our former generals were inept. They were gutless when they ordered the termination of Diệm and his brother Nhu. They feared reprisal had he been saved by the Americans." He fished out a much-bent cigarette from his shirt pocket. He lit it from the spurting flames under the *goz* can. "You might know who killed both Diệm and his brother. He was a captain. Our airborne unit carried out the mission to kill him. We beat him to death. Then we hung him. People thought he committed suicide."

That night I lay awake. May nothing serious happen to Bee. I kept that thought turning over and over in my mind, and the more I thought about the warden's shenanigans, the more I became aware of our vulnerability to their guile. If you confront them, you would be the egg hurled against a wall.

Then I thought back to the year President Diệm was killed.

At that time, I had been with the CIO barely a year. It was formed in 1961, signed by President Diệm, and I was recruited to the CIO in 1962 after graduating from the College of Science in Saigon. I was detailed to the Chiêu Hồi Program when it came into being in 1963. In my two-year stint with the program, I spent most of my time in the deep south, working with the program's newly formed propaganda offices. Most members in our section had a high school diploma, and the rest were college graduates. Our office reported directly to the Office of the President. The CIO had two sections: Study Section and Implementation Section. Study Section was in charge of the logistics as well as intelligence analysis; Implementation Section carried out the infiltration missions and espionage assignments.

It all began with the Viet Cong flyers showing up at local schools in early 1963, when I was in the Open Arms program. Then my Special Commissioner sent me to the deep south where the Viet Cong slowly encroached. Some nights I would watch barges pulling a string of sampans, covered with cajeput firewood, coming into the Hậu River, where the firewood was distributed to steam ships that went up and down the Mekong River. I acquainted myself with a number of locals who worked on those steam ships, and half of them were Viet Cong sympathizers. Some of them got sick and died during those long sea journeys, and their bodies were thrown overboard. I was not married then and spent most of my evenings in the town's cafés or at a movie house that showed more and more American movies with John Wayne or Charles Chaplin. Every day a buggy would come through town, sounding the drum to catch attention to its billboards featuring American actors, actresses, and a kid running alongside handing out the movie program printed with pictures and fancy words on green paper. There were many canals and creeks that brought to towns new faces, new lives among the old ones. I did not know where they came from and where they went. By the time I was able to take the pulse of those towns in the deep south, I knew most of those firewood dinghies carried arms and medical supplies to be stashed somewhere for the Viet Cong.

On that night, I could not sleep. Listening to the former major I felt nostalgic. My peaceful, fertile South. All ruined now because of the soulless communists. I thought of writing a letter to notify Âu's family of his death. It had been more than a week, and I could only blame myself for not making time to dash off just a letter. I lay awake. I wrote the letter in my head, expressing my condolences to his family. I kept it short so that in the morning I could simply write it down from memory.

We had a few ethnic Chinese inmates, and one of them in our shack was Mr. Zhao Fang.

A former wealthy merchant of rice in Cholon, the Chinese quarter of Saigon, he had back home a young and pretty wife—second wife. He told me his name, Zhao Fang, had a phonetic name in Vietnamese: Triệu Phương.

He was small in stature, pink-cheeked, with a white beard. Looking at him, I thought of Zhang Guolao, one of the eight immortals. I was very fond of him when I was growing up. One story my mother had read to me about him described him always riding a white mule, and the man and the mule would travel a thousand *li* a day; before night came, he would fold his mule up into a piece of paper and put it in his pocket. In the morning, before he set out, he sprinkled water on the inanimate mule and it woke and regained its form.

What Mr. Fang lacked in occult power he made up with his wealth, which afforded him a hassle-free life in the camp. Never complaining about his fate, he once said to me, "If you are still alive, you shall get another chance to start over." Coming from a tycoon like him, his words had ingrained in my mind like a morale booster.

He could deal with anyone. Easygoing yet reserved. If you carped on about someone, he would find some positives in that person to balance your view.

There was this Chinese businessman, Mr. Chou Ling, from Cholon, who was also a former rice dealer, and he had had his rice supply transported regularly into the Viet Cong sanctuaries. Still, after the North seized the South, they classified him as comprador bourgeoisie, the profitmaking bourgeoisie allied with foreign investors, multinational corporations, bankers, and military interests. They seized his assets and sent him to the reform camp. I had seen inmates trying to bum a cigarette from him only to be told, "It's my last cigarette."

He had a box of hard candies his wife brought him amongst many other items. He found a vial, and kept a half-sucked candy in it for the next time. Once, Mr. Ling did not cap it tight and ants came, and it was the only time he parted with his unfinished candy. Another time he dropped a small clump of white rice on the earthen floor, then picked it up and put it into his mouth. Someone said to him, "This floor is filthy." He nodded and said, "If eight hundred million Chinese each wastes a clump of rice, how many hungry people could you feed with eight hundred million clumps of rice?"

He collected the shrink-wraps from his ramen packets; he would flatten the wrappings and put them in his bag. Nobody knew what he saved them for. When a shack mate asked him to spare one of them for kindling wild tobacco, he said to him, "I am selfish by habit, but I am wise to respect my habit of following my nature." His daily job was to feed the pigs, and every morning you would see him, a bucket in hand, going from shack to shack asking for rice leftovers. None of us had enough to feed ourselves, much less to spare for the camp pigs.

One of our shack fellows had received from his wife a cotton facecloth, hand-sewn with two red hearts, one eclipsing the other. One day after an unannounced personal property search by the camp guards, he found out that his washcloth was gone. The shack leader asked everyone to comply with the camp's regulations by letting the man go through their personal items. He found it in the Chinese rice dealer's rucksack, who casually said to him, "It's mine. But I can cut it in half and you can have one half if that pleases you." Someone later called Mr. Ling a thief, a miser, and hearing that Mr. Fang said to me, "Better to be a thief than an informant; better to be miser than a usurer." He was not cynical in his insinuation of squealers, because we had had a handful of them among us and none of those snitches were Chinese.

Mr. Fang could read facial features as a physiognomist, as well as *Tử Vi Đẩu Số*—Destiny Astrology. I laughed when he said that Lê Duẩn, General Secretary of the Central Committee of the Communist Party of Vietnam, was born to become a butcher, literally; and truly, he was later responsible for the massive casualties of both sides in 1972 Easter Offensive, the Sino-Viet border war, and the Cambodia-Vietnam war.

At first, I thought what Mr. Fang shared with me about Lê Duẩn was historical facts I already knew. We were at that time in 1981. Then, one day, Mr. Fang read the natal chart of my neighbor shack mate. Cung was a former airborne major. There was an incident and afterward I felt bound to him with sympathy. One night not too long past, he received a packet of gifts from his wife. Back in our shack, he sat down on his cot and opened the packet. Inside were two cakes of brown sugar, one pouch of tobacco for hand-rolled cigarettes, and one jar of shrimp paste. One of the two sugar cakes had little nicks. Cung kept the nicked one and gave me the intact one. I thanked him profusely as he opened the pouch of tobacco, shook it, sniffed it. It was like gold amongst us. There was a white piece of paper peeking through the brown shreds. A much-folded piece of paper. Then we both knew that his wife had hidden her note in the pouch. He read the note. Afterward he sat slumped, shaking his head.

"What's wrong?" I asked him.

It took him a great effort to tell me that his wife had donated their house to the local authorities and took their three children, aged six to nine, to the train station and boarded down under a tree. Their abode was rigged up with sheets of corrugated iron, its entrance covered by a tarp, the dirt floor lined with burlaps taken from old military sandbags. There was a bamboo cot for her and their six-year-old son, the rest sleeping on the burlap-covered ground. She made ends meet during the day as a coolie, hauling firewood that the train brought in later to be distributed to retailers who would sell them to local wholesalers.

He stopped and picked up the nicked sugar cake. He gazed at the little nicks without saying a word. Finally, he said to me, "My youngest son gnawed at this while my wife wasn't around . . ." He could not say any more. He saved that brown-sugar cake and did not look at it for three days. One sultry afternoon, coming back from the field for lunch break, when the shack was cooking with high noon heat, he opened the packet and sat there dumbfounded. His brown-sugar cake had melted.

Now Mr. Fang offered Cung a cup of tea and waited until his guest drank it up. "I want to tell you what you might not wish to hear," Mr. Fang said to Cung in a neutral tone of voice. "Most, if not all, people only expect something good coming out of their charts. I have not seen anyone who came to hear something bad. I only speculate that I might be wrong in reading your chart and I would feel better if I am wrong. But according to your chart, you will not die in this camp or any other reform camp, not even at home."

Even the camp commander had consulted Mr. Fang on Destiny Astrology and Eastern Horoscope. Such study of planets correlating with human behaviors was deemed as fortune-telling and, thus, forbidden in the camp. Yet from the camp commander to the wardens, they were all anxious to know what destiny might hold for them, quite fitting with their worries about their regime's vagaries.

Mr. Fang was in a quandary for a few days. I asked him why he could not interpret the commander's natal chart. He shook his head in dismay. "This man won't live past his fortieth. I'm not Kong Ming. Even he would not be able to change this man's destiny."

Kong Ming was one of my favorite historical persons in the history of China. Those of us who read Chinese classics, knew of Zhuge Liang or Kong Ming. During the Three Kingdoms period, he served Liu Bei of the state of Shu Han as a military strategist. But his knowledge in astrology was what fascinated me—and millions of Asian admirers. A mathematical genius to whom supernatural powers such as controlling the wind and foretelling the future were ascribed, he was an expert in astronomy.

"Then tell him his future is rosy," I said, grinning. "That someday he'll be a major figure in Hanoi, chauffeured in a black Volga."

"I wish it was that uncomplicated."

"Or tell the truth. Then spend the next two weeks in an isolation cell."

Mr. Fang did not smile.

What I enjoyed immensely when drinking tea with Mr. Fang was relaxing while he recited *The Tale of Kiều* or *Lament of a Royal Concubine*, our two epic poems of the 19th and 18th centuries. I was one of a few fans of his repertoire of Vietnamese classic literature. Most men in the shack loved swashbuckling tales, especially those from Jin Yong's novels. But Mr. Fang didn't mind a small audience.

During a break from reciting *The Tale of Kiều*, Mr. Fang went back to his water pipe. He drew deeply on the water pipe when someone raised his voice. "Can you verify something for me?"

"What is something you wish for me to verify?" Mr. Fang peered up groggily.

"In the annals of our nation, we have this scholar named Mạc Đỉnh Chi. He was the intellectual at the age of twenty-four who scored the highest in the Imperial examination. When our king was officially crowned by the emperor Buyantu Khan of Yuan dynasty, he anointed Mạc Đỉnh Chi as envoy to China in order to pay respects to the Yuan emperor for the crowning. After the palace feast, Mạc Đỉnh Chi happened upon a tapestry in the hall. A sparrow perching on a bamboo branch. It was so real he reached out to touch the sparrow, but this made the Mongol officials roar with laughter. Quickly he ripped down the tapestry and tore it. He turned to meet the stunned faces, among them, the emperor's. He said, 'The sparrow represents a small-minded person; the bamboo symbolizes a nobleman. Do we wish to allow the former to be above the latter?' The Yuan emperor pondered. Before Mạc Đỉnh Chi returned home, he was bestowed with the highest honor: Scholar of the Yuan. Our annals recorded his dual title as 'Two-Nation Scholar.'" The man cleared his throat. "Mr. Fang, was this fact recorded in the Chinese history?"

Mr. Fang broke away from the pipe, blinked a few times. "It could be. But again, it could be removed by the Chinese Communist Party."

"Why?"

"They wouldn't wish to see you smarter than they are."

In the snickering, Mr. Fang resumed his smoking.

CHAPTER 9

Sơn La

Summer 1983–84

I am but mad north-north-west. When the wind is southerly, I know a hawk from a handsaw.
—William Shakespeare

The first time I noticed him was the night we all tossed and turned because of the sultry heat. A voice drawled across the shack. "Bless you if you were born with a father and a mother who were there to see you grow up. I wasn't born with a father. Never know him. Even Mother didn't know him. She only guessed that he must be one of the fishermen who bottom-fished, for the night she woke in her riverside shack somebody was on top of her. He smelled of mud and river silt, and he overpowered her until he satisfied his lust."

I ran into him again a day later. The meal break at noon was over, but there had been no sound of a gong to send us back out to the work sites where we harvested manioc tubers. Every one of us reform inmates stayed put in our shacks, listening. Then out on the baked courtyard appeared a man. Cao—our eccentric shack mate. He stood hatless, surveying the camp. No guards in the watchtower; not a soul in the camp's personnel quarters. "They've left." He raised his voice, heading toward our shack. "Let's pack our gear, gentlemen, and get ready to work for our transitional government. I'll assign tasks to each of you." We cringed. Someone stepped out and called to him, "Get back in here, you fool! They're due back soon."

I looked at Cao, who was still standing in the sun like a general, deluding himself into another reality—a reality where he was empowered to lead a new government. Was he really insane as many of us had thought?

Another day at noon, after my midday meal, I went outside to the latrine and saw Cao stalking the camp dog, the chief warden's dog. He had a broom in his hand, but he had stopped sweeping, man and dog moving silently across the bright courtyard. The dog had, in its jaw, a manioc tuber it must have picked up from the kitchen. Cao swung his broom and the dog slunk off, dropping the tuber on the ground. He picked up the tuber and sat down in the shade of a tree. I believed the tuber was what he was after. The dog was known to have eaten our human waste in the morning. But I had seen worse.

When I came out of the latrine, a warden was standing over Cao. He seemed impervious to the warden. I could hear him talking to himself. "Eagle, this is Tiger calling. Permission to bring down thunders. Level it. We take full responsibility. Over."

The warden raised his voice. "Who were you talking to?"

"Who else?" Cao did not even look up. "My artillery support. I've got the coordinates of this camp. You just watch."

The other inmates were coming out of their shacks for roll call before our afternoon labor trip. Cao pointed at them. "I know who you are. You disguised CIA goons!" The men looked off. He continued to rant. "I know you. You've been on CIA payroll since before 1975. You've been selling information to the CIA."

The warden grimaced. Just the word CIA startled them.

Cao slept three cots from mine. He dreaded water. The fellow next to him always complained about Cao's body odor. "You smell like a skunk!" Then every time afterward, Cao would wake up at midnight and ask his neighbor to go with him to wash themselves in the latrine where he had saved a bucket of fresh water. His neighbor had stopped bothering him ever since.

On this night, I woke to somebody's ringing laugh. Someone was cursing in the dark. "What were you laughing about?"

Cao's neighbor answered, "He's talking to himself. Come listen."

I remained on my cot. The shack was quiet, save the snoring. I could hear Cao speaking as if in a trance:

Down with Thiệu regime, but then we could buy anything every bit
Long live Hồ Chí Minh, now we can't buy a nail without a permit.

I was wary of some snitch in the shack. What else could the camp do with a man like Cao after having recurrently seen his cuckoo behaviors?

Cao droned on. "I told them their leaders are imbeciles and they locked me up in a reform camp for three years for being reactionary, and for indefinite detention for telling the truth."

A few days later, I happened upon him in the meeting hall. The afternoon heat quivered, and the camp was in siesta. He was alone in the dim, cool hall, his hands folded behind his back, gazing at Uncle Hồ's framed photograph on the wall. He saw me and asked casually, "How much does it cost, that picture?"

"It's not for sale," I said. "Not like those pocket pictures they sold in Saigon in seventy-five." Back then, the victor's Military Administrative Committee had issued a decree that every urban house hang a yellow-star red flag and Uncle's picture side by side.

"I know what his picture cost back then," he said, nodding. "I asked this woman vendor and she said 'Twenty piasters' and I said 'This tiny print? Why so expensive? A wee piece of crap paper with this goateed man? How about ten?' and she said 'Done. Take him away. I left my home in the North to go to the South just because of this goat, and now here he is again, right in the South!'"

Alarmed, I put a finger to my lips. "Tone it down!"

"There's nobody here," he said, grinning. His glasses glinted. "My wife visited me just last week. She told me a local security cadre came into our house to inspect our altar. He ordered her to put Uncle's picture on the top tier, which she'd always reserved for our ancestors. What did he say to her? 'Have any of these folks done anything more revolutionary, nobler and grander than Uncle? Why then is Uncle's picture on the lower tier? Re-arrange it to show your political attitude, your respect toward Uncle and the Revolution. I shall be back next week for re-inspection.' My wife pondered this quandary for a whole night. The next day, she put Uncle's picture on the top tier. She moved her parents' pictures—her father was denounced as a feudal landlord during Land Reform and buried alive; her mother died of grief—to the lower tier. But every night, she put this goateed man's picture in the kitchen near the chicken coop."

The more he talked, the more nervous I became. I cut him off. "What were you doing in here at this hour?"

"What are you?" he asked me.

"I thought it'd be cooler in here for a nap." Looking at him I did not detect anything out of sync; his faculties seemed sound. "Did your wife bring any good news from back home?"

"Yeah," he said, calm yet irked. "She hasn't been asked to move to the New Economic Zone. Not yet. But if your husband is in a reform camp and you have a house, they'll hound you until you move out of it. Like evicting a tenant. You see, everyone tries to keep a low profile now, down to their attire. No more bright, colorful garments. Just drab brown or gray. Like those in the North. If you're in the street, keep your head down, talk to no one. They also changed many street names to names they brought from where they came. I wish I had the time and means to look up their names. To see what each of them has done for this country and its people, so that I can show my respect properly without being tendentious."

I left the hall unsure what to think of his behavior.

One morning, I received a letter. My very first in all the years since my imprisonment. It was not from home. It was from Âu's family, written by his daughter. It had been nearly eight months since I sent them my letter on behalf of our team. She wrote:

> Dear chú,
>
> Ma said she could not answer to thank you for your condolences. I am writing for her. Ma cried when she first tried to write a letter. Dear chú, she said to me before Ba died, that we must save enough money to go to the North to visit Ba. We never had enough for the travel expenses. One family in our town did save up and eventually made the trip north to visit their father. But, chú ơi, when they got there he had died just a week before. I was so sad to hear the news. I could never imagine that for our family. I helped Ma every day to make ends meet. Ma got up very early in the morning to make dumplings so I could take them to the commune market to sell. I have been doing this since I was ten. I am sixteen now. Chú ơi, thank you for saying good things about my Ba. Ma said she was grateful from the bottom of her heart.

Something about the letter gave me pause. I felt touched by the tone of his daughter. But what kept me going back to the letter was her telling me about her daily life, and about how her mother and she tried to eke out a living. I kept the letter in my knapsack and reread it when I was in bed, using a borrowed lighter to make out the girl's small handwriting. Finally, I wrote back. I told her I was in Sóc Trăng eight years before, and I knew about the seaside there. As inmates, I told her, we were to bring the camp's produce to the local commune where we sold them and used the profit to buy necessary items the camp was lacking. I wished her and her mother well. In closing, I asked for her name.

At this camp, I was fortunate to see Mr. Liên again. Seeing him always reminded me of my late father. There were not many people of their generation left. Mr. Liên and Mr. Thạch and Dr. Đàm belonged to that endangered species.

Mr. Liên knew my wife had left me. He patted me on the back. "Well, it's been years now since that last moment of pleasure, huh? Have you missed it? Thrust and squeezed?"

I shook my head vehemently. "No! Can't even get a hit of wild tobacco and you're talking about *that*? Thrust-and-squeezed fairy tale!"

"Listen, those girls back home will wait for you and welcome you with open arms. They'll be willing to take ten years off your age. So how old will you be then? Still in your forties."

"They'll call me Uncle." I glanced at his silver-haired head. "What worries me is not age but morality, from young to old, Mr. Liên. They're all changed. Not for the better, mind you. Where I came from, back then, a criminal accused of a petty offense would deny it. They were ashamed of it. Now, look at those youths in the common-criminal camps. Depraved, foul-mouthed. They take pride in committing an offense and brag about it. The longer their stay in these camps, the worse they turn out to be."

Now Mr. Liên scratched his head. He studied his dirt-rimmed nails and began flicking at them with his thumb. "Son, you don't sound like you have a solution, do you? I've thought about it. Hunger leads to depravity. Build a society that can feed the people, then empathy and kindness will be aplenty."

"That's the ideal, Mr. Liên," I said then quickly looked around us. "It's a principle to which people aspire. Can it be done? I doubt it. What do you think happens when those cadres arrive in the South and witness firsthand its wealth? In the Mekong Delta, people even pounded rice to feed their pigs. Here in the North, people eat hog feed to stave off starvation. How'd those cadres react? Disillusioned! What'd they think? Damn the Party! All lies. They'll hurry to make up for what's kept them in poverty for many years, courtesy of the Party's lies. And whatever they do to enrich themselves, they claim they do it for the People, for the Revolution."

A frown pinched Mr. Liên's face. "Son, I agree with you. Saigon in no time will look like Hanoi. A slattern." He squinted at me behind his cigarette's smoke. "My daughter is about your age. A Hanoi girl. Prim and cultured. She'll be a good match for you. So just hold your bladder."

I listened to him, not certain if he was serious. The glow of his cigarette slowly dimmed in the dark. He coughed then said, "Want to hear a commie joke?"

I leaned over, whispered into his ear, "Keep it down, will you, Mr. Liên?"

We knew some snitches in our shack, but they were sleeping toward the other end of the room.

"So," he began, his voice phlegmy, "Nikita Khrushchev asks his advisor, 'Our Communist Party of the Soviet Union deems religion as opium. We persecuted Christian, Muslim, and Buddhist clergies. But we failed to take away their faith, while our comrades have shown little belief in our Party. Why?'

"His advisor said, 'Comrade First Secretary, the sole difference between us and them is the concept of Heaven. Marx and Lenin and you, Comrade Secretary-General, have drilled into our people this notion of communist heaven existing right here in the Soviet Union. But them, the religions we badger, place Heaven where it should be: Up there!'

"'What's wrong with that?'

"'Our people have had a taste of Heaven right here. Hunger, no bread. Freezing, no clothing. Those religious followers of other sects have kept their faiths alive, because none of them has ever been to Heaven.'"

In August our food supplies dwindled again.

So, when the camp, on the August Revolution Commemoration Day, announced there would be fresh meat for everyone come dinner, we were exalted. The day before, the camp sent a warden and four inmates to the local commune to buy a horse. They came back with a scruffy looking horse. It was a scrawny horse, so lean I could see its rib cage under its hide. Having been promised a meat feast in the past, I remembered the pigs and the death of the youth guard. But this time it would be horse meat. None of us had tasted horse meat, but we would welcome any type of meat.

Before noon, the team that brought back the horse led it to the courtyard. There, the horse was tethered to a pole. Unlike Cổng Trời, this camp had only one pole in the center of the court. It did not use the pole to bind an offender butterfly style; instead, the pole was almost exclusively for execution by firing squad.

I watched the horse stepping nervously back and forth. It must sense death, because its rheumy eyes looked sad. The crowd looked on nervously. The scene reminded me of a medieval execution: the arena our courtyard. One man wielding a sledgehammer walked up to the horse. He appeared lost. I must say that none of us had been a butcher in our former lives. Rather, we had been in slaughterhouses from camp to camp, and I empathized with the horse as if seeing my own self.

"Hit it," the warden yelled.

The man raised the sledgehammer and brought it down. The horse jerked its head to one side. The blow landed on his neck. It got skittish, jerked away from the pole only to be yanked back by the rope.

"Harder!" the warden commanded. "You're a man."

The man hit the horse again. I cringed. But the horse withstood the blow. The warden ordered another man to tie the horse's head to a stake, so it would not dodge.

"You have one more chance," the warden deadpanned.

The man swung the sledgehammer and crushed the horse's head with a solid thump. The animal slumped, forelegs crumbling under it. The warden motioned for one man to bring him a bamboo culm, one end diagonally cut into a spear-head. Another man quickly brought up a brass pan which he lay where the horse's neck rested. Two more pans, stacked up, lay nearby. The warden, squatting, drove the bamboo cane into the horse's throat. With a loud grunt, he pushed it downward into the horse's neck. Blood poured in rivulets. Quickly the pan filled. The men swapped pans until all three were filled.

The next day I noticed blood in my discharge. My body was listless. Our team leader agreed to take me to the infirmary where the nurse examined me to verify my illness. He sent me to the one cot left unoccupied. I asked what would happen if more patients were admitted, where would they sleep, and the nurse said, "You share cots, or sleep on the floor."

That year diarrhea killed many inmates. The carpenter could not make coffins fast enough for the dead, the four-man burial team did not have time to bury corpses lined side by side by the carpentry shack.

The administrator decreed that the death rate must be brought under control. "The policy of the Party is to treat the sick and save lives. Get the sick back on their feet and send them out to the fields."

When flies buzzed over me, one after another alighting on the crotch of my pants and on the stained cot, I knew my life was hanging by a thread. I understood now why inmates called this place the Death Pending Room. Then, like a miracle, Dr. Đàm arrived.

I heard Dr. Đàm say to the nurse, "Give him an injection. You still have Tetracycline?"

"No. And I've never tried my hand at injection."

Dr. Đàm said nothing and came to my bed. He looked at me without saying a word then left. In the afternoon he came back. He knelt on the floor by my cot. I could see him blurrily. He said, "I've got five tablets of Stovarsol. At best, it'll stop the infection. At worst . . ."

I shook my head. "This is for syphilis . . ."

"It's antibiotic." He grinned. "But now is the time to treat that too."

I could not smile at his humor. "I'd be glad to catch it from a female cadre . . . Any of them around?"

Dr. Đàm helped me sit up. I took one tablet with a sip of water. "One a day," he said, then shook his head. "I went back and ask around in your shack and none of them had anything to give. One of them said to me, 'Doesn't he have plenty? I saw it.' I found out he was one of the fellows you've given Reostop to. I had to go to other shacks to get these."

The only vial of antibiotic pills I had received was from my wife during her first and only visit. Then I started dispensing them to some of our sick men. Now I looked at Dr. Đàm, stooped and gray, and felt enormous gratitude swell up in me. I had heard one male nurse ask him, "In the South, how many *lạng* of rice were you allowed a day?"

The irony struck me. Everyone in the North was preoccupied with their own bellies. All the rice allocations were measured by *lạng*, 100 grams, based on the Party's echelons, the seniority, and the loyalty. One could look at the daily allowance as a barometer of a social status. The nurse then inquired further about the meat allotment to a person during Tết, our Lunar New Year. I could only hope that when Dr. Đàm fell sick, there would be help around for him.

CHAPTER 10

Sơn La

Winter 1985–86

Think only of the past as its remembrance gives you pleasure.
—Jane Austen

Cao bought a hen from a guard who told him to let the kitchen tend it. Behind the kitchen was a pen, and the staff took turns feeding the fowls they raised.

Cao worked around the camp instead of the usual work sites. It had taken but one incident on a work site: The warden caught him creeping up behind another inmate, an axe in his hand. As he was poised to strike, the warden rushed up to seize his arm. "You dimwit," the warden yelled. "Why? Why?" Cao looked at him serenely and said, "There's a gnat on the back of his head." He pointed, but the gnat must have disappeared. "Gnats are bloodsuckers." After that, he was given lighter duties, mostly working on his own.

Of late I had not seen much of him. He would be gone in the morning and return mid-afternoon, often in the company of guards and cadres whose jobs were to sell the camp's produce or barter for goods at the commune. I heard that he was used as a coolie, hauling and loading heavy bags of rice, peanuts, beans; sometimes sugar and salt. He was quick and accurate with arithmetic; more than once, the warden would double-check his figures and always conclude that all was well. Occasionally the warden would allow a quick exchange of goods—produce we had grown in the camp—for money and give him petty cash. He would bring back sugar and wild tobacco, and the sight of our general returning to the shack was always a good omen for the evening.

Once, we were building a shack for the incoming cadres and we ran out of nails. I rode with the warden on his bicycle to get some, followed by a guard and Cao. I knew how to sit on the rear saddle of a bicycle, both feet to one side being the norm for bicycle passengers in the North. When I looked back, I saw Cao straddling the seat behind the guard. We were coming into the market. Some women vendors were pointing at us, laughing. Old black-turbaned women with snaggled, black-lacquered teeth. The guard soon glanced back and shouted at Cao, "Devil you!" He braked, swerving. "Both feet to one side! How uncivilized you are!"

It had been two years since that night when I first noticed him. Because he frequently left and returned to the camp with the guards and cadres, he had become a familiar face to the folks in the neighboring areas. Then came the idea of escape. He told me he had explored the area and talked with these folks. Names of hamlets and villages he mentioned all sounded alien to me.

"Didn't they discriminate against you because you're a *ngụy* element?" I asked him. "You even speak with a southern accent."

"None of that," he said, blinking behind his never-wiped glasses. "I've been giving them foodstuff. Those that'd cost them a fortune at the commune." He handed me a pack of cigarettes, still unopened. It was a Điện Biên brand, unfiltered, its pack illustrated with green figures of the bộ đội flying a victory flag on top of the French commanding bunker. I politely declined because I did not smoke. He squinted at me. "I saw you smoke with Mr. Thạch."

"That was wild tobacco. And only during social hours."

"I've heard that he's a chess master."

"Yes. I could never beat him. Not even close."

"Ask him if he wants to play with me."

I told him that I would.

Two nights later, we gathered around Mr. Thạch's cot—Cao did not know that the old man was an ex-communist hardliner who had been incarcerated for his radical thoughts against the Party's vision—to watch him play chess against Cao. It was a cold night. In the center of the shack, a metal drum burned with firewood, smelling foul. I sat on a cot next to Mr. Thạch's, wrapped in my blanket. The old commie, too, was bundled in two layers of shirts and a quilted jacket. Only Cao was sparse in his clothing. It was the first time I saw him put on the camp shirt buttoned up to the neck. He sat on the floor, wrapped in a burlap sack. He looked like a cormorant at rest.

The match started after the final gong that signaled bedtime. The men who huddled around the cot talked in small voices. The board became clear of most of the chess pieces, the red belonging to the general, the black to Mr. Thạch. Cao drank his tea from his own cup, tea Mr. Thạch had brewed. I noticed Cao only took three sips before abandoning the cup on the floor. The two players said not a word, taking a moment to ponder each move, brisk and resolute. I counted the pieces on the board. With seven pieces left, Mr. Thạch was attacking.

Cao had nine pieces deployed on both sides of the river. The next move Mr. Thạch made was to buy time by advancing his cannon one square. I could tell that his plan, after Cao's move, was to jump his horse in front of his cannon to checkmate.

Cao scratched his head. It was the only time he did. The whole night he had sat immobile, meditating on the board. He moved one of his chariots, anticipating Mr. Thạch's next move, to take out his opponent's horse when it jumped. Mr. Thạch moved his other cannon to align for the next strike. He was one step too late. Cao, with his last move of the chariot, jumped his horse to checkmate. Now the board became clear.

With his pawn already on the edge of Mr. Thạch's king palace, the horse move to checkmate finalized the game. It was midnight. Mr. Thạch shook hands with the man who had just beaten him—perhaps the only man in a long time who had done so.

The winter of 1986 was stark.

It had been ten years for me. Ten years since we lost to the northern commies. Worse, each of us, from the highest to the lowest, had volunteered to attend these prisons. I'd had no concept of time ever since. Only despair slowly replaced by physical hunger. In their flashing images—the potatoes, the manioc, the bo bo, the greens of wild vegetables—I felt a stab of self-hate for having stolen things to calm hunger, seeing theft done by others, and feeling worthless because of a collective shame.

But one morning a letter addressed to me arrived. I saw the handwriting and felt a rare joy. The letter came from Âu's daughter. She wrote in longhand and each line slanted upward toward the right edge. Her handwriting was small and neat. She said she knew about the reform camp in her home province and the beach I had described. She said she crossed the vast sand flat every morning on her way to the commune. Her name was Hải Yến, she wrote, as she ended her letter.

Cung, my cot neighbor, was a big man with a healthy appetite. The former airborne major saved up his allowance of manioc tubers and made himself a perforated metal sheet to grate them. He stuffed the grated manioc into a bamboo culm and baked it. That did not last long for him. He told me back home in Saigon he breakfasted on two king-size bowls of *phở*, sometimes three, having to leave one stall for another to avoid embarrassment. With the camp's permission, he, among us, foraged wild herbs and plants and boiled them to make his light meals seem fuller. I would watch him go through his dining ritual. He picked each ear of corn, each grain of cooked rice—on an auspicious day when rice was heaven-sent—and chewed until they tasted sweet, and that was his discovery.

Then one day his limbs started swelling up, until they became distended—even his testicles were a sight to see—though he was not exempted from daily labor. Our team leader simply assigned him to the basketry team when his mobility had become an issue. Even Dr. Đàm admitted that, without diuretic medication to eliminate excess fluid, it was only a matter of time.

We stayed up late one night when I shared with him a boiled potato. It came from Mr. Thạch who had given me and Cung most of his evening meal. We were grateful and happy at the same time for Mr. Thạch who had recently received gifts from home. Cung took only two bites and his half of potato was gone. I broke my share in half and gave one part to him. He wolfed it down and tried to turn onto his side. Even this movement proved a struggle for him.

"Brother Khang," he said, blinking, "I'd trade half of my life to eat a bowl of phở at this moment. Oh, those pristine mornings in Saigon when you can't wait for them phở stalls to open."

I simply nodded. I pictured in my head a big man, on the handsome side, sitting on a stool under a tarpaulin hung overhead to keep sun and rain out, bending over a steaming bowl of phở, oblivious to the pedestrians and the traffic beginning to clog up the sidewalks and avenues. Here was a man whose loyalty to President Diệm had led him to execute the fellow who murdered his boss and the boss' brother. Now he was only half a shadow of his old self.

"Don't you miss the old time, Brother Khang?" he asked me.

"Don't mention it," I said, chuckling. "Our peace time was short but sweet. We die, but our memories don't."

"Our feelings don't die either. Why? I don't know. Maybe we feed them with memories."

"Yes, brother." I hated recalling those years. But memories were carbon copies which retained everything. Out of 30,000 prisoners, both military and civilian, we released to the North as part of the Paris Peace Accords, and then found out two-thirds of them were re-planted back into the communist troops already stationed in our South. Indelible facts of the North's doubling the installations of fuel pipelines along the Hồ Chí Minh Trail. Indelible satellite photographs of increasing ammunition depots and provisions warehouses in the South's jungles. Indelible facts of our South's dwindling supplies of fuel and ammunition once the Americans had departed.

I felt sick again, haunted by gray ghosts.

Three days later, on a crude litter, I helped carry Cung to a shack outside the camp. It sat at the bottom of a hill, not a ward but a transitory place we called "Death Dwelling." Dr. Đàm went there to check on him a few times, then he stopped going. Then, one evening before meal time, I could hear the pounding of a hammer from the carpentry shack. The sound was familiar, reminiscent of the time I spent in the coffin-making shack at Cổng Trời.

Cung died shortly after he was placed in the death dwelling. It did not occur to me that his death was any different from any other death I had seen. But that night, with his cot empty next to mine, it came to me what Mr. Zhao Fang had said after reading Cung's natal chart: "You would not die in this camp or any other reform camp, not even at home."

Cung, indeed, died not in the camp, but outside of it.

CHAPTER 11

Sơn La

Summer 1987

Remember me and smile . . .
—Dr. Seuss

Summer arrived.

I now worked in the carpentry team, a stint I had undertaken at Cổng Trời. Day after day we went into the woods to fell cedars and thornless bamboo and carried them back together with bundles of elephant grasses. We cut timbers and smoothed them to make beams and rafters and support posts, and thatched the roof with grass which had been laid out in the sun for several days to dry.

Upon returning to the camp in the late afternoon, we were summoned in front of the camp administrator. "This house was built for all of you, the camp attendees," he spoke to us. "What is it for? It's for your family visitation. But unlike the visitation shack by the camp entrance, this house will provide lodging for the night when your families visit you. Now beware. Only those of you who have shown progress toward the Revolution will receive the privilege to stay overnight with your families."

We had had several rearrangements of residents since winter. I had a new cot neighbor and Cao was moved to another shack. Fortunately, though, Bee stayed with me.

One afternoon, too hot to nap before going back to the work site, I sat outside under the thatched eave and opened my wallet and looked at the picture of my baby girl and my wife. Opening my wallet always made me nostalgic for the days back home. In those days, none of us had thin wallets. There would be a healthy sheaf of banknotes, family photographs, bank cards, membership cards, prescription cards, business cards. Now my wallet was thin and worn. Its contents had been registered and held under care of the bursar.

I was gazing at the picture, imagining what my baby girl now looked like, when someone sat down beside me. He put his finger on the picture and I looked at him. Cao, our General.

"You know her too?" He pressed his finger on my wife's face.

"Of course."

"Since when?"

"Since I married her."

"Good for her. I thought she'd never marry after sleeping with me and my buddies in our unit."

It must be the heat that wreaked havoc on the man's brain. During wintertime he seemed more at peace. I put my wallet away. To test his faculties, I pointed toward the freshly sculpted bust of Hồ Chí Minh that the camp had recently installed outside the meeting hall.

"You know who that is?" I asked him.

"Who else but that nitwit again!" He pushed his glasses up the bridge of his nose. "Individualism is morally harmful to the Revolution and socialism. That's what these commies believe in. Tell me, why this halfwit's bust? Why do people have to bow to him? I knew him. I was drafted and graduated to an officer rank. He failed. Just an imbecile."

"You realize who you're talking about?"

"Yeah. The same goateed slimeball hung on the wall in the meeting hall."

He tapped the side of his head as his glasses slipped down on the bridge of his nose. "Do you know that Hồ Chí Minh was blessed?"

"With?"

"Freedom."

"From?"

"Living in reform camps like us. If he had, do you think he'd ever become revered 'Uncle'?"

I fixed him with a stare. His face was impassive. Finally, I shrugged. "Here we're dangling between human and animal. We're losing humaneness. The Buddha said, 'All Buddhas evolve from hungry ghosts—the preta.' You think Hồ Chí Minh could beat it and rise like the Buddha?"

"I know where he'd end up. One day when I'm out of this hellhole, I'll go into business making toilets."

"You must be sick of the Revolution toilets here."

"No. I like them. Fresh air. But the toilets I'd manufacture would be modeled after Hồ Chí Minh's head."

"Careful now."

"His mouth is the drain hole."

He rose and headed toward the infirmary. Bareheaded, barefooted as always. I followed him, curious to see what he was up to. He stopped outside the sick bay, picked up a broken branch on the ground, and, using it as a cane, entered the shack. There were sick inmates on every cot, everyone napping. Cao kept jabbing his stick at the ceiling.

"What's wrong with the stick?" the male nurse asked.

"What's wrong with Heaven?" Cao asked in return. "I was questioning Him."

"About what?"

"Why he picked Trường Chinh instead of me to succeed Lê Duẩn."

"That's our General Secretary you're blaspheming." Then the nurse hissed, "Shut your trap."

He, our General Cao, was indeed up to date with recent political events, I could tell. Now he stood, leaning on his stick, watching as the middle-aged nurse acting as the camp's official doctor picked up a syringe. The nurse tapped the syringe a few times and held it in midair to inspect any bubbles left inside. Cao shook his head and said, "Your hand shakes like a rat's tail. How can you hold the syringe steady to finish your job? I'll have you handcuffed once you're done."

I traded half of my evening meal and five packs of cigarettes I had saved for a handmade comb. It was a comb cut from aluminum used to frame doors. Our artisan had meticulously filed away the metal into fine teeth and shaped the comb's handle with a graceful curve.

That Sunday I wrote Hải Yến a letter. I was careful in writing letters. The camp security read every letter we sent. They also read every letter we received. I never wanted to reveal my identity for fear of complications, should the security office take it the wrong way. I simply asked her if, after all these years, she still sold dumplings her mother made. I worded my letter to praise the Party and the State for a day in the future when I had successfully reformed myself and returned to the civilization as a new man. Then I expressed my wish to visit her. I mentioned again the seaside and my desire to live there. Then I brought my letter and the comb to my shack leader and asked him to put them in care of the camp's security office where outgoing mail was inspected.

Someone from our shack came back and told us that the Hanoi radio broadcast had announced that inmates were being released. He must have caught the news in our proctor committee's office where he was carpentering. Then he added, "It also said those who owe a blood debt to the people and are considered incorrigible won't be released." I recalled my meeting with the administrator of Cổng Trời camp, that black-inked word stamped on a sheet in my personal file: "Incorrigible."

The day after I heard the news, I ran into Cao. Past noon, the heat was sultry, the air still, shimmering. He was lying in a crude hammock made from rice sacks and hung between two trees.

I could see that he was reading a magazine. It was the *Communist Review*, a monthly government journal featuring articles on political theory and, sometimes, economic and cultural developments. He must have gained enough trust from the camp officials to borrow this type of journal.

"What're you reading?" I asked, sitting down by his hammock.

"Here, let me read to you a quote by Hồ Chí Minh," he said, adjusting his glasses.

I stopped him. "Are you sure it's from him?"

"Are you sure all the wise Buddha's quotes actually come from the Buddha?"

"What did Uncle say?" I said.

"He said, 'It is well known that the black race is the most oppressed and most exploited of the human family. It is well known that the spread of capitalism and the discovery of the New World led to, as an immediate result, the rebirth of slavery which was, for centuries, a scourge for the Negroes and a bitter disgrace for mankind. What everyone does not perhaps know, is that after sixty-five years of so-called emancipation, American Negroes still endure atrocious moral and material sufferings, of which the most cruel and horrible is the custom of lynching.' Tell me, brother, isn't this what they're doing to us? *Nothing is more precious than independence and liberty*? Isn't that what we're supposed to have now? Emancipation?"

For one moment I did not see him as being cuckoo at all. I leaned in and said, "There's news that they're going to set many of us free."

"I'll believe it when I see it."

That was what I thought too, knowing these commies. He took out a lighter, a rare commodity among us. He flicked it on, hovering the orange flame over the pages he was reading.

"Be careful with that lighter," I said warily.

"I only want to model myself after our great leaders. They're great arsonists."

"Take it easy. Don't you ever wish to be out of here and be somewhere else?"

"Then who'll be here to rebuild our country? You must burn everything to the ground and build it back up. Two stages. We're at stage one now. Do you believe evil has morality?"

"Where're you heading with this?"

"To find out what evil truly is, you must burn everything to the ground. Our great leaders are doing just that. Great men can't be judged on morality."

I narrowed my eyes. "Are you really crazy?"

"Imagine all the fires burning." He flicked his lighter and watched the tiny flame. "Beautiful."

It was mealtime at midday. Everyone looked forward to having their naps. I sat outside with my *Guigoz* can filled with sweetened lemonade and saw Cao wandering by himself in the sunbaked courtyard. He looked up at the guard tower and back at the inmates' shacks.

"I lost my hen yesterday, a hen with white flecks on her head. Whoever stole it, if you're one of those from our shacks, your next three generations shall be slaves; if you're one of those from the camp, you shall live in the jungles and mate with monkeys for the rest of your life . . ."

Startled, I watched him. I had seen him feed his hen behind the kitchen. He fed it with cooked rice grains. A luxury. He let it drink water from his cupped hands.

Then someone from his shack ran out and pulled on his arm. "Get back in, will you?" he pleaded with Cao. "Your hen's gone. All feathers and gizzards. Don't waste your breath."

Cao turned away. He raised his face to the watchtower where a guard was watching him. He raved on. "I curse you so you'll remember, eh? I curse you so you'll change, eh? Prick up your ears and listen, eh? Stand up in a straight line. You up there get down here on the ground. You in your cool shacks get out here and kneel. Go sleep on the bare ground for three months and ten days. Fast. Bring all your kin, your mother's kin, your father's kin, boys and girls, men and women, your living and your dead. Bring them here, eh? You from Hell put on your hats and be here, eh? You from Heaven put on your dresses and be in line, eh? If you're hungry, I shall feed you, eh? If you're thirsty, I shall hydrate you, eh? All of you, your pathetic lot, your barefaced lot, your depraved lot, you can't fool me."

Watching him moving in circles like a true madman, I did feel for him. Perhaps one of those guards had thieved his hen. It was much harder for us inmates to steal a fowl and make a meal out of it.

Within two weeks, I received news. It was not good. A snitch from another shack told Bee that Bee and another fellow inmate were about to be moved somewhere else. Shortly after I found out from Bee that his to-be-transferred companion was an elderly former chief judge of the court of appeals.

That night I sat on Bee's cot, between us a chess board. We played, neither saying a word. He moved one pawn after another across the river. I captured all of them. Finally, he leaned back, shaking his head:

Pity those pawns
Crossing the river, all vanished.

I reflected on his verse, then said, "Aren't we all?"

"The day I'm released, I'll smoke one cigarette a day."

Bee smoked a pack a day before 1975. Here he smoked occasionally because of the cigarette ration. I pressed him on his vow. "Can you quit smoking when this 'ism' has ceased to exist in our country?"

"That's not unreasonable for an oath," he said, his face solemn. "Everything is possible. I used to smoke two packs a day. Remember the Cotab and Golden Club? Then after I met you, I cut it down to one pack, since you didn't smoke. Everything has an end. The law of nature."

I looked at the chessboard then made a move to checkmate him. He did not bother to look. He lay down on his back. The cot creaked. Where the mat came short of the cot's edge, there were dried blood stains, perhaps from the crushing of lice by one body after another of those who had slept on this cot. We said nothing. There was nothing to say. After a while he said, "Me and the judge from this shack and a few others from other shacks. A small number though. Leaving tomorrow."

He certainly did not know where. I believed even the proctor committee had no knowledge about it.

The next day, during our meal time in the shack at noon, our warden came in and called out Bee's name and the judge's.

"Pack up your belongings," he said. "Move out."

The judge was already at the door. He had everything packed up the night before. Bee took his time to toss everything into his cloth sack. The last item was his *goz* can. He flung his worn towel over his shoulder as he walked out. He passed my cot, stopped, and handed me a folded piece of paper.

"Keep it as a parting gift," he said. "And don't die!" Then he headed for the door where he stopped and raised his voice. "Anyone here want me to pass along your good wishes to our people?"

Some snickered. Some shook their heads. The warden snapped at him. "Do not try to rise above your lowly self, or you shall go to a penal cell for blasphemy."

Bee patted his small sack. "Yes, sir warden."

"Is that all you have?" asked the warden.

"I'm classless, homeless. Except for what I wear as clothes, I own nothing else. One big O." He tilted his face up and let his words tumble out.

Thirteen kilos of rice a month in our pipe dreams,
We slurp on congee year round,
Forty meters of cloth as yard goods per year in our fantasy,
We're clad in our own skin to keep warm.

The warden shook a finger at him. "Listen here. Do you wish to go back to where you belong or spend your next two weeks in a disciplinary cell?"

"I'm not a reactionary, sir warden," Bee calmy replied, "if it means I'm against Marxism-Leninism, or any regime built on that theory. It's merely a disagreement of ideals between the enforcer and the believer. And I'm the believer who does not believe in the enforcer's belief. Sir warden, in a democratic society, I can't be arrested for that, let me assure you."

I kept his piece of paper and during the day on the labor site I kept my mind on my job. Every time my mind started wandering, I worked harder to drive the thought of him out of my mind. After our evening meal, it was the first time I let my gaze fall on the empty cot on which he had slept. I opened the piece of paper. A poem.

Tonight my shack mate
Celebrated my going away
We sat beneath a chinaberry
Under a starless sky
On the ground between us
Sat a bowl of sorghum millet
And a cup of diluted saltwater.

Outside the shack I sat down leaning against the wall. Distant stars, just dots, like in a child's eyes. Yet what I saw was simply blackness.

Of all the eyes watching the sky this night, how many naked eyes welled up with tears?

On Saturday I received Hải Yến's letter. It was always a joy for me to see her neat handwriting. Over the years it no longer looked childish. Still her longhand would slant upward toward the paper's edge. She said she adored the handicraft she received as a gift from me. She could never believe we inmates could make such beautiful handiwork. I was happy to find out she now had a stall in the commune market where she sold not only dumplings but steam buns and sesame baked buns like the Chinese Hujiao bing. Sometimes on the way to the commune, by crossing the beach, she would have customers who would make her load lighter by the time she arrived at her market stall. She hung a bell from her shoulder pole and upon hearing it, people would know who was coming.

Toward the end of April, the heat made our outdoor labor much harder. The only respite we received from the camp was on Reunification Day, April 30, the anniversary of the day our South fell to communism. Ironically, on this day all of us rejoiced. Banks and government offices and schools closed, and in Hanoi people would visit Uncle's mausoleum. The kitchen told us we would have meat, a treat for those already ravaged by year-round physical hardship. We had meat on other major holidays such as Tết, International Workers' Day, Uncle's Birthday, and National Day. Not only did we get meat on those celebrated holidays, we also got rice.

The night before the celebration, all the shacks were in a festive mood. We could sleep late and did not have to rise at the first gong at dawn. I spent the evening in Mr. Thạch's shack. There, I saw Cao again. He was carousing with the men. They were telling jokes and smoking wild tobacco. Cao never smoked it. He did not even smoke cigarettes. He sat among them, the only bespectacled one, with the camp shirt on and a fresh haircut.

One man was telling a story. "The Pacific Ocean froze that extreme winter of 1972 after a run of US bombing in the North. There was a ship stranded off-coast that could be seen from San Francisco Bay. The ship carried a North Vietnamese delegate whose head had a fear of flying; their mission was to seek settlement with the US."

His tall tale had everyone laughing. Cao piped up, "Legends do exaggerate. But in those elaborate untruths, there's always a grain of truth."

The men turned and appraised him with questioning stares. He shrugged. "Are you in a mood for another tall tale?"

It took one brief moment before some men nodded, while some just shook their heads.

"You all have seen Uncle Hồ's goatee? Haven't you?" asked Cao.

Many of the men nodded. None said a word. Beware of the snitch was the motto.

"Did you know that each of his goatee strands is priceless?" Cao scanned the faces and they all looked impassive. "Did you know that a tiger's whisker is priceless too?"

At last, someone volunteered an answer. "Folklore says you can make poison out of it. Not sure if it's true though."

"True or untrue," Cao said, cackling. "Stick that whisker into a bamboo shoot and weeks later it turns into a black worm, and its excretion is poisonous. Drop a speck of it into a water tank like the one we draw water from every day, and you can kill this whole camp, or any fool who drinks that water. Now—" He paused and cleared his throat. "Some personal aide of Uncle Hồ was curious to find out what a priceless strand of goatee from our most revered Uncle could do compared to the effect of a tiger's whisker. So, one morning, from the wash pan Uncle used to clean his face, the aide found a goatee strand. Lo and behold, he got hold of a bamboo shoot and . . .you know the rest . . ." This drew blank looks from all the faces around him.

"What happened?" A man grinned at him. "I don't know what the rest means. Any of you here?"

Cao took a healthy sip of tea from his *goz* then put it down. "What came out of the bamboo sprout was a blood-red worm. The curious aide decided to keep it in a jar with a broken neck. He cut his finger on it one day and blood dripped into the jar. That seemed to excite the worm out of its dormant state. Soon, there was no trace of blood left in the jar. The aide experimented with the worm and concluded that it was a bloodsucker. Word got to Uncle and he ordered his aide to surrender the bloodworm."

Cao said nothing after that, asking for the wild tobacco pipe and taking one deep hit. That was the first time I saw him smoke wild tobacco. Then he lay down, closing his eyes.

"What the hell?" someone sneered. "Is that it?"

"What happened to the worm?" someone else asked mockingly. "Did Uncle kill it?"

Cao opened his eyes slowly. "That would've been a lifesaver. He chose to keep it and nourish it."

"How?" said the man who just laughed. "With his own blood?"

"Are you stupid?" Cao scowled. "He's got millions of people he can draw blood from."

The men looked at one another; none showed any emotion, none laughed. Cao finally nodded toward them. "Look at me. My wife's left me, my older son died at sea during a boat escape, and my youngest son, only twelve, begs on the streets, barred from school due to his father's record. Keep feeding that worm with our blood, and we'll all rot in here eventually."

Cao must know that at least one of the listeners was a snitch, I thought. But the thing I did not know, I would find out the next morning.

There was a bustling air toward noon the next day. I stood outside the meeting hall, watching the carpentry team bring in the last table they had finished the night before. One then two of them pointed at a banner on the wall before motioning for the guards. Then curses and shouts ensued, and guards rushed in to take the banner down.

During the night, some saboteur had altered the sacred message on the banner. The red banner, lettered in yellow, had read: "*The Great President Hồ Lives Forever in Our Lifetime.*" Someone had blotched the word "Lives" with soot and written "Dies" above it.

Commotion broke out after another guard came upon the altar on which rested the sculpted head of Uncle. Someone had placed on the altar a chipped bowl of manioc tubers cooked with rice. Glued to Uncle's brow with rice paste was a stained piece of brown paper and on it was a scribble:

Best farewell wishes to the ravenous Party
And to Uncle, my only bowl of manioc-mixed rice!

For the next few hours, we could sense the eyes and ears of the camp's sneaks wherever we went.

During the bustling celebration later that day came the news that Cao had disappeared. That was the word the wardens used. They would not admit his escape. Nor did they mention the Citroën DS-19 that had disappeared with him. The camp had sent him to the commune to pick up several items for the Unification Day celebration. I recalled having seen him leaving the camp in the morning by himself. In the car. He was wearing a clean shirt and a clean pair of shoes. He waved at me and some other men in the courtyard, and I remembered he'd once told me that he saved his shirt and shoes for a special occasion. "To honor the victory and the surrender," he said as he departed, grinning like a devil. If his fellow inmates felt insulted, the camp overseers would be gleeful. That was my last remembrance of him.

The camp overseers now paid a dear price for slighting Cao. They would be held accountable for his disappearance; yet no one questioned or interrogated us afterward. We understood. Why admit your fatuity by exposing it under the sun?

After his perfect escape, I then understood. Shortly after he'd lost his hen, I'd happened upon Cao standing hatless in the courtyard, gazing at a banner that hung over the gate. It read: *Không Có Gì Quý Hơn Độc Lập Tự Do.* "Nothing Is More Precious Than Freedom and Independence." He was mumbling. Then he pointed at the banner. "It should read 'Không Có Gì Qúy Bằng Độc Lập Tự Do. Nothing Is As Precious As Freedom and Independence,'" he said. "Every time I read that line, I can't help remembering another line I saw on the door of a brothel in Saigon: Không Có Gì Qúy Hơn Tiết Trinh. *Nothing Is More Precious Than Virginity.*"

I glanced up at the watchtower. The guard had withdrawn because of the heat. Cao, without looking at me, continued, "The way they phrase it, freedom and independence are ultimate, if we understand these words to mean the absence of external impediments and the ability to decide for oneself. But there are other qualities a human is born for, with or without freedom. The inviolate family unit, for example; one's human rights. These things are absolute but not ultimate. Not even independence can be ultimate, only absolute among other absolutes."

Months later, on April 30, Unification Day, the day the camp sent him to town by himself to fetch supplies for the celebration and he put on that clean shirt and pair of shoes, Cao drove out through the gate over which that banner hung. He never returned.

CHAPTER 12

Hàm Tân

Winter 1989

> But the rain
> Is full of ghosts tonight.
>
> —Edna St. Vincent Millay

The day was bleak.

Yet the crowd of inmates, a thousand strong, gathered in the courtyard half an hour before the proctor committee appeared, all bundled up in quilted jackets and earflap hats. Finally, the chief warden began reading out the names on the list held in his hand. At times he stopped when an inmate stood up, only to hear clarification that the name just called belonged to another inmate. The list seemed endless. The chief warden came to the last name on the list. Three hundred and fifty-five inmates were to be released on this day. My name was not on the list.

The cold day did not bother those soon to leave for home. They shook hands. They called out to one another. They bantered. Laughs. Tears. People went in and out of the shacks, carrying with them most of their belongings; the rest they gave away to those who remained behind. I watched them, even shaking hands with some, as I stood outside my shack. The longer I watched them, the hollower I felt. Many of them were my friends. Their imminent departure had already left a void in me. We were one big family, though none of us admitted it. The word "family" was reserved for our close-knit family back home. But I had spent nearly one third of my life with men I called brother and had bonded with them over the years. I had hoped for my name to be called from that list. It was wishful thinking. I had to come to grips with my incorrigible status. It had been fourteen years. Based on the magic number three, going from three to nine to twelve years, there was hope. Next year, my fifteenth, would mark my release.

Six months later, now autumn, we were gathered in the same courtyard, under a cloudy sky of a chill morning, to hear our names called again with trepidation. The list was much longer this time, and when the chief warden read out the last name on it, there was a total of six hundred and twenty inmates to be relocated to the South. My name was on that list.

I was relieved. We were not being released; we were being transferred. The saving grace was that we were going back to our beloved South. As I packed my sparse belongings, holding the spare camp shirt up to look at the black "CT" initials, I tried to remember how many camp shirts I had gone through over the years. All of them had weathered sweat, sun, and rain, and eventually were disposed of as rags to wipe myself in the latrines. One morning, not too far back, I was carpentering in the administrator's office when I saw an old man. White-haired, he looked dignified in his black vest and gray trousers. He sat on one chair in a corner, quietly watching me mending the administrator's cabinet. When I packed up my tools to leave, I turned to face him and politely said to him, "Sir, I'm done. Please send my best wishes to our administrator." He nodded then said, "Please lie low. Play the jester's role to fool them. One day you shall return home again." I did not know who he was. Later, I found out he was the administrator's father.

I went to see Mr. Thạch and then Mr. Liên. They both remained. I told them I had nothing worthy to leave behind for them and they told me not to worry. They had withstood their internment, whose years of imprisonment put together was nearly twice my age. I shook their hands and quickly left. When I was back in my shack, I sat down on my cot among many others, now empty. I felt like crying.

The afternoon came and we cleared out of our shack, parting ways with several personal items we were not allowed to bring with us to the new camp. I gave a friend a cloth bag in which I hid potatoes, manioc tubers, cabbage, bo bo, and some rice grains. Some of them were cadres' gifts as tokens of their appreciation for work done at their personal request. It was chilly in October, and while sitting on my knapsack in the courtyard I put on another shirt, the most decent one, though it was threadbare and mended in multicolored patches. In my bag I had two prisoner outfits—one badly worn out, the other fairly intact. I had cut off the bottom part of my poncho so I could use it as a lining beneath my mat to ward off lice. My canteen and my *goz* can were tied to the side of my rucksack as I sat on it, waiting.

The convoy of Molotova trucks passed through mostly empty roads, rutted with dips and potholes, and each bone-jarring thump had our heads banging one another's. I would spot a Honda motorbike now and then on the roads, those introduced from the once-wealthy-and-free South to the northerners, most of whom possessed only a bicycle, and considered them luxuries. Fourteen years had passed now after the war, and what the communists extolled as "progress" was laid bare in front of our eyes.

I caught glimpses of the train station, its low-wattage lights receding in melancholic yellow. Something about the yellow lights of the socialist north made me brood. Twelve years in the North, sometimes in the wilderness, sometimes in the wooded mountains, finally broke my teeth on the North's socialist civilization. We were Neanderthals. We had made everything with our hands because we were encouraged to do so. Everything we had made came from wood and bamboo.

There were times when I felt I had been haphazardly transported to another dimension, where, one morning after roll call, a camp cadre spoke to us: "Have you ever seen anywhere else, the western world included, a meeting hall built with virtua*nn*y no nails? This hall, which could seat over five hundred people, was constructed with mortise and tenon joints, with timbers and bamboo. Now you know why we don't need plastic to make pails and baskets. Now you rea*n*ize how genuine*n*y progressive our socia*n*ist State is."

We were dumbstruck. We simply watched him, his bucktoothed grin, the enraptured expression that passed over his face. How proud he must be to rephrase what he had been drilled with since he was a child. From a boy to a man, he must not have seen civilization in all its colors outside his tiny world. Had he seen a tractor we used in the South to plow our fields, he would have jumped on it and, like a child in a toy store, grabbed this and touched that, to figure out how to operate it so he could till his land without the aid of a buffalo, or worse, a human that replaced a beast of burden. And that was what we had seen one day. Two little boys bending in front of a plow, pulling it through muddy, ankle-high water in a rice plot, while a woman was pushing from behind. Then it became our reality when we, the inmates, had gone in pairs to pull our plow. We plowed and tilled day after day in those leech-infested valleys, where the soil was blackish with odorous mud that sucked at our bare feet as we replaced buffalos to break ground for a new crop, to have our feet and legs covered with blood-swollen leeches, while many of us would come down with strange fevers and full-bodied rashes that killed.

By late afternoon, the convoy crossed the Thăng Long bridge over Red River into Hanoi. We saw more Honda motorbikes and the cheerful colors of urban people's attire. "Look at our southern fashion," a man in the truck yelled and was immediately warned by the security escort. Those fashions were banned in the South shortly after the communists seized it.

I could see as far as the horizon where the Red River was hazy and gray. It was empty, save for a ferry gliding across the reddish-brown water. It dawned on me that the bridge we were crossing was the only bridge, and there were no others over that vast body of water. When we were moved to Sơn La camp ten years earlier, we had waited half the morning in the Molotova trucks until they were all ferried across the Red River by motorboat-pulled barges. Rusty and noisy, the motorboats managed to tow the barges, each carrying only two trucks at a time.

We reached Phủ Lý train station at midnight. Dimly lit by a single low-wattage bulb, the station had a run-down look. While we were waiting, a cadre approached us, smiling. He wore army-green pants, a white shirt, and his pith helmet sat snugly on his head. "You will stay on the train whenever we stop at a station. It is for your safety. We do not want you to be abused by the people who still hate you. Understood?"

Herded by the security escorts, we climbed back onto the train in pairs, handcuffed by the wrists to each other. The inmates filled up three railcars. Most of us sat on the floor, for each bench was only wide enough for three bodies. Chained to a partner, we managed to lean on each other as we dozed off. Many of us refrained from emptying our bladders; but some had to drag his partner with him to an odorous latrine.

At three in the morning the train departed.

The coal-burning train passed several small stations without stopping. It only slowed down for safety, attracting a horde of vendors—women and children—to run alongside the train, calling out their wares. At the first station we passed, no windows were opened—that was the guards' order. But they relented afterward and allowed us to peek out at the next station. Some vendors recognized us as reform inmates and told us to take their treats and keep our money. I bought two fried bananas and offered my partner one. As the sweetness of the banana seeped into my tastebuds, I realized it had been a long time since I had treated myself to such a luxury. When they ordered us to pull down the shades as the train moved on, I tried to doze again. But in my head dinged the words, "All for socialism." They had robbed us of our assets, our wealth. They had preyed on their own people to build an inhuman regime devoid of morality. "All for socialism."

Sometimes we passed a local train with only a few cars, but each was packed with passengers, some hanging on the steps. Some rough-looking faces stood out among the crowds. My stomach turned. This was what the wives had to endure during each trip north they made; those long, agonizing trips that put them at risk against the thieves, robbers, rapists, who rode those trains to prey on helpless victims.

The day was gray when the train crossed the bridge over Bến Hải River. My heart throbbed. Many of us pressed our faces against the windowpanes and gazed out. We were leaving the North and entering our South. The landscape became familiar to me. The river, the national highway, the citadel of Quảng Trị. They had not changed. Only I had changed.

Late in the afternoon, the train stopped in Huế and it was there that we were allowed to disembark the train to eat. A mist hung over the station, the lampposts shone yellow, and perched on them were crows, hunched. We lined up in pairs, handcuffed, on the narrow platform. Soon a small crowd gathered. They were young and old women. Some cried out, "*Tù! Tù!*" That was who we were. Prisoners. Not camp attendees. They came nearer, appraising us with their eyes. They were food peddlers, selling cakes and dumplings and *bánh mì*. I paid for a loaf of bánh mì and the old woman told me to keep my money. She gazed at me and my partner then looked off, shaking her head sadly. "Those vile communists! Look at these men! You call it reform?"

Then came children and teenagers. I watched them peddling around and thought of my daughter. A girl's voice startled me. "Chú!"

She was in her early teens, wearing only a patched blouse. It was chilly in the late afternoon. She gave me a packet of roasted peanuts, a packet of Bastos cigarettes.

"I don't smoke, *cháu*," I said. Neither did my partner. But hearing her calling me "chú" revived my past. I had not heard that honorific for many years in the North.

"Chú," she said again, her eyes earnest and innocent, "don't pay me."

I hurriedly pulled out my wad of money with my free hand and managed to put a bill into her hand. She closed her fist. "No, chú."

A sudden whistle pierced the air. The guards, the cadres ordered everyone back on to the train. Some of the youths tossed us packets of dried foods and cigarettes and cured pork. The train pulled out. They ran alongside the train until they could not keep up with it. I looked back and the gray mist was all I saw.

That night we were herded into a shack where we were to have our supper before resuming our journey. On the floor were ten rubber pails, those we used to wash our clothes in. The seven sky-blue pails were filled with rice mixed with cooked manioc; two of the three orange pails contained murky broth in which floated the green stems of water spinach, and the other pail had salt water, a substitute for our *nước mắm*.

Before noon, the train pulled in at the last station in Nha Trang. We raised the shades and, shocked at what we saw, shouted back and forth among ourselves. Lining up along the tracks were thousands of people. Soon we could tell they were not passengers waiting for the train as they called out to us, hands and handkerchiefs waving frantically, as they tossed all kinds of gifts onto the train. Many ran along the slowing train, yelling out the names of their loved ones, and behind them the lights in the houses were all lit up and the people were greeting us like heroes returning home.

On the train I had learned that many of us, from captain to major to lieutenant colonel, were being shipped back to the South. We had run into one another at train stations on the way south, and it was the first time since 1975 that many of us had seen one another. Late in the afternoon, after all of us had disembarked at the final station, we were trucked to Hàm Tân in Bình Thuận province. It was our new camp.

The southern camp at Hàm Tân was called Z30D. The locals called this region *Rừng Lá*, fan-palm jungle, an eponymous name given because of the profusion of fan palm.

My new cot neighbor was a former major who'd specialized in "thought correction" to rehabilitate the Viet Cong hồi chánh. He had been here several months before I arrived. One night he showed me his bare back. It looked like a wrinkled parchment scratched with a sharp pen. Purplish scars striped his bony frame. They were scars inflicted from the electric wire whipping by a sadist camp security cadre. "Stealing crops from the camp," he said to me. "Crops grown by us, by our labor, our sweat. You know that too, don't you?" I did. I was no stranger to this so-called stealing. I did stealthily eat raw peanuts after cracking their shells, then swallowed them with their papery skin. I had eaten them raw or boiled. I was a thief with a recurrent vice. He continued, "After whipping me, they asked my teammates to punish me for my behavior."

Not so long after I knew him, I saw him with his young daughter during an allowed visit. The daughter was crying into his arms. That evening in the shack he confided in me that his wife had left him for another man, and that she'd told their daughter not to tell him.

In autumn, hummingbird trees flowered red and white along the only road going to the camp. We would pluck their flowers and cook them to supplement our meals. Along the road when we went out to the labor site, I would see among the greenery the red-tiled roofs of the cadres' dwellings, the administrator's house, the personnel offices. Farther toward Highway One, the road cut through the fan-palm jungle, brown-trunked and pinecone-scaled, then the woodland populated with Burmese rosewood and flamewood and blackwood. Among them were sometimes ebony and guava crepe myrtle. The locals used fan palms to thatch the roofs of their dwellings. In autumn, the palms' creamy-white flowers had wilted, their toxic drupes dried and fallen to the ground, and the locals used them as fish bait.

Returning to camp in the late afternoon, we would pass the mess hall outside the entrance gate. I was in the mess hall on one occasion when the kitchen detail ran short of help. The food I helped bring to the dining hall was cooked rice and bo bo and water-diluted soy sauce. I thought they were for us, but the cook said otherwise. I stood in the airy hall and admired the mosaic-tiled walls, the gleaming tiled floor in blue and white as the cadres started filing in, each holding a ceramic bowl, a pair of chopsticks. Those who had money went to the counter to buy a small bottle of authentic fish sauce or soy sauce to enhance their meals. In that moment, I saw the thin veneer of their affluence.

That afternoon, the same cook came back with unusual news. The diners, while drifting in and out of the mess hall, all spotted some graffiti on the wall.

Inside are ngụy prisoners; outside are us custodians-turned-prisoners

Whispers spread quickly among the inmates. *Fancy façade*, someone said under his breath. *Rotten food every day.* We could see they were no better than us the inmates, except for their freedom.

Our camp had sub-camps, separated by a swift-flowing stream. It was wide, and during the rainy season sometimes it crested, the water roiled with twigs and brown bark and became impassable. Before we came, the inmates of both sub-camps pooled resources and built a bridge. In the autumn, the stream was serene and we would come here to bathe or wash ourselves after a day's work.

One late afternoon, I stopped at the stream and the creeper-crawling bank was already full of inmates bathing. I spotted Bee among them. Unable to contain myself, I ran to him.

"Lau!" I yelled.

He turned. His gray hair was wet as he was standing waist deep in the stream. He threw his arms up. "It's you!"

I got into the water and grasped his hands. He shook his head and blurted out, "Damnation!" Then he leaned back to take me in, still shaking his head. "Where're you staying now?"

I told him. We were separated by this stream. As a rule, we were not allowed to cross between camps. "We'll find a way," Bee said, as the whistle blew for roll call before each team was to head back to its camp. I had barely time to dry myself as he lined up with his team and walked single file across the bridge to the other bank. He waved. Just a silhouette.

I did not run into Bee again until a month passed and, as I was coming out of the kitchen carrying a tub of food for our team, I saw him.

"Damnation!" Bee's face beamed. "I've been looking for you. What shack are you in?"

I told him. The first shack. His was the last out of ten.

"We're cattle," Bee said. "The pasture's the same." He added he had barely settled in. "Guess who I share the shack with?"

I could not pull any name from my memory. Bee slapped my arm. "Remember Mr. Zhao Fang?"

How could I forget him? I told Bee that I missed him as much as I missed Mr. Thạch and Mr. Liên. Bee nodded. "Those two gentlemen aren't like us," Bee said. "They're hardcore commies and will never be let out of sight. Well, I'd better get going. We'll get together on Sunday."

On Sunday, Bee brought me a small red can. The gold lettering read "Beurre Bretel." The rich, luxuriant French butter. I gasped. "How did you get this?"

"From home," Bee said. "I'm always worried about you and your eating, or lack of it."

"Eating, huh?" I raised my eyebrows.

"Aren't we all reduced to that? A living proof of dialectical materialism?"

There was some truth in it, I thought, unless you were someone like *thầy* Thanh Tâm who had transcended the conflicts caused by material needs. Bee clamped his hands over mine, still clutching the can. "We've done fourteen years," he said. "Don't ruin it by acting foolish while you're here."

If he meant planning an escape, he was wrong. I knew better. I had learned my lesson.

The next Sunday, Bee bought me a small bottle which used to contain cough medicine. In it was some clear liquid.

"Don't tell anyone," he said. "We'll drink it tonight."

"What's in it?" I asked.

"Sugarcane wine."

I stared at him, wide-eyed. He grinned. His grin reminded me of Cao's grin the morning he waved at me before driving out of the camp in its Citroën DS-19. I asked how he managed to lay his hands on it.

"A fellow I know," said Bee, "works in the cane field. They'd press the canes then process the juice to make sugar. He stole some and let it ferment. And that's what you've got here." He paused and grinned again. "If I learn how to distill it, I can make rum."

That night we drank the wine in my shack. It had been a long time since I tasted wine. Buoyed, I thanked Bee as we shared a pipe of wild tobacco he brought with him. A few cots from me, two fellows were playing Chinese chess. It brought back memories.

"Remember Cao?" I said to Bee. "The cuckoo man? Our General?"

"How could I not?" Bee said. "Was he in this camp?"

"No. He was long gone before our transfer." Then I told Bee the rest of Cao's story.

"I bet he must've gotten someone to make a fake ID for him. I saw his wife once when she visited him."

That must have been the only visit Cao received. Like me. I shared with him some unnamed anguish, a hankering for something nameless, once there and now gone.

"Do you think he was really cuckoo?" I asked Bee.

"If you were him," said Bee, "wife left you, one son died at sea, the other not allowed to school, and you're stuck there rotting in prison . . . if you're sane then something's wrong with you."

I mentally agreed. Perhaps Cao talked to himself to keep himself sane.

We finished the wine. Bee took another hit on the pipe and leaned back, his face clouded with smoke as he gazed at me.

"You still remember the poem I gave you at Sơn La?" It was about the two friends sharing a pot of tea before parting.

"Yeah," I said.

"I had an ending to that poem. And it's about you." Bee nodded, took a sip then added. "And for you." In a soft, scratchy voice, he recited:

In God I found love,
In Karl Marx I found Marxism,
In you I found passion.
But God promised me a paradise,
Marx promised me a classless utopia,
As they taught me in countless reform camps.
And what have you promised me, my love?
A love utopia until we die?
Each day I toiled with a glimmer of hope,
In this hell hole,
Fenced in with barbed wire.
And in that hell hole,
One day I heard that you have found
a new love
A utopia forever denied of me.

Mr. Zhao Fang gave me a firm handshake when I visited him in his shack the next Sunday. He was jovial as ever. I envied him. He was a man who had accepted his fate by living in peace with the life chosen for him. In that sense, he chose not to deny it. In Sơn La he kept a low profile. I never saw him on the front row in the meeting hall. In a work group he disappeared among others. He was a worm. You touch it, it would coil. No wardens ever singled him out. He gave others his gifts, even to some cadres, not to curry favor but to make peace. I could never imagine him as a former tycoon.

On that day, Mr. Zhao Fang had received visitation gifts which were a fortune in the eyes of everyone else in the shack. Weighing a nylon pack in his hand Mr. Fang said to me, "This is the best remedy on a hot day. Mix one teaspoon of this in water and fill your *goz* with it when you go out to labor. Best way to fight dehydration." It was granulated white sugar finely blended with lemon powder. He opened a baguette-shaped rice roll, wrapped so tightly for the long journey it was still fresh when Mr. Fang unwrapped the banana leaves. Then he sliced the rice roll and offered me a piece. We sprinkled it with fermented shrimp paste and lemongrass.

We sat on his cot, a teapot and two teacups between us. Mr. Fang smiled like in the old times. "You see, Brother Khang" he said to me, "even now I'm truly a proletariat. Own nothing. Am nothing. But I'm still here."

"We're still here," I said, amused by his raillery, "because we've followed our creed: Never admit your crime for the sake of self-preservation."

"I am old. But you are still young. You might outlast their regime. It is rotten at the core and has an unkempt odor. Even their rank and file can smell it. They adhere to their duties but privately to their relatives, especially those in the South, they would tell them what is true in their hearts. Valuable advice. Buy gold. Do not hoard paper currency, for it can be replaced by new currency, hence leading those who are short-sighted to bankruptcy. Stay in the cities. Do not go to the New Economic Zones. I have shared their advice with my relatives back home."

It stirred pity in me to relive the memory of 1975. Only five months after their victory—every day, long North-bound trains leaving the South loaded with looted goods—the socialist regime changed the currency in the South: One liberation đồng was worth five hundred old southern đồng. Each southern household was allowed to exchange their old money for up to two hundred đồng of the new currency. That equals 100,000 old southern đồng; the rest of their wealth must be deposited with the National Bank of Vietnam. To withdraw some money, they must submit applications to their ward council, and whether or not the ward council would approve depended on the withdrawn amount. It was robbery in disguise; a time of bankruptcy and suicide for many southerners. The communist doctrine stressed equality, because we were all equal now in poverty.

"I'm not so sure," I said to Mr. Fang in a subdued tone, "about outlasting the regime. Not when I wake up every morning on an empty stomach and don't know where my next meal will come from. But one thing I know for certain is the rationing of my meals. Mr. Fang, if you live on a half-empty stomach day after day, you won't outlast those who put you there."

"You must know one thing, Brother Khang," he said, relaxing his jaw. "What's rotten will die in the end. It might be a slow death, but death is inevitable nevertheless."

How could I tell him that he was possibly going senile in his old age? Perhaps my cynicism was not misplaced. When I looked around, all I saw was the People's Security Force.

Citizens had to report to their civil security city block while all the cafés and restaurants had to account for the daily number of customers they received, the regulars and newcomers, and particularly those who socialized with each other. In those busiest cafés and restaurants, sometimes you could spot new faces who were not customers, but waiters or waitresses or cashiers. They moved about, eavesdropping on the customers, for these new faces were security incognitos who had supplanted the usual workers. Even the boy who looked after your scooter parked outside the café was planted to spy on any likely dissident.

I could pick on Mr. Fang's brain for his sagacity, but I could never share his view of communism. To him, there was light at the end of the tunnel in every issue he examined. The glass was half full in his eyes. Perhaps I was a pessimist, but I was a pessimist with a sense of place, fact, scene. I saw, and therefore I believed. I was more aligned with Mr. Liên, for he was a true believer in the evil of communism. Take those secret police in a city. They could, by the power vested in them from the State, pull you out of a group and demand a written confession. What did you talk about among yourselves? Each one in such a group had to write a confession. If these confessions did not match, prison would be next. There were few gatherings, and citizens walked with their heads down, their lips pinched. A quiet city. Should you gather, decide among yourselves what topic you would talk about in case a confession is called for. The secret police could arrest you by merely calling you "reactionary." Once arrested, you were guilty—the Party was never wrong. And because the Party was never wrong, it became the shackles without keys. It was therefore easier to arrest than to release. To set you free, the Ministry of Public Security or the City Committee must find you not guilty. But without a trial there was no sentence, and without a sentence, you were in limbo in prison.

Perhaps Mr. Fang's self-preservation was the profundity I had never learned, a wisdom that transcended all probity. In mid-summer, he was released among one hundred and twenty inmates. When we bid farewell, I told him about Cung, our former airborne major, where he died, all true to Mr. Fang's reading of his natal chart. Mr. Fang noted the fact with a nod then said, "Many of your compatriots came to me with the same question: When would I be released? But you, Brother Khang, you never came. Why?"

"It's not that I don't believe in it, Mr. Fang," I said, smiling. "But if I know it, what then?"

"You cannot change anything, Brother Khang. But treat that knowing as therapy. Many need it."

I wished him well.

Two months passed. Then the camp announced another release. Over three hundred inmates received the good news. Bee was one of them. We looked at each other as if we could read each other's thought. Finally, he said, "Don't do anything rash."

"Patience is a virtue I've acquired," I said.

The next day, past noon, I walked with him to the security shack. I waited at the door while he signed the release paper and received twenty đồng as his travel fare. Behind the cadre's table was a banner lettered red: "Socialist Republic of Vietnam – People's Public Security of Bình Thuận Province." The cadre sitting behind the table handed him the release paper and the money, then capped his pen and clipped it in his shirt pocket. "Now you are pardoned. Be grateful."

"I'm being released, not pardoned, sir cadre." Bee still held the paper in his hand. "These two words must be distinguished from each other. We're not pardoned when we're released, because we were not criminals."

The cadre rose to his feet. "Do you want to forfeit your release?"

"No, sir cadre." Bee turned to leave.

I silently cursed him. He stopped outside the shack and peered up at the portrait of Hồ Chí Minh hung under a red flag. He saluted Uncle. "Stay well, old goat," he said under his breath.

We both turned to head out to the gate when the cadre called out from behind. "Stop!" He rushed out, his face hardened. "What did you just say to Uncle?"

Bee shrugged. "I said, 'Thank you, Uncle.' Sir cadre, I was elated and enthusiastic, for having paid my debt to Uncle and the Party, and for their clemency that has granted me this opportunity to reform myself and prepare me to be reunited with my family."

"Wait here. Let us look into this."

He went back inside and telephoned someone. Within minutes a warden arrived. They interrogated Bee inside while the first group of inmates being released had already boarded the trucks and left. I was angry with him and let him know it as we headed back to the shacks.

After two days Bee had written a confession to answer the question: "What did you say to Uncle?" I thought his fate was doomed. His curse had ruined the fourteen years he had paid the Party and State.

Then on the third day he came back from the security shack and said to me, "I'm set to go." Grinning, he put a hand on my shoulder. "I won't say goodbye to Uncle this time."

CHAPTER 13

Hàm Tân

Winter 1990

Blow on a dead man's embers
And a live flame will start.
—Robert Graves

In winter, the days were cool. At night I could sleep with a blanket without having to don two layers of clothing. But those stark winters in the North were an undying memory. There were many empty cots now in my shack, and the camp decided to merge shacks to reduce the number of guards and supervisors. There were two shacks in the end.

In the mornings, we did not have to trek to distant labor sites. Instead, we worked around the camp, planting and growing vegetables and fruits. I would bring back bitter gourds or sometimes cabbage I grew myself in my own plot. That was our privilege now, which made us feel like petite bourgeoisie. When I sat on my cot, taking time to slice each wax gourd or squash, smelling its fresh aroma, I did not fear being watched. I could cook without rushing myself. I could eat unhurriedly without darting my eyes around like a mouse. I did not have to get up in the night to check on the fire in the metal drum. Sometimes I thought I heard the frightful norther and woke up disoriented. After coming to myself, I knew I was alive.

There were no more than fifty of us left in both shacks. I knew all the faces now and I felt a chill. They were generals, colonels and high-profile intelligence officers. This was the lot I now belonged to. I wondered if Mr. Thạch and Mr. Liên had ever thought they would spend over seventy years combined in prison when they were incarcerated. Like them, I had moved from camp to camp, and the years added up. I did not know how to pray; even if I did, whom would I pray to?

We did not talk among ourselves about current events whenever we met. Years had passed and hopes waned. I could, however, read journals and newspapers in the camp's library, and there were times I could listen to the radio alongside

Cadre Kim who, like us, was anxious for change. What change, I did not know. But when you felt ill, you would wish for a remedy. Sometimes, sitting together to catch a voice from a broadcast, I would enrich Cadre Kim's knowledge with what I knew about certain countries, their cultures, their cuisines, their languages. Slowly the outside world passed by me through those broadcasts. In Russia, President Mikhail Gorbachev had put into effect the *glasnost* and *perestroika* policies; and I explained to Cadre Kim that Russia was now allowing freedom of expression and of information, and at the same time decentralizing economic decision-making and democratizing the Soviet political system to allow multi-candidate contests. Then, one day I caught news of the Berlin Wall coming down to allow for the reunification of East and West Germany. Cadre Kim's face had a glassy look when I explained to him the beginning of the fall of communism in Eastern and Central Europe. How astonished he must feel toward the about-face of Russia, their mentor. In those recent years I had heard of the death of his Party's long-time general secretary Lê Duẩn, then his next general secretary Trường Chinh also died, and someone named Nguyễn Văn Linh was now the new general secretary.

It was a day like any other when we were called into the meeting hall one morning. I had been to so many of these meetings and endured enough of their rehearsed routines, the speeches learned by rote, that I knew how to tune them out. I simply sat, eyes unfocused, and let my mind go blank.

Then the words "transfer" and "release" snapped me out of my stupor. On the podium, the chief warden was reading out the names of those to be relocated. Hearing each one made my heart flutter. How dreadful that we were to be moved again. Each name called was like a hammer, and I simply felt exhausted. I lifted my gaze when the chief warden concluded the list. Mercy. Now I could stay. He began reading the next list of those to be released. I heard names I recognized. In that moment, I felt tremors in my hands. After all these years, did my hope of release ever die?

"Trần Khang," announced the chief warden, speaking my name like any other on the list.

I remained in my seat. The fellow next to me nudged me. "It's you. Stand up."

I rose to my feet. The chief warden stared at me, waiting. The fellow pushed me in the back. "Go get your papers."

My feet felt heavy as I made a great effort to get to the podium. I thanked the chief warden when he handed me a piece of paper.

Outside it was bright, and the courtyard was full of people milling about. Those who stayed walked quietly back to their shacks. Seeing them, I saw my distant self manifest from years past, having walked with nothing on my mind, returning to a shack with nothing awaiting me.

Back in my shack, I sat down on my cot. Finally. Afraid to read what was on the piece of paper, I simply sat there. After regaining myself, I looked at the paper. I felt a sharp jab at the first words "Order of Release." I was actually being released. A moment passed. I read on. My exit paper had been signed by the camp's senior lieutenant of security on the ninth of June, 1990, following the order of release dated on the thirty-first of May, 1990. I saw that I could have been a free man nine days earlier. The paper said my crime was that of being an intelligence officer of the Central Intelligence Office. I knew it was not an error. In fact, our careers under the *nguy* regime were classified as transgression, regardless.

Evening came. Two of my shack mates suggested to me that we should have a meal together before we bade farewell in the morning. It should be a decent meal. I thought of Cadre Kim and together we went to his shack outside the camp. I told him our wish and said to him, "May we pay for two bowls of rice grains, if you can spare us that much?"

He signaled for me to follow him into the interior of his shack where I saw a lidded bin. He opened the bin. Then he shook his head. "Brother Khang, I have bad news for you . . ."

I could see that the bin was empty. "Are you going to have your meal at the mess hall, sir cadre?" I asked and now felt bad that I had seen how humbly he and his family had lived. I took out two đồng and offered it to him. "Please accept this as my farewell gift for your daughter."

He did not know how to react. Then reluctantly he took it. "Do you have money for food on the way home?"

"I still have some, sir cadre. They gave me twenty đồng."

That night I lay awake. Many of us could not sleep.

All, including myself, had in his pocket a Certificate of Interim Release to return home to live in a bigger prison. We had no identification cards, belonged to no family registers, could work only menial jobs. Bee's wife, he had told me, still had in her family's possessions the long-time refrigerator that churned out ice cubes day after day for her to sell in her neighborhood. "Do not think about our children," he had said. "They have no future if they are not northerners." I had not given much thought to my future. Several years into my detention, I had thought that being sentenced to death would be more of a blessing than serving an indefinite stay in the reeducation camp.

In fact, I had not, for a number of years, looked at myself in a mirror, because there weren't any. At times I saw my reflection in a glass-framed picture in the camp's office. The face I saw was aged, a bearded man with a gloomy visage. That night, though tired, I felt revived. Then I let myself come face to face with a fact: I was a man in his prime at thirty-five when I went to prison. My daughter was only three when I left. She was now eighteen and living overseas with my wife who had left me.

The train left the station at noon the next day. The day was humid and bright and cicadas were ringing in the treetops. There were a dozen of us sitting together in a railcar. Among us was a former general. The night before, a cadre responsible for buying us our train tickets came into our shack. The general said to him, "Sir cadre, would you be so kind to get me a berth? I'm an old man and the long trip will be arduous for me." He gave the cadre forty đồng. That was ten đồng short of the cadre's monthly salary. The general would sleep the whole afternoon.

I was, however, more cautious with my personal possessions—all that was returned to me included my old money now converted to the new currency, a wristwatch, a hat, two shirts, two pairs of pants. I still had my wedding ring and kept my *goz* can because nobody wanted it; theirs were ceramic-lidded bowls and pottery jars their families had brought them. The moment I signed my release paper in the security office, I felt as transparent as glass. Outside, the air seemed sharper. I felt unbound, weightless. I had no wish to go anywhere. Perhaps I had been successfully reformed despite my thoughts otherwise. I felt threadbare. Where is my home?

In the clattering of the train, I closed my eyes. Bee's family had vouched before the Urban Civil Committee for my stay with them. My personal file had been sent to the district of my impending residency. Upon my arrival, I would report to the local security office to apply for my name to be on Bee's household registry. In that application I must include a summary of my past three generations, my release paper, Bee's approval form for my name on his family register, plus my marriage certificate with a note explaining my spouse had left Vietnam for

America. Attached to this application would be my assertion stating the truth of my non-reactionary activities.

The train stopped at a station on the way to Saigon. It had a new name now: Hồ Chí Minh City, named after a man much maligned among us.

I slept and woke to the singsong voice of a girl on the train. "Cigarettes and dumplings!" She was a young teen with her hair in two plaits. She was wearing a simple floral blouse.

A few men bought cigarettes then fell back asleep. She stopped before me.

"How about you, chú? Would you have a pack of cigarettes?" She handed me a Hoa Mai pack.

"I don't smoke, cháu," I said.

"How about some dumplings, chú?" She smiled. Her dimpled smile cheered me up.

"I'll take two."

She told me how much each was and I paid her. She put another wrapped dumpling in my hand. "Chú can have it. No charge."

I shook my head. "I can't take it, cháu."

"It's free, chú."

"Then how d'you make money by giving these away?"

"It's fine. My dad's tù like chú. He's not home yet."

Something stabbed me and I could not speak. "What did he do before the war?"

"Mom said he taught the Viet Cong men to become better men. They used to be bad, and they surrendered to us."

"He was with the Chiêu Hồi Program?" I asked, then smiled. "I know what he did."

"His name is Lê Quang Minh. Have chú ever met him?"

"Was he sent to the North?"

"Yes, chú." She counted her fingers on one hand, then lay down the tray and counted them on the other hand. "Many years now."

I simply shook my head. His bones might have rotted in one of those stark places in the North. I said to her, "Someday he'll be back. Like me."

I lay awake. The girl had awoken a memory.

At sunset, the train arrived at the station in Hồ Chí Minh City. My final destination. I recognized the surroundings as I stood on the platform, my knapsack on my back, watching passengers calling out to those who had been waiting for them. Had I been here before? I knew I had, and yet I felt like I didn't belong.

Something as old as the earth rose up in my memory, and in that instant, I was merely a specter revisiting his old haunt.

I shook hands with my companions and we wished each other well. One asked me where I was headed in the city. I said I didn't know, and he looked at me as if I'd had a memory lapse. I said I needed some time to reacquaint myself with it.

Dusk fell, and I walked the streets inquiring about overnight lodging. In an alley a woman answered the door of a yellow-stuccoed dwelling. I asked for an overnight stay.

"Where's your travel pass?" she asked.

"I don't have it," I said, standing in the dimly lit doorway. "I have my release paper though."

"You were tù, weren't you?"

I nodded.

"Give it to me in case they do a house search." She scowled. "Another way to make extra money for them. Understood?"

Again, I nodded.

"You pay in advance." She told me how much and I paid. "First room upstairs on the left. You're responsible for your belongings. Make sure to lock the door of your room and tuck in the mosquito netting. We have roaches and rats here."

As I mounted the stairs, I heard her from behind, "Don't forget to get your release paper back from me in the morning."

Thinking of the girl named Hải Yến, something struck me. I turned to ask her, "Are there any buses going to Sóc Trăng during the day?"

"Two. One leaving at eleven, the other at two. Walk five blocks, turn left and go six blocks toward the river. That's where the train and bus station is."

The desolation of the train station had a jaundiced look in the morning sun, bronzing the tiled roof of a shack built for the stationmaster. Having heard about the prisoners' release, more than a dozen women vendors milled around, squatting on their haunches, waiting for the train. On their trays were dumplings, baguettes, and yellow bananas. Most of them only pined to glimpse a familiar face behind the train's window. A son. A husband. To know that they were still alive after all these years.

At eleven I boarded a bus. I ate the three dumplings I had bought on the train the day before. Afterward, I slept. I woke and slept again, my body aching. Once,

I smelled the muddy odor of a river and woke and slowly gathered myself to watch the landscape of mangrove swamps lying beyond the river. On the loamy riverbank, cajeput flowers were white in brush like bunches.

Sometime in the afternoon, it rained and then stopped. The bus turned and followed a canal silty red in the afternoon sun. Along the banks were dense groves of bananas and papayas, green and dangling with fruits. The noise of the bus stirred some cormorants to wake, and from deep in the groves a flock of painted stork took to the air. The bus arrived at an open-air market and the sun, now a red orb, hovered over the western horizon.

I got off the bus and asked the driver how far to the sea from the market town. An hour's walk, he said. I asked if he knew there was a reform camp half an hour on foot from the Hậu river. It was no longer there after 1977, he told me, then said, "Aren't you a reform tù?"

"How d'you know?"

"I know. When I was released many moons ago, I was dressed just like you. Always walked around with a backpack." He offered me a light blue Bastos cigarette which I declined. In the North, most of the men—inmates and cadres—smoked Điện Biên or Vàm Cỏ cigarettes, which they disliked for their flat taste. He took a quick puff. "How long were you detained?"

"Fifteen years."

He said nothing. Then he frowned. "You must be very bad."

"Or badly reformed."

He cracked a grin. "If you want to find a place to stay, ask the woman in that café over there. If you want to unwind after all these years without a woman, ask her too."

I thanked him and left the market. The streetlights had come on when I arrived at the café. It overlooked the river; beyond the opposite bank was an island. Sampans and boats glided up and down, their lanterns hung over the bows flickered yellow, casting reflections in the water. It got dark quickly after sunset. In the shrubbery of bear's breeches and threeleaf derris blinked white dots of fireflies.

I ate a bowl of caramel pork cooked with a hardboiled egg and thin slices of coconut. There were a few customers. The woman owner asked me if I was passing through and I did not know if I was. In fact, I had no place to go to. "Sis," I said to her, "I was just released from a reeducation camp."

"You have family here in Sóc Trăng?" she asked and pulled out the chair across from me. She looked in her forties and was wearing a red-and-blue polka-dotted blouse, her hair rolled up inside a headscarf.

"No, sis." I leaned back in the low-backed chair. "I used to have a family in Saigon, though."

Hearing the tone of my voice, she did not press. "I understand. I've seen many men like you. Came and left. Like migratory birds. Yeah. Those birds sometimes fall and die halfway on their journey." She watched me play with the empty bowl. "You want something else? Café sữa đá or plain black?"

"Just black, sis. What time do you close?"

"I close whenever I feel like. Usually late. Do you have a place to sleep tonight?"

"No, sis." I looked quickly over the café. It was fairly small, with barely half a dozen tables. The interior behind the eating area was dark, curtained by a square sheet of blue cloth. "Do you live here?"

She glanced back to the interior and nodded. "I'll get you coffee." As she rose to her feet, she pointed toward the river where some boats had docked for the night. There were lantern lights inside their rattan domes. "Some of them rent a cot for an overnight stay. Just ask them."

She brought me a cup of black coffee with no saucer. As she cleaned the table she peered at me. "You need a companion for the evening?"

I looked at her. She smiled a friendly smile. Then after some thinking, I nodded. "Drink your coffee," she said. "I'll be back."

I sat back and sipped. I could hear the sound of bamboo clapping as a boat glided downriver. It must be a vendor boat selling something at night. The breeze came in and brought a fresh smell of vegetation after the late afternoon rain. Soon the woman returned, and with her was a girl in her twenties. The girl was slender. Her short hair was cut on a slant along her jawline and her oval face was tanned and fresh. She caught my gaze and smiled. I noticed her eyetooth which made her smile all the more charming.

The woman seemed to appraise me with her gaze. "You like her?"

I nodded. The girl blinked. She was dressed in a simple collarless, lemon-yellow blouse and white pantaloons. The woman gestured toward the interior behind the cloth curtain. "The room on the right," she said. "Just follow her."

I rose. "How long can I stay?"

"As long as you want," the woman said. "As long as no one else asks for her." She nodded toward the girl. "She's popular."

The room was dark. The girl pulled a cord in the center of the room and light came on from a low-wattage single naked bulb. A cot padded with a thin pallet sat low in a corner. The girl sat down. I lowered myself to sit next to her when she took my hand and put it on her belly. "Be gentle, *anh*."

Suddenly it hit me. I understood. "How many months?"

"Three."

"What's your name?"

"Bích Nhi."

"How old are you?"

"Twenty-four."

I glanced at her belly. "You're not married?"

"No, anh."

I did not want to ask what did not concern me.

Sometime in the evening, when I lay with her in the dark, hearing the clap-clapping bamboo of a downriver boat, I heard men's voices and the woman's voice. The girl told me it must be some local bộ đội seeking pleasure for the night. I listened and heard one man asking the woman, "Is she available tonight?" He had a northern accent that I detested, even though I was born there.

"No, she's in there with a customer."

"Get him out. I want her."

A silence. Then I heard the woman again, softer this time. "She's with a senior lieutenant. He just arrived from Hồ Chí Minh City."

"The whole night?" The northern accent had an edge in it.

"Yeah. He paid for the whole night."

They left. I lay in the dark with her head on my shoulder. She was soft and gentle, and she asked me where I was headed, and I said I needed to find someone in the vicinity and described to her the area where I used to travel on foot from that nameless camp, and how I would cut through the dunes to go across the salt flat to a commune. The girl said she knew the commune and had heard of the reform camp once there. "I was only ten."

I imagined her age and thought of Hải Yến; there was something so poignant about the idea of these children living in this iniquitous society that I couldn't sleep thinking about it. I told her I wished I could stay with her all night, and she said she would ask the woman. She rose and went out and then came back and said I could. "Just pay her a little extra," the girl said as she lay down in the dark beside me. "She's closing for the night."

In the early morning, I woke and went outside. The woman was not in the café. In the rear, Bích Nhi was washing herself by an earthen vat. The morning breeze was fresh. Her bare shoulders had a gentle slope as she bent to pour water over them. There was a scent of holy basil on the breeze. It came from the water she had boiled in a brass pan. She let me use the rest of it to wash myself. It was getting bright now, and the kapok blossoms were crimson red against a blue sky. Something I had thought during the night while I dried myself came back to me.

"Is there anything around here I can do to make some extra money?" I asked her.

She wrapped herself around the shoulders with a towel. "In the marketplace, anh," she said, and pointed back over her shoulder toward the river. "Plenty of boats carry stuff to the market every day. They always need a helping hand to load and unload stuff."

I thanked her. She said, "Anh can find a place to sleep at night in one of those boats." She added that it was safer to sleep there because the local security rarely searched the boats for those who possessed no travel passes. "When does your release paper expire, anh?"

"Soon," I said. "I don't intend to go back to Hồ Chí Minh City."

The girl said goodbye and left after the woman owner returned. The woman told me which boat would take me to the seaside. By boat, she said, it would take half an hour.

As the boat pulled out, she stood at the door waving. Over her the sign in red lettering said, "Pleasure Café." I was thinking of some simple, down-to-earth name to replace it, then realized I was no longer living in the traditional society which I'd left all those years ago.

It had rained the night before, though I did not hear rain in my sleep. Toward the sea where the river emptied itself, the turbulent water roiled red. A mist was veiling the water. Heat was rising. In the bushes along the riverbank, birds were keeping themselves away from the heat. One or two would fly out, hovering over riverhemp shrubs yellow as corn.

It was eight in the morning when I found my way to the seaside and saw the dunes. Years before, I would arrive here about this time and rest on a dune, and the little girl would soon appear. Now I sat alone, breathing in the briny air. After all these years, was she still selling dumplings? I pictured her, an adult now, crossing the beach, a bell hung on her shoulder pole so that, upon hearing it, people would know who was coming. After a while I went down to the sandy flat when the sun was high. The green weed covering the rocks began to dry, turning the weed white and stringy, and the gulls stirred awake from their slumber and stepped gingerly along the cove's rocks, probing for crabs and snails under the crinkly heaps of weed. An acrid odor hung over the drying rocks.

I waited for a long time until the sun became too hot and I returned to the town. To save money, I walked back.

For days I loitered in the marketplace and found odd jobs that paid me a modest sum. At night I slept in a boat whose owner was a man in his fifties, Bee's age. He ferried farm produce from those who grew crops year round. Sometimes I helped him load up his boat from a distant farmhouse and then unload sacks of produce at the town's market. There were days I did not have time to visit the seaside, but I always thought about it. There were also days I sat on a dune with the sun in my eyes and watched the beach for the girl. She must be Bích Nhi's age now. I would listen to the sound of the bell but hear none. The boom of waves came and went, a brief lull, and I could hear the soughing pine needles in the wind.

One early morning, I found myself back on the beach after the high tide. There was no sign of rock-dwellers—the barnacles, the snails—only the gulls perching on ledges of rocks above the tide mark, their shapes white, yellow bills tucked into their breasts, dozing in the sun. I sat for a long time on a dune until my shirt became dried of sweat and my eyes tired from watching the empty white sand. Then, in the breeze, came the sound of a bell.

A girl shouldering two round baskets balanced on a pole appeared around the bend of a dune. She walked quick footed, the bell clinking.

I left the dune and went down. I stood on the shore, feeling the spray of crashing waves on my face and on the sand, several crabs were washed out of their burrows and kicking in the liquefying sand.

The girl came toward me. Her bell tinkled. She wore a bright orange blouse the color of the stains on the sea-facing rocks. She lifted her gaze and I could see her face now.

I recognized her.

Acknowledgments

I am not a historian; I am a novelist. But in writing this novel I felt as if I was recording part of the history. As a historian, one studies written records of history and evaluates information from oral sources, often poring over printed documents, gleaning them to form some sort of foundation for his historical account. A historian gives readers a grasp of the past and a sense of a part of the history. When it comes to historical novels, however, the same readers will feel that part of the past differently. They now live in it. "It is as important to me as a writer as it is to historians that my readers are given a picture of a real past, not of a past that never was" (Virginia Warner Brodine).

Though the fictional world created in this novel adhered to the dimension of time and place, historically true, I am not bound by it. Some historical figures were mentioned for the sake of the narrative; but they were not used as fictional characters. My job as a novelist was to open a door for readers to glimpse the unvarnished truths of the wasted and unvaried horror of the Vietnamese communist labor-camp system. My burden then was to trace a man's life from reveille to retreat, not one day in his life as lived by Ivan Denisovich Shukhov, but five thousand four hundred and seventy-nine days—four leap-year days accounted for. Last, my hope is to free my soul of the unbearable burden of seeing the long-suppressed truths about human abuses and justice violations by the Vietnamese communists for the evils of their labor camps. This is not a novel of *ism* excoriation; it is, in fact, a story that seeks questions to the truths of life and asks the question: "How can you expect a man who's warm to understand a man who's cold?"[1]

I am grateful to many authors whose works have shed lights on the nature and truths of the reform program instituted by the Vietnamese communist government as their instrument of security police oppression and corporeal punishment to run the reeducation camps throughout Vietnam after 1975. For their books, articles, memoirs, and interviews from which I have culled insightful information to shape my story line regarding events, tales, which sustained my imagined world of an enormous network of penal camps disguised as reeducation camps, I wish to thank the following authors:

Trại Tập Trung, Duyên Anh; *Trại Giam Cổng Trời,* Mặc Lâm; *Cổng Trời Cán*

1 *One Day in the Life of Ivan Denisovich* by Alexander Solzhenitsyn.

Tỷ, Kiều Duy Vĩnh; *Hỏa Lò,* Nguyễn Chí Thiện; *Trại Cổng Trời,* Trần Nhu; *Trại Kiên Giam,* Nguyễn Chí Thiệp; *Những Người Tù Cuối Cùng,* Phạm Gia Đại; *Trại Tù T4,* Quỳnh Hương; *Tôi Đi "Cải Tạo" 1975–1984,* Nguyễn Văn Thái; *Ký Sự Trong Tù,* Phạm Bá Hoa; *Những Người Tù Bất Khuất,* Trịnh Tiếu; *Đường Vào Địa Ngục,* Phan Tuấn Sơn; *Như Chuyện Không Tưởng,* Chung Tử Bửu; *Interview with Nguyễn Xuân Phong,* Richard Burks Verrone; *Ai giết Cha Tôi?* and *Cuối Tầng Địa Ngục,* Đỗ Văn Phúc; "Đỗ Lệnh Dũng", Lê Thiệp; *Cái Lon, Chiếc Nón & Nùi Giẻ Rách,* Tưởng Năng Tiến; *Tháng Ba Định Mệnh,* Võ Đức Nhuận; *Thượng Tọa Thiên Lương,* Nguyễn Đức Tâm; *Những Tiếng Hát Bừng Sáng A20* and *Thiên Thần Trong Ngục Tối,* Phạm Đức Nhì; *Hồi Ký Chí Hoà* and *Thân Phận Người Lính Gãy Súng,* Vĩnh Khanh; *Nhật Ký Người Tù Cải Tạo,* Vương Văn Ba; *Huấn Nhục,* Hồ Minh Đức; *Trại Đầm Đùn,* Trần Văn Thái; *Làm Người Là Khó,* Đoàn Duy Thành; *Tù Nhân Chính Trị Tại Việt Nam (1975–1979),* Cố Bác Sĩ Trần Vỹ; *Hoàng Liên Sơn: Núi Rừng Trùng Điệp* and *Long Giao: Một Bước Đổi Đời, Phan Quân*; *Giấc Mộng Kinh Hoàng,* Phan Đức Minh; *Đại úy Khinh Binh* and *Vết Nám,* Hoàng Long Hải; *Tôi Đi Học (Tập),* Khúc Ruột Ngàn Dặm; *Tôi Là Vô Sản* and *Lên Rừng Thăm Bạn,* Lâm Chương; *Tù Sơn La* and *Người Tù Kiệt Xuất,* Phan Lạc Phúc; *Cái Lạnh Ngoài Trại Tù Yên Bái,* Nguyễn Minh Châu; *Tháng Tư Đen Nối Dài: Đoạn Trường Cải Tạo,* Lê Tân Văn; *Bài Hoan Ca Ở A38,* Chu Trầm Nguyên Minh; *Tôi Đi Tìm Tự Do,* Nguyễn Hữu Chí; *Viên Ngọc Nát,* Vương Mộng Long; *Trên Chuyến Tàu Xuôi Nam,* Hải Triều; *Mẹ Việt Nam Ơi, Dân Ta Có Tội Tình Gì?* Pierre Darcourt; *How the Steel Was Tempered,* Nikolai Ostrovsky; *Hành Trình Vào Địa Ngục Đỏ,* Nguyễn Ngọc Luyến; *Tôi Bị Bắt,* Trần Vàng Sao; *Trận Lụt Vàng,* Ngô Viết Trọng; *Chuyến Tàu Ra Miền Bắc* and *Những Người Tù Đói,* Tạ Thành Lộc; *Những Năm Tháng Tù Đày,* Xuyến Trịnh; *Chuyện Tù Cải Tạo Nhiều Người Muốn Biết,* Trần Văn; *Tết Trong Tù Cải Tạo,* Nguyễn Mạnh Tiến; *Những Kỷ Niệm Trong Tù Với Chưởng Môn Việt Võ Đạo* and *Đêm Noel Trong Xà Lim Số 6,* Vũ Ánh; *Người Tù Điên* and *Đêm Xuân Trong Trại Tù Cao Lãnh,* Phạm Hồng Ân; *Thanh Tâm Tuyền Những Điều Nhớ,* Ninh Hạ; *Tôi đi gỡ mìn,* Đặng Văn Xin; *Để Vinh Danh Một Cái Chết* and *Nhà Ri,* Bác Sĩ Tôn Thất Sang; *Đêm Thánh Vô Cùng,* Nguyên Lập; *Người Tù Chăn Bò Ở Gia Trung,* Phan Thái Yên; *Đêm Xuân Trong Trại Tù Cao Lãnh,* Phạm Hồng Ân; *Phiên Tòa Đầu Tiên,* Đông Vân; *Một Cái Tết Không Thể Quên,* Phùng Ngọc Sa; *Về Nam* and *Con Suối Nhớ,* Nguyên Huy; *Cai Tù Việt Cộng,* Phạm Kim Khôi; *Từ U Minh Đến Cần Thơ,* Sơn Nam; *Xuân Trong Rừng Thẳm,* Phương Duy; *Hồi Ức Tù Cải Tạo,* Nguyễn Huy Hùng; *Thung Lũng Tử Thần!* Phạm Trần Anh; *Nghẹn Ngào,* Nguyễn Trác Hiếu; *Trong Những Trại Tù VC Sau Cùng,* Kiều Công Cự; *Ngày*

Trở Về, Trần Nhật Kim; *Đời Sống Người Tù Cải Tạo*, Nguyễn Ý-Đức; *Tử Tù Tự Xử Lý*, Trần Thư; *Cầu Tre Lắc Lẽo*, Hoàng Chính; *Nhớ Chuyện Trong Tù*, Thủy Lan Vy; *Chuyện Trong Tù*, Lê Hùng; *Đi Tìm Cái Tôi Đã Mất*, Nguyễn Khải; *Hồi Ký*, Võ Long Triều; *Tù Binh Và Hòa Bình*, Phan Nhật Nam; *Lương Y Như Từ Mẫu*, Chu Tất Tiến; *Đêm Noel Vùng Dậy Tại Suối Máu*, Võ Văn Sáu; *Những Trại Tù Cải Tạo đã In Dấu Chân Tôi*, Huy Vũ; *Chuyến Đò Tốc Hành*, Nguyễn Lê Hồng Hưng; *Ngục Tù Cộng Sản*, Giang Văn Nhân; *Chuyện Vui Trong Tù*, THG; *Bài Ca Lý Chuồn Chuồn*, Cai Hạnh; *Chuyện Gối Đầu*, Huỳnh Văn Phú; *Những Xác Chết Trên Mãnh Đất Hình Cong Chữ S*, J. Nguyễn; *Kha Tư Giáo — Người Chiến Sĩ Bất Khuất Của Tự Do*, Trần Văn Giang; *Trong Lao Tù Cộng Sản*, Admin; *Người Tù Chiến Hữu*, Hồ Hoàng Hạ; *Người Không Nhận Tội*, Duy Nhân; *Người Bạn Bất Thường*, Ninh Thuận.

I am particularly indebted to Lê Anh Kiệt's *17 Năm Trong Các Trại Cải Tạo Của CSVN*; Hà Thúc Sinh's *Đại Học Máu;* Nguyễn Hữu Lễ's *Tôi Phải Sống* and *Địa Ngục Trần Gian*; Vũ Thư Hiên's *Đêm Giữa Ban Ngày* and *Cái Chết Của Người Tù Già;* Duyên Anh's *Nhà Tù;* Rachel Carson's *The Edge of the Sea*. Xuân Đỗ's *Tiếng Đàn;* Duyên Anh's *Trại Tập Trung*; Hàn Giang Trần Lệ Tuyền's *Những Dòng Nước Mắt;* Lâm Chương's *Con Sâu Đỏ;* Nguyễn Quang Hữu's *Ký Sự*; Bích Huyền's *Đường Ra Vĩnh Phú*; Thích Thiện Minh's *26 Năm Lưu Đày Dưới Chế Độ Cộng Sản*; Dương Hoài Ninh's *Chuyện Vui Buồn Cải Tạo;* Điền Đông Phương's *Đời Cải Tạo;* Tôn Thất Phú Sĩ's *Ngày Về*.

All the quoted poems which I translated came from public domain: page 46, *Lời mẹ dặn* by Phùng Quán; page 242 by HVL. The lyrics on page 160 were by Eugène Pottier, translated by Charles H. Kerr. A snapshot of Mr. Thạch was fictionalized from my maternal uncle's life, courtesy of his son, Tôn Thất Phương, who is my cousin.

A special thanks to Jordan Mulligan and Hà Lệ Thúy. I am also grateful to Kate Gale, Rebeccah Sanhueza, Annalisa Zox-Weaver, and Victoria De Leon for their staunch support.

A word on the Vietnamese most common names. All Vietnamese words in this novel are diacritically marked except for those most commonly seen in the media, e.g., Saigon, Hanoi, Vietnam, Viet Minh.

Finally, I have no ambition to write the history of the post-1975 Vietnamese communist labor camps; yet, without this novel recreating that historic period, I would have done disservice to those whose bones were still unclaimed, though many having been discovered, and chiefly to their descendants. This novel pays tribute to all of them.

Biographical Note

Award-winning author Khanh Ha is a ten-time Pushcart nominee. He is the recipient of the Sand Hills Prize for Best Fiction, The Robert Watson Literary Prize, The Orison Anthology Award, The James Knudsen Prize, The C&R Press Fiction Prize, The EastOver Fiction Prize, The Blackwater Press Fiction Prize, The Gival Press Novel Award, The Cai Emmons Fiction Award, The Unleash Creatives Fiction Prize, and The Next Generation INDIE Book Award. He lives in New Jersey.